WANT ME, COWBOY

MAISEY YATES

MILLION DOLLAR BABY

JANICE MAYNARD

MILLS & BOON

First Published in Great Britain 2018
by Mills & Boon, an imprint of HarperCollinsPublishers,
1 London Bridge Street, London, SE1 9GF

Want Me, Cowboy © 2018 Maisey Yates
Million Dollar Baby © 2018 Harlequin Books S.A.

Special thanks and acknowledgement are given to Janice Maynard for her contribution to the *Texas Cattleman's Club: Bachelor Auction* series.

ISBN: 978-0-263-93625-4

1118

Maisey Yates is a *New York Times* bestselling author of more than thirty romance novels. She has a coffee habit she has no interest in kicking, and a slight Pinterest addiction. She lives with her husband and children in the Pacific Northwest. When Maisey isn't writing she can be found singing in the grocery store, shopping for shoes online and probably not doing dishes. Check out her website: www.maiseyyates.com.

USA TODAY bestselling author **Janice Maynard** loved books and writing even as a child. After multiple rejections, she finally sold her first manuscript! Since then, she has written fifty-plus books and novellas. Janice lives in Tennessee with her husband, Charles. They love hiking, traveling and family time. You can connect with Janice at janicemaynard.com, Twitter.com/janicemaynard, Facebook.com/janicemaynardreaderpage, Facebook.com/janicesmaynard and Instagram.com/janicemaynard.

Also by Maisey Yates

Take Me, Cowboy
Hold Me, Cowboy
Seduce Me, Cowboy
Claim Me, Cowboy
Shoulda Been a Cowboy (prequel novella)
Part Time Cowboy
Brokedown Cowboy
Bad News Cowboy
A Copper Ridge Christmas (ebook novella)
The Cowboy Way

Also by Janice Maynard

A Not-So-Innocent Seduction
Baby for Keeps
Christmas in the Billionaire's Bed
Twins on the Way
Second Chance with the Billionaire
How to Sleep with the Boss
For Baby's Sake
His Heir, Her Secret
On Temporary Terms

Discover more at millsandboon.co.uk

WANT ME, COWBOY

MAISEY YATES

One

November 1, 2018
Location: Copper Ridge, Oregon

WIFE WANTED—

Rich rancher, not given to socializing. Wants a
wife who will not try to change me. Must be tolerant of moods, reported lack of sensitivity and
the tendency to take off for a few days' time in
the mountains. Will expect meals cooked. Also,
probably a kid or two. Exact number to be negotiated. Beard is nonnegotiable.

November 5, 2018
Revised draft for approval by 11/6

WIFE WANTED—

~~Rich rancher, not given to socializing.~~ Successful rancher searching for a wife who enjoys rural

living. ~~Wants a wife who will not try to change me. Must be tolerant of moods, reported lack of sensitivity, and the tendency to take off for a few days' time in the mountains.~~ Though happy with my life, it has begun to feel lonely, and I would like someone to enhance my satisfaction with what I have already. I enjoy extended camping trips and prefer the mountains to a night on the town. ~~Will expect meals cooked. Also, probably a kid or two. Exact number to be negotiated. Beard is nonnegotiable. I~~ I'm looking for a traditional family life, and a wife and children to share it with.

"This is awful."

Poppy Sinclair looked up from her desk, her eyes colliding with her boss's angry gray stare. He was holding a printout of the personal ad she'd revised for him and shaking it at her like she was a dog and it was a newspaper.

"The *original* was awful," she responded curtly, turning her focus back to her computer.

"But it was all true."

"Lead with being less of an asshole."

"I *am* an asshole," Isaiah said, clearly unconcerned with that fact.

He was at peace with himself. Which she admired on some level. Isaiah was Isaiah, and he made no apologies for that fact. But his attitude would be a problem if the man wanted to find a wife. Because very few other people were at peace with him just as he was.

"I would never say I want to—" he frowned "'—enhance my enjoyment.' What the hell, Poppy?"

Poppy had known Isaiah since she was eighteen years old. She was used to his moods. His complete lack of subtlety. His gruffness.

But somehow, she'd never managed to get used to *him*. As a man.

This grumpy, rough, bearded man who was like a brick wall. Or like one of those mountains he'd disappear into for days at a time.

Every time she saw him, it felt as if he'd stolen the air right from her lungs. It was more than just being handsome—though he was. A lot of men were handsome. His brother Joshua was handsome, and a whole lot easier to get along with.

Isaiah was… Well, he was her very particular brand of catnip. He made everything in her sit up, purr…and want to be stroked.

Even when he was in full hermit mode.

People—and interacting with them—were decidedly not his thing. It was one reason Poppy had always been an asset to him in his work life. It was her job to sit and take notes during meetings…and report her read on the room to him after. He was a brilliant businessman, and fantastic with numbers. But people… not so much.

As evidenced by the ad. Of course, the very fact that he was placing an ad to find a wife was both contradicting to that point—suddenly, he wanted a wife!—and also, somehow, firmly in affirmation of it. He was placing an ad to find her.

The whole situation was Joshua's fault. Well, probably Devlin and Joshua combined, in fairness.

Isaiah's brothers had been happy bachelors until a

couple of years ago when Devlin had married their sister Faith's best friend, Mia.

Then, Joshua had been the next to succumb to matrimony, a victim of their father's harebrained scheme. The patriarch of the Grayson family had put an ad in a national newspaper looking for a wife for his son. In retaliation, Joshua had placed an ad of his own, looking for an unsuitable wife that would teach his father not to meddle.

It all backfired. Or…front fired. Either way, Joshua had ended up married to Danielle, and was now happily settled with her and her infant half brother who both of them were raising as their son.

It was after their wedding that Isaiah had formed his plan.

The wedding had—he had explained to Poppy at work one morning—clarified a few things for him. He believed in marriage as a valuable institution, one that he wanted to be part of. He wanted stability. He wanted children. But he didn't have any inclination toward love.

He didn't have to tell her why.

She *knew* why.

Rosalind.

But she wouldn't speak her foster sister's name out loud, and neither would he. But she remembered. The awful, awful fallout of Rosalind's betrayal.

His pain. Poppy's own conflicted feelings.

It was easy to remember her conflicted feelings, since she still had them.

He was staring at her now, those slate eyes hard and glinting with an energy she couldn't quite pin down. And with coldness, a coldness that hadn't been there before Rosalind. A coldness that told her and any other woman—loud and clear—that his heart was unavailable.

That didn't mean her own heart didn't twist every time he walked into the room. Every time he leaned closer to her—like he was doing now—and she got a hint of the scent of him. Rugged and pine-laden and basically lumberjack porn for her senses.

He was a contradiction, from his cowboy hat down to his boots. A numbers guy who loved the outdoors and was built like he belonged outside doing hard labor.

Dear God, he was problematic.

He made her dizzy. Those broad shoulders, shoulders she wanted to grab on to. Lean waist and hips—hips she wanted to wrap her legs around. And his forearms…all hard muscle. She wanted to lick them.

He turned her into a being made of sensual frustration, and no one else did that. Ever. Sadly, she seemed to have no effect on him at all.

"I'm not trying to mislead anyone," he said.

"Right. But you *are* trying to entice someone." The very thought made her stomach twist into a knot. But jealousy was pointless. If Isaiah wanted her…well, he would have wanted her by now.

He straightened, moving away from her and walking across the office. She nearly sagged with relief. "My money should do that." As if that solved every potential issue.

She bit back a weary sigh. "Would you like someone who was maybe…interested in who you are as a person?"

She knew that was a stupid question to ask of Isaiah Grayson. But she was his friend, as well as his employee. So it was kind of…her duty to work through this with him. Even if she didn't want him to do this at all.

And she didn't want him to find anyone.

Wow. Some friend she was.

But then, having…complex feelings for one's friend made emotional altruism tricky.

"As you pointed out," he said, his tone dry, "I'm an asshole."

"You were actually the one who said that. I said you *sounded* like one."

He waved his hand. "Either way, I'm not going to win Miss Congeniality in the pageant, and we both know that. Fine with me if somebody wants to get hitched and spend my money."

She sighed heavily, ignoring the fact that her heart felt an awful lot like paper that had been crumpled up into a tight, mutilated ball. "Why do you even *want* a wife, Isaiah?"

"I explained that to you already. Joshua is settled. Devlin is settled."

"Yes, they are. So why now?"

"I always imagined I would get married," he said simply. "I never intended to spend my whole life single."

"Is your biological clock ticking?" she asked drily.

"In a way," he said. "Again, it all comes back to logic. I'm close to my family, to my brothers. They'll have children sooner rather than later. Joshua and Danielle already have a son. Cousins should be close in age. It just makes sense."

She bit the inside of her cheek. "So you…just think you can decide it's time and then make it happen?"

"Yes. And I think Joshua's experience proves you can make anything work as long as you have a common goal. It *can* be like math."

She graduated from biting her cheek to her tongue. Isaiah was a numbers guy unto his soul. "Uh-huh."

She refused to offer even a pat agreement because she just thought he was wrong. Not that she knew much of anything about relationships of…any kind really.

She'd been shuffled around so many foster homes as a child, and it wasn't until she was in high school that she'd had a couple years of stability with one family. Which was where she'd met Rosalind, the one foster sibling Poppy was still in touch with. They'd shared a room and talked about a future where they were more than wards of the state.

In the years since, Poppy felt like she'd carved out a decent life for herself. But still, it wasn't like she'd ever had any romantic relationships to speak of.

Pining after your boss didn't count.

"The only aspect of going out and hooking up I like is the hooking up," he said.

She wanted to punch him for that unnecessary addition to the conversation. She sucked her cheek in and bit the inside of it too. "Great."

"When you think about it, making a relationship a transaction is smart. Marriage is a legal agreement. But you don't just get sex. You get the benefit of having your household kept, children…"

"Right. Children." She'd ignored his first mention of them, but… She pressed her hands to her stomach unconsciously. Then, she dropped them quickly.

She should not be thinking about Isaiah and children or the fact that he intended to have them with another woman.

Confused feelings was a cop-out. And it was hard to deny the truth when she was steeped in this kind of reaction to him, to his presence, to his plan, to his talk about children.

The fact of the matter was, she was tragically in love with him. And he'd never once seen her the way she saw him.

She'd met him through Rosalind. When Poppy had turned eighteen, she'd found herself released from her foster home with nowhere to go. Everything she owned was in an old canvas tote that a foster mom had given her years ago.

Rosalind had been the only person Poppy could think to call. The foster sister she'd bonded with in her last few years in care. She'd always kept in touch with Rosalind, even when Rosalind had moved to Seattle and got work.

Even when she'd started dating a wonderful man she couldn't say enough good things about.

She was the only lifeline Poppy had, and she'd reached for her. And Rosalind had come through. She'd had Poppy come to Rosalind's apartment, and then she'd arranged for a job interview with her boyfriend, who needed an assistant for a construction firm he was with.

In one afternoon, Poppy had found a place to live, gotten a job and lost her heart.

Of course, she had lost it, immediately and—in the fullness of time it had become clear—irrevocably, to the one man who was off-limits.

Her boss. Her foster sister's boyfriend. Isaiah Grayson.

Though his status as her boss had lasted longer than his status as Rosalind's boyfriend. He'd become her fiancé. And then after, her ex.

Poppy had lived with a divided heart for so long. Even after Isaiah and Rosalind's split, Poppy was able to care for them both. Though she never, ever spoke to Rosalind in Isaiah's presence, or even mentioned her.

Rosalind didn't have the same embargo on mentions of Isaiah. But in fairness, Rosalind was the one who had cheated on him, cost him a major business deal and nearly ruined his start-up company and—by extension—nearly ruined his relationship with his business partner, who was also his brother.

So.

Poppy had loved him while he'd dated another woman. Loved him while he nursed a broken heart because of said other woman. Loved him when he disavowed love completely. And now she would have to love him while she interviewed potential candidates to be his wife.

She was wretched.

He had said the word *sex* in front of her like it wouldn't do anything to her body. Had talked about children like it wouldn't make her...yearn.

Men were idiots. But this one might well be their king.

"Put the unrevised ad in the paper."

She shook her head. "I'm not doing that."

"I could fire you." He leaned in closer and her breath caught. "For insubordination."

Her heart tumbled around erratically, and she wished she could blame it on anger. Annoyance. But she knew that wasn't it.

She forced herself to rally. "If you haven't fired me yet, you're never going to. And anyway," she said, narrowing her tone so that the words would hit him with a point, "I'm the one who has to interview your prospective brides. Which makes this my endeavor in many ways. I'm the one who's going to have to weed through your choices. So I would like the ad to go out that I think has the best chance of giving me less crap to sort through."

He looked up at her, and much to her surprise seemed to be considering what she said. "That is true. You will be doing the interviews."

She felt like she'd been stabbed. She was going to be interviewing Isaiah's potential wife. The man she had been in love with since she was a teenage idiot, and was still in love with now that she was an idiot in her late twenties.

There were a whole host of reasons she'd never, ever let on about her feelings for him, Rosalind and his feelings on love aside.

She loved her job. She loved Isaiah's family, who she'd gotten to know well over the past decade, and who were the closest thing she had to a family of her own.

Plus, loving him was just…easy to dismiss. She wasn't the type of girl who could have something like that. Not Poppy Sinclair whose mother had disappeared when she was two years old and left her with a father who forgot to feed her.

Her life was changing though, slowly.

She was living well beyond what she had ever imagined would be possible for her. Gray Bear Construction was thriving; the merger between Jonathan Bear and the Graysons' company a couple of years ago was more successful than they'd imagined it could be.

And every employee on every level had reaped the benefits.

She was also living in the small town of Copper Ridge, Oregon, which was a bit strange for a girl from Seattle, but she did like it. It had a different pace. But that meant there was less opportunity for a social life. There were fewer people to interact with. By default she, and the other folks in town, ended up spending a lot of their free time with the people they worked with every day. There was nothing wrong with that. She loved Faith, and she had begun getting close to Joshua's wife recently. But it was just… Mostly there wasn't enough of a break from Isaiah on any given day.

But then, she also didn't enforce one. Didn't take one. She supposed she couldn't really blame the small-town location when the likely culprit of the entire situation was *her*.

"Place whatever ad you need to," he said, his tone abrupt. "When you meet the right woman, you'll know."

"I'll know," she echoed lamely.

"Yes. Nobody knows me better than you do, Poppy. I have faith that you'll pick the right wife for me."

With those awful words still ringing in the room, Isaiah left her there, sitting at her desk, feeling numb and ill used.

The fact of the matter was, she probably *could* pick him a perfect wife. Someone who would facilitate his life, and give him space when he needed it. Someone who was beautiful and fabulous in bed.

Yes, she knew exactly what Isaiah Grayson would think made a woman the perfect wife for him.

The sad thing was, Poppy didn't possess very many of those qualities herself.

And what she so desperately wanted was for Isaiah's perfect wife to be *her*.

But dreams were for other women. They always had been. Which meant some other woman was going to end up with Poppy's dream.

While she played matchmaker to the whole affair.

Two

"I put an ad in the paper."

"For?" Isaiah's brother Joshua looked up from his computer and stared at him like he was waiting to hear the answers to the mystery of the universe.

Joshua, Isaiah and their younger sister, Faith, were sitting in the waiting area of their office, enjoying their early-morning coffee. Or maybe enjoying was overstating it. The three of them were trying to find a state of consciousness.

"A wife."

Faith spat her coffee back into her cup. "What?"

"I placed an ad in the paper to help me find a wife," he repeated.

Honestly, he couldn't understand why she was having such a large reaction to the news. After all, that was how Joshua had found his wife, Danielle.

"You can't be serious," Joshua said.

"I expected you of all people to be supportive."

"Why *me*?"

"Because that's how you met Danielle. Or you have you forgotten?"

"I have not forgotten how I met my wife. However, I didn't put an ad out there seriously thinking I was going to find someone to marry. I was trying to prove to dad that *his* ad was a stupid idea."

"But it turned out it wasn't a stupid idea," Isaiah said. "I want to get married. I figured this was a hassle-free way of finding a wife."

Faith stared at him, dumbfounded. "You can't be serious."

"I'm serious."

The door to the office opened, and Poppy walked in wearing a cheerful, polka-dotted dress, her dark hair swept back into a bun, a few curls around her face.

"Please tell me my brother is joking," Faith said. "And that he didn't actually put an ad in the paper to find a wife."

Poppy looked from him back to Faith. "He doesn't joke, you know that."

"And you know that he put an ad in the paper for a wife?" Joshua asked.

"Of course I know," Poppy responded. "Who do you think is doing the interviews?"

That earned him two slack-jawed looks.

"Who else is going to do it?" Isaiah asked.

"You're not even doing the interview for your own wife?" Faith asked.

"I trust Poppy implicitly. If I didn't, she wouldn't be my assistant."

"Of all the… You are insane." Faith stormed out of the room. Joshua continued to sit and sip his coffee.

"No comment?" Isaiah asked.

"Oh, I have plenty. But I know you well enough to know that making them won't change a damn thing.

So I'm keeping my thoughts to myself. However," he said, collecting his computer and his coffee, "I do have to go to work now."

That left both Isaiah and Poppy standing in the room by themselves. She wasn't looking at him; she was staring off down the hall, her expression unreadable. She had a delicate profile, dark, sweeping eyelashes and a fascinating curve to her lips. Her neck was long and elegant, and the way her dress shaped around her full breasts was definitely a pleasing sight.

He clenched his teeth. He didn't make a habit of looking at Poppy that way. But she was pretty. He had always thought so.

Even back when he'd been with Rosalind he'd thought there was something...indefinable about Poppy. Special.

She made him feel... He didn't know. A little more grounded. Or maybe it was just because she treated him differently than most people did.

Either way, she was irreplaceable to him. In the running of his business, Poppy was his barometer. The way he got the best read on a situation. She did his detail work flawlessly. Handled everything he didn't like so he could focus on what he was good at.

She was absolutely, 100 percent, the most important asset to him at the company.

He would have to tell her that sometime. Maybe buy her another pearl necklace. Though, last time he'd done that she had gotten angry at him. But she wore it. She was wearing it today, in fact.

"They're right," she said finally.

"About?"

"The fact that you're insane."

"I think I'm sane enough."

"Of course you do. Actually—" she let out a long, slow breath "—I don't think you're insane. But, I don't think this is a good idea."

"Why?"

"This is really how you want to find a wife? In a way that's this…impersonal?"

"What are my other options? I have to meet someone new, go through the process of dating… She'll expect a courtship of some kind. We'll have to figure out what we have in common, what we don't have in common. This way, it's all out in the open. That's more straightforward."

"Maybe you deserve better than that," she said, her tone uncharacteristically gentle.

"Maybe this is better for *me*."

She shook her head. "I don't know about that."

"When it comes to matters of business, there's no one I trust more than you. But you're going to have to trust that I know what will work best in my own life."

"It's not what I want for you."

A strange current arced between them when she spoke those words, a spark in her brown eyes catching on something inside him.

"I appreciate your concern."

"Yes," she echoed. "My concern."

"We have work to do. And you have wife applications to sort through."

"Right," she said.

"Preference will be given to blondes," he said.

Poppy blinked and then reached up slowly, touching her own dark hair. "Of course."

And then she turned and walked out of the room.

* * *

Isaiah hadn't expected to receive quite so many responses to his ad. Perhaps, in the end, Poppy had been right about her particular tactic with the wording. It had certainly netted what felt to him to be a record number of responses.

Though he didn't actually know how many women had responded to his brother's personal ad.

He felt only slightly competitive about it, seeing as it would be almost impossible to do a direct comparison between his and Joshua's efforts. Their father had placed an ad first, making Joshua sound undoubtedly even nicer than Poppy had made Isaiah sound.

Thereafter, Joshua had placed his own ad, which had offered a fake marriage and hefty compensation.

Isaiah imagined that a great many more women would respond to that.

But he didn't need quantity. He just needed quality.

And he believed that existed.

It had occurred to him at Joshua and Danielle's wedding that there was no reason a match couldn't be like math. He believed in marriage; it was romance he had gone off of.

Or rather, the kind of romance he had experience with.

Obviously, he couldn't dispute the existence of love. His parents were in love, after all. Forty years of marriage hadn't seemed to do anything to dampen that. But then, he was not like his mother. And he wasn't like his father. Both of them were warm people. *Compassionate*. And those things seemed to come easily to them.

Isaiah was a black-and-white man living in a world

filled with shades of gray. He didn't care for those shades, and he didn't like to acknowledge them.

But he wasn't an irrational man. Not at all.

Yet he'd been irrational once. Five years with Rosalind and they had been the best of his life. At least, he had thought so at the time.

Then she had betrayed him, and nearly destroyed everything.

Or rather, he had.

Which was all he had needed to learn about what happened to him and his instincts under the influence of love.

He'd been in his twenties then, and it had been easy to ignore the idea that his particular set of practices when it came to relationships meant he would be spending his life without a partner. But now he was in his thirties, and that reality was much more difficult to ignore. When he'd had to think about the future, he hadn't liked the idea of what he was signing himself up for.

So, he had decided to change it. That was the logical thing to do when you found yourself unhappy with where you were, after all. A change of circumstances was not beyond his reach. And so, he was reaching out to grab it.

Which was why Poppy was currently on interview number three with one of the respondents to his ad. Isaiah had insisted that anyone responding to the ad come directly to Copper Ridge to be interviewed. Anyone who didn't take the ad seriously enough to put in a personal appearance was not worthy of consideration, in his opinion.

He leaned back in his chair, looking at the neat expanse of desk in front of him. Everything was in its place in his office, as it always was. As it should be. And soon, everything in his personal life would be in place too.

Across the hall, the door to Poppy's office opened and a tall, willowy blonde walked out. She was definitely his type in the physical sense, and the physical mattered quite a bit. Emotionally, he might be a bit detached, but physically, everything was functioning. Quite well, thank you.

In his marriage-math equation, sex was an important factor.

He intended to be faithful to his wife. There was really no point in making a lifelong commitment without fidelity.

Because of that, it stood to reason that he should make sure he chose in accordance with his typical physical type.

By the time he finished that thought process the woman was gone, and Poppy appeared a moment later. She was glaring down the hall, looking both disheveled and generally irritated. He had learned to recognize her moods with unerring accuracy. Mostly because it was often a matter of survival. Poppy was one of the few people on earth who wasn't intimidated by him. He should be annoyed by that. She was his employee, and ought to be a bit more deferential than she was.

He didn't want her to be, though. He liked Poppy. And that was a rarity in his world. He didn't like very many people. Because most people were idiots.

But not her.

Though, she looked a little bit like she wanted to kill him at the moment. When her stormy, dark eyes connected with his across the space, he had the fleeting thought that a lesser man would jump up and run away, leaving his boots behind.

Isaiah was not that man.

He was happy to meet her. Steel-capped toe to pointy-toed stiletto.

"She was stupid," Poppy pronounced.

He lifted a brow. "Did you give her an IQ test?"

"I'm not talking about her intelligence," Poppy said, looking fierce. "Though, the argument could be made that any woman responding to this ad…"

"Are you about to cast aspersions on my desirability?"

"No," she said. "I cast those last week, if you recall. It would just be tiresome to cast them again."

"Why is she stupid?" he pressed.

"Because she has no real concept of what you need. You're a busy man, and you live in a rural…area. You're not going to be taking her out to galas every night. And I know she thought that because you're a rich man galas were going to be part of the deal. But I explained to her that you only go to a certain number of business-oriented events a year, and that you do so grudgingly. That anyone hanging on your arm at such a thing would need to be polished, smiling, and, in general, making up for you."

He spent a moment deciding if he should be offended by that or not. He decided not to be. Because she was right. He knew his strengths and his limitations.

"She didn't seem very happy about those details. And that is why I'm saying she's stupid. She wants to take this…job, essentially. A job that is a life sentence. And she wants it to be about her."

He frowned. "Obviously, this marriage is not going to be completely about me. I am talking about a *marriage* and not a position at the company." Though, he supposed he could see why she would be thinking in those terms. He had placed an ad with strict requirements. And he supposed, as a starting point, it *was* about him.

"Is that true, Isaiah? Because I kind of doubt it. You don't want a woman who's going to inconvenience you."

"I'm not buying a car," he said.

"Aren't you?" She narrowed her eyes, her expression mean.

"No. I realize that."

"You're basically making an arranged marriage for yourself."

"Consider it advanced online dating," he said. "With a more direct goal."

"You're having your assistant choose a wife for you." She enunciated each word as if he didn't understand what he'd asked of her.

Her delicate brows locked together, and her mouth pulled into a pout. Though, she would undoubtedly punch him if he called it a pout.

In a physical sense, Poppy was not his type at all. She was not tall, or particularly leggy, though she did often wear high heels with her 1950s housewife dresses. She was petite, but still curvy, her hair dark and curly, and usually pulled back in a loose, artfully pinned bun that allowed tendrils to slowly make their escape over the course of the day.

She was pretty, in spite of the fact that she wasn't the type of woman he would normally gravitate toward.

He wasn't sure why he was just now noticing that. Perhaps it was the way the light was filtering through the window now. Falling across her delicately curved face. Her mahogany skin with a bit of rose color bleeding across her cheeks. In this instance, he had a feeling the color was because she was angry. But, it was lovely nonetheless.

Her lips were full—pouty or not—and the same rose color as her cheeks.

"I don't understand your point," he said, stopping his visual perusal of her.

"I'm just saying you're taking about as much of a personal interest in finding a wife as someone who was buying a car."

He did not point out that if he were buying a car, he would take it for a test drive, and that he had not suggested doing anything half so crass with any of the women who'd come to be interviewed.

"How many more women are you seeing today?" he asked, deciding to bypass her little show of indignation.

"Three more," she said.

There was something in the set of her jaw, in the rather stubborn, mulish look on her face that almost made him want to ask a question about what was bothering her.

But only almost.

"Has my sister sent through cost estimates for her latest design?" he asked.

Poppy blinked. "What?"

"Faith. Has she sent through her cost estimates? I'm going to end up correcting them anyway, but I like to see what she starts with."

"I'm well aware of the process, Isaiah," Poppy said.

"I'm just surprised that you moved on from wife interviews to your sister's next design."

"Why would you be surprised by that? The designs are important. They are, in fact, why I am a billionaire."

"Yes. I know," Poppy said. "Faith's talent is a big reason why we're all doing well. Believe me, I respect the work. However, the subject change seems a bit abrupt."

"It *is* a workday."

Deep brown eyes narrowed in his direction. "You're really something else, do you know that?"

He did. He always had. The fact that she felt the need to question him on it didn't make much sense to him.

"Yes," he responded.

Poppy stamped.

She stamped her high-heel-clad foot like they were in a black-and-white movie.

"No, she hasn't sent it through," Poppy said.

"You just stomped your foot at me."

She flung her arms wide. "Because you were just being an idiot at me."

"I don't understand you," he said.

"I don't need you to understand me." Her brow furrowed.

"But you *do* need me to sign your paychecks," he pointed out. "I'm your boss."

Then, all the color drained from her cheeks. "Right. Of course. I do need that. Because you're my boss."

"I am."

"Just my boss."

"I've been your boss for the past decade," he pointed out, not quite sure why she was being so spiky.

"Yes," she said. "You have been my boss for the past decade."

Then, she turned on her heel and walked back into her office, shutting the door firmly behind her.

And Isaiah went back to his desk.

He had work to do. Which was why he had given Poppy the task of picking him a wife. But before he chased Faith down for those estimates, he was going to need some caffeine. He sent a quick text to that effect to Poppy.

There was a quick flash of three dots at the bottom of the message box, then they disappeared.

It popped up again, and disappeared again. Then finally there was a simple: of course.

He could only hope that when he got his coffee it wasn't poisoned.

Three hours and three women later, Poppy was wishing she had gone with her original instinct and sent the middle finger emoji to Isaiah in response to his request for coffee.

This was too much. It would be crazy for anyone to have their assistant pick their wife—a harebrained scheme that no self-respecting personal assistant should have to cope with. But for her especially, it was a strange kind of emotional torture. She had to ask each woman questions about their compatibility with Isaiah. And then, she had to talk to them about Isaiah. Who she knew better than she knew any other man on the face of the earth. Who she knew possibly better than she knew anyone else. And all the while his words rang in her ears.

I'm your boss.

She was his *employee*.

And that was how he saw her. It shouldn't surprise her that no-nonsense, rigid Isaiah thought of her primarily as his employee. She thought of him as her friend.

Her best friend. Practically family.

Except for the part of her that was in love with him and had sex dreams about him sometimes.

Though, were she to take an afternoon nap today, her only dreams about Isaiah would involve her sticking a pen through his chest.

Well, maybe not his chest. That would be fatal. Maybe his arm. But then, that would get ink and blood on his shirt. She would have to unbutton it and take it off him…

Okay. Maybe she was capable of having both dreams at the same time.

"Kittens are my hard line," the sixth blonde of the day was saying to her. All the blondes were starting to run together like boxes of dye in the hair care aisle.

"I…" Poppy blinked, trying to get a handle on what that meant. "Like… Sexually… Or?"

The woman wrinkled her nose. "I mean, I need to be able to have a kitten. That's nonnegotiable."

Poppy was trying to imagine Isaiah Grayson with a kitten living in his house. He had barn cats. And he had myriad horses and animals at his ranch, but he did not have a kitten. Though, because he already had so many animals, it was likely that he would be okay with one more.

"I will… Make a note of that."

"Oh," the woman continued. "I can also tie a cherry stem into a knot with my tongue."

Poppy closed her eyes and prayed for the strength to not run out of the room and hit Isaiah over the head with a wastebasket. "I assume I should mark that down under special skills."

"Men like that," the woman said.

Well, maybe that was why Poppy had such bad luck with men. She couldn't do party tricks with her tongue. In fairness, she'd never tried.

"Good to know," Poppy continued.

Poppy curled her hands into fists and tried to keep herself from... She didn't even know what. Screaming. Running from the room.

One of these women who she interviewed today might very well be the woman Isaiah Grayson slept with for the rest of his life. The last woman he ever slept with. The one who made him completely and totally unavailable to Poppy forever.

The one who finally killed her fantasy stone-cold.

She had known that going in. She had. But suddenly it hit her with more vivid force.

I am your boss.

Her boss. Her boss. He was her boss. Not her friend. Not her lover. Never her lover.

Maybe he didn't see his future wife as a new car he was buying. But he basically saw Poppy as a stapler. Efficient and useful only when needed.

"Well, I will be in touch," Poppy stated crisply.

"Why are *you* interviewing all the women? Is this like a sister wives thing?"

Poppy almost choked. "No. I am Mr. Grayson's assistant. Not his wife."

"I wouldn't mind that," Lola continued. "It's always

seemed efficient to me. Somebody to share the work-
load of kids and housework. Well, and sex."

"Not. His. Wife." Poppy said that through clenched
teeth.

"He should consider that."

She tightened her hold on her pen, and was surprised she didn't end up snapping it in half. "Me as
his wife?"

"Sister wives."

"I'll make a note," Poppy said drily.

Her breath exited her body in a rush when Lola finally left, and Poppy's head was swimming with rage.

She had thought she could do this. She had been
wrong. She had been an idiot.

I am your boss.

He was her boss. Because she worked for him. Because she had worked for him for ten years. Ten years.

Why had she kept this job for so long? She had job
experience. She also had a nest egg. The money was
good, she couldn't argue that, but she could also go get
comparable pay at a large company in a city, and she
now had the experience to do that. She didn't have to
stay isolated here in Copper Ridge. She didn't have to
stay with a man who didn't appreciate her.

She didn't have to stay trapped in this endless hell
of wanting something she was never going to have.

No one was keeping her here. Nothing was keeping her here.

Nothing except the ridiculous idea that Isaiah had
feelings for her that went beyond that of his assistant.

Friends could be friends in different cities. They
didn't have to live in each other's pockets. Even if he
had misspoken and he did see them as friends—and

really, now that she was taking some breaths, she imagined that was closer to the truth—it was no excuse to continue to expose herself to him for twelve hours a day.

He was her business life. He was her social life. He was her fantasy life. That was too much for one man. Too much.

She walked into his office, breathing hard, and he looked up from his computer screen, his gray eyes assessing. He made her blood run hotter. Made her hands shake and her stomach turn over. She wanted him. Even now. She wanted to launch herself across the empty space and fling herself into his arms.

No. It had to stop.

"I quit," she said, the words tumbling out of her mouth in a glorious triumph.

But then they hit.

Hit him, hit her. And she knew she could take them back. Maybe she should.

No. She shouldn't.

"You *quit*?"

"It should not be in my job description to find you a wife. This is ludicrous. I just spent the last twenty minutes talking to a woman who was trying to get me to add the fact that she could tie a cherry stem into a knot with her tongue onto that ridiculous, awful form of yours underneath her '*skills*.'"

He frowned. "Well, that is a skill that might have interesting applications…"

"I know that," she said. "But why am I sitting around having a discussion with a woman that is obviously about your penis?"

Her cheeks heated, and her hands shook. She could

not believe she had just… Talked about his penis. In front of him.

"I didn't realize that would be a problem."

"Of course you didn't. Because you don't realize *anything*. You don't care about anything except the bottom line. That's all you ever see. You want a wife to help run your home. To help organize your life. By those standards *I* have been your damned wife for the past ten years, Isaiah Grayson. Isn't that what you're after? A personal assistant for your house. A *me* clone who can cook your dinner and…and…do wife things."

He frowned, leaning back in his chair.

He didn't speak, so she just kept going. "I quit," she repeated. "And you have to find your own wife. I'm not working with you anymore. I'm not dealing with you anymore. You said you were my boss. Well, you're not now. Not anymore."

"Poppy," he said, his large, masculine hands pressing flat on his desk as he pushed himself into a standing position. She looked away from his hands. They were as problematic as the rest of him. "Be reasonable."

"No! I'm not going to be reasonable. This situation is so unreasonable it isn't remotely fair of you to ask me to be reasonable within it."

They just stayed there for a moment, regarding each other, and then she slowly turned away, her breath coming in slow, harsh bursts.

"Wait," he said.

She stopped, but she didn't turn. She could feel his stare, resting right between her shoulder blades, digging in between them. "You're right. What I am looking for is a personal version of you. I hadn't thought about it that way until just now. But I am looking for a PA. In all areas of my life."

An odd sensation crept up the back of her neck, goose bumps breaking out over her arms. Still, she fought the urge to turn.

"Poppy," he said slowly. "I think you should marry me."

Three

When Poppy turned around to face him, her expression was still. Placid. He wasn't good at reading most people, but he knew Poppy. She was expressive. She had a bright smile and a stormy frown, and the absence of either was…concerning.

"Excuse me?"

"You said yourself that what I need is someone like you. I agree. I've never been a man who aims for second best. So why would I aim for second best in this instance? You're the best personal assistant I've ever had."

"I doubt you had a personal assistant before you had me," she said.

"That's irrelevant," he said, waving a hand. "I like the way we work together. I don't see why we couldn't make it something more. We're good partners, Poppy."

Finally, her face moved. But only just the slightest bit. "We're good partners," she echoed, the words hollow.

"Yes," he confirmed. "We are. We always have been.

You've managed to make seamless transitions at every turn. From when we worked at a larger construction firm, to when we were starting our own. When we expanded, to when we merged with Jonathan Bear. You've followed me every step of the way, and I've been successful in part because of the confidence I have that you're handling all the details that I need you to."

"And you think I could just… Do that at your house too?"

"Yes," he said simply.

"There's one little problem," Poppy said, her cheeks suddenly turning a dark pink. She stood there just staring for a moment, and the color in her face deepened. It took her a long while to speak. "The problem being that a wife doesn't just manage your kitchen. *That* is a housekeeper."

"I'm aware of that."

"A wife is supposed to…" She looked down, a pink blush continuing to bleed over her dark skin. "You don't feel that way about me."

"Feel what way? You know my desire to get married has nothing to do with love and romance."

"Sex." The word was like a mini explosion in the room. "Being a wife does have something to do with sex."

She was right about that, and when he had made his impromptu proposal a moment earlier, he hadn't been thinking of that. But now that he was…

He took a leisurely visual tour of her, similar to the one he had taken earlier. But this time, he didn't just appreciate her beauty in an abstract sense. This time, he allowed it to be a slightly more heated exploration.

Her skin looked smooth. He had noticed how lovely

it was earlier. But there was more than that. Her breasts looked about the right size to fit neatly into his hands, and she had an extremely enticing curve to her hips. Her skirts were never short enough to show very much of her leg, but she had nice ankles.

He could easily imagine getting down on his knees and taking those high heels off her feet. And biting one of her ankles.

That worked for him.

"I don't think that's going to be a problem," he said.

Poppy's mouth dropped open and then snapped shut. "We've never even… We've never even kissed, Isaiah. We've never even almost kissed."

"Yes. Because you're my assistant."

"Your assistant. And you're my foster sister's ex-fiancé."

Isaiah gritted his teeth, an involuntary spike of anger elevating his blood pressure. Poppy knew better than to talk about Rosalind. And hell, she had nothing to do with Poppy. Not in his mind, not anymore.

Yes, she was the reason Poppy had come to work for him in the first place, but Poppy had been with him for so long her presence wasn't connected with the other woman in any way.

He wasn't heartbroken. He never had been, not really. He was angry. She'd made a fool of him. She'd caused him to take his focus off his business. She'd nearly destroyed not only his work, but his brother's. And what would eventually be their sister's too.

All of it, all the success they had now had nearly been taken out by his own idiocy. By the single time he'd allowed his heart to control him.

He would never do that again.

"Rosalind doesn't have anything to do with this," he said.

"She's in my life," Poppy pointed out.

"That's a detail we can discuss later." Or not at all. He didn't see why they were coming close to discussing it now.

"You don't want to marry me," Poppy said.

"Are you questioning my decision-making, Poppy? How long have you known me? If there's one thing I'm not, it's an indecisive man. And I think you know that."

"You're a dick," Poppy said in exasperation. "How dare you... Have me interviewing these women all day... And then... Is this some kind of sick test?"

"You threatened to quit. I don't *want* you to quit. I would rather have you in all of my life than in none of my life."

"I didn't threaten to quit our friendship."

"I mostly see you at work," he said.

"And you value what I do at work more than what you get out of our friendship, is that it?"

That was another question he didn't know how to answer. Because he had a feeling the honest answer would earn him a spiked heel to the forehead. "I'm not sure how the two are separate," he said, thinking he was being quite diplomatic. "Considering we spend most of our time together at work, and my enjoyment of your company often dovetails with the fact that you're so efficient."

Poppy let out a howl that would not have been out of place coming from an enraged chipmunk. "You are... You are..."

Well, if her objection to the marriage was that they had never kissed, and never almost kissed, and he didn't want to hear her talk anymore—and all those things were true—he could only see one solution to the entire situation.

He made his way over to where Poppy was standing like a brittle rose and wrapped his arms around her waist. He dragged her to him, holding her in place as he stared down at her.

"Consider this your almost-kiss," he said.

Her brown eyes went wide, and she stared up at him, her soft lips falling open.

And then his heart was suddenly beating faster, the unsettled feeling in his gut transforming into something else. Heat. Desire. He had never looked at Poppy this way, ever.

And now he wondered if that had been deliberate. Now he wondered if he had been purposefully ignoring how beautiful she was because of all the reasons she had just mentioned for why they shouldn't get married.

The fact she was his assistant. The fact that she was Rosalind's foster sister.

"Isaiah…"

He moved one hand up to cup her cheek and brought his face down closer to hers. She smelled delicate, like flowers and uncertainty. And he found himself drawn to her even more.

"And this will be your kiss."

He brought his lips down onto hers, expecting… He didn't know what.

Usually, sexual attraction was a straightforward thing for him. That was one of the many things he liked about sex. There was no guesswork. It was honest. There was never anything shocking about it. If he saw a woman he thought was beautiful, he approached her. He never wondered if he would enjoy kissing her. Because he always wanted to kiss her before he did. But Poppy...

In the split second before their mouths touched, he wondered. Wondered what it would be like to kiss this woman he had known for so long. Who he had seen as essential to his life, but never as a sexual person.

And then, all his thoughts burned away. Because she tasted better than anything he could remember and her lips just felt right.

It felt equally right to slide his fingertips along the edge of her soft jawline and tilt her face up farther so he could angle his head in deep and gain access. It felt equally right to wrap both arms around her waist and press her body as tightly to his as he possibly could. To feel the soft swell of her breasts against his chest.

And he waited, for a moment, to see if she was going to stick her claws into him. To see if she was going to pull away or resist.

She did neither. Instead, she sighed, slowly, softly. Sweetly. She opened her mouth to his.

He took advantage of that, sliding his tongue between her lips and taking a taste.

He felt it, straight down to his cock, a lightning bolt of pleasure he'd had no idea was coming.

Suddenly, he was in the middle of a violent storm when only a moment ago the sky had been clear.

He had never experienced anything like it. The idea that Poppy—this woman who had been a constant in his world—was a hidden temptress rocked him down to his soul. He had no idea such a thing was possible.

In his world, chemistry had always been both

straightforward and instant. That it could simply exist beneath the surface like this seemed impossible.

And yet, it appeared there was chemistry between himself and Poppy that had been dormant all this time.

Her soft hands were suddenly pressed against his face, holding on to him as she returned his kiss with surprising enthusiasm.

Her enthusiasm might be surprising, but he was damn well going to take advantage of it.

Because if chemistry was her concern, then he was more than happy to demolish her worry here and now.

He reversed their positions, turning so her back was to his desk, and then he walked her backward before sliding one arm beneath her ass and picking her up, depositing her on top of the desk. He bent down to continue kissing her, taking advantage of her shock to step between her legs.

Or maybe he wasn't taking advantage of anything. Maybe none of this was calculated as he would like to pretend that it was. Maybe it was just necessary. Maybe now that their lips had touched there was just no going back.

And hell, why should they? If she couldn't deny the chemistry between them… If it went to its natural conclusion…she had no reason to refuse his proposal.

He slid one hand down her thigh, toward her knee, and then lifted that leg, hooking it over his hip as he drew her forward and pressed himself against her.

Thank God for the fullness of her skirt, because it was easy to make a space for himself right there between her legs. He was so hard it hurt.

He was a thirty-six-year-old man who had a hell

of a lot more self-control now than he'd ever had, and yet, he felt more out of control than he could ever remember being before.

That did not add up. It was bad math.

And right now, he didn't care.

Slowly, he slid his other hand up and cupped her breast. He had been right. It was exactly the right size to fill his palm. He squeezed her gently, and Poppy let out a hoarse groan, then wrenched her mouth away from his.

Her eyes were full of hurt. Full of tears.

"Don't," she said, wiggling away from him.

"What?" he asked, drawing a deep breath and trying to gain control over himself.

Stopping was the last thing he wanted to do. He wanted to strip that dress off her, marvel at every inch of uncovered skin. Kiss every inch of it. He wanted her twisting and begging underneath him. He wanted to sink into her and lose himself. Wanted to make her lose herself too.

Poppy.

His friend. His assistant.

"How dare you?" she asked. "How dare you try to manipulate me with… wth *sex*. You're my friend, Isaiah. I trusted you. You're just…trying to control me the way you control everything in your life."

"That isn't true," he said. It wasn't. It might have started out as…not a manipulation, but an attempt to prove something to both of them.

But eventually, he had just been swept up in all this. In her. In the heat between them.

"I think it is. You… I quit."

And then she turned and walked out of the room,

leaving him standing there, rejected for the first time in a good long while.

And it bothered him more than he would have ever imagined.

Poppy was steeped in misery by the time she crawled onto the couch in her pajamas that evening.

Her little house down by the ocean was usually a great comfort to her. A representation of security that she had never imagined someone like her could possess.

Now, nothing felt like a refuge. Nothing at all. This whole town felt like a prison.

Her bars were Isaiah Grayson.

That had to stop.

She really was going to quit.

She swallowed, feeling sick to her stomach. She was going to quit and sell this house and move away. She would talk to him sometimes, but mostly she had to let the connection go.

She didn't mean to him what he did to her. Not just in a romantic way. Isaiah didn't... He didn't understand. He didn't feel for people the way that other people felt.

And he had used the attraction she felt for him against her. Her deepest, darkest secret.

There was no way a woman without a strong, pre-existing attraction would have ever responded to him the way she had.

It had been revealing. Though, now she wondered if it had actually been revealing at all, or if he had just always known.

Had he known—all this time—how much she wanted him? And had he been…laughing at her?

No. Not laughing. He wouldn't do that. He wasn't cruel, not at all. But had he been waiting until it was of some use to him? Maybe.

She wailed and dragged a blanket down from the back of the couch, pulling it over herself and curling into a ball.

She had kissed Isaiah Grayson today.

More than kissed. He had… He had touched her.

He had *proposed* to her.

And, whether it was a manipulation or not, she had felt…

He had been hard. Right there between her legs, he had been turned on.

But then, he was a man, and there were a great many men who could get hard for blowup dolls. So. It wasn't like it was that amazing.

Except, something about it felt kind of amazing.

She closed her eyes. Isaiah. He was… He was absolutely everything to her.

She could marry him. She could keep another woman from marrying him.

Great. And then you can be married to somebody who doesn't love you at all. Who sees you as a convenience.

She laughed aloud at that thought. Yes. Some of that sounded terrible. But… She had spent most of her life in foster care. She had lived with a whole lot of people who didn't love her. And some of them had found her to be inconvenient. So that would put marrying Isaiah several steps above some of the living situations she'd had as a kid.

Then there was Rosalind. Tall, blond Rosalind who was very clearly Isaiah's type. While Poppy was...not.

How would she ever...cope with that? With the inevitable comparisons?

He hates her. He doesn't hate you.

Well. That was true. Rosalind had always gone after what she wanted. She had devastated Isaiah in the process. So much so that it had even hurt Poppy at the time. Because as much as she wanted to be with Isaiah, she didn't want him to be hurt.

And then, Rosalind had gone on to her billionaire. The man she was still with. She traveled around the world and hosted dinner parties and did all these things that had been beyond their wildest fantasies when they were growing up.

Rosalind wasn't afraid of taking something just for herself. And she didn't worry at all about someone else's feelings.

Sometimes, that was a negative. But right about now... Poppy was tempted—more than a little bit tempted—to be like Rosalind.

To go after her fantasy and damn the feelings and the consequences. She could have him. As her husband. She could have him...kissing her. She could have him naked.

She could be *his*.

She had been his friend and his assistant for ten years. But she'd never been his in the way she wanted to be.

He'd been her friend and her boss.

He'd never been hers.

Had anyone ever been hers?

Rosalind certainly cared about Poppy, in her own

way. If she didn't, she wouldn't have bailed Poppy out when she was in need. But Rosalind's life was very much about her. She and Poppy kept in touch, but that communication was largely driven by Poppy.

That was…it for her as far as family went. Except for the Graysons.

And if she married Isaiah…they really would be her family.

There was a firm, steady knock on her door. Three times. She knew exactly who it was.

It was like thinking about him had conjured him up.

She wasn't sure she was ready to face him.

She looked down. She was wearing a T-shirt and no bra. She was definitely not ready to face him. Still, she got up off the couch and padded over to the door. Because she couldn't *not*…

She couldn't not see him. Not right now. Not when all her thoughts and feelings were jumbled up like this. Maybe she would look at him and get a clear answer. Maybe she would look at him and think, *No, I still need to quit*.

Or maybe…

She knew she was tempting herself. Tempting him.

She hoped she was tempting him.

She scowled and grabbed hold of her blanket, wrapping it tightly around her shoulders before she made her way to the door. She wrenched it open. "What are you doing here?"

"I came to talk sense into you."

"You can't," she said, knowing she sounded like a bratty kid and not caring at all.

"Why not?"

"Because I am an insensible female." She whirled

around and walked back into her small kitchen, and Isaiah followed her, closing the front door behind him.

She turned to face him again, and her heart caught in her throat. He was gorgeous. Those cold, clear gray eyes, his sculpted cheekbones, the beard that made him more approachable. Because without it, she had a feeling he would be too pretty. And his lips…

She had kissed those lips.

He was just staring at her.

"I'm emotional."

He said nothing to that.

"I might actually throw myself onto the ground at any moment in a serious display of said emotion, and you won't like it at all. So you should probably leave."

Those gray eyes were level with hers, sparking heat within her, stoking a deep ache of desire inside her stomach.

"Reconsider." His voice was low and enticing, and made her want to agree to whatever commandment he issued.

"Quitting or marrying you?" She took a step back from him. She couldn't be trusted to be too close to him. Couldn't be trusted to keep her hands to herself. To keep from flinging herself at him—either to beat him or kiss him she didn't know.

"Both. Either."

Just when she thought he couldn't make it worse.

"That's not exactly the world's most compelling proposal."

"I already know that my proposal wasn't all that compelling. You made it clear."

"I mean, I've heard of bosses offering to give a

raise to keep an employee from leaving. But offering marriage…"

"That's not the only reason I asked you to marry me," he said.

She made a scoffing sound. "You could've fooled me."

"I'm not trying to fool you," he said.

Her heart twisted. This was one of the things she liked about Isaiah. It was tempting to focus on his rather grumpy exterior, and when she did that, the question of why she loved him became a lot more muddled. Because he was hot? A lot of men were hot. That wasn't it. There was something incredibly endearing about the fact that he said what he meant. He didn't play games. It simply wasn't in him. He was a man who didn't manipulate. And that made her accusation from earlier feel…wrong.

Manipulation wasn't really the right way to look at it. But he was used to being in charge. Unquestioned.

And he would do whatever he needed to do to get his way, that much she knew.

"Did you take the kiss as far as you did because you wanted to prove something to me?"

"No," he said. "I kissed you to try and prove something to *me*. Because you're right. If we were going to get married, then an attraction would have to be there."

"Yes," she said, her throat dry.

"I can honestly say that I never thought about you that way."

She felt like she'd just been stabbed through the chest with a kitchen knife. "Right," she said, instead of letting out the groan of pain that she was tempted to issue.

"We definitely have chemistry," he said. "I was genuinely caught off guard by it. I assume it was the same for you."

She blinked. He really had no idea? Did he really not know that her response to him wasn't sudden or random?

No. She could see that he didn't.

Isaiah often seemed insensitive because he simply didn't bother to blunt his statements to make them palatable for other people. Because he either didn't understand or care what people found offensive. Which meant, if backed into a corner about whether or not he had been using the kiss against her, he would have told her.

"I'm sorry," she said.

Now he looked genuinely confused. "You're apologizing to me. Why?"

"I'm apologizing to you because I assumed the worst about you. And that wasn't fair. You're not underhanded. You're not always sweet or cuddly or sensitive. But you're not underhanded."

"You like me," he pointed out.

He looked smug about that.

"Obviously. I wouldn't have put up with you for the past ten years. Good paying job or not. But then, I assume you like me too. At least to a degree."

"We're a smart match," he said. "I don't think you can deny that."

"Just a few hours ago you were thinking that one of those bottle blondes was your smart match. You can see why I'm not exactly thrilled by your sudden proposal to me."

"Are you in love with someone else?"

The idea was laughable. She hadn't even been on a date in…

She wasn't counting. It was too depressing.

"No," she said, her throat tightening. "But is it so wrong to want the possibility of love?"

"I think love is good for the right kind of people. Though my observation is that people mostly settle into a partnership anyway. The healthiest marriage is a partnership."

"Love is also kind of a thing."

He waved a hand. "Passion fades. But the way you support one another… That's what matters. That's what I've seen with my parents."

She stared at him for a long moment. He was right in front of her, asking for marriage, and she still felt like he was standing on the other side of a wall. Like she couldn't quite reach him. "And you're just…never going to love anyone."

"I *have* loved someone," he said simply.

There was something so incredibly painful about that truth. That he had loved someone. And she had used the one shot he was willing to give. It wasn't fair. That Rosalind had gotten his love. If Poppy would have had it, she would have preserved it. Held it close. Done anything to keep it for always.

But she would never get that chance. Because her vivacious older foster sister had gotten it first. And Rosalind hadn't appreciated what she'd had in him.

It was difficult to be angry at Rosalind over what had happened. Particularly when her and Isaiah being together had been painful for Poppy anyway. But right now… Right now, she was angry.

Because whole parts of Isaiah were closed off to Poppy because of the heartbreak he'd endured.

Or maybe that was silly. Maybe it was just going to take a very special woman to make him fall in love. And she wasn't that woman.

Well, on the plus side, if you don't marry him, you'll give him a chance to find that woman.

She clenched her teeth, closing her eyes against the pain. She didn't think she could handle that. It was one terrible thing to think about watching him marry another woman. But it was another, even worse thing to think about him falling in love with someone else. If she were good and selfless, pure and true, she supposed that's what she would want for him.

But she wasn't, and she didn't. Because if he fell in love, that would mean she wasn't going to get what she wanted. She would lose her chance at love. At least, the love she wanted.

How did it benefit her to be that selfless? It just didn't.

"I'll think about it," she said.

Four

"I'm not leaving here until I close this deal," he said.

"I'm not a business deal waiting to happen, Isaiah."

He took a step toward her, and she felt her resolve begin to weaken. And then, she questioned why she was even fighting this at all.

He was the one driving this train. He always was.

Because she loved him.

Because he was her boss.

Because he possessed the ability to remain somewhat detached, and she absolutely did not.

She could watch him trying to calculate his next move. She could see that it was difficult for him to think of this as something other than a business deal.

No, she supposed that what Isaiah was proposing *was* a business deal. With sex.

"You can't actually be serious," she said.

"I'm always serious."

"I get that you think you can get married and make it not about…*feelings*. But it's… I can't get over the sex thing, Isaiah. I can't."

There were many reasons for that, not the least of

which being her own inexperience. But she was not going to have that discussion with him.

"The kiss was good." He said it like that solved everything. Like it should somehow deal with all of her concerns.

"A kiss isn't sex," she said lamely. As if pointing out one of the most obvious things in the world would fix this situation.

"Do you think it's going to be a problem?"

"I think it's going to be weird."

Weird was maybe the wrong word. Terrifying.

Able to rip her entire heart straight out of her chest.

"You're fixating," he said simply. "Let's put a pin in the sex."

"You can't put a pin in the sex," she protested.

"Why can't I put a pin in the sex?"

"Because," she said, waving her hand in a broad gesture. "The sex is like the eight-hundred-pound gorilla in the room. In lingerie. It will not be ignored. It will not be…pinned."

"Put a pin in it," he reiterated. "Let's talk about everything else that a marriage between the two of us could offer you."

She sputtered. "Could offer *me*?"

"Yes. Of course, I don't expect you to enter into an arrangement that benefits only me. So far, I haven't presented you with one compelling reason why marriage between the two of us would be beneficial to you."

"And you think that's my issue?"

"I think it's one issue. My family loves you. I appreciate that. Because I'm very close to my family. Anyone I marry will have to get along with my family. You already do. I feel like you love my family…"

She closed her eyes. Yes. She did love the Grayson family. She loved them so much. They were the only real, functional family she had ever seen in existence. They were the reason she believed that kind of thing existed outside the land of sitcoms. If it weren't for them, she would have no frame of reference for that kind of normalcy. A couple who had been together all those years. Adult children that loved their parents enough to try to please them. To come back home and visit. Siblings who worked together to build a business. Who cared for each other.

Loud, boisterous holiday celebrations that were warm and inviting. That included her.

Yes, the Grayson family was a big, fat carrot in all of this.

But what Isaiah didn't seem to understand was that he was the biggest carrot of all.

An inescapably sexual thought, and she had been asked to put a pin in the sex. But with Isaiah she could never just set the sex aside.

"You love my ranch," he said. "You love to come out and ride the horses. Imagine. You would already be sleeping there on weekends. It would be easy to get up and go for a ride."

"I love my house," she protested.

"My ranch is better," he said.

She wanted to punch him for that. Except, it was true.

His gorgeous modern ranch house with both rustic and modern details, flawlessly designed by his sister, was a feat of architectural engineering and design. There was not a single negative thing she could say about the place.

Set up in the mountains, with a gorgeous barn and

horses and all kinds of things that young, daydreamer Poppy would have given her right arm to visit, much less inhabit.

He had horses. And he'd taught her to ride a year earlier.

"And I assume you want children."

She felt like the wind had been knocked out of her. "I thought we weren't going to talk about sex."

"We're not talking about sex. We're talking about children."

"Didn't your parents tell you where babies come from?"

His mouth flattened into a grim line. "I will admit there was something I missed when I was thinking of finding a wife through an ad."

She rolled her eyes. "Really?"

"Yes. I thought about myself. I thought about the fact that I wanted children in the abstract. But I did not think about what kind of mother I wanted my children to have. You would be a wonderful mother."

She blinked rapidly, fighting against the sting of sudden tears. "Why would you think that?"

"I know you. I've watched the way you took care of me and my business for the last ten years. The way you handle everything. The details in my professional life, Joshua and Faith's, as well. I've seen you with Joshua's son."

"I was basically raised by wolves," she pointed out. "I don't know anything about families."

"I think that will make you an even better mother. You know exactly what not to do."

She huffed out a laugh. "Disappearing into a heroin haze is a good thing to avoid. That much I know."

"You know more than that," he said. "You're good with people. You're good at anticipating what they want, what they need. You're organized. You're efficient."

"You make me sound like an app, Isaiah."

"You're warm and…and sometimes sweet. Though, not to me."

"You wouldn't like me if I were sweet," she pointed out.

"No. I wouldn't. But that's the other thing. You know how to stand up to me." The sincerity on his face nearly killed her. "We would be good together."

He sounded so certain. And she felt on the opposite side of the world from certain.

This was too much. It really was. Too close to everything she had ever dreamed about—without one essential ingredient. Except… When had she really ever been allowed to dream?

She had watched so many other people achieve their dreams. While she'd barely allowed herself to imagine…

A life with Isaiah.

Children.

A family of her own.

Isaiah had simply been off-limits in her head all this time. It had made working with him easier. It had made being his friend less risky.

But he was offering her fantasy.

How could she refuse?

"Your parents can't know it's fake," she said.

"Are you agreeing?"

She blinked rapidly, trying to keep her tears back. "They can't know," she repeated.

"It's not fake," he said simply. "We'll have a real marriage."

"They can't know about the ad. They can't know that you just… Are hiring me for a new position. Okay?"

"Poppy…"

"They can't know you're not in love with me."

She would die. She would die of shame. If his wonderful, amazing parents who only ever wanted the best for their children, who most certainly wanted deep abiding love for Isaiah, were to know this marriage was an arrangement.

"It's not going to come up," he said.

"Good. It can't." Desperation clawed at her, and she wasn't really sure what she was desperate for. For him to agree. For him to say he had feelings for her. For him to kiss her. "Or it's off."

"Agreed."

"Agreed."

For a moment she thought he *was* going to kiss her again. She wasn't sure she could handle that. So instead, she stuck her hand out and stood there, staring at him. He frowned but took her offered hand, shaking it slowly.

Getting engaged in her pajamas and ending it with a handshake was not the romantic story she would need to tell his family.

He released his hold on her hand, and she thought he was going to walk away. But instead, he reached out and pulled her forward, capturing her mouth with his after all, a flood of sensation washing over her.

And then, as quickly as it began, the kiss ended.

"No. It's not going to be a problem," he said.

She expected him to leave then. He was supposed

to leave. But instead, he dipped his head and kissed her again.

She felt dizzy. And she wanted to keep on kissing him. This couldn't be happening. It shouldn't be happening.

But they were engaged. So maybe this had to happen.

She didn't know this man, she realized as he let out a feral growl and backed her up against her wall. This was not the cool, logical friend she had spent all these years getting to know. This was…

Well, this was Isaiah as a man.

She had always known he was a man. Of course she had. If she hadn't, she wouldn't have been in love with him. Wouldn't have had so many fantasies about him. But she hadn't *really* known. Not like this. She hadn't known what it would be like to be the woman he wanted. Hadn't had any idea just how hot-blooded a man as detached and cool as he was on a day-to-day basis could be when sex was involved.

Sex.

She supposed now was the time to bring up her little secret.

But maybe this was just a kiss, maybe they weren't going to have sex.

He angled his head then, taking the kiss deeper. Making it more intense. And then he reached down and gripped the hem of her T-shirt, pulling it up over her head.

She didn't have a bra on underneath, and she was left completely exposed. Her nipples went tight as he looked at her, as those familiar gray eyes, so cold and rational most of the time, went hot.

He stared at her, his eyes glittering. "How did I not know?"

"How did you not know what?" Her teeth chattered when she asked the question.

Only then did she realize she was afraid this would expose her. Because while she could handle keeping her love for Isaiah in a little corner of her heart while she had access to his body—while she claimed ownership of him, rather than allowing some other woman to have him—she could not handle him knowing how she felt.

She'd had her love rejected too many times in her life. She would never subject herself to that again. Ever.

"How did I not know how beautiful you were?" He was absolutely serious, his sculpted face looking as if it was carved from rock.

She reached out, dragged her fingertips over his face. Over the coarse hair of his beard.

She could touch him now. Like this.

The kiss in his office had been so abrupt, so shocking, that while she had enjoyed it, she hadn't fully been able to process all that it meant. All the changes that came with it.

She didn't touch Isaiah like this. She didn't touch him ever.

And now… She finally could.

She frowned and leaned forward, pressing her lips slowly against his. They were warm, and firm, and she couldn't remember anything in the world feeling this wonderful.

Slowly, ever so slowly, she traced the outline of his bottom lip with her tongue.

She was tasting him.

Ten years of fantasies, vague and half-realized, and they had led here. To this. To him.

She slid her hands back, pushing them through his hair as she moved forward, pressing her bare breasts to his chest, still covered by the T-shirt he was wearing.

She didn't want anything between them. Nothing at all.

Suddenly, pride didn't matter.

She pulled away from him for a moment, and his eyes went straight down to her breasts again.

That would be her salvation. The fact that he was a man. That he was more invested in breasts than in feelings.

He was never going to see how she felt. Never going to see the love shining from her eyes, as long as he was looking at her body. And in this, in sex, she had the freedom to express everything she felt.

She was going to.

Oh, she was going to.

She wrapped her arms around his neck and pushed forward again, claiming his mouth, pouring everything, every fantasy, into that moment.

He growled, his arm wrapping around her waist like a steel band, the other one going down to her thighs as he lifted her up off the ground, pulling her against him. She wrapped her legs around his waist and didn't protest at all when he carried them both from the kitchen back toward her bedroom.

She knew exactly where this was going.

But it was time.

If she were totally, completely honest with herself, she knew why she hadn't done this before.

She was waiting for him.

She always had been.

A foolish, humiliating truth that she had never allowed herself to face until now. But it made pausing for consideration pointless.

She was going to marry him.

She was going to be with him.

There was nothing to think about.

There was a small, fragile bubble of joy in her chest, something she had never allowed herself to feel before. And it was growing inside her now.

She could have this. She could have him.

She squeaked when he dropped her down onto the bed and wrenched his shirt up over his head. She lay back, looking at him, taking in the fine, sculpted angles of his body. His chest was covered with just the right amount of dark hair, extending in a line down the center of his abs, disappearing beneath the waistband of his jeans.

She was exceptionally interested in that. And, for the first time, she hoped she was going to have those questions answered. That her curiosity would be satisfied.

He moved his hands to his belt buckle and reality began to whisper in her ear as he worked through the loops.

She didn't know why reality had showed up. It was her knee-jerk reaction to good things, she supposed.

In her life, nothing stayed good for long. Not for her. Only other girls got what they wanted.

The fact of the matter was, she wasn't his second choice after her much more beautiful foster sister.

She wasn't even his tenth choice.

She had come somewhere down the line of she-didn't-even-want-to-know-how-many bar hookups and the women who had been in her office earlier today.

On the list of women he might marry, Poppy was below placing an ad as a solution.

That was how much of a last resort she was.

At least this time you're a resort at all. Does it really matter if you're the last one?

In many ways, it didn't. Not at all.

Because she wanted to be chosen, even if she was chosen last.

He slowly lowered the zipper on his jeans and all of her thoughts evaporated.

Saved by the slow tug of his underwear, revealing a line of muscle that was almost obscene and a shadow of dark hair before he drew the fabric down farther and exposed himself completely, pushing his pants and underwear all the way to the floor.

She tried not to stare openmouthed. She had never seen a naked man in person before. And she had never counted on seeing Isaiah naked. Had dreamed about it, yes. Had fantasized about it, sure. But, she had never really imagined that it might happen.

"Now it's your turn," he said, his voice husky. Affected.

"I…"

She was too nervous. She couldn't make her hands move. Couldn't find the dexterity to pull her pajama pants down. And, as skills went, taking off pajama pants was a pretty easy one.

He took pity on her. He leaned forward, cupping her chin and kissing her, bringing himself down onto the bed beside her and pressing his large, warm palm between her shoulder blades, sliding his hand down the line of her back, just beneath the waistband of those pajamas. His hand was hot and enticing on her ass, and she arched her hips forward, his erection brushing against the apex of her thighs.

She gasped, and he kissed her, delving deep as he did, bringing his other hand around to cup her breast, his thumb sliding over her nipple, drawing it into an impossibly tight bud.

She pressed her hands against his chest, and just stared at them for a moment. Then she looked up at his face and back down at her hands.

She was touching his bare chest.

Isaiah.

It was undeniable.

He was looking down at her, his dark brows locked together, his expression as serious as it ever was, and it was just...*him*.

She slid her hands downward, watching as they traveled. Her mouth went dry when she touched those ab muscles, when her hands went down farther. She paused, holding out her index finger and tracing the indention that ran diagonally across his body, straight toward that place where he was most male.

She avoided touching him there.

She didn't know *how*.

But then, he took hold of her hand, curved his fingers around it and guided her right toward his erection.

She held back a gasp as he encouraged her to curl her fingers around his thick length.

He was so hot. Hot and soft and hard all at once. Then she looked back up, meeting his eyes, and suddenly, it wasn't so scary. Because Isaiah—a man who was not terribly affected by anything at all in the world, who seemed so confident in his ability to control everything around him—looked absolutely at a loss.

His forehead had relaxed, his eyes fluttering closed, his lips going slack. His head fell back. She squeezed him, and a groan rumbled in his chest.

Right now, she had the control, the power.

Probably for the first and only time in their entire relationship.

She had never felt anything like this before. Not ever.

A pulse began to beat between her legs, need swamping her. She felt hollow there, the slickness a telltale sign of just how much she wanted him too. But she didn't feel embarrassed about it. It didn't make her feel vulnerable. They were equals in this. It felt…exhilarating. Exciting. Right here in her little bed, it felt safe. To want him as much as she did.

How could it not, when he wanted her too?

Experimentally, she pumped her hand along his length, and he growled.

He was beautiful.

Everything she'd ever wanted. She knew he'd been made for her. This man who had captured her heart, her fantasies, from the moment she'd first met him.

But she didn't have time to think about all of that, because she found herself flipped onto her back, with Isaiah looming over her. In an easy movement, he reached between them and yanked off her pants and underwear.

He made space for himself between her legs, gripping his arousal and pressing it through her slick folds, the intimacy of the action taking her breath away, and then the intense, white-hot pleasure that assaulted her when he hit that perfect spot cleared her mind of anything and everything.

He did it again, and then released his hold on himself, flexing his hips against her. She gasped, grabbing his shoulders and digging her fingers into his skin.

His face was a study in concentration, and he cupped her breast, teasing her nipple as he continued to flex his hips back and forth across that sensitive bundle of nerves.

Something gathered low in her stomach, that hollow sensation between her legs growing keener...

And he didn't stop. He kept at it, teasing her nipple, and moving his hips in a maddening rhythm.

The tension within her increased, further and further until it suddenly snapped. She gasped as her climax overtook her, and he captured that sound of pleasure with his mouth, before drawing back and pressing the himself into the entrance of her body. And then, before she had a chance to tense up, he pressed forward.

The shocking, tearing sensation made her cry out in pain.

Isaiah's eyes clashed with hers.

"What the hell?"

Five

Isaiah was trying to form words, but he was completely overtaken by the feel of her around his body. She was so tight. So wet. And he couldn't do anything but press his hips forward and sink even deeper into her in spite of the fact that she had cried out with obvious pain only a second before.

He should stop. But she was kissing him again. She was holding him against her as she moved her hips in invitation. As her movements physically begged him to stay with her.

Poppy was a virgin.

He should stop.

He *couldn't* stop.

He couldn't remember when that had ever happened to him before. He didn't know if it ever had. He was all about control. It was necessary for a man like him. He had to override his emotions, his needs.

Right now.

But she was holding him so tight. She felt…so good. He had only intended to give her a kiss before he left.

And he *had* intended to go. But he'd been caught up…
in her. Not in triumph over the fact that he had convinced her to marry him.

No, he had been caught up in *her*.

In the wonder of kissing her. Uncovering her. Exploring her in a way he had never imagined he might.

But he'd had no idea—none at all—that she was this inexperienced.

Poppy was brash. She gave as good as she got. She didn't shy away from anything. And she hadn't shied away from this either.

She still wasn't.

Her hands traveled down to cup his ass, and she tugged at him, as if urging him on.

"Isaiah," she whispered. "Isaiah, please."

And he had no choice but to oblige.

He moved inside her, slowly at first, torturing them both, and trying to make things more comfortable for her.

He had no idea how he was supposed to have sex with a damned virgin. He never had before.

He had a type. And Poppy was against that type in every single way.

But it seemed to be working just fine for him now.

She pressed her fingertips to his cheek, then pulled him down toward her mouth. She kissed him. Slow and sweet, and he forgot to have control.

He would apologize later. For going too fast. Too hard. But she kept making these sounds. Like she wanted it. Like she liked it. She wrapped her legs around his hips and urged him on, like she needed it. And he couldn't slow down. Couldn't stop. Couldn't make it better, even if he should.

He should make her come at least three more times before he took his own pleasure, but he didn't have the willpower. Not at all.

His pleasure overtook him, squeezing down on his windpipe, feeling like jaws to his throat, and he couldn't pull back. Not now. When his orgasm overtook him, all he could hear was the roar of his own blood in his ears, the pounding of his heartbeat. And then Poppy arched beneath him, her nails in his shoulders probably near to drawing blood as she let out a deep, intense cry, her internal muscles flexing around him.

He jerked forward, spilling inside her before he withdrew and rolled over onto his back. He was breathing hard, unable to speak. Unable to think.

"Poppy..."

"I don't want to talk about it," she said, crawling beneath a blanket beside him, covering herself up. She suddenly looked very small, and he was forced to sit there and do the math on their age difference. It wasn't that big. Well, eight years. But he had never thought about what that might mean.

Of course, he had never known her to have a serious relationship. But then, he had only had the one, and he had certainly been having sex.

"We should talk about it."

"Why?" Her eyes were large and full of an emotion he couldn't grab hold of. But it echoed in him, and it felt a lot like pain. "There's really nothing to talk about. You know that my... My childhood was terrible. And I don't see why we have to go over all the different issues *that* might've given me."

"So you've been avoiding this."

It suddenly made sense why she had been so fixated on the sex aspect of his proposal. He'd been with a lot of women. So he had taken for granted that sex would be sex.

Of course, he had been wrong. He looked down at her, all vulnerable and curled into a ball. He kissed her forehead.

It hadn't just been sex. And of course poor Poppy had no reference at all for what sex would be like anyway.

"I'm sorry," he said.

"Don't be sorry. But I... I need to be alone."

That didn't sit well with him. The idea of leaving her like this.

"Please," she said.

He had no idea how to handle a woman in this state. Didn't know how to...

He usually wasn't frustrated by his difficulty connecting with people. He had a life that suited him. Family and friends who understood him. Who he knew well enough to understand.

Usually, he understood Poppy. But this was uncharted territory for the two of them, and he was at a loss for the right thing to do.

"If you really need that."

She nodded. "I do."

He got up, slowly gathering his clothes and walking out of the bedroom. He paused in her living room, holding those clothes in his hands. Then he dropped them. He lay down on her couch, which he was far too tall for, and pulled a blanket over himself.

There. She could be alone. In her room. And tomorrow they would talk. And put together details for their upcoming wedding.

He closed his eyes, and he tried not to think about what it had felt like to slide inside her.

But that was all he thought about.

Over and over again, until he finally fell asleep.

Poppy's eyes opened wide at three in the morning. She padded out into the hall, feeling disoriented. She was naked. Because she'd had sex with Isaiah last night.

And then she had sent him away.

Because… She didn't know why. She hated herself? She hated him? And everything good that could possibly happen to her?

She'd panicked. That was the only real explanation for her reaction.

She had felt stripped and vulnerable. She had wanted—needed—time to get a hold of herself.

Though, considering how she felt this morning, there probably wasn't enough time in the entire world for her to collect herself.

She had asked him to leave. And he'd left.

Of course he had.

She cared for that man with a passion, but he was not sensitive. Not in the least. Not even a little bit.

You asked him to go. What do you want from him?

It was silly to want anything but exactly what she had asked for. She knew it.

She padded out toward the living room. She needed something. A mindless TV show. A stiff drink. But she wasn't going to be able to go back to sleep.

When she walked into the living room, her heart jumped into her throat. Because there was a man-shaped something lying on her couch.

Well, it wasn't just man-shaped. It *was* a man.

Isaiah. Who had never left.

Who was defying her expectations again.

He'd been covered by a blanket, she was pretty sure, considering the fact that there was a blanket on the floor bunched up next to him. But he was still naked, sprawled out on her couch and now uncovered. He was...

Even in the dim light she could see just how incredible he was. Long limbs, strong muscles. So hard. Like he was carved from granite.

He was in many ways a mystery to her, even though she knew him as well as she knew anyone. If not better.

He was brilliant with numbers. His investments, his money management, was a huge part of what made Gray Bear Construction a success. He wasn't charismatic Joshua with an easy grin, good with PR and an expert way with people. He wasn't the fresh-faced wunderkind like Faith, taking the architecture world by storm with designs that outstripped her age and experience. Faith was a rare and unique talent. And Jonathan Bear was the hardest worker she had ever met.

And yet, Isaiah's work was what kept the company moving. He was the reason they stayed solvent. The reason that everything he had ever been involved with had been a success in one way or another.

But he was no pale, soft, indoor man. No. He was rugged. He loved spending time outdoors. Seemed to thrive on it. The moment work was through, Isaiah was out on his ranch. It amazed her that he had ever managed to live in Seattle. Though, even then, he had been hiking on the weekends, mountain biking and staying in cabins outside the city whenever he got the chance.

She supposed in many ways that was consistent enough. The one thing he didn't seem to have a perfect handle on was people. Otherwise, he was a genius.

But he had stayed with her.

In spite of the fact that she had asked him not to. She wasn't sure if that was an incredible amount of intuition on his part or if it was simply him being a stubborn ass.

"Are you just going to stand there staring at me?"

She jumped. "I didn't know you were awake."

"I wasn't."

"You knew I was looking at you," she said, shrinking in on herself slightly, wishing she had something to cover up her body.

Isaiah, for his part, looked completely unconcerned. He lifted his arms and clasped his hands, putting them behind his head. "Are you ready to talk?"

"I thought it was the woman who was supposed to be all needy and wanting to talk."

"Traditionally. Maybe. But this isn't normal for me. And I'm damn sure this isn't normal for you. You know, on account of the fact that you've never done this before."

"I said I didn't want to talk about my hymenal status."

"Okay."

He didn't say anything. The silence between them seemed to balloon, expand, becoming very, very uncomfortable.

"It wasn't a big deal," she said. "I mean, in that I wasn't waiting for anything in particular. I was always waiting for somebody to care about me. Always. But then, when I left home… When I got my job with you…" She artfully left out any mention of Rosalind.

"That was when I finally felt like I fit. And there just wasn't room for anything else. I didn't want there to be. I didn't need there to be."

"But now, with me, you suddenly changed your mind?"

She shifted, covering herself with her hand as she clenched her thighs more tightly together. "It's not that I changed my mind. I didn't have a specific No Sex Rule. I just hadn't met a man I trust, and I trust you and…and I got carried away."

"And that's never happened to you before," he said, keeping his tone measured and even. The way he handled people when he was irritated but trying not to show it. She knew him well enough to be familiar with that reaction.

"No," she admitted. Because there was no point in not telling him.

"You wanted this," he said, pushing into a sitting position. "You wanted it, didn't you?"

"Yes," she said. "I don't know how you could doubt that."

"Because you've never wanted to do this before. And then suddenly… You did. Poppy, I knew I was coercing you into marriage, but I didn't want to coerce you into bed."

"You didn't. We're engaged now anyway and… It was always going to be you," she blurted out and then quickly tried to backtrack. "Maybe it was never going to happen for me if I didn't trust and know the person. But I've never had an easy time with trusting. With you, it just kind of…happened."

"Sex?"

"Trust."

"Come here."

"There?"

He reached out and took hold of her wrist, and then he tugged her forward, bringing her down onto his lap in an elegant tumble. "Yes."

He was naked. She was naked. She was sitting on his lap. It should feel ridiculous. Or wrong somehow. This sudden change.

But it didn't feel strange. It felt good.

He felt good.

"I'm staying," he said.

"I asked you to leave," she pointed out.

"You didn't really want me to."

"You can't know that," she said, feeling stubborn.

It really wasn't fair. Because she *had* wanted him to stay.

"Normally, I would say that's true. But I know you. And I knew that you didn't really want me to leave you alone *alone*."

"You knew that?"

"Yes, even I knew that," he said.

She lifted her hand, let it hover over his chest. Then he took hold of it and pressed it down, over his heart. She could feel it thundering beneath her palm.

"I guess you can stay," she whispered.

"I'm too tall for this couch," he pointed out.

"Well, you can sleep on the floor."

That was when she found herself being lifted into the air as Isaiah stood. "I think I'll go back to your bed."

She swallowed, her heart in her throat, her body trembling. Were they really going to… Again?

"It's not a very comfortable bed," she said weakly.

"I think I can handle it."

Then he kissed her, and he kept on kissing her until they were back in her room.

Whatever desire she had to protect herself, to withdraw from him, was gone completely.

For the first time in her life, she was living her dream in Isaiah's arms. She wasn't going to keep herself from it.

Six

Poppy was not happy when he insisted they drive to work together the next day.

But it was foolish for them to go separately. He was already at her house. She was clearly resisting him taking over every aspect of the situation, and he could understand that. But it didn't mean he could allow for impracticality.

Still, she threw him out of the bedroom, closed herself in and didn't emerge until it was about five minutes to the time they were meant to be there.

She was back in her uniform. A bright red skirt that fell down to her knees and a crisp, white top that she had tucked in. Matching red earrings and shoes added to the very Poppy look.

"Faith and Joshua are going to have questions," she said, her tone brittle as she got into the passenger seat of his sports car.

"So what? We're engaged."

"We're going to have to figure out a story. And… We're going to have to tell your parents. Your parents are not going to be happy if they're the last to know."

"We don't have to tell my siblings we're engaged."

"Oh, you just figure we can tell them we knocked boots and leave it at that?" Her tone told him she didn't actually think that was a good idea.

"Or not tell them anything. It's not like either of them keep me apprised of their sexual exploits."

"Well, Joshua is married and Faith is your little sister."

"And?"

"You are an endless frustration."

So was she, but he had a feeling if he pointed that out at the moment it wouldn't end well for him.

This wasn't a real argument. He'd already won. She was here with him, regardless of her protestations. He'd risk her wrath when it was actually necessary.

"Jonathan will not be in today, if that helps. At least, he's not planning on it as far as I know."

She made a noise halfway between a snort and clearing her throat. "The idea of dealing with Jonathan bothers me a lot less than dealing with your siblings."

"Well. We have to deal with them eventually. There's no reason to wait. It's not going to get less uncomfortable. I could probably make an argument for the fact that the longer we wait the more uncomfortable we'll get."

"You know. If you could be just slightly less practical sometimes, it would make us mere mortals feel a whole lot better."

"What do you mean?"

"Everything is black-and-white to you. Everything is…easy." She looked like she actually meant that.

"That isn't true," he said. "Things are easy for me when I can line them out. When I can make categories and columns, so whenever I can do that, I do it. Life has variables. Too many. If you turn it into math, there's one answer. If the answer makes sense, go with that."

"But life *isn't* math," she said. "There's not one answer. We could hide this from everyone until we feel like not hiding it. We could have driven separate cars."

"Hiding it is illogical."

"Not when you're a woman who just lost her virginity and you're a little embarrassed and don't necessarily want everyone to know."

"You know," he said, his tone dry, "you don't have to walk in and announce that you just lost your virginity."

"I am aware of that," she snapped. She tapped her fingernails on the armrest of the passenger door. "You know. You're a pretty terrible cowboy. What with the sports car."

"I have a truck for the ranch. But I also have money. So driving multiple cars is my prerogative."

She made a scoffing sound. And she didn't speak to him for the rest of the drive over.

For his part, Isaiah wasn't bothered by her mood. After she had come to speak to him in the early hours of the morning, he had taken her back to bed where he had kept her up for the rest of the night. She had responded to every touch, every kiss.

She might be angry at him, but she wanted him. And that would sustain them when nothing else would.

The whole plan was genius, really.

Now that they'd discovered this attraction between them, she really was the perfect wife for him. He liked her. She would be a fantastic mother. She was an amazing partner, and he already knew it. And then there was this…this heat.

It was more than he'd imagined getting out of a relationship.

So he could handle moments of spikiness in the name of all they had going for them.

They drove through the main street of town in silence, and Isaiah took stock of how the place looked, altered for Christmas. All the little shops adorned with strings of white lights and evergreen boughs.

It made him wonder about Poppy's life growing up. About the Christmases she might have had.

"Did you celebrate Christmas when you were a child?" he asked.

"What?"

"The Christmas decorations made me wonder. We did. Just…very normal Christmases. Like movies. A tree, family. Gifts and a dry turkey."

She laughed. "I have a hard time believing your mother ever made a dry turkey."

"My grandma made dry turkey," he said. "She died when I was in high school. But before then…"

"It sounds lovely," Poppy said. "Down to the dry turkey. I had some very nice Christmases. But there was never a routine. I also had years where there was no celebration. I don't have…very strong feelings about Christmas, actually. I don't have years of tradition to make into something special."

When they pulled into the office just outside of town, he parked, and Poppy wasted no time in getting out of the car and striding toward the building. Like she was trying to outrun appearing with him.

He shook his head and got out of the car, following behind her. Not rushing.

If she wanted to play a game, she was welcome to it. But she was the one who was bothered. Not him.

He walked into the craftsman-style building behind her, and directly into the front seating area, where his sister, Faith, was curled on a chair with her feet underneath her and a cup of coffee beside her.

Joshua was sitting in a chair across from her, his legs propped up on the coffee table.

"Are you having car trouble?" Faith directed that question at Poppy.

Poppy looked from Isaiah to Joshua and then to Faith. And he could sense when she'd made a decision. Her shoulders squared, her whole body became as stiff as a board, as if she were bracing herself.

She took a deep breath.

"No," she said. "I drove over with your brother because I had sex with him last night."

Then she swept out of the room and stomped down the hall toward her office. He heard the door slam decisively behind her.

Two heads swiveled toward him, wide eyes on his face.

"What?" his sister asked.

"I don't think she could have made it any clearer," he said, walking over to the coffeepot and pouring himself a cup.

"You had sex with Poppy," Joshua confirmed.

"Yes," Isaiah responded, not bothering to look at his brother.

"You... *You.* And Poppy."

"Yes," he said again.

"Why do I know this?" Faith asked, covering her ears.

"I didn't know she was going to make a pronouncement," Isaiah said. He felt a smile tug at his lips. "Though, she was kind of mad at me. So. I feel like this is her way of getting back at me for saying the change in our relationship was simple."

Faith's eyes bugged out. "You told her that it was simple. The whole thing. The two of you...*friends*... *Poppy*, an employee of the past ten years... *Sleeping together*." Faith was sputtering.

"It was good sex, Faith," he commented.

Faith's look contorted into one of abject horror, and she withdrew into her chair.

"There's more," Isaiah said. "I'm getting married to her."

"You are...*marrying Poppy*?" Now Faith was just getting shrill.

"Yes."

"You don't have to marry someone just because you have sex with them," Joshua pointed out.

"I'm aware of that, but you know I want to get married. And considering she and I have chemistry, I figured we might as well get married."

"But... Poppy?" Joshua asked.

"Why *not* Poppy?"

"Are you in love with her?" Faith asked.

"I care about her more than I care about almost anyone."

"You didn't answer my question," Faith said.

"Did no one respond to your ad?" Joshua was clearly happy to skip over questions about feelings.

Isaiah nodded. "Several women did. Poppy interviewed six of them yesterday."

Joshua looked like he wanted to say something that he bit back. "And you didn't like any of them?"

"I didn't meet any of them."

"So," Faith said slowly, "yesterday you had her interviewing women to marry you. And then last night you…hooked up with her."

"You're skipping a step. Yesterday afternoon she accused me of looking for a wife who was basically an assistant. For my life. And that was when I realized… She's actually the one I'm looking for."

"That is… The least romantic thing I've ever heard," Faith said.

"Romance is not a requirement for me."

"What about Poppy?"

He lifted a shoulder. "She could have said no."

"Could she have?" Faith asked. "I mean, no offense, Isaiah, but it's difficult to say no to you when you get something in your head."

"You don't want to hear this," Isaiah said, "but particularly after last night, I can say confidently that Poppy and I suit each other just fine."

"You're right," Faith said, "I don't want to hear it." She stood up, grabbing her coffee and heading back toward her office.

"I hope you know what you're doing," Joshua said slowly.

Isaiah looked over at his brother. "What about any of this doesn't look like I know what I'm doing?"

"Getting engaged to Poppy?" Joshua asked.

"You like Poppy," Isaiah pointed out.

"I do," Joshua said. "That's my concern. She's not like you. Your feelings are on a pretty deep freeze, Isaiah. I shouldn't have to tell you that."

"I don't know that I agree with you," he said.

"What's your stance on falling in love?"

"I've done it, and I'm not interested in doing it again."

"Has Poppy ever been in love before?" Joshua pressed.

Isaiah absolutely knew the answer to this question, not that it was any of his brother's business how he knew it. "No."

"Maybe she wants to be. And I imagine she wants her husband to love her."

"Poppy wants to be able to trust someone. She knows she can trust me. I know I can trust her. You can't get much better than that."

"I know you're anti-love… But what Danielle and I have…"

"What you and Danielle have is statistically improbable. There's no way you should have been able to place an ad in the paper for someone who is the antithesis of everything you should need in your life and fall madly in love with her. Additionally, I don't want that. I want stability."

"And my life looks terribly unstable to you?" Joshua asked.

"No. It doesn't. You forget, I was in a relationship for five years with a woman who turned out to be nothing like what I thought she was."

"You're still hung up on Rosalind?"

Isaiah shook his head. "Not at all. But I learned from my mistakes, Joshua. And the lesson there is that you can't actually trust those kinds of feelings. They blind you to reality."

"So you think I'm blind to reality?"

"And I hope it never bites your ass."

"What about Mom and Dad?"

"It's different," he said.

"How?"

"It's different for you too," Isaiah said. "I don't read people like you do. You know how to charm people. You know how to sense what they're feeling. How to turn the emotional tide of a room. I don't know how to do that. I have to trust my head because my heart doesn't give me a whole lot. What works for you isn't going to work for me."

"Just don't hurt her."

"I won't."

But then, Isaiah suddenly wasn't so sure. She was already hurt. Or at least, annoyed with him. And he wasn't quite sure what he was supposed to do about it.

He walked back toward Poppy's office and opened the door without knocking. She was sitting in her chair at her desk, not looking at anything in particular, and most definitely fuming.

"That was an unexpected little stunt," he said.

"You're not in charge of this," she pointed out. "If we are going to get married, it's a partnership. You don't get to manipulate me. You're not my boss in our marriage."

His lips twitched. "I could be your boss in the bedroom."

The color in her cheeks darkened. "I will allow that. However, in real life…"

"I get it."

He walked toward her and lowered himself to his knees in front of her, taking her chin in his hand. "I promise, I'm not trying to be a dick."

"Really?" He felt her tremble slightly beneath his touch.

He frowned. "I never try to be. I just am sometimes."

"Right."

"Joshua and Faith know. I mean, they already knew about the ad, and there was no way I was getting it by them that this wasn't related to that in some way."

"What did they say?"

"Joshua wants to make sure I don't hurt you."

She huffed a laugh. "Well. I'm team Joshua on that one."

"When do you want to tell my parents?" he asked. "We have our monthly dinner in three weeks."

"Let's…wait until then," she said.

"You want to wait that long?"

"Yes," she said. "I'm not…ready."

He would give her that. He knew that sometimes Poppy found interactions with family difficult. He'd always attributed that to her upbringing. "I understand. In the meantime, I want you to move your things into my house."

"But what about *my* house?" she asked.

"Obviously, you're coming to live on my ranch."

"No sex until we get married." The words came out fast and desperate.

He frowned. "We've already had sex. Several times."

"And that was…good. To establish our connection. It's established. And I want to wait now."

"Okay," he said.

She blinked. "Good."

He didn't think she'd hold to that. But Poppy was obviously trying to gain a sense of power here, and he was happy to give it to her.

Of course, that didn't mean he wouldn't try to seduce her.

Seven

Poppy didn't have time to think much about her decision over the next few days. Isaiah had a moving company take all of her things to his house, and before she knew it, she was settling into a routine that was different from anything she had ever imagined she'd be part of.

They went to work together. They spent all day on the job, being very much the same Poppy and Isaiah they'd always been. But then they went home together.

And sexual tension seemed to light their every interaction on fire. She swore she could feel his body heat from across the room.

He had given her a room, her own space. But she could tell he was confused by her abstinence edict.

Even she was wondering why she was torturing herself.

Being with him physically was wonderful. But she felt completely overwhelmed by him.

She'd spent ten years secretly pining for him. Then in one moment, he'd decided he wanted something dif-

ferent, something more, and they'd been on their way
to it. Isaiah had snapped his fingers and changed her
world, and she didn't recognize even one part of it
anymore.

Not even the ceiling she saw every morning when
she opened her eyes.

She had to figure out a way to have power in this
relationship. She was the one who was in love, and that
meant she was at a disadvantage already. He was the
one who got to keep his house. He was the one with
the family she would become a part of.

She had to do something to hold on to her sanity.

It was hard to resist him though. So terribly hard.

When she felt lonely and scared at night, worrying
for the future in a bedroom that was just down the hall
from his, she wished—like that first night—that he
would do a little less respecting of her commandments.
That he would at least try to tempt her away from her
resolve. Because if he did, she was sure it would fail.

But he didn't. So it was up to her to hang on to that
edict.

No matter what.

Even when they had to behave like a normal couple
for his parents' sakes.

And she was dreading the dinner at his parents'
house tonight. With all of her soul.

Dreading having to tell a vague story about how
they had suddenly realized their feelings for each other
and were now making it official.

The fact that it was a farce hurt too badly.

But tonight they would actually discuss setting a
wedding date.

A wedding date.

She squeezed her eyes shut for a moment, and then looked up at the gorgeous, custom-made cabinets in Isaiah's expansive kitchen. Maybe she should have a glass of wine before dinner. Or four. To calm her nerves.

She was already dressed and ready to go, but Isaiah had been out taking care of his horses, and she was still waiting for him to finish showering.

Part of her wished she could have simply joined him. But she'd made an edict and she should be able to stick to it.

She wondered if there was any point in preserving a sanity that was so frazzled as it was. Probably not.

Isaiah appeared a moment later, barefoot, in a pair of dark jeans with a button-up shirt. He was wearing his cowboy hat, looking sexy and disreputable, and exactly like the kind of guy who had been tailor-made for her from her deepest fantasies.

Or, maybe it was just that *he* was her fantasy.

Then he reached into his pocket and pulled out a black velvet box.

"No," she said.

He held it up. "No?"

"I didn't… I didn't know you were going to…"

"You have to have a ring before we see my parents."

"But then I'm going to walk in with a ring and they're going to know." As excuses went, it was a weak one. They were going to inform his parents of their engagement anyway.

They were engaged.

It was so strange. She didn't feel engaged to him. *Maybe because you won't sleep with him?* *No. Because he doesn't love me.*

She had a snotty response at the ready for her internal critic. Because really.

"They won't know you're engaged to me. And even so, were not trying to make it a surprise. We're just telling them in person."

The ring inside the box was stunning. Ornately designed, rather than a simple solitaire.

"It's vintage," he said. "It was part of a museum collection, on display in Washington, DC. I saw it online and I contacted the owner."

"You bought a vintage ring out of a museum." It wasn't a question so much as a recitation of what he'd just said.

"It was a privately owned collection." As if that explained it. "What?" he asked, frowning after she hadn't spoken for a few moments. "You don't look happy."

She didn't know how to describe what she was feeling. It was the strangest little dream come true. Something she would never have even given a thought to. Ever. She never thought about what kind of engagement ring she might want. And if she had, she would have asked for something small, and from the mall. Not from…*a museum collection*.

"I know how much you like vintage. And I know you don't like some of the issues surrounding the diamond trade."

She had gone on a small tirade in the office after seeing the movie *Blood Diamond* a few years ago. Just once. It wasn't like it was a cause she talked about regularly. "You…listened to that?"

"Yes," he responded.

Sometimes she wondered if everybody misunderstood him, including her. If no one knew just how deeply he held on to each moment. To people. Remembering a detail like that wasn't the mark of an unemotional man. It seemed...remarkably sentimental for him to remember such a small thing about her. Especially something that—at the time—wouldn't have been relevant to him.

She saw Isaiah as such a stark guy. A man who didn't engage in anything unnecessary. Or hold on to anything he didn't need to hold on to.

But that was obviously just what he showed the world. What he showed her.

It wasn't all of him.

It was so easy to think of him as cold, emotionless. He would be the first person to say a relationship could be a math equation for him, after all.

But remembering her feelings on diamonds wasn't math. It was personal.

There was no other man on earth—no other person on earth—who understood her the way Isaiah Grayson did.

She hadn't realized it until this moment. She'd made a lot of accusations about him being oblivious, but she was just as guilty.

And now...

She wanted to wear his ring. The ring he'd chosen for her with such thought and...well, extravagance. Because who had ever given her that kind of thought before? No one.

And certainly no one had ever been so extravagant for her.

Only him.

Only ever him.

He walked over to where she was sitting and took

the ring out of the box, sliding it onto her finger. He didn't get down on one knee. But then, that didn't surprise her.

More to the point, it didn't matter.

The ring itself didn't even matter. It was the thought.

It was the man.

Her man.

It was how much she wanted it that scared her. That was the real problem. She wanted to wear his ring more than she wanted anything in the world.

And she was going to take it.

"Are you ready to go to dinner?"

She swallowed hard, looking down at the perfect, sparkly rock on her finger.

"Yes," she said. "I'm ready."

Isaiah felt a sense of calm and completion when they pulled into his parents' house that night. The small, modest farmhouse looked the same as it ever did, the yellow porch light cheery in the dim evening. It was always funny to him that no matter how successful Devlin, Joshua, Faith or Isaiah became, his parents refused to allow their children to buy them a new house. Or even to upgrade the old one at all.

They were perfectly happy with what they had.

He envied that feeling of being content. Being so certain what home was.

He liked his house, but he didn't yet feel the need to stop changing his circumstances. He wasn't settled.

He imagined that this new step forward with Poppy would change that. Though, he would like it if she dropped the sex embargo.

He wasn't quite sure why she was so bound by it,

though she had said something about white weddings
and how she was a traditional girl at heart, even though
he didn't believe any of it since she had happily jumped
into bed with him a few weeks earlier.

It was strange. He'd spent ten years not having sex
with Poppy. But now that they'd done it a few times, it
was damn near impossible to wait ten days, much less
however long it was going to be until their wedding.
He was fairly confident she wouldn't stick to her proclamation that whole time, though. At least, he had been
confident until nearly three weeks had passed without
her knocking on his bedroom door.

But then, Poppy had been a twenty-eight-year-old
virgin. Her commitment to celibacy was much greater
than his own. He might have spent years abstaining
from relationships, but he had not abstained from sex.

They got out of the car, and she started to charge
ahead of him, as she had done on the way into the office that first morning after they'd made love. He was
not going to allow that this time.

He caught up with her, wrapping his arm around her
waist. "If you walk into my parents' living room and
announce that we had sex I may have to punish you."

She turned her head sharply, her eyes wide. "Punish me? What sort of caveman proclamation is that?"

"Exactly the kind a bratty girl like you needs if
you're plotting evil."

"I'm *not* plotting evil," she said, her cheeks turning pink.

He examined her expression closely. Knowing
Poppy like he did, he could read her better than he
could read just about anyone else. She was annoyed

with him. They certainly weren't back on the same footing they had been.

But she wanted him. She couldn't hide that, even now, standing in front of his parents' home.

"But you're a little bit intrigued about what I might do," he whispered.

She wiggled against him, and he could tell she absolutely, grudgingly was intrigued. "Not at all."

"You're a liar."

"You have a bad habit of pointing that out." She sounded crabby about that.

"I don't see the point of lies. In the end, they don't make anything less uncomfortable."

"Most people find small lies a great comfort," she disagreed.

"I don't," he said, a hot rock lodging itself in his chest. "I don't allow lies on any level, Poppy. That, you do have to know about me."

He'd already been in a relationship with a woman who had lied to him. And he hadn't questioned it. Because he'd imagined that love was somehow the same as having two-way trust.

"I won't lie to you," she said softly, brushing her fingertips over his lips

Instantly, he felt himself getting hard. She hadn't touched him in the weeks since he'd spent the night in her bed. But now was not the time.

He nodded once, and then tightened his hold on her as they continued to walk up the porch. Then he knocked.

"Why do you knock at your parents' house?"

"I don't live here."

The door opened, and his mother appeared, looking between the two of them, her eyes searching.

"Isaiah? Poppy."

"Hi," Poppy said, not moving away from his hold.

"Hi, Mom," Isaiah said.

"I imagine you have something to tell us," his mom said, stepping away from the door.

Isaiah led Poppy into the cozy room. His father was sitting in his favorite chair, a picture of the life he'd had growing up still intact. The feeling it gave him… It was the kind of life he wanted.

"We have something to tell you," Isaiah said.

Then the front door opened again and his brother Devlin and his wife, Mia, who was heavily pregnant, walked into the room.

"We brought chips," Mia said, stopping cold when she saw Isaiah and Poppy standing together.

"Yay for chips," Poppy said.

Then Joshua, Danielle and baby Riley came in, and with the exception of Faith, the entire audience was present.

"Do you want to wait for Faith?" his mom asked.

"No," Isaiah said. "Poppy and I are engaged."

His mother and father stared at them, and then his mother smiled. "That's wonderful!" She closed the distance between them and pulled him in for a hug.

She did the same to Poppy, who was shrinking slightly next to him, like she was her wilting namesake.

His father made his way over to them and extended his hand; Isaiah shook it. "A good decision," his dad said, looking at Poppy. And then, he hugged her, kissing her on the cheek. "Welcome to the family, Poppy."

Poppy made a sound that was somewhere between a gasp and a sob, but she stayed rooted next to his side.

This was what he wanted. This feeling. There was warmth here. And it was easy. There was closeness.

And now that he had Poppy, it was perfect.

Poppy didn't know how she made it through dinner. The food tasted like glue, which was ridiculous, since Nancy Grayson made the best food, and it always tasted like heaven. But Poppy had a feeling that her taste buds were defective, along with her very soul. She felt…wonderful and awful. All at once.

The Graysons were such an amazing family, and she loved Isaiah's parents. But they thought Isaiah and Poppy were in love. They thought Isaiah had finally shared his heart with someone.

And he didn't understand their assumptions. He thought they wanted marriage for him. A traditional family. But that wasn't really what they wanted.

They wanted his happiness.

And Isaiah was still… He was still in the same place he had always been, emotionally. Unwilling to open up. Unwilling to take a risk because it was so difficult. They thought she'd changed him, and she hadn't.

She was…enabling him.

She was enabling him and it was terrible.

After dinner, Poppy helped Nancy clear the dishes away.

"Poppy," she said. "Can I talk to you?"

Poppy shifted. "Of course."

"I've always known you would be perfect for him," Nancy said. "But I'm hesitant to push Isaiah into anything because he just digs in. They're all like that to a degree… But he's the biggest puzzle. He always has been. Since he was a boy. Either angry and very emotional, or seemingly emotionless. I've always known that wasn't true. People often find him detached, but I think it's because he cares so much."

Poppy agreed, and it went right along with what she'd been thinking when he'd given her the ring. That there were hidden spaces in him he didn't show anyone. And that had to be out of protection. Which showed that he did feel. He felt an awful lot.

"He's a good man," Nancy continued. "And I think he'll be a good husband to you. I'm just so glad you're going to be the one to be his wife, because you are exactly what he needs. You always have been."

"I don't… He's not difficult." Poppy looked down at her hands, her throat getting tight. "He's one of the most special people I know."

Nancy reached out and squeezed Poppy's hands. "That's all any mother wants the wife of her son to think."

Poppy felt even more terrible. Like a fraud. Yes, she would love Isaiah with everything she had, but she wasn't sure she was helping him at all.

"I have something for you," Nancy said. "Come with me."

She led Poppy back to the master bedroom, the only room in the house Poppy had never gone into. Nancy walked across the old wooden floor and the threadbare braided rug on top, moving to a highboy dresser and opening up a jewelry box.

"I have my mother's wedding band here. I know that you like…old-fashioned things. It didn't seem right for Danielle. And I know Faith won't want it. You're the one it was waiting for." Nancy turned, holding it out to Poppy.

Poppy swallowed hard. "Thank you," she said. "I'll save it until the… Until the wedding."

"It can stay here, for safekeeping, if you want."

"If you could," Poppy said. "But I want to wear it. Once Isaiah and I are married." Married. She was going to marry Isaiah. "Thank you."

Nancy gave Poppy another hug, and Poppy felt like her heart was splintering. "I know that your own mother won't be at the wedding," Mrs. Grayson said. "But we won't make a bride's side and a groom's side. It's just going to be our family. You're our family now, Poppy. You're not alone."

"Thank you," Poppy said, barely able to speak.

She walked back out into the living room on numb feet to find Isaiah standing by the front door with his hat on. "Are you ready to go?" he asked.

"Yes," she said.

She got another round of hugs from the entire family, each one adding weight to her already burdened conscience.

When they got out, they made their way back to the car, and as soon as he closed the door behind them, Poppy's insides broke apart.

They pulled out of the driveway, and a tear slid down her cheeks, and she turned her face away from him to keep him from seeing.

"I can't do this."

Eight

"What?"

"I can't do this," she said, feeling panic rising inside her now. "I'm sorry. But your parents think that I've... transformed you in some way. That I'm healing you. And instead, I'm enabling you to keep on doing that thing you love to do, where you run away from emotion and make everything about..."

"Maybe I just don't feel it," he said. "Maybe I'm not running from anything because there isn't anything there for me to run from. Why would you think differently?"

"Because you loved Rosalind..."

"Maybe. Or maybe I didn't. You're trying to make it seem like I feel things the exact same way other people do, and that isn't fair. I don't."

"I'm not trying to. It's just that your parents think—"

"I don't give a damn what my parents think. You were the one who wanted them to believe this was a normal kind of courtship. I don't care either way."

"Of course you don't."

"This is ridiculous, Poppy. You can't pull out of our agreement now that everybody knows."

"I could," she said. "I could, and I could quit. Like I was going to do."

"Because you would find it so easy to leave me?"

"No!"

"You're doing this because you feel guilty? I don't believe it. I think you're running away. You accuse me of not dealing with my feelings. But you were a twenty-eight-year-old virgin. You've refused to let me touch you in the time since we first made love, and now that you've had to endure hugs from my entire family suddenly you're trying to escape like a feral cat."

"I am not a feral cat." The comparison was unflattering.

And a little bit too close to the truth.

"I think you are. I think you're fine as long as somebody leaves a can of tuna for you out by the Dumpster, but the minute they try to bring you in the house you're all claws and teeth."

"No one has ever left me a can of tuna by a Dumpster." If he wanted claws, she was on the verge of giving them to him. This entire conversation was getting ridiculous.

"This isn't over." He started to drive them back toward his house.

"It is," she protested.

"No."

"Take me back to *my* house," she insisted.

"My house *is* your house. You agreed to marry me."

"And now I'm *un*agreeing," she insisted.

"And I think you're full of shit," he said, his tone so sharp it could have easily sliced right through her. "I think you're a hypocrite. Going on about what I need to do. Worrying about my emotional health when your own is in a much worse place."

She huffed, clenching her hands into fists and looking away from him. She said nothing for the rest of the drive, and then when they pulled up to the house, Isaiah was out of the car much quicker than she was, moving over to her side and pulling open the door. Then he reached into the car, unbuckled her and literally lifted her out as though she were a child. Holding her in his arms, he carried her up the steps toward the house.

"What the hell are you doing?" she shouted.

"What I should have done weeks ago."

"Making the transformation from man to caveman complete?"

He slid his hand down toward her ass and heat rioted through her. Even now, when she should be made of nothing but rage, she responded to him. Dammit.

"Making you remember why we're doing this."

"For your convenience," she hissed.

"Because I can't want another woman," he said, his voice rough, his eyes blazing. "Not now. And we both know you don't want another man."

She made a poor show of kicking her feet slightly as he carried her inside. She could unman him if she wanted to, but she wouldn't. And they both knew it.

"You can't do this," she protested weakly. "It violates all manner of HR rules."

"Too bad for you that I own the company. I *am* HR."

"I'm going to organize an ethics committee," she groused.

"This is personal business. The company has nothing to do with it."

"Is it? I think it's business for you, period, like everything else."

"It's personal," he ground out, "because I've been inside you. Don't you dare pretend that isn't true. Though it all makes sense to me now. Why you wanted me to stay away from you for the past few weeks."

"Because I'm just not that into you?" she asked as he carried her up the stairs.

"No. Because you're *too* into it."

She froze, ice gathering at the center of her chest. She didn't want him to know. He had been so clueless up until this point.

"You're afraid that I'll be able to convince you to stay because the sex is so good."

Okay. Well, he was a little bit onto it. But not really.

Just a little bit off base, was her Isaiah.

"You're in charge of everything," she said. "I didn't think it would hurt you to have to wait."

"I don't play games."

"Sadly for you, the rest of the world does. We play games when we need to. We play games to protect ourselves. We play games because it's a lot more palatable than wandering around making proclamations like you do."

"I don't understand games," he said. He flung open the door to his bedroom and walked them both inside. "But I understand this." He claimed her mouth. And she should have… She should have told him no. Because of course he would have stopped. But she didn't.

Instead, she let him consume her.

Then she began to consume him back. She wanted him. That was the problem. As much as everything that had happened back at the Grayson house terrified her, she wanted him.

Terrified. That wasn't the word she had used before. Isaiah was the one who had said she was afraid. And maybe she was. But she didn't know what to do about it.

It was like the time she had gone to live with a couple who hadn't been expecting a little girl as young as she was. They had been surprised, and clearly, their house hadn't been ready for a boisterous six-year-old. There had been a list of things she wasn't allowed to touch. And so she had lived in that house for all of three weeks, afraid to leave feet print on the carpet, afraid of touching breakable objects. Afraid that somehow she was going to destroy the beautiful place she found herself in simply because of who she was.

Because she was the wrong fit.

That was what it had felt like at the Graysons' tonight. Like she was surrounded by all this lovely, wonderful love, and somehow, it just wasn't for her. Wasn't to be.

There was more to it than that, of course, but that was the *real* reason she was freaking out, and she knew it.

But it didn't make her *wrong*.

It also didn't make her want to stop what was happening with Isaiah right now.

She was lonely. She had been a neglected child, and then she had lived in boisterous houses full of lots of children, which could sometimes feel equally lonely. She had never had a close romantic relationship as an adult. She was making friends in Copper Ridge, but moving around as often as she had made it difficult for her to have close lifelong friends. Isaiah was that friend, essentially.

And being close to him like this was a balm for a wound that ran very, very deep.

"You think this is fake?" he asked, his voice like gravel.

He bent down in front of her, grabbing hold of her skirt and drawing it down her legs without bothering to take off her shoes. Her shirt went next.

"Sit down," he commanded, and her legs were far too weak to disobey him. He looked up at her, those gray eyes intent on hers. "Take your bra off for me."

With shaking hands, she found herself obeying him.

"I imagine you're going to report me to HR for this too." The smile that curved his lips told her he didn't much care.

"I might," she responded, sliding her bra down her arms and throwing it onto the floor.

"Well, then I might have to keep you trapped here so you can't tell anyone."

"This is a major infraction."

"Maybe. But then again. I am the boss. I suppose I could choose to reprimand you for such behavior."

"I… I suppose you could."

"You're being a very bad girl," he said, hooking his fingers in the waistband of her panties and pulling them down to her knees. "Very bad."

Panic skittered in her stomach, and she had no idea how to respond. To Isaiah being like this, so playful. To him being like this and also staring at her right where he was staring at her.

"You need to remember who the boss is," he said, moving his hands around her lower back and sliding them down to cup her ass. Then he jerked her forward, and she gasped as he pressed a kiss to the inside of her thigh.

Then he went higher, and higher still, while she trembled.

She couldn't believe he was about to do this. She wanted him to. But she was also scared. Self-conscious. Excited. It was a whole lot of things.

But then, everything with Isaiah was a lot.

He squeezed her with both hands and then moved his focus to her center, his tongue sliding through her slick folds. She clapped her hand over her mouth to keep from making an extremely embarrassing noise, but she had a feeling he could still hear it, muffled or not.

Because he chuckled.

Isaiah, who was often humorless, chuckled with his mouth where it was, and his filthy intentions were obvious even to her.

And then he started to show her what he meant by punishment. He teased her with his tongue, with his fingers, with his mouth. He scraped her inner thigh with the edge of his teeth before returning his attention to where she was most needy for him. But every time she got close he would back off. He would move somewhere else. Kiss her stomach, her wrist, her hand. He would take his attention off of exactly where she needed him.

"Please," she begged.

"Bad girls don't get to come," he said, the edge in his voice sharp like a knife.

Those words just about pushed her over the edge all on their own.

"I thought you said you didn't play games," she choked out.

"Let me rephrase that," he said, looking up at her, a wicked smile curving his mouth. "I only play games in the bedroom."

He pressed two fingers into her before laughing at her again with his tongue, taking her all the way to the edge again before backing off. He knew her body better than she did, knew exactly where to touch her, and where not to. Knew the exact pressure and speed. How to rev her up and bring her back.

He was evil, and in that moment, she felt like she hated him as much as she had ever loved him.

"Tell me what you want," he said.

"You *know*."

"I do," he responded. "But you have to tell me."

"You're mean," she panted.

"I'm a very, very mean man," he agreed, sounding unrepentant as he slid one finger back through her folds. Tormenting. Teasing. "And you like it."

"I don't," she insisted.

"You do. Which is your real problem with all of this. You want me. And you want this. Even though you know you probably shouldn't."

"Well, what about you?" she asked, breathing hard. "You want it too. Or you wouldn't be trying so hard to convince me to go through with this marriage. Maybe *you* should beg."

"I'm on my knees," he said. "Isn't that like begging?"

"That's not—"

But she was cut off because his lips connected with that most sensitive part of her again. She could do nothing but feel.

She was so wet, so ready for him, so very hollow and achy that she couldn't stand for him to continue. It was going to kill her.

Or she was going to kill him. One of the two.

"Tell me," he whispered in her ear. "Tell me what you want."

"You," she said.

"Me?"

"You. Inside me. Please."

She didn't have to ask him twice.

Instead, she found herself being lifted up, brought down onto the bed, sitting astride him. He maneuvered her so her slick entrance was poised just above his hardness. And then he thrust up, inside her.

She gasped.

"You want to be in charge? Go ahead."

It was a challenge. And it gave her anything but control, when she was so desperate for him, when each move over him betrayed just how desperate she was.

He knew it too. The bastard.

But she couldn't stop, because she was so close, and now that she was on top she could...

Stars exploded behind her eyes, her internal muscles pulsing, her entire body shaking as her orgasm rocked her. All it had taken was a couple of times rocking back and forth, just a couple of times applying pressure where it was needed.

He growled, flipping her over and pinning her hands above her head. "You were just a bit too easy on me."

He kissed her then, and it was like a beast had been unleashed inside him. He was rough and untamed, and his response called up desire inside her again much sooner than she would have thought possible.

But it was Isaiah.

And with him, she had a feeling it would always be like this.

Always?

She pushed that mocking question aside.

She wasn't going to think about anything beyond this, right now.

She wasn't going to think about what she had told him before he carried her upstairs. About what she believed she deserved or didn't, about what she believed was possible and wasn't.

She was just going to feel.

This time, when the wave broke over her, he was swept up in it too, letting out a hoarse growl as he found his own release.

And when it was over, she didn't have the strength to get up. Didn't have the strength to walk away from him.

Tomorrow. Tomorrow would sort itself out.

Maybe for now she could hang on to the fantasy.

Poppy woke up in the middle of the night, curled around Isaiah's body. Something strange had woken her, and it wasn't the fact that she was sharing a bed with Isaiah.

It wasn't the fact that her resolve had weakened quite so badly last night.

There was something else.

She couldn't think what, or why it had woken her out of a dead sleep. She rolled away from him and padded into the bathroom that was just off his bedroom. She stood there for a moment staring at the mirror, at the woman looking back at her. Who was disheveled and had raccoon eyes because she hadn't taken her makeup off before allowing Isaiah to rock her world last night.

And then it suddenly hit her.

Because she was standing in a bathroom and staring at the mirror, and it felt like a strange kind of déjà vu.

It was the middle of the month. And she absolutely should've started her period by now.

She was two days late.

And she and Isaiah hadn't used a condom.

"No," she whispered.

It was too coincidental.

She went back into the bedroom and dressed as quickly and quietly as possible. And then she grabbed her purse and went downstairs.

She had to know.

She wouldn't sleep until she did. There were a few twenty-four-hour places in Tolowa, and she was going over there right now.

And that was how, at five in the morning in a public restroom, Poppy Sinclair's life changed forever.

Nine

When Isaiah woke up the next morning, Poppy wasn't in bed with him. He was irritated, but he imagined she was still trying to hold on to some semblance of control with her little game.

She was going to end up agreeing to marry him. He was fairly confident in that. But what he'd said about her being like a stray cat, he'd meant. She might not like the comparison, but it was true enough. Now that he wanted to domesticate her, she was preparing to run.

But her common sense would prevail. It didn't benefit her *not* to marry him.

And she couldn't deny the chemistry between them. He wasn't being egotistical about that. What they had between them was explosive. It *couldn't* be denied.

When he got downstairs, he saw Poppy sitting at the kitchen table. She was dressed in the same outfit she'd been wearing last night, and she was staring straight ahead, her eyes fixed on her clenched fists.

"Good morning," he said.

"No, it isn't," she responded. She looked up at him, and then she frowned. "Could you put a shirt on?"

He looked down at his bare chest. He was only wearing a pair of jeans. "No."

"I feel like this is a conversation we should have with your shirt on." She kept her gaze focused on the wall behind him.

He crossed his arms over his chest. "I've decided I like the conversations I have with you without my shirt better."

"I'm not joking around, Isaiah."

"Then you don't have time for me to go get a shirt. What's going on?"

"I'm pregnant." She looked like she was delivering the news of a death to him.

"That's…" He let the words wash over him, took a moment to turn them over and analyze what they made him feel. He felt…calm. "That's good," he said.

"Is it?" Poppy looked borderline hysterical.

"Yes," he said, feeling completely confident and certain now. "We both want children."

It was sooner than he'd anticipated, of course, but he wanted children. And…there was something relieving about it. It made this marriage agreement feel much more final. Made it feel like more of a done deal.

Poppy was his.

He'd spent last night in bed with her working to affirm that.

A pregnancy just made it that much more final.

"I broke up with you last night," she pointed out.

"Yes, you did a very good impression of a woman who was broken up with me. Particularly when you cried out my name during your… Was it your third or fourth orgasm?"

"That has nothing to do with whether or not we should be together. Whether or not we should get married."

"Well, now there's no question about whether or not we're getting married. You're having my baby."

"This is not 1953. That is not a good enough reason to get married."

He frowned. "I disagree."

"I'm not going to just jump into marriage with you."

"You're being unreasonable. You were more than willing to jump into marriage with me when you agreed to my proposal. Now suddenly when we're having a child you can't *jump into* anything? You continually *jump into* my bed, Poppy, so you can't claim we don't have the necessary ingredients to make a marriage work."

"Do you love me?" There was a challenge in her eyes, a stubborn set to her chin.

"I care very much about you," he responded.

It was the truth. The honest truth. She was one of the most important people in his life.

"But you're not in love with me."

"I already told you—"

"Yes. You're not going to do love. Well, you know what? I've decided that it feels fake if we're not in love."

"The fact that you're pregnant with my child indicates it's real enough."

"You don't understand. You don't understand anything."

"You sound like a sixteen-year-old girl having an argument with her parents. You would rather have some idealistic concept that may never actually happen than make a family with me?"

"I would rather... I would rather none of this was happening."

It felt like a slap, and he didn't know why.

That she didn't want him. Didn't seem to want the baby. He couldn't sort out the feeling it gave him. The sharp, stabbing sensation right around the area of his heart.

But he could reason through it. He was right, and her hysterics didn't change that.

There was an order to things. An order of operations, like math. That didn't change based on how people felt.

He understood...nothing right now. Nothing happening inside him, or outside him.

But he knew what was right. And he knew he could count on his brain.

It was the surest thing. The most certain.

So he went with that.

"But it is happening," he said, his voice tight. "You are far too practical to discard something real for some silly fantasy."

Her face drained of color. "So it's a *fantasy* that someone could love me."

"That isn't what I meant. It's a fantasy that you're going to find someone else who can take care of you like I can. Who is also the father of your child. Who can make you come the way that I do."

"Maybe it's just easy for me. You don't know. Neither do I. I've only had the one lover."

That kicked up the fire and heat in his stomach, and

he shoved it back down because this was not about what he felt. Not about what his body wanted.

"Trust me," he bit out. "It's never this good."

"I can't do this." She pressed a balled-up fist to her eyes.

"That's too bad," he said. "Because you will."

Resolve strengthened in him like iron. She was upset. But there was only one logical way forward. It was the only thing that made sense. And he was not going to let her take a different route. He just wasn't.

"I don't have to, Isaiah."

"You want your child growing up like you did? Being shuffled between homes?"

She looked like he'd hit her. "Foster care is not the same as sharing custody, and you know that. Don't you dare compare the two. I would have been thrilled to have two involved parents, even if I did have to change houses on the weekends. I didn't have that, and I never have had that. Don't talk about things you don't understand."

"I understand well enough. You're being selfish."

"I'm being *reasonable*!"

Reasonable.

Reasonable to her was them not being together. Reasonable to her was shoving him out of her life now that he'd realized just how essential she was.

"How is it reasonable to deny your child a chance at a family?" he asked. "All of us. Together. At my parents' house for dinners. Aunts and uncles and cousins. How is it unreasonable for me to want to share that with you instead of keeping my life and yours separate?"

"Isaiah…"

He was right, though. And what he wanted wasn't really about what he wanted. It was about logic.

And he wasn't above being heavy-handed to prove that point.

"If you don't marry me, I'm going to pursue full custody of our child," he said, the words landing heavily in the room.

Her head popped up. "You what?"

"And believe me, I'll get it. I have money. I have a family to back me up. I can make this very difficult for you. I don't want to, Poppy. That's not my goal. But I will have my way."

The look on her face, the abject betrayal, almost made him feel something like regret. Almost.

"I thought you were my friend," she said. "I thought you cared about me."

"I do. Which is why I'm prepared to do this. The best thing. The right thing. I'm not going to allow you to hurt our child in the name of friendship. How is that friendship?"

"Caring about someone doesn't just mean running them over until they do what you want. Friendship and caring goes both ways." She pressed her hand to her chest. "What I feel—*what I want*—has to matter."

"I know what you *should* want," he insisted.

If she would only listen. If she could, she'd understand what he was doing. In the end, it would be better if they were together. There was no scenario where their being apart would work, and if he had to play hardball to get her there, he damn well would.

"That isn't how wanting works. It's not how feelings work." She stood up, and she lifted her fist and slammed it down onto his chest. "It's not how any of this works, you robot."

He drew back, shock assaulting him. Poppy was one of the only people who had never looked at him that way before. Poppy had always taken pains to try to understand him.

"I'm a robot because I want to make sure my child has a family?" he asked, keeping his voice low.

"Because you don't care about what I want."

"I *want* you to want what *I* want," he said, holding her fist against his chest where she had hit him. "I want for this to work. How is that not feeling?"

"Because it isn't the *right feeling*."

Those words were like a whip cracking over his insides.

He had *never* had the right feelings. He already knew that. But with Poppy his feelings hadn't ever felt wrong before. *He* hadn't felt wrong before.

She'd been safe. Always.

But not now. Not now he'd started to care.

"I'm sorry," he said, his voice low. "I'm sorry I can't open up my chest and rearrange everything for you. I'm sorry that you agreed to be engaged to me, and then I didn't transform into a different man."

"I never said that's what I wanted."

"It *is* what you wanted. You wanted being with me to look like being with someone else. And you know what? If you weren't pregnant, I might've been able to let you walk away. But it's too late now. This is happening. The wedding is not off."

"The wedding *is* off," she insisted.

"Look at me," he said, his voice low, fierce. "Look

at me and tell me if you think I was joking about taking custody."

Her eyes widened, her lips going slack. "I've always cared about you," she said, her voice shaking. "I've always tried to understand you. But I think maybe I was just pretending there was a heart in your chest when there never was."

"You can fling all the insults you want at me. If I'm really heartless, I don't see how you think that's going to make a difference."

Then she let out a frustrated cry and turned and fled the room, leaving him standing there feeling hollowed out.

Wishing that he was exactly what she had accused him of being.

But if he were heartless, then her words—her rejection—wouldn't feel like a knife through his chest.

If he were a robot, he wouldn't care that he couldn't find a way to order his feelings exactly to her liking.

But he did care.

He just had no idea what to do about it.

Ten

Ultimately, it wasn't Isaiah's threats that had her agreeing to his proposal.

It was what he'd said about family.

She was angry that it had gotten inside her head. That it had wormed its way into her heart.

No. Angry was an understatement.

She was *livid*.

She was also doing exactly what he had asked her to do.

The date for their wedding was now Christmas Eve. Of all the ridiculous things. Though, she supposed that would give her a much stronger association with the holiday than she'd had before.

His family was thrilled.

Poppy was not.

And she was still sleeping in her own room.

After that lapse when she had tried to break things off with him a week earlier, she had decided that she really, *really* needed Isaiah not to touch her for a while.

For his part, he was seething around the house with an intensity that she could feel.

But he hadn't tried to change her mind.

Which was good. Because the fact of the matter was he *would* be able to change her mind. With very little effort.

And besides the tension at home, she was involved in things that made her break out in hives.

Literally.

She had been itchy for three days. The stress of trying to plan a wedding that felt like a death march was starting to get to her.

The fact that she was going wedding-dress shopping with Isaiah's mother and sister was only making matters worse.

And yet, here she was, at Something New, the little bridal boutique in Gold Valley, awaiting the arrival of Nancy and Faith.

The little town was even more heavily decorated for the holidays than Copper Ridge. The red brick buildings were lined with lights, wreaths with crimson bows on every door.

She had opted to drive her own car because she had a feeling she was going to need the distance.

She sighed heavily as she walked into the store, the bell above the door signaling her arrival. A bright, pretty young woman behind the counter perked up.

"Hi," she said. "I'm Celia."

"Hi," Poppy said uncomfortably. "I have an appointment to try on dresses."

"You must be Poppy," she said.

"I am," Poppy said, looking down at her hands. At the ring that shone brightly against her dark skin. "I'm getting married."

"Congratulations," Celia said, as though the inane announcement wasn't that inane at all.

"I'm just waiting for…" The words died on her lips. Her future mother-in-law and sister-in-law. That was who she was waiting for.

Isaiah's family really would be her family. She knew that. It was why she'd said yes to this wedding. And somehow it hadn't fully sunk in yet. She wondered if it ever would.

The door opened a few moments later and Faith and Nancy came in, both grinning widely.

"I'm so excited," Faith said.

Poppy shot her an incredulous look that she hoped Nancy would miss. Faith of all people should not be that excited. She knew Isaiah was only marrying Poppy because of the ad.

Of course, no one knew that Isaiah was also marrying her because she was pregnant.

"So exciting," Poppy echoed, aware that it sounded hollow and lacking in excitement. She was a great assistant, but she was a lousy actress.

Celia ushered them through endless aisles of dresses and gave them instructions on how to choose preferred styles.

"When you're ready," Celia said, "just turn the dresses out and leave them on the rack. I'll bring them to you in the dressing room."

Poppy wandered through her size, idly touching a few of the dresses, but not committing to anything. Meanwhile, Faith and Nancy were selecting styles left and right.

She saw one that caught her eye. It looked as though it was off the shoulder with long sleeves that came to a point over the top of her hand and loops that would go over her middle finger. It was understated, sedate. Very Grace Kelly, which was right in Poppy's wheelhouse. The heavy, white satin was unadorned, with a deep sheen to it that looked expensive.

She glanced at the price tag. *Incredibly* expensive.

It was somewhat surprising that there was such an upscale shop in the small community of Gold Valley, but then the place had become something of a destination for brides who wanted to make a day of dress shopping, and the cute atmosphere of the little gold rush town, with its good food and unique shops, made for an ideal girls' day out.

"Don't worry about that," Nancy said.

"I can't not worry about it," Poppy said, looking back at the price.

"Isaiah is going to pay for all of it," Nancy said. "And he made sure I was here to reinforce that."

"I know it's silly to be worked up about it," Poppy said. "Considering he signs my paychecks. But the thing is… I don't necessarily want to just take everything from him. I don't want him to think that…"

"That you're marrying him for his money?" Faith asked.

"Kind of," Poppy said.

"He isn't going to think that," Nancy said with authority. "He knows you."

"Yes," Poppy said slowly. "I just…" She looked at them both helplessly. "He's not in love with me," she said. Faith knew, and there was no reason that Poppy's future mother-in-law shouldn't know too. She'd thought she wanted to keep it a secret, but she couldn't bear it anymore, not with the woman she was accepting as family.

"I love him," Poppy said. "I want to make that clear. I love him, and I told him not to let on that this was…a convenient marriage. For my pride. But I can't lie to you." She directed that part to his mother. "I can't lie to you and have you think that I reached him or changed him in a way that I haven't. He still thinks this marriage is the height of practicality. And he's happy to throw money at it like he's happy to throw money at any of his problems. He's not paying for this wedding because he cares what I look like in the wedding dress."

She swallowed hard. "He's paying for it because he thinks that making me his wife is going to somehow magically simplify his life."

Nancy frowned. "You love him."

"I do."

"You've loved him for a long time, haven't you?"

Poppy looked down. She could see Faith shift uncomfortably out of the corner of her eye.

"Yes," Poppy confirmed. "I've loved him ever since I met him. He's a wonderful person. I can see underneath all of the… Isaiah. Or maybe that's not the right way of putting it. I don't even have to see under it. I love who he is. And that…not everybody can see just how wonderful he is. It makes it like a secret. My secret."

"I'm not upset with you," Nancy said, taking hold of the wedding dress Poppy was looking at and turning it outward. "I'm not upset with you at all. You love him, and he came barreling at you with all of the intensity that he has, I imagine, and demanded that you marry him because he decided it was logical, am I right?"

"Very."

"I don't see what woman in your position could have resisted."

If only his mother knew just how little Poppy had resisted. Just how much she wasn't resisting him...

"I should have told him no."

"Does he know that you love him?" Faith asked.

"No," Poppy said.

And she knew she didn't have to tell either of them to keep it a secret. Because they just would.

"Maybe you should tell him," Faith pointed out.

Poppy bit back a smart remark about the fact that Faith was single, and had been for as long as Poppy had known her, and Faith maybe didn't have any clue about dealing with unrequited love.

"Love isn't important to him," Poppy said. "He *likes* me. He thinks that's enough."

Nancy shook her head. "I hope he more than likes you. Otherwise that's going to be a cold marriage bed."

Faith made a squeaking sound. "Mom. Please."

"What? Marriage is long, sweetheart. And sometimes you get distant. Sometimes you get irritated with each other. In those times all you've got is the spark."

Faith slightly receded into one of the dress racks. "Please don't tell me any more about your spark."

"You should be grateful we have it," Nancy said pointedly at her daughter. "It's what I want for you in your marriage, whenever you get married. And it's certainly what I want for Poppy and Isaiah."

Poppy felt her skin flushing. "We're covered there."

"Well, that is a relief."

She wasn't going to tell them about the baby. Not now. She was just going to try on wedding dresses.

Which was what they did.

For the next two hours, Poppy tried on wedding dresses. And it all came down to The One. The long-sleeved beauty with the scary price tag and the perfect train that fanned out behind her like a dream.

Celia found a veil and pinned it into Poppy's dark hair. It was long, extending past the train with a little row of rhinestones along the edge, adding a hint of mist and glitter.

She looked at herself in the mirror, and she found herself completely overwhelmed with emotion.

She was glowing.

There, underneath the lights in the boutique, the white dress contrasted perfectly with her skin tone. She looked like a princess. She felt like one.

And she had…

She looked behind her and saw Nancy and Faith, their eyes full of tears, their hands clasped in front of them.

She had a family who cared about this. Who was here watching her try on dresses.

Who cared for her. For her happiness.

Maybe Isaiah didn't love her, but she loved him. And… His mother and sister loved her. And that offered Poppy more than she had ever imagined she might have.

It was enough. It would be.

Nancy came up behind Poppy and put a hand on Poppy's shoulder. "This is the one. Let him buy it for you. Believe me, he'll cause enough trouble over the course of a lifetime with him that you won't feel bad about spending his money this way."

Poppy laughed, then wiped at a tear that fell down her cheek. "I suppose that's true."

"I'm going to try to keep from hammering advice at you," Nancy said. "But I do have to say this. Love is an amazing thing. It's an inexhaustible resource. I've been married a long time. And over the course of that many decades with someone, there are a lot of stages. Ebbs and flows. But if you keep on giving love, as much as you have, you won't run out. Give it even when it's not flowing to you. Give it when you don't feel like it. If you can do that... That's the best use of love that I can think of. It doesn't mean it's always easy. But it's something you won't regret. Love is a gift. When you have it, choosing to give it is the most powerful thing you can do."

Poppy looked back at her reflection. She was going to be a bride. And more than that, she was going to be Isaiah's wife. He had very clear ideas about what he wanted and didn't want from that relationship. He had very definite thoughts on what he felt and didn't feel.

She had to make a decision about that. About what she was going to let it mean to her.

The problem was, she had spent a lot of years wanting love. Needing love. From parents who were unable to give it for whatever reason. Because they were either too captivated by drugs, or too lost in the struggle of life. She had decided, after that kind of childhood, after the long years of being shuffled between foster homes, that she didn't want to expose herself to that kind of pain again.

Which was exactly what Isaiah was doing.

He was holding himself back. Holding his love back because he'd been hurt before. And somehow… somehow she'd judged that. As if she was different. As if she was well-adjusted and he was wrong.

But that wasn't true.

It was a perfect circle of self-protection. One that was the reason why she had nearly broken the engagement off a week ago. Why she was holding herself back from him now.

And they would never stop.

Not until one of them took a step outside that self-created box.

She could blame her parents. She could blame the handful of foster families who hadn't been able to care for her the way she had needed them to. She could blame the ones who had. The ones she had loved deeply, but whom she had ultimately had to leave, which had caused its own kind of pain.

She could blame the fact that Isaiah had been unavailable to her for all those years. That he had belonged to Rosalind, and somehow that had put him off-limits.

But blame didn't matter. The reasons didn't really matter

The only thing that mattered was whether or not she was going to change her life.

No one could do it for her.

And if she waited for Isaiah to be the first to take that step, then she would wait forever.

His mother was right. Love was a gift, and you could either hoard it, keep it close to your chest where it wouldn't do a thing for anyone, or you could give it.

Giving her love was the only thing that could possibly open up that door between them. If she wanted him to love her, wanted him to find the faith to love her, she'd have to be the first one to stop protecting herself.

Poppy would have to open up her arms. Stop holding them in front of her, defensive and closed off.

Which was the real problem. Really, it had been all along.

That deeply rooted feeling of unrequited love that she'd had for Isaiah had been incredibly important to her. It had kept her safe. It had kept her from going after anyone else. It had kept her insulated.

But she couldn't continue that now.

Not if she wanted a hope at happiness. Not if she wanted even the smallest chance of a relationship with him.

Someone was going to have to budge first. And she could be bitter about the fact that it had to be her, but there was no point to that.

It was simple.

This wasn't about right or wrong or who should have to give more or less. Who should have to be brave.

She could see that she should.

And if she loved him… Well. She had to care more for him and less for her own comfort.

"I think I might need to give a little bit more love," Poppy said softly.

"If my son doesn't give back to you everything that you deserve, Poppy, you had better believe that I will scar him myself."

"I do believe it," Poppy said.

And if nothing else, what she had learned in that moment was invaluable.

Somebody was in her corner.

And not only had she heard Nancy say it, Poppy believed it. She couldn't remember the last time that had been true.

This was family.

It was so much better than she had ever imagined it could be.

Eleven

It was late, and Isaiah was working in his home office. His eyes were starting to get gritty, but he wasn't going to his room until he was ready to pass out. It was the only way he could get any sleep at all these days.

Lying in bed knowing she was just down the hall and he couldn't have her was torture. Distance and exhaustion were the only things he could do to combat the restlessness.

He looked up, catching his reflection in the window, along with the reflection of the lamp on his desk.

It was dark out. So dark he couldn't see anything. But he knew the view well. The mountains and hills that were outside that window. A view he had carefully curated after growing tired of the gray landscape of Seattle.

Poppy had been out shopping all day, and he hadn't seen her since she'd left that morning. But he had been thinking about her.

It was strange. The way his feelings for her were affected. A borderline obsession with a woman who should feel commonplace to him in many ways. She had been a part of his office furniture for the past decade.

Except, she'd always been more than that.

Yes. That was true. She always had been.

She was remarkable, smart and funny. Funny in a way he could never really manage to be. More than once, he had wished he could capture that sweetness and hold it to himself just for a little while.

Not that she was saccharine. No. She had no issues taking strips off his hide when it was necessary.

She was also so damn sexy he couldn't think of anything else, and she was starting to drive him insane.

He didn't have any practice with restraint. Over the years, he had been involved mostly in casual hookups, and the great thing about those was they could absolutely happen on his schedule. If the woman didn't matter, then all that was needed was time spent in an appropriate location, and a woman—any woman— would eventually indicate she was available.

But now, he was at the point where not just any woman would do. He needed Poppy.

She was still withholding herself from him, and he supposed he could understand. What with the fact that he had made threats to take her child away if she didn't fall in line. It was entirely possible he wasn't her favorite person at the moment.

That bothered him.

He wasn't very many people's favorite person. But Poppy liked him. At least, she had always seemed to. And now, he had found a very unique way of messing that up.

He'd had a lot of friendships not go the distance. Admittedly, this was quite the most creative way he'd had one dissolve. Proposing, getting that same friend pregnant, and then forcing her to marry him.

Not that he was *forcing* her. Not *really*. He was simply giving her a set of incredibly unpleasant options. And forcing her to choose the one she found the least unpleasant.

He supposed he could take some small measure of comfort in the fact that he wasn't the *least* pleasant option.

But then, that had more to do with the baby than with him.

He sighed heavily.

He'd never felt this way about a woman before. The strange sense of constant urgency. To be with her. To fix things with her. The fact that she was angry with him actively bothered him even when she wasn't in the room displaying that anger.

He could feel it.

He could actually feel someone else's emotion. Stronger than his own.

If he wasn't so fed up, he might marvel at that.

He didn't know what was happening to him.

He was obsessing about the desire. Fixated on it. Because that he understood. Sex, he understood.

This need to tear down all the walls inside him so that he could...

He didn't know.

Be closer to her? Have her feel him, his emotions, so difficult and hard to explain, as keenly as he felt hers?

They'd been friends for ten years. Now they were lovers.

His feelings were like nothing he'd ever felt for a friend or a lover.

The door opened behind him, and he didn't have to turn to see that it was Poppy standing in the doorway. She was wearing her favorite red coat that had a high collar and a tightly belted waist, flaring out at her hips. Her hands were stuffed in her pockets, her eyes cast downward.

"How was your day?"

Her voice was so soft it startled him. He turned. "Good. I wish it were over."

"Still working?"

"Yes. Faith is interested in taking on a couple more projects. I'm just trying to make sure everything balances out."

"I chose a wedding dress."

He had half expected her to say that she had chosen a burlap sack. Or nothing at all. As a form of protest.

"I'm glad to hear it," he said, not quite sure what she wanted him to say. Not quite sure where this was leading at all.

"I've missed you."

The words landed softly, then seemed to sing down deep into his heart. "I've seen you every day for the past week."

"That isn't what I meant." A small crease appeared between her brows as she stared at him. "I'm not going to say I miss the way we used to be. Because I don't. I like so much of what we have now better. Except...we don't have it right now. Because I haven't let you get close to me. I haven't let you touch me."

She pushed away from the door jamb and walked slowly toward him. His eyes were drawn downward, to the wicked, black stilettos on her feet. And to her bare legs. Which was odd, because she was wearing a coat as if she had been outside in the cold, and he would have thought she would have something to cover her skin.

"I've missed you touching me," she said, her voice growing husky. "I've missed touching you."

She lifted her hands, working the button at the top of her coat, and then the next, followed by the next. It exposed a V of brown skin, the soft, plump curve of her breasts. And a hint of bright yellow lace.

She made it to the belt, working the fabric through the loop and letting the coat fall open before she undid the button behind it, and the next button, and the next. Until she revealed that she had nothing on beneath the coat but transparent yellow lace. Some sort of top that scooped low around her full breasts and ended above her belly button, showing hints of dark skin through the pattern, the darker shadows of her nipples.

The panties were tiny. They covered almost nothing, and he was pleased with that. She left the heels on, making her legs look impossibly long, shapely and exactly what he wanted wrapped around him.

"What did I do to deserve this?" he asked.

It wasn't a game. Not a leading question. He genuinely wanted to know.

"Nothing," she said. She took a step toward him, lifted the delicate high heel up off the ground and pressed her knee into the empty space on the chair, just beside his thigh.

She gripped the back of the chair, leaning forward. "You haven't done anything at all to deserve this. But I want it. I'm not sure why I shouldn't have it. I think… I think this is a mess." Her tongue darted out, slid over her lips, and he felt the action like a slow lick. "*We* are a mess. We have been. For a long time. Together. Apart. But I'd rather be a mess with you than just a mess who lives in your house and wears your ring. I'd rather be a mess with you inside of me. We're going to get married. I'm having your baby. We're going to have to be a family. And I don't know how to…fix us. I don't know how to repair the broken spaces inside of us. I don't know if it's possible. But nothing is going to be fixed, nothing at all if we're just strangers existing in the same space. If I'm still just your personal assistant when I'm at work."

"What are you going to be when you're at work?"

"Your personal assistant. And your fiancée. And later, your wife. We can't separate these things. Not anymore. We can't separate ourselves."

She pressed her fingertips against his cheek and dragged her hand back, sliding her thumb over his lower lip. "I'm so tired of being lonely. Feeling like… nobody belongs to me. That I don't belong to anyone."

Those words echoed inside him, and they touched something raw. Something painful. He felt… He felt as if they could be words that were coming out of his own mouth. As if she was putting voice to his own pain, a pain he had never before realized was there.

"I want you," she said.

He reached out, bracing his hands on her hips, marveling at the erotic sight of that contrast. His paler hand over the deep rich color of her skin.

A contrast. And still a match.

Deep and sexual and perfect.

He leaned forward and pressed a kiss to her breast, to the bare skin just above the edge of lace. And she gasped, letting her head fall back. It was the most erotic sight. Perfect and indulgent, and something he wanted to hold on to and turn away from with matching intensity.

He wanted her to make him whole. He wanted to find the thing that she was talking about. That depth. That sense of belonging.

Of not being alone.

Of being understood.

He had never even made that a goal. Not even when he'd been with Rosalind. He'd never imagined that a woman might…understand him. He didn't quite understand himself. No one ever had.

He was different. That was all he knew.

He didn't know how to show things the way other people did. Didn't know how to read what was happening right in front of him sometimes.

Was more interested in the black-and-white numbers on a page than the full-color scene in front of him.

He couldn't change it. Didn't know if he would even if he could. His differences were what had made him successful. Made him who he was. But there were very few people willing to put up with that, with him.

But Poppy always had.

She had always been there. She had never—except for the day when she'd hit him in the chest and called him a robot—she had never acted like him being different was even a problem.

Maybe she was the one who could finally reach him. Maybe she was the one he could hold on to.

"I want you," he said, repeating her words back to her.

"I'm here," she said, tilting his face up, her dark eyes luminous and beautiful as she stared down at him. "I'm giving myself to you." She leaned forward, her lips a whisper from his. "Can I be yours, Isaiah?"

"You already are."

He closed the distance between them and claimed her mouth with his.

It was like a storm had exploded. He pulled her onto his lap, wrapping his arms around her tightly as he kissed her. As he lost himself in her. He wanted there to be nothing between them. Not the T-shirt and jeans he was wearing, not even the beautiful lace that barely covered her curves.

Nothing.

Nothing but her.

A smile curved his lips. She could maybe keep the shoes. Yes, he would love for her to have those shoes on when he draped her legs over his shoulders and thrust deep inside her.

"I want you so much," he said. The words were torn from him. Coming from somewhere deep and real that he wasn't normally in touch with. "I think I might die if I don't have you."

"I've been in front of you for ten years," she whispered, kissing the spot right next to his mouth, kissing his cheek. "Why now?"

Because he had seen her. Because she had finally kissed him. Because…

"I don't see the world the way everyone else does," he whispered. "I know that. Sometimes it takes an act of God for me to really notice what's happening in front of me. To pull me out of that space in my head. I like it there. Because everything makes sense. And I put people in their place, so I can navigate the day with everything just where I expect it. I can never totally do that with you, Poppy. You always occupied more spaces than you were supposed to.

"I hired you, but you were never only my assistant.

You became my friend. And then, you wouldn't stay there either. I put control above everything else. I always have. It's the only way to… For me to make the world work. If I go in knowing exactly what to expect, knowing what everything is. What everyone is. And that's how I didn't see. But then…the minute our lips touched, I knew. I knew, and I can't go back to knowing anything different."

"You like blondes," she pointed out.

"I don't," he responded.

"Rosalind was blonde," Poppy said, brazenly speaking the name she usually avoided at all costs. "And there have been a string of them ever since."

"I told you. I like certainty. Blondes are women I'm attracted to. At least, that was an easy way to think of it. I like to bring order to the world in any way I can."

"And that kept you from looking at me?"

He searched her face, trying to get an idea of what she was thinking. He searched himself, because he didn't know the answer. She was beautiful, and the fact that he hadn't been obsessed with her like this for the past decade was destined to remain a mystery to him.

"Maybe."

She touched his face, sliding her palms back, holding him. "You are not difficult," she said. "Not to me. I like you. All of you."

"No," he responded, shaking his head. "You… You put up with me, I'm sure. And I compensate for the ways that I'm difficult by…"

"No, Isaiah. I like all of you. I always have. There's no putting up with anything."

He hadn't realized how much words like that might mean. Until they poured through him like sunshine dipping down into a low, dark valley. Flooding him with light and warmth.

When he'd been younger, he'd had a kind of boundless certainty in his worldview. But as he'd gotten older—as he'd realized that the way he saw things, the way he perceived interactions and emotions, was often different from the other people involved—he'd started questioning himself.

The older he'd gotten the more he'd realized. How difficult people found it to be his friend. How hard he found it sometimes to carry on a conversation another person wanted to have when he just wanted to charge straight to the point.

How much his brother Joshua carried for him, with his lightning-quick response times and his way with words.

Which had made him wonder how much his parents had modified for him back before he'd realized he needed modification at all.

And with that realization came the worry. About how much of a burden he might be.

But not to Poppy.

He reached up and wrapped his fingers around her slender wrists, holding her hands against his face. He looked at her. Just looked. He didn't have words to respond to what she had said.

He didn't have words.

He had nothing but his desire for her, twisting in his gut, taking him over. Control was the linchpin in his life. It was essential to him. But not now. Now, only Poppy was essential. He wanted her to keep touching him.

Control could wait. It could be set aside for now.

Because letting go so he could hold on to this—to her—was much more important.

It was necessary.

He slid her hands back, draping her arms over his shoulders so she was closer to him, so she was holding on to him. Then he cradled her face, dragging her mouth to his, claiming her, deep and hard and long. Pouring everything that he felt, everything he couldn't say, into this kiss. Into this moment.

He pulled away, sliding his thumb across her lower lip, watching as heat and desire clouded her dark eyes. He could see her surrender to the same need that was roaring through him.

"I always have control," he mumbled, pressing a kiss to her neck, another, and then traveling down to her collarbone. "Always."

He pressed his hand firmly to the small of her back, holding her against him as he stood from the chair, then lowered them both down onto the floor.

He reached behind her and tugged at the top she was wearing. He didn't manage to get hold of the snaps, and he tore the straps, the elastic popping free, the cups falling away from her breasts.

He didn't have to tell her he was out of control. She knew. He could see it. In the heat and fire burning in her dark eyes, and in the subtle curve of her full lips.

She knew that he was out of control, for her. And she liked it.

His efficient, organized Poppy had a wild side. At least, she did with him.

Only for him.

Suddenly, the fact that she had never been with another man before meant everything. This was his.

She was his.

And it mattered.

More than he would have ever thought it could. He had never given thought to something like that before. He didn't know why he did now. Except... Poppy.

Poppy, who had always been there.

She was a phenomenon. Someone he couldn't understand, someone he wasn't sure he wanted to understand. He didn't mind her staying mysterious. An enigma he got to hold in his arms. As long as this burning bright glory remained.

If he stopped to think, she might disappear. This moment might vanish completely, and he couldn't bear that.

She tore at his clothes too, wrenching them away from his body, making quick work of his shirt before turning her attention to his pants.

As she undressed him, he finished with her clothes, capturing her nipple in his mouth, sucking it in deep. Tasting her. Relishing the feel of her, that velvet skin under his tongue. The taste of her.

It wasn't enough. It never would be. Nothing ever would be.

He felt like his skin was hypersensitized, and that feeling ran all the way beneath his skin, deeper. Making him feel...

Making him *feel*.

He pressed his face into the curve of her neck, kissing her there, licking her. She whimpered and shifted beneath him, wrapping her fingers around his thick length, squeezing him. He let his head fall back, a hoarse groan on his lips.

"Not like that," he rasped. "I need to… No, Poppy. I need you."

"But you have me." She looked innocent. Far too innocent for the moment.

She stroked him, sliding her fingers up and down his length. Then she reached forward, planting her free hand in the center of his chest and pushing him backward slightly. He didn't have to give. He chose to. Because he wanted to see what she would do. He was far too captivated by what might be brewing beneath the surface.

Her breasts were completely bare for him. And then she leaned forward, wrapping her lips around the head of his erection, sliding down slowly as she took all of him into her mouth.

He gritted his teeth, her name a curse on his lips as he grabbed hold of her dark curls and held on tightly while she pleasured him with her mouth. He was transfixed by the sight of her. By the way she moved, unpracticed but earnest. By the way she made him feel.

"Have you ever done this before?" He forced the words out through his constricted throat.

The answer to that question shouldn't matter. It was a question he never should have asked. He'd never cared before, if one of his partners had other lovers. He would have said he preferred a woman with experience.

Not with Poppy. The idea of another man touching her made him insane.

She licked him from base to tip like a lollipop, and then looked up at him. "No."

He swore, letting his head fall back as she took him in deep again.

"Does that matter to you?" she asked, angling her head and licking him.

"Don't stop," he growled.

"Does it matter, Isaiah?" she repeated. "Do you want to be the only man I've ever touched like this? Do you want to know you that you're the only man I've ever seen naked?"

His stomach tightened, impossibly. And he was sure he was going to go right over the edge as her husky, erotic words rolled over him.

"Yes," he bit out.

"Why?"

"Because I want you to be mine," he said, his tone hard. "Only mine."

"I said I was yours," she responded, stoking the length of him with her hand as she spoke. "You're the only man I've ever wanted like this."

His breath hissed out through his teeth. "Me?"

"The only one. From the time you hired me when I was eighteen. I could never... I wanted to date other men. But I just couldn't. I didn't want them. Isaiah, I only wanted you."

Her dark eyes were so earnest as she made the confession, so sincere. That look touched him, all the way down. Even to those places he normally felt were closed off.

She kissed his stomach, up higher to his chest, and then captured his lips again.

"I want you," she said. "Please."

She didn't have to ask twice. He lowered her onto her back and slipped his fingers beneath the waistband of those electric yellow panties, sliding his fingers through her slick folds slowly, slowly, drawing out all that slick wetness, drawing out her pleasure. Until she was whimpering and bucking beneath him. Until she was begging him.

Then he slipped one finger deep inside her, watched as her release found her. As it washed over her like a wave. It was the most beautiful thing he'd ever seen.

But it wasn't enough.

He pulled her panties off and threw them onto the floor, positioning himself between her thighs, pressing himself to the entrance of her body and thrusting in, rough and decisive. Claiming her. Showing her exactly who she belonged to.

Just as he belonged to her.

He lost himself completely, wrapped in her, consumed by her. That familiar scent, vanilla and spice, some perfume Poppy had always worn, mingling with something new. Sweat. Desire. Skin.

What they had been collided with what they were now.

He gripped her hips, thrust into her, deep and hard, relishing her cry of pleasure as he claimed her. Over and over again.

She arched underneath him, crying out his name, her fingernails digging into his skin as her internal muscles pulsed around him.

And he let go. He came on a growl, feral and unrestrained, pleasure like fire over his skin, in his gut.

And when it was over, he could only hold her. He couldn't speak. Couldn't move. Didn't want to.

He looked down at her, and she smiled. Then she pressed her fingers to his lips.

He grabbed her wrist, kissed her palm. "Come to bed with me," he said.

"Okay."

Twelve

At three in the morning, Isaiah decided that they needed something to eat. Poppy sat on the counter wearing nothing but his T-shirt, watching as he fried eggs and bacon.

She wondered if this was…her life now. She could hardly believe it. And yet, she didn't want to believe anything different.

She ached just looking at this man.

He was so…him. Undeniably. So intense and serious, and yet now, there was something almost boyish about him with his dark hair falling into his eyes, his expression one of concentration as he flipped the eggs in the pan flawlessly without breaking a yolk.

But then, he was shirtless, wearing a pair of low-slung gray sweatpants that seemed perilously close to falling off. His back was broad and muscular, and she enjoyed the play of those muscles while he cooked.

Just that one moment, that one expression on his face, could come close to being called boyish. The rest of him was all man.

He served up the eggs and bacon onto a plate, and he handed Poppy hers, then set his on the counter beside her. He braced himself on the counter, watching her expectantly.

"Do you often have midnight snacks?" she asked.

"No," he said. "But then, tonight isn't exactly routine. Eat."

"Are you trying to fortify me so we can have sex again?"

His lips curved upward. "Undoubtedly."

"This bacon is tainted with ulterior motives," she said, happily taking a bite.

"You seem very sad about that."

"I am." She looked down, then back up, a bubble of happiness blooming in her chest.

"I wanted to make sure you were taken care of," he said, his voice suddenly serious. "Do you feel okay?"

"Yes," she said, confused for a moment.

"No...nausea, or anything like that?"

Right. Because of the baby. So he wasn't only concerned about her. She fought off a small bit of disappointment.

"I feel fine," she said.

"Good," he said.

"Because if I had morning sickness I'd have to miss work?" she asked, not quite certain why she was goading him.

"No. Because if you were sick it would upset me to see you like that."

Suddenly, she felt achingly vulnerable sitting here like this with him.

Isaiah.

She was having his baby. She'd just spent the past

couple of hours having wild sex with him. And now she just felt…so acutely aware of who she was. With her hair loose and curly, falling into her face that was free of makeup. Without her structured dresses and killer high heels.

She was just Poppy Sinclair, the same Poppy Sinclair who'd bounced from home to home all through her childhood. Who had never found a family who wanted her forever.

Her throat ached, raw and dry.

His large hand cupped her chin, tilted her face upward. "What's wrong?"

Her heart twisted. That show of caring from him made the vulnerability seem like it might not be so bad. Except…even when he was being nice, it hurt.

She definitely liked a little bit of opposition in her life, and Isaiah was always around to provide that. Either because of her unrequited feelings, or because he was such an obstinate, hardheaded man.

Somehow, all of that was easier than…feeling. It was all part of remaining closed off.

This…opening up was hard, but she had expected that. She hadn't expected it to be painful even when nothing bad was happening.

"I was just thinking," she said.

"About?"

"Nothing specifically," she said.

Just about who she was, and why it was almost ludicrous that she was here now. With him. With so many beautiful things right within her reach.

A family. A husband. A baby.

Passion.

Love.

"You can tell me," he said, his gray eyes searching.

"Why do you *want* me to tell you?" she pressed.

"Because you're mine. Anything that is bothering you… Give it to me. I want to…help. Listen."

"Isaiah…" Her eyes burned.

"Did I make you cry?" He looked genuinely concerned by that. He lifted his hand, brushed his thumb beneath the corner of her eye, wiping away a tear she hadn't realized was there.

"You didn't," she said. She swallowed hard. "I was just… It's stupid."

"Nothing is stupid if it makes you cry."

"I was thinking, while I was sitting here watching you take care of me, that I don't remember what it's like to have someone care for me like this. Because… I'm not sure anyone ever really has. People definitely showed me kindness throughout my life—I'm not saying they didn't. There were so many families and houses. They blur together. I used to remember everyone's names, but now the earlier homes are fading into a blur. Even the people who were kind.

"I remember there was a family… They were going to take me to the fair. And I'd never been before. I was so excited, Isaiah. So excited I could hardly contain myself. We were going to ride a Ferris wheel, and I was going to have cotton candy. I'd never had it before." She took another bite of her bacon and found swallowing difficult.

"The next day, that family found out that the birth mother of a sibling group they were fostering had given birth to another baby. Child services wanted to arrange to have the baby brought in right away. And…that required they move me. The baby had to be with her half siblings. It was right. It made sense."

"You didn't get to go to the fair."

She blinked and shook her head. A tear rolled down her cheek, and she laughed. "It's stupid to still be upset about it. I've been to the fair. I've had cotton candy. But I just… I can remember. How it hurt. How it felt like the world was ending. Worse, I think, is that feeling that nothing in the world is ever stable. That at any moment the rug is going to be pulled out from underneath me. That everything good is just going to vanish. Well, like cotton candy once it hits your tongue."

"I want to take care of you," he said, looking at her, his gray eyes fierce. "Always."

"Don't make promises you can't keep," she said, her stomach churning.

"Don't you trust me?"

She wanted to. But he didn't love her. And if they didn't share love, she wasn't sure what the bond was supposed to be. They had one. She didn't doubt that. And she loved him more than ever.

They would have the baby.

Once they were married it would feel better. It would feel more secure.

"I don't know if you can…understand. But… You've been one of the most constant people I've ever had in my life. Rosalind and I don't see each other very often, but she made sure I was taken care of. She didn't forget me. She's my family. And you… You're my family too."

"If you want to invite Rosalind to the wedding you can," he said.

She blinked. Stunned, because usually any mention of Rosalind's name earned her nothing but stony silence or barely suppressed rage. "She can come to our...wedding?"

"She matters to you," Isaiah said. "And what happened between the two of us isn't important anymore."

"It isn't?" Hope bloomed in her heart, fragile and new, like a tiny bud trying to find its way in early spring. "But she...broke your heart," Poppy finished.

"But now I have you. The rest doesn't matter."

It wasn't the declaration she wanted, but it was something. Better than the promise of a fair or cotton candy or anything like it.

And she wanted to hope.

So she did.

And she leaned forward and kissed him. With each pass of his lips over hers, she let go of a little more of the weight she carried and held on to him a little bit tighter.

Thirteen

Isaiah had actually taken a lunch break, which wasn't like him, and then it had turned into a rather long lunch. In fact, he had been out of the office for almost two hours, and Poppy couldn't remember the last time he had done that in the middle of the day. She was almost sure he never had, unless he'd taken her with him because it was a working lunch and he had needed somebody to handle the details.

It made her edgy to have him acting out of character.

At least, that's what she told herself. In reality, she just felt a little edgy having him out of her sight. Like he might disappear completely if she couldn't keep tabs on him. Like everything that had happened between them might be imaginary after all.

She tried to relax her face, to keep her concern from showing. Even though there was no one there to see it. It was just… The situation made her feel tense all over. And she shouldn't. Last night had been…

She had never experienced anything like it. Never before, and the only way she would again was if…

If they actually got married.

If everything actually worked out.

She placed her hand lightly on her stomach and sent up a small prayer. She just didn't want to lose any of this.

She'd never had so much.

She sighed and stood up from her desk. She needed some coffee. Something to clear her head. Something to make her feel less like a crazy lady who needed to keep a visual on her fiancé at all times.

Of course, she *was* a crazy lady who wanted a visual on her fiancé at all times, but, it would be nice if she could pretend otherwise.

Then the door to her office opened and she turned and saw Isaiah standing there in the same black T-shirt and jeans he'd been wearing when he left. But his arm was behind his back, and his expression was...

She didn't think she had ever seen an expression like that on his face before.

"What are you doing?" she asked.

"I went out looking for something for you," he said, his expression serious. "It was harder to find than I thought it would be."

"Because you didn't know what to get me?"

"No. Because it turns out I had no idea where to find what I was looking for."

She frowned. "What's behind your back?"

"Roses would have been easy," he said, and then he moved his hand and she saw a flash of pink. He held out something that was shaped like a bouquet but was absolutely not.

She stood there and just...stared for a moment.

Another diamond ring wouldn't have affected her as deeply as this gesture.

Seemingly simple and inexpensive.

To her...it was priceless.

"Cotton candy," she breathed.

"I just wanted to find you some to have with lunch." He frowned. "But now of course it isn't lunchtime anymore."

Isaiah in his most intense state, with his dark brows and heavy beard, holding the pinkest, fluffiest candy in the world, was her new favorite, absurd sight.

She held back a giggle. "Where did you go to get this?"

"There's a family fun center in Tolowa that has it, funnily enough."

"You drove all the way to... Isaiah." She took hold of the cotton candy, then wrenched it from his hand and set it on her desk before wrapping her arms around his neck and kissing him.

"It's going to melt," he said against her lips.

"Cotton candy doesn't melt."

"It shrinks," he pointed out.

"I love cotton candy, don't get me wrong. But I'd rather eat you," she returned.

"I worked hard for that."

She laughed and reached behind her, grabbing hold of the cotton candy and taking a bite, the sugar coating her lips and her tongue. Then she kissed Isaiah again, a sugary, sweet kiss that she hoped expressed some of what she felt.

But not all of it.

Because she hadn't told him.

She was afraid to.

Last night had been a big step of faith, approaching him and giving herself to him like that. It had been her *showing* him what was in her heart. But she knew that wasn't enough. Not really. She needed to say it too.

It had to be said.

She cupped his face and kissed him one more time, examining the lines by his gray eyes, the weathered, rugged look his beard gave him, that sharp, perfect nose and his lips... Lips she was convinced had been made just for her.

Other women had kissed them. She'd seen them do it. But it didn't matter. Because those lips weren't for those women. They were for her. They softened for her. Smiled for her. Only she reached those parts of Isaiah, and she had been the only one for a long time.

And yes, Rosalind had reached something in him Poppy hadn't managed to reach, but if she could do all these other things to him, if she could make him lose control, make him hunt all over creation for cotton candy, then maybe in the future...

It didn't matter. What might happen and what might not. There was only one thing that was certain. And that was how she felt.

She'd loved him for so long. Through so many things. Growing his business, enduring a heartbreak. Long hours, late nights. Fighting. Laughing. Making love.

She'd loved him through all of that.

And she'd love him forever.

Not telling him...worrying about what might happen was just more self-protection, and she was done with that.

"I love you," she said.

He went stiff beneath her touch, but she truly hadn't expected a different reaction. It was going to take him time. She didn't expect a response from him right away; she didn't even want one.

"I've always loved you," she said. "In the beginning, even when you were with Rosalind. And it felt like a horrible betrayal. But I wanted you. And I burned with jealousy. I wanted to have your intensity directed at me. And then when she… The fact that she got to be the only one to ever have it… It's not fair.

"I want it. I love you, Isaiah. I've loved you for ten years, I'll love you for ten more. For all my years. You're everything I could ever want. A fantasy I didn't even know I could create. And I just… I love you. I loved you before we kissed. Before we made love. Before you proposed to me and before I was pregnant. I just…love you."

His expression hadn't changed. It was a wall. Impenetrable and flat. His mouth was set into a grim line, his entire body stiff.

"Poppy…"

"Don't. Don't look at me like you pity me. Like I'm a puppy that you have to kick. I've spent too much of my life being pitied, Isaiah, and I don't want to be pitied by you."

"You have me," he said. "I promise that."

"You don't love me," she said.

"I can't," he said.

She shook her head, pain lancing her heart. "You won't."

"In the end, does it make a difference?"

"In the end, I suppose it doesn't make a difference, but on the journey there, it makes all the difference.

Can't means there's nothing… Nothing on heaven or earth that could make you change. Won't means you're choosing this. You're choosing to hold on to past hurts, to pain. You're choosing to hold on to another woman instead of holding on to me. You accused me of clinging to a fantasy—of wanting a man who might love me, instead of taking the man who was right in front of me. But what you're doing is worse. You're hanging on to the ghosts of the past rather than hanging on to something real. I think you could love me. I think you might. But you have it buried so far down, underneath all this protection…"

"You don't understand," he said, turning away from her and pushing his fingers through his hair. "You don't understand," he repeated, this time more measured. "It's easy for you. You don't have that disconnect. That time it takes to translate someone's facial expression, what the words beneath their words are, and what it all means. Rosalind was the clumsiest liar, the clumsiest cheat in the entire world, and I didn't know. Because she said she loved me, and so I believed it."

Poppy let out a harsh, wounded breath. "And you don't believe me?"

"I didn't say that."

"But that's what it is. You don't trust me. If you trusted me, then this wouldn't be an issue."

"No," he said. "That isn't true. I felt like a tool when everything happened with Rosalind. She broke places in me I hadn't realized were there to be broken. I don't think you can possibly understand what it's like to be blindsided like that."

Her vision went fuzzy around the edges, her heart pounding so hard she thought she might faint.

"You don't… I just told you one small piece of what it was like to grow up like I did. How anticipating what might happen tomorrow was dangerous because you might be in a whole new house with a bunch of strangers the next day. My life was never in my control. Ever. It was dangerous to be comfortable, dangerous to care. There was a system, there were reasons, but when I was a child all I knew was that I was being uprooted. Again and again."

"I'm sorry. I didn't mean…"

"We've all been hurt. No one gives us a choice about that. But what are you going to do about it? What is the problem? Say it out loud. Tell me. So that you have to hear for yourself how ridiculous this all is."

"It changed something in me," he said. "And I can't… I can't change it back."

"You *won't*. You're a coward, Isaiah Grayson. You're running. From what you feel. From what you *could* feel. You talk about these things you can't do, these things you can't feel. These things you can't understand. But you understand things other people never will. The way you see numbers, the way you fit it all together—that's a miracle. And if your brain worked like everyone else's, then you wouldn't be that person. You wouldn't be the man I love. I don't want you to change who you are. Don't you understand that? That's not what I'm asking for. I'm asking for you to hold on to me instead of her."

He took a step back, shaking his head slowly. "Poppy…"

"Where's my big, scary, decisive boss? My stubborn friend who doesn't back down? Or is this request terrifying because I'm asking for something that's not in your head? Something that's in your heart?"

Her own heart was breaking, splintering into a thousand pieces and falling apart inside her chest. She thought she might die from this.

She hadn't expected him to be able to give her a response today, but she hadn't known he was going to launch into an outright denial of his ability to ever, ever love her.

"Maybe I don't have a heart," he said, his voice hard. "Maybe I'm a robot, like you said."

"I don't think that's true. And I shouldn't have said that in the first place."

"But maybe you were closer to the truth than you want to believe. Maybe you don't love me like I am, Poppy. Maybe you just see things in me that aren't there, and you love those. But they aren't real."

She shook her head, fighting back tears. "I don't think that's true. I've been with you for a decade, Isaiah." She looked at his face, that wonderful, familiar face. That man who was destroying everything they'd found.

She wanted to hit him, rage at him. "I *know you*. I know you care. I've watched you with your family. I've watched you work hard to build this business with Joshua and Faith, to take it to the next level with the merger. You work so hard, and that's not…empty. Everything you've done to support Faith in her dream of being an architect…"

"It's her talent. I can't take the credit."

"Without you, the money wouldn't flow and that would be the end of it. You're the main artery, and you give it everything. You might not express how you care the way other people do, but you express it in a real, tangible way." He didn't move. Didn't change his expression. "You can love, Isaiah. And other people love you."

He said nothing. Not for a long moment.

"I would never take our child from you," he said finally.

"What?"

"I won't take our child from you. Forcing you to marry me was a mistake. This is a mistake, Poppy."

She felt like that little girl who had been promised a carnival, only to wake up in the morning and have her bags packed again.

The disappointment even came complete with cotton candy.

"You don't want to marry me?"

"I was forcing it," he said. "Because in my mind I had decided that was best, and so because I decided it, it had to be true. But… It's not right. I won't do that to you."

"How dare you? How dare you dump me and try to act like it's for my own good? After I tell you that I love you? Forcing me to marry you was bad enough, but at least then you were acting out of complete emotional ignorance."

"I'm always acting out of emotional ignorance," he said. "Don't say you accept all of me and then act surprised by that."

"Yeah, but sometimes you're just full of shit, Isaiah. And you hide behind those walls. You hide behind that brain. You try to outwit and outreason everything, but life is not a chess game. It's not math. None of this is. Your actions least of all. Because if you added up everything you've said and done over the past few weeks, you would know that the answer equaled love. You would know that the answer is that we should be together. You would know that you finally have what you want and *you're giving it away*.

"So don't try to tell me you're being logical. Don't try to talk to me like I'm a hysterical female asking something ridiculous of you. You're the one who's scared. You're the one who's hysterical. You can stand there with a blank look on your face and pretend that somehow makes you rational, but you aren't. You can try to lie to me. You can try to lie to yourself. But I don't believe it. I refuse."

She took a deep breath. "And I quit. I really do quit this time. I'm not going to be here for your convenience. I'm not going to be here to keep your life running smoothly, to give you what you want when you want it while I don't get my needs met in return. If you want to let me go, then you have to let me go."

She picked up the cotton candy. "But I'm taking this." She picked up her coat also, and started to walk past him and out of the room. Then she stopped. "I'll be in touch with you about the baby. And I will pay you back for the wedding dress if I can't return it. Please tell… Please tell your mom that I'm sorry. No. Tell them you're sorry. Tell them you're sorry that you let a woman who could never really love you ruin your chance with one who already does."

And then she walked out of the office, down the hall, past Joshua's open door and his questioning expression, through the lobby area, where Faith was sitting curled up in a chair staring down at a computer.

"Goodbye," Poppy said, her voice small and pained.

"What's going on?" Faith asked.

"I quit," Poppy said. "And the wedding is off. And… I think my heart is breaking. But I don't know what else to do."

Poppy found herself standing outside the door, waiting for a whole new life to start.

And, like so many times before, she wasn't confident that there would be anything good in that new life.

She took a breath. No. There would be something good. This time, there was the certainty of that.

She was going to be a mother.

Strangely, out of all this heartbreak, all this brokenness, came a chance at a kind of redemption she had never really let herself believe in.

She was going to be a mother.

It would be her only real chance at having a good mother-daughter relationship. And yes, she would be on the other side of it. But she would give her child the best of herself.

A sad smile touched her lips. Even without meaning to, Isaiah had given her a chance at love. It just hadn't been the kind of love she'd been hoping for.

But…it was still a gift.

And she was going to cling to it with everything she had.

Fourteen

Isaiah wasn't a man given to excessive drinking, but tonight he was considering it.

By the time he had gotten home from work, Poppy had cleared out her things. He supposed he should have gone after her. Should have left early. But he had been…

He had been frozen.

He had gone through the motions all day, trying to process what had happened.

One thing kept echoing in his head, and it wasn't that she loved him, though that had wrapped itself around his heart and was currently battering at him, making him feel as though his insides had been kicked with a steel-toed boot.

Or maybe just a stiletto.

No, the thing that kept going through his mind was what she'd said about his excuses.

He had known even as he said it out loud that he didn't really believe all the things he'd said. It wasn't true that he couldn't love her.

She had asked if he didn't trust her. And that wasn't the problem either.

He didn't trust himself.

Emotion was like a foreign language to him. One he had to put in effort to learn so he could understand the people around him. His childhood had been a minefield of navigating friendships he could never quite make gel, and high school and college had been a lot of him trying to date and inadvertently breaking hearts when he missed connections that others saw.

It was never that he didn't feel. It was just that his feelings were in another language.

And he often didn't know how to bridge the gap.

And the intensity of what he felt now was so sharp, so intense that his natural inclination was to deny it completely. To shut it down. To shut it off. It was what he often did. When he thought of those parts of himself he couldn't reach...

He chose to make them unreachable.

It was easier to navigate those difficult situations with others if he wasn't also dealing with his own feelings. And so he'd learned. Push it down. Rationalize the situation.

Emotion was something he could feel, hear, taste and smell. Something that overtook him completely. Something that became so raw and intense he wanted to cut it off completely.

But with her... He couldn't.

When he was making love with her, at least there was a place for all those feelings to go. A way for them to be expressed. There was something he could do with them. With that roaring in his blood, that sharp slice to his senses.

How could he give that to someone else? How could he... How could he trust himself to treat those emotions the way that they needed to be treated?

He really wanted a drink. But honestly, the explosion of alcohol with his tenuous control was likely a bad idea. Still, he was considering it.

There was a heavy knock on his front door and Isaiah frowned, going down the stairs toward the entry.

Maybe it was Poppy.

He jerked the door open and was met by his brother Joshua.

"What are you doing here?" Isaiah asked.

"I talked to Faith." Joshua shoved his hands in his pockets. "She said Poppy quit."

"Yes," Isaiah said. He turned away from his brother and walked toward the kitchen. He was going to need that drink.

"What did you do?"

"You assume I did something?" he asked.

Isaiah's anger rang a little bit hollow, considering he knew that it was his fault. Joshua just stared at him.

Bastard.

Was he so predictably destructive in his interpersonal relationships?

Yes.

He knew the answer to that without thinking.

"I released her from her obligation," Isaiah said. "She was the one who chose to leave."

"You released her from her obligation? What the hell does that mean?"

"It means I was forcing her to marry me, and then I decided not to." He sounded ridiculous. Which in and of itself was ridiculous, since *he* never was.

His brother pinched the bridge of his nose. "Start at the beginning."

"She's pregnant," Isaiah said.

Joshua froze. "She's…"

"She's pregnant," Isaiah repeated.

"How…"

"You know exactly how."

"I thought the two of you had an arrangement. Meaning I figured you weren't going to go…losing control," Joshua said.

"We had something like an arrangement. But it turned out we were very compatible. Physically."

"Yes," Joshua said, "I understood what you meant by compatible."

"Well, how was I supposed to know? You were just standing there staring at me." He rubbed his hand over his face. "We were engaged, she tried to break it off. Then she found out she was pregnant. I told her she had to marry me or I would pursue full custody—"

"Every woman's fantasy proposal. I hope you filmed it so you'll always have a memory of that special moment."

Isaiah ignored his brother. "It was practical. But then…then she wanted things I couldn't give, and I realized that maybe forcing a woman to marry me wasn't the best idea."

"And she's in love with you."

Isaiah sighed heavily. "Yes."

"And you said you couldn't love her back so she left?"

"No," he said. "I said I couldn't love her and I told her I wouldn't force her to marry me. And then she left."

"You're the one who rejected her," Joshua said.

"I don't know how to do this," Isaiah said, his voice rough. "I don't know how to give her what she wants while…while making sure I don't…"

He didn't want to say it because it sounded weak, and he'd never considered himself weak. But he was afraid of being hurt, and if that wasn't weakness, he didn't know what was.

"You can't," Joshua said simply, reading his mind. "Loving someone means loving them at the expense of your own emotional safety. Sorry. There's not another alternative."

"I can't do that."

"Because one woman hurt you?"

"You don't understand," Isaiah said. "It has nothing to do with being hurt once. Rosalind didn't just hurt me, she made a fool out of me. She highlighted every single thing that I've struggled with all my life and showed me how inadequate I am. Not with words. She doesn't even know what she did."

He took a deep breath and continued, "Connecting with people has always been hard for me. Not you, not the family. You all…know how to talk to me. Know how to deal with me. But other people? It's not easy, Joshua. But with her I thought I finally had something. I let my guard down, and I quit worrying. I quit worrying about whether or not I understood everything and just…was with someone for a while. But what I thought was happening wasn't the truth. Everything that should've been obvious was right in front of me."

"But that's not your relationship with Poppy. And it isn't going to be. She's not going to change into something else just because you admit that you're in love with her."

"Poppy is different," Isaiah said. "Whatever I thought I felt then, this is different."

"You love her. And if you don't admit that, Isaiah? Maybe you won't feel it quite so keenly, but you won't have her. You're going to…live in a separate place from the woman you love?"

"I won't be a good father anyway," Isaiah said.

"Why do you think that?"

"How am I going to be a good father when I can't… What am I going to teach a kid about relationships and people? I'm not wired like everyone else."

"And maybe your child won't be either. Or maybe my child will be different, and he'll need his uncle's help. Any of our children could need someone there with him who understands. You're not alone. You're not the only person who feels the way that you do."

Isaiah had never thought about that. About the fact that his own experiences might be valuable to someone else.

"But Poppy…"

"Knows you and loves you. She doesn't want you to be someone else."

Isaiah cleared his throat. "I accused her of that."

"Because she demanded you pull your head out of your ass and admit that you love her?"

"Yes," he admitted.

"Being alone is the refuge of cowards, Isaiah, and you're a lot of things, but I never thought you were a coward. I understand trying to avoid being hurt again. After everything I went through with my ex, I didn't want anything to do with a wife or another baby. But now I have Danielle. I have both a wife and a son. And I'm glad I didn't let grief be the deciding factor in my life. Because, let me tell you something, that's easy. It's easy to let the hard things ruin you. It's a hell of a lot braver to decide they don't get to control you."

"It hurts to breathe," Isaiah said, his voice rough. "When I look at her."

"If you aren't with her, it'll still hurt to breathe. She just won't be beside you."

"I didn't want a wife so I could be in love," Isaiah said. "I wanted one to make my life easier."

"You don't add another person to your life to make it easier. Other people only make things harder, and you should have a better understanding of that than most. You accept another person into your life because you can't live without them. Because easy isn't the most important thing anymore. She is. That's love. And it's bigger than fear. It has to be, because love itself is so damned scary."

"Why does anyone do it?" Isaiah asked.

"You do it when you don't have a choice anymore. I almost let Danielle walk away from me. I almost ruined the best thing I'd ever been given because of fear. And you tell me why a smart man would do that? Why does fear get to be the biggest emotion? Why can't love win?"

Isaiah stood there, feeling like something had shifted under his feet.

He couldn't outrun emotion. Even when he suppressed it, there was an emotion that was winning: fear.

He'd never realized that, never understood it, until now.

"Think about it," Joshua said.

Then he turned and walked out of the house, leaving Isaiah alone with his obviously flawed thinking.

He loved Poppy.

To his bones. To his soul.

He couldn't breathe for the pain of it, and he had no idea what the hell he was supposed to do with the damned fear that gnawed at his gut.

This had all started with an ad for a wife. With the most dispassionate idea any man had ever hatched.

Him, divorcing himself from feeling and figuring out a way to make his life look like he wanted it to look. To make it look like his parents' lives. His idea of home.

Only now he realized he'd left out the most important thing.

Love.

It was strange how his idea of what he wanted his life to be had changed. He had wanted to get married. He had wanted a wife. And he'd found a way to secure that.

But now he just wanted *Poppy*.

Whether they were married or not, whether or not they had perfect, domestic bliss and Sunday dinners just like his parents, whether they were in a little farmhouse or his monstrosity of a place... It didn't matter. If she was there.

Wherever Poppy was...that was his home.

And if he didn't have her, he would never have a home.

He could get that drink now. Stop the pain in his chest from spreading further, dull the impending realization of what he'd done. To himself. To his life. But he had to feel it. He had to.

He braced himself against the wall and lowered his head, pain starting in his stomach, twisting and turning its way up into his chest. Like a shard of glass had been wedged into the center of his ribs and was pushed in deeper with each breath.

He'd never lost love before.

He'd had wounded pride. Damaged trust.

But he'd never had a broken heart.

Until now.

And he'd done it to himself.

Poppy had offered him all he needed in the world, and he'd been too afraid to take it.

Poppy had lived a whole life filled with heartbreak. With being let down. He'd promised to take care of her, and then he hadn't. He was just another person who'd let her down. Another person who hadn't loved her like she should have been loved.

He should have loved her more than he loved himself.

He clenched his hand into a fist. He was done with this. With this self-protection. He didn't want it anymore.

He wanted Poppy.

Now. Always.

More than safety. More than breathing.

But he'd broken her trust. She'd already loved and lost so many people in her life, had been let down by parades of people who should have done better, and there was no logical reason for her to forgive him.

He just had to hope that love would be stronger than fear.

Fifteen

Poppy was a study in misery.

She had taken all her easily moved things and gone back to her house.

She wasn't going to flee the town. She loved her house, and she didn't really have anywhere else to go at the moment. No, she was going to have to sort that out, but later.

She wasn't entirely sure what she wanted. Where she would go.

She would have to find another job.

She could, she knew that. She had amply marketable skills. It was just that… It would mean well and truly closing the door on the Isaiah chapter of her life. Possibly the longest chapter she even had.

So many people had cycled in and out of her life. There had been a few constants, and the Graysons had been some of her most cherished friends. It hurt. Losing him like this. Losing them. But this was just how life went for her. And there was nothing she could do about it. She was always, forever at the mercy of people who simply couldn't…

She swallowed hard.

There was no real furniture left in her house after she'd moved to Isaiah's ranch. She had gathered a duffel bag full of clothes and a sleeping bag. She curled up in the sleeping bag on the floor in the corner of her bedroom and grabbed her cell phone.

There was one person she really owed a phone call.

She dialed her foster sister's number and waited.

"Hello?"

"I hope it's not too late," Poppy said, rolling to her side and looking out the window at the inky black sky.

It had the audacity to look normal out there. Clear and crisp like it was just a typical December night and not a night where her world had crashed down around her.

"Of course not. Jason and I were just getting ready to go out. But that can wait. What's going on?"

"Oh. Nothing… Everything."

"What's going on?" Rosalind repeated, her voice getting serious. "You haven't called in a couple of months."

"Neither have you," Poppy pointed out.

"I know. I'm sorry. I've never been very good at keeping in touch. But that doesn't mean I don't like hearing from you."

"I'm pregnant," Poppy blurted out.

The pause on the other end was telling. But when Rosalind finally did speak, her voice was shot through with excitement. "Poppy, congratulations. I'm so happy for you."

"I'm single," she said as a follow-up.

"Well, I figured you would have altered your announcement slightly if you weren't."

"I don't know what I'm going to do." She pulled her knees up and tucked her head down, holding her misery to her chest.

"If you need money or a place to stay... You know you can always come and stay with me and Jason."

Poppy did know that. Maybe that was even why she had called Rosalind. Because knowing that she had a place with her foster sister made her feel slightly less rootless.

She wouldn't need to use it. At least, she *shouldn't* need to use it. But knowing that Rosalind was there for her helped.

Right now, with the only other anchor in her life removed and casting her mostly adrift, Rosalind was more important than ever.

"Isaiah isn't being a terror about it, is he?" Rosalind asked.

"Not... Not the way you mean," Poppy said slowly. "It's Isaiah's baby."

The silence stretched even longer this time. *"Isaiah?"*

"Yes," Poppy said. "And I know... I know that's... I'm sorry."

"Why are you apologizing to me?" Rosalind sounded genuinely mystified.

"Because he's your...your ex. And I know I don't have a lot of experience with family, but you're the closest thing I have to a sister, and I know you don't... go dating your sister's ex-boyfriends."

"Well. Yes. I suppose so. But he's my *ex*. From a long time ago. And I'm with someone else now. I've moved on. Obviously, so has he. Why would you keep yourself from something you want just because...just because it's something other people might not think was okay? If you love him…"

Poppy realized that the guilt she felt was related to the fact that her feelings for Isaiah had most definitely originated when Isaiah had not been Rosalind's ex.

"I've had feelings for him for a long time," Poppy said quietly. "A really long time."

"Don't tell me you feel bad about that, Poppy," Rosalind said.

"I do," Poppy said. "He was your boyfriend. And you got me a job with him. In that whole time…"

"You didn't *do* anything. It's not like you went after him when were together."

"No."

"I'm the cheater in that relationship." Rosalind sighed heavily. "I didn't handle things right with Isaiah back then. I cheated on him, and I shouldn't have. I should have been strong enough to break things off with him without being unfaithful. But I wasn't."

They'd never talked about this before. The subject of Isaiah had always been too difficult for Poppy. She'd been so angry that Rosalind had hurt him, and then so resentful that her betrayal had claimed such a huge part of his heart.

But Poppy had never really considered…how Rosalind's past might have informed what she'd done.

And considering happiness had made Poppy act a lot like a feral cat, she should have.

"He was the first person who treated me really well, and I felt guilty about it," Rosalind continued. "But gratitude isn't love. And what I felt for him was gratitude. When I met Jason, my whole world kind of turned over, and what I felt for him was something else. Something I had never experienced before.

"I caused a lot of trouble for Isaiah, and I feel bad about it. But you certainly shouldn't feel guilty over having feelings for him. You should… You should be with him. He's a great guy, Poppy. I mean, not for me. He's too serious and just…not *right* for me. But you've known him in a serious way even longer than I have, and if you think he's the guy for you…"

"We were engaged," Poppy said. "But he broke it off."

"What?"

"It's a long story." Poppy laughed. "A very Isaiah story, really. We got engaged. Then we slept together. Then I broke up with him. Then I got pregnant. Then we slept together again. Then we kind of…got back engaged… But then he…broke up with me because I told him I was in love with him."

"We really need to not have so much time between phone calls," Rosalind said. "Okay. So… You being in love with him…scared him?"

"Yes," Poppy said slowly.

She wasn't going to bring up Rosalind's part in the issues between Poppy and Isaiah. Mostly because Poppy didn't actually believe they were a significant part. Not specifically. The issues that Isaiah had with love and feelings were definitely on him.

"And you're just going to…let him walk away from what you have?"

"There's nothing I can do to stop him. He said he doesn't love me. He said he doesn't… He doesn't want a relationship like that. There's nothing I can do to change how he feels."

"What did you do when he said that?"

"I yelled at him. And then… I left."

"If I was in love with a guy, I would camp out on his doorstep. I would make him miserable."

"I have some pride, Rosalind."

"I don't," Rosalind said. "I'm a crazy bitch when it comes to love. I mean, I blew up a really good thing to chase after Jason."

"This is… It's different."

"But you love him."

"How many times can I be expected to care for someone and lose them? You know. Better than anyone, you understand what growing up was like for me. For us. People were always just…shuffling us around on a whim. And I just… I can't handle it. Not anymore."

"There's a really big difference between now and then," Rosalind pointed out. "We are not kids. This is what I realized, though a little bit late with Isaiah. I wasn't a child. I didn't have to go along. I had a choice. Child services and foster families and toxic parents don't get to run our lives anymore, Poppy. We are in charge now. You're your own caseworker. You are the one who gets to decide what kind of life you want to have. Who you want to live with. What you'll settle for and what you won't. You don't have to wait for someone to rescue you or accept it when someone says they can't be with you."

"I kind of do. He said…"

"What's the worst that could happen if you fight for him one more time? Just one more?"

Poppy huffed out a laugh. "I'll die of humiliation."

"You won't," Rosalind said. "I guarantee you, humiliation isn't fatal. If humiliation were fatal, I would have died twice before Jason and I actually got married. At *least*. I was insecure and clingy, and a lot of it was because of how our relationship started, which was my own fault. My fear of getting him dirty and losing him dirty, that kind of thing. But…now we've been married for five years, and…none of that matters. Now all that matters is that we love each other. That we have each other. Everything else is just a story we tell and laugh about."

"You know Isaiah. He was very certain."

"I don't actually know Isaiah as well as you do. But you're going to have a baby with him. And… Whether or not you get him in the end, don't you think what you want is worth fighting for? Not for the sake of the baby, or anything like that. But for you. Have you ever fought for *you* before, Poppy?"

She had started to. When Isaiah had broken things off. But…

She didn't know if she really had.

Maybe Rosalind was right. Maybe she needed to face this head-on. Again.

Because nobody controlled the show but her. Nobody told her when to be done except for her.

And pride shouldn't have the last word.

"I love you," Poppy said. "I hope you *know* that. I know we're different. But you've been family to me. And… You're responsible for some of the best things I have in life."

"Well, I'm going to feel guilty if Isaiah breaks your heart."

"Even if he does… I'll be glad he was in my life for as long as he was. I love him. And…being able to love someone like this is a gift. One I don't think I fully appreciated. With our background, just being able to admit my love without fear, without holding back... That's something. It's special. It's kind of a miracle."

"It really is," Rosalind said. "I had a rocky road to Jason. I had a rocky road to love, but Poppy, it's so worth it in the end. I promise you."

"I just hope Isaiah realizes how special it is. How amazing it is. His parents always loved him. He grew up in one house. He...doesn't know that not everyone has someone to love them."

"He might have had all of that, Poppy, but he's never had you. Don't sell yourself short."

Poppy tried to breathe around the emotion swelling in her chest. "If it all works out, you're invited to the wedding," Poppy said decisively.

"Are you sure?"

"Of course. You're my family. And the family I've created is the most important thing I have."

"Good," Rosalind said. "Then go fight for the rest of it."

Poppy would do that. She absolutely would.

Isaiah didn't know for sure that he would find Poppy at her house. He could only hope that he would.

If not, he would have to launch a search of the entire town, which everyone was going to find unpleasant. Because he would be getting in faces and asking for access to confidential records. And while he was confident that ultimately he would get his way, he would rather not cut a swath of rage and destruction through the community that he tried to do business in.

But, desperate times.

He felt like he was made entirely of feelings. His

skin hurt from it. His heart felt bruised. And he needed to… He needed to find Poppy and tell her.

He needed to find her and he needed to fix this.

It was 6:00 a.m., and he had two cups of coffee in his hand when he pounded on the door of her house with the toe of his boot.

It took a couple of minutes, but the door finally opened and revealed Poppy, who was standing there in baggy pajama pants with polar bears on them, and a plain shirt. Her hair was exceptionally large and sticking out at all angles, one curl hanging in her face. And she looked…

Not altogether very happy to see him.

"What are you doing here?"

"I brought you coffee."

"Yesterday you brought me cotton candy, and you were still a dick. So explain to me why I should be compelled by the coffee." She crossed her arms and treated him to a hard glare.

"I need to talk to you."

"Well, that works, because I need to talk to you too. Though, I was not going to talk to you at six in the morning."

"Were you asleep?"

"Obviously. It's six in the morning." Then her shoulders slumped and she sighed, backing away from the door. "No. I wasn't sleeping."

He found himself relieved by that.

"I couldn't sleep at all," she continued. "Because I kept thinking about you. You asshole."

He found that extraordinarily cheering.

"I couldn't sleep either," he said.

"Well, of course not. You lost your assistant. And

you had to get your own coffee as a result. Life is truly caving in around you, Isaiah."

"That isn't why I couldn't sleep," he said. "I talked to my brother last night."

"Which one?"

"Joshua. Who was not terribly impressed with me, I have to say."

"Well, I'm not sure who could be terribly impressed with you right at the moment."

She wasn't letting him off easy. And that was all right. He didn't need it to be easy. He just needed to fix it.

"I do feel," he said, his voice coming out so rough it was like a stranger's. "I feel a lot. All the time. It's just easier when I don't. So I'm very good at pushing down my emotions. And I'm very good at separating feelings from a moment. That way I have time to analyze what I feel later, instead of being reactionary."

"Because being reactionary is bad?"

"Yes. Especially when… When I might have read a situation wrong. And I do that a lot, Poppy. I'm a perfectionist. I don't like being wrong."

"This is not news to me," she said.

"I know. You've also known me long enough that you seem to know how to read me. And I… I'm pretty good at reading you too. But sometimes I don't get it right. Feelings are different for me. But it doesn't mean I don't have them. It does mean that sometimes I'm wrong about what's happening. And… I hate that. I hate it more than anything. I hate feeling like everything is okay and finding out it isn't. I hate feeling like something is wrong only to find out that it's not."

"You know everyone makes those mistakes," she

said gently. "Nobody gets it completely right all the time."

"I do know that," he said. "But I get it wrong more often than most. I've always struggled with that. I've found ways to make it easier. I use organization. My interest in numbers. Having an assistant who helps me with the things I'm not so great at. All of those things have made it easier for me to have a life that functions simply. They've made it so I don't have to risk myself. So I don't have to be hurt.

"But I'm finding that they have not enabled me to have a full life. Poppy, I don't just want easy. That was a mistake I made when I asked you to find me a wife. I thought I wanted a wife so I could feel the sense of completeness in my personal life that I did my professional life. But what I didn't realize was that things felt complete in my professional life because I was with you every day."

He took a step toward her, wanting to touch her. With everything he had.

"I had you in that perfect space I created for you. And I got to be with you all the time," he continued. "Yours was one of the first faces I saw every morning. And you were always one of the last people I saw before I went home. There was a rightness to that. And I attributed it to…the fact that you were efficient. The fact that you were organized. The fact that I liked you. But it was more than that. And it always has been. It isn't that I didn't think of you when I decided to put an ad in the paper for a wife. You were actually the reason I did it. It's just that… I'm an idiot."

He paused and watched her expression.

"Are you waiting for me to argue with you?" She blinked. "I'm not going to."

"I'm not waiting for you to argue. I just want you to… I want you to see that I mean this. I want you to understand that I didn't do it on purpose. There's just so many layers of protection inside me, and it takes me days sometimes to sort out what's happening in my own chest.

"You are right. I hated it because it wasn't in my head. I hated it because it all comes from that part of me that I find difficult. The part that I feel holds me back. It is amazing to have a brother like Joshua. Someone who's a PR expert. Who seems to navigate rooms and facial expressions and changes in mood seamlessly. I've had you by my side for that. To say the right thing in a meeting when I didn't. To give me your rundown on how something actually went so that I didn't have to."

"I already told you it's not hard for me to do that for you. The way you are doesn't bother me. It's just you. It's not like there's this separate piece of you that has these challenges and then there's you. It's all you. And I could never separate it out. I wouldn't even want to. Isaiah, you're perfect the way you are. Whether there is a label for this or not. Whether it's a disorder or it isn't. It doesn't matter to me. It's all you."

"I bet you resented it a little bit yesterday."

"You hurt me. You hurt me really badly. But I still think you're the best man I know. I still… Isaiah, I love you. You saying terrible things to me one day is not going to undo ten years of loving you."

The relief washing through him felt unlike anything he'd ever experienced before. He wanted to drop to his knees. He wanted to kiss her. Hold her. He wanted to unlock himself and let everything he felt pour out.

Why wasn't he doing that? Why was he standing there stiff as a board when that wasn't at all what he felt?

So he did.

He dropped down to his knees and he wrapped his arms around her, pressing his face against her stomach. Against Poppy and the life that was growing inside her.

"I love you," he whispered. "Poppy, I love you."

He looked up at her, and she was staring down at him, bewildered, as he continued, "I just... I was so afraid to let myself feel it. To let myself want this. To let myself have it. I can't help but see myself as an emotional burden. When I think of everything you do for me... I think of you having to do that in our lives, and it doesn't feel fair. It feels like you deserve someone easier. Someone better. Someone you don't have to act as a translator for."

"I've had a long time to fall in love with other men, Isaiah. But you are the one I love. You. And I already told you that I don't see you and then the way you process emotion. It's all you. The man I love. All your traits, they can't be separated. I don't want them to be. You're not my project. You... You have no idea what you give to me. Because I've never told you. I talked with Rosalind last night."

"You did?"

"Yes." Poppy crouched down, so that they were eye to eye. "She told me I needed to fight for you. That we are not foster children anymore, and I can't live like someone else is in control of my destiny. And she's right. Whether or not you showed up at my house this morning, we were going to talk. Because I was going to come find you. And I was going to tell you again that I love you."

"I'm a lot of work," he said, his voice getting rough.

"I don't care. It's my privilege to have the freedom to work at it. No one is going to come and take me away and move me to a different place. No one is controlling what I do but me. If I choose to work at this, if I choose to love you, then that's my choice.

"And it's worth it. You mean everything to me. You hired me when I was an eighteen-year-old girl who had no job experience, who had barely been in one place for a year at a time. You introduced me to your family, and watching them showed me how love can function in those kinds of relationships. Your family showed me the way people can treat each other. The way you can fight and still care. The way you can make mistakes and still love."

"That's my family. It isn't me."

"I haven't gotten to you yet." She grabbed hold of his chin, her brown eyes steady on his. "You've told me how difficult it is for you to navigate people. But you still do it. You are so loyal to the people in your life. Including me.

"I watched the way you cared for Rosalind. Part of that was hiring me, simply because it meant something to her. Part of that was caring for her, and yes, in the end you felt like you made a mistake, like she made a fool out of you, but you showed that you had the capacity to care deeply.

"You have been the most constant steady presence in my life for the past decade. You've shown me what it means to be loyal. You took me with you to every job, every position. Every start-up. You committed to me in a way that no one else in my life ever has. And I don't know if you can possibly understand what that means for a foster kid who's had more houses than she can count."

Poppy stroked his face, her heart thundering hard, her whole body trembling. She continued, "You can't minimize the fact that you taught me that people can care that deeply. That they might show it in different ways, but that doesn't mean they don't care.

"I *do* know you have feelings, Isaiah. Because your actions show them. You are consistent month to month, year to year. It doesn't matter whether I misinterpret your reaction in the moment. You're always in it for the long haul. And that seems like a miracle to me." Her voice got thick, her eyes shiny. "You are not a trial, Isaiah Grayson. You are the greatest gift I've ever been given. And loving you is part of that gift."

The words washed over him, a balm for his soul. For his heart.

"I was afraid," he said. "Not just of being too much for you—" the words cut his throat "—but of losing you. I wish I were that altruistic. But I'm not. I was afraid because what I feel for you is so deep… I don't know what I would do if I lost you. If I… If I ruined it because of… Because of how I am."

"I *love* how you are." Poppy's voice was fierce. "It's up to me to tell you when something is wrong, to tell you when it's right. It doesn't matter how the rest of the world sees things, Isaiah. It matters how *we* see things. Here. Between us.

"Normal doesn't matter. Neither of us is normal. You're going to have to deal with my baggage. With the fact that I'm afraid I don't know how to be a mother because I never had one of my own. With the fact that sometimes my first instinct is to protect myself instead of fighting for what I feel. And I'm going to have to learn your way of communicating. That's love for everyone. Sometimes I'll be a bigger burden. And sometimes you will be. But we'll have each other. And that's so much better than being apart."

"I think I've loved you for a very long time. But it felt necessary to block it out. But once I touched you... Once I touched you, Poppy, I couldn't deny it. I can't keep you or my feelings for you in a box, and that terrifies me. You terrify me. But in a good way."

She lifted her hand, tracing a line down the side of his face. "The only thing that terrifies me is a life without you."

"Will you marry me? This time I'm asking. Not because you're pregnant. Not because I want a wife. Because I want you."

"I will marry you," she said. "Not for your family. Not in spite of you, but because of you. Because I love you."

"I might be bad when it comes to dealing with emotion, but I know right now I'm the happiest man in the world."

His heart felt like it might burst, and he didn't hide from it. Didn't push it aside. He opened himself up and embraced all of it.

"There will have to be some ground rules," Poppy said, smiling impishly.

"Ground rules?"

"Yes. Lines between our personal and professional lives. For example, at home, I'm not making the coffee."

"That's a sacrifice I'm willing to make."

"Good. But that won't be the only one."

He wrapped his arms around her and pulled them both into a standing position, Poppy cradled against his chest. "Why don't I take you into your bedroom and show you exactly what sorts of sacrifices I'm prepared to make."

"I don't have a bed in there," she protested as he carried her back toward her room. "There's just a sleeping bag."

"I think I can work with that."

And he did.

Epilogue

December 24, 2018

WIFE FOUND—

Antisocial mountain man/businessman Isaiah Grayson married his assistant, his best friend and his other half, Poppy Sinclair, on Christmas Eve.

She'll give him a child or two, exact number to be negotiated. And has vowed to be as tolerant of his mood as he is of hers. Because that's how love works.

She is willing to stay with him in sickness and in health, in a mountain cabin or at a fancy gala. As long as she is with him. For as long as they both shall live.

She's happy for him to keep the beard.

They opted to have a small, family wedding on a mountain.

The fact that Poppy was able to have a family wedding made her heart feel like it was so full it might burst. The Grayson clan was all in attendance, standing in the snow, along with Rosalind and her husband.

Poppy peeked out from around the tree she was hiding behind and looked at Isaiah, who was standing next to Pastor John Thompson. The backdrop of evergreens capped with snow was breathtaking, but not as breathtaking as the man himself.

He wasn't wearing a suit. He was wearing a black coat, white button-up shirt and black jeans. He also had on his black cowboy hat. He hadn't shaved.

But that was what she wanted.

Him.

Not some polished version, but the man she loved.

This would be her new Christmas tradition. She would think of her wedding. Of their love. Of how her whole life had changed because of Isaiah Grayson.

For her part, Poppy had on her very perfect dress and was holding a bouquet of dark red roses.

She smiled. It was the fantasy wedding she hadn't even known she wanted.

But then, she supposed that was because she hadn't known who the groom might be.

But this was perfectly them. Remote, and yet surrounded by the people they loved most.

There was no music, just the deep silence of the forest, the sound of branches moving whenever there was a slight breeze. And Poppy came out from behind the tree when it felt like it was time.

She walked through the snow, her eyes never leaving Isaiah's. She felt like she might have been walking down a very long aisle toward him for the past ten years. And that each and every one of those years had been necessary to bring them to this moment.

Isaiah didn't feel things the way other people did. He felt them deeper. It took longer to get there, but she knew that now she had his heart, she would have it forever.

She trusted it. Wholly and completely.

Just like she trusted him.

He reached out and took her hand, and the two of them stood across from each other, love flooding Poppy's heart.

"I told you an ad was a good idea," he whispered after they'd taken their vows and the pastor had told him to kiss the bride.

"What are you talking about?"

"It's the reason I finally realized what was in front of me the whole time."

"I think we would have found our way without the ad."

"No. We needed the ad."

"So you can be right?" she asked, holding back a smile.

He grinned. "I'm always right."

"Oh, really? Well then, what do you think is going to happen next?"

He kissed her again, deep and hard and long. "I think we're going to live happily-ever-after."

He was right. As always.

* * * * *

MILLION DOLLAR
BABY

JANICE MAYNARD

For the artists and dreamers among us…
May you always find ways to keep your
creative spirit alive. The world needs you!

One

A dimly lit bar filled with rowdy patrons was an uncomfortable place to be on a Thursday night near the witching hour…if you were a woman without a date and too shy to make eye contact with anyone. The music was loud, masking Brooke's unease.

She was lonely and so very tired of being the forgotten Goodman child. She'd spent her entire life toeing some invisible line, and what had it gotten her? Neither of her parents respected her. Her two older brothers were out conquering the world. And where was Brooke? Stuck at home with Mom and Dad in Royal, Texas. Held hostage by their expectations and her own eager-to-please personality. The whole situation sucked.

She nursed her virgin strawberry daiquiri and stared at the tiny seeds nestling in the ice. Impulsive decisions were more her style than drunken peccadilloes. Brooke had seen too many of her friends almost ruin their lives with a single alcohol-fueled mistake. She might be crazy, but she was clearheaded.

Suddenly, she realized that the band had vacated the

stage. The remaining plaintive music—courtesy of the lone guitar player—suited Brooke's mood. She didn't even mind the peanut-strewn floor and the smell of stale beer. At the same moment, she saw a man sitting alone at the bar, three empty stools on either side of him. Something about his broad shoulders made the breath catch in her throat. She had seen him walk in earlier. Instantaneous attraction might be a quirk of pheromones, but yearning had curled in the pit of her stomach even then. Sadly, the dance floor had been too crowded, and she had lost sight of him before she could work up the courage to introduce herself.

Now, here he was. All the scene needed was a shaft of light from heaven to tell her *this* was the man. *This* was her moment. She wanted him.

Butterflies fluttered through her. *Oh, God.* Was she really going to do it? Was she really going to pick up a stranger?

There was little question in her mind that he was her type. Even seated, she could tell that he was tall. His frame was leanly muscled and lanky, his posture relaxed. His dark blond hair—what she could see of it beneath the Stetson— was rumpled enough to be interesting and had a slight curl that gave him an approachable charm. Unfortunately, she couldn't gauge the color of his eyes from this distance.

Before she could change her mind, she lurched to her feet, frosty glass in hand, and made her way across the room. Not a single person stopped her. Not a single person joined the solitary man at the bar.

Surely it was a sign.

Taking a deep breath, she set her drink and her tiny clutch purse on the polished mahogany counter and hopped up on the leather-covered stool. No need to panic. It was only a conversation so far. That's all.

Now that she was close to him, she felt a little dizzy.

She gnawed her bottom lip and summoned a smile. "Hello, Cowboy. Mind if I join you?"

Austin glanced sideways and felt a kick of disappointment. The little blonde was a beauty, but she was far too young for him. Her gray eyes held an innocence he had lost years ago.

He shot her a terse smile. "Sorry, ma'am. I was about to leave."

Her face fell. "Oh, don't go. I thought we could chat."

He lifted an eyebrow. "Chat?"

Mortification stained her cheeks crimson. "Well, you know…"

"I *don't* know," he said. "That's the point. This could be a sorority prank, or maybe you're a not-quite-legal girl trying to lose her virginity. You look about sixteen, and I'm not keen to end up in jail tonight."

She scowled at him. "That's insulting."

"Not at all. You reek of innocence. It's a compliment, believe me. Unfortunately, I'm not the guy you're looking for."

"Maybe I want one who doesn't end sentences with prepositions."

The bite in her voice made him grin. "Are you insinuating that I'm uneducated?"

"Don't change the subject. For your information, I'm twenty-six. Plenty old enough to know my own mind." She took a deep breath. "I'm in the mood for romance."

"I think you mean sex."

He drawled the five words slowly, for nothing more than the pleasure of watching all that beautiful creamy skin turn a darker shade of dusky pink. "Sex?" The word came out as a tiny high-pitched syllable. Huge, smoky, thickly lashed eyes stared up at him.

This time he hid the grin. Poor kid was petrified.

He couldn't deny that he was tempted. She was genuine and sweet and disarmingly beautiful…in a healthy, girl-next-door kind of way. Her pale blond hair was caught up in a careless ponytail, and her royal-blue silk shirt and skinny jeans were nothing pretentious. Even her ballerina flats were unexceptional. She was the kind of woman who probably looked exactly this good when she rolled out of bed in the morning.

That thought took him down a road he needed to avoid. His sex hardened, making his pants uncomfortable. He held out his hand, attempting to normalize the situation. "I'm Au—"

She slapped her hand over his mouth, interrupting his polite introduction. "No," she said, sounding desperate and anxious all at the same time. "I'll call you Cowboy. You can call me Mandy."

He took her wrist and moved her hand away. "Not your real name?"

"No."

"Ah. Aliases. Intriguing."

"You're making fun of me." Her face fell.

"Maybe a little." He smiled to let her know he was teasing.

Without warning, their flirtatious repartee was rudely curtailed. A tall, statuesque redhead took the bar stool at his right shoulder and curled an arm around his waist. "Buy me another beer, will you? Sorry I was gone so long. Who the hell thinks it's a good idea to build a ladies' room with only a single stall?"

Austin groaned inwardly. *Damn.* He'd actually forgotten about Audra for a moment. "Um…"

Poor *Mandy* went dead white and looked as if she were going to throw up. "Excuse me," she said, with all the politeness of a guest at high tea with the queen. "It was a pleasure to meet you, but I have to go now."

Thank God Audra was a quick study. She sized up the situation in a glance. Her eyes widened. "Oh, crap. I'm sorry. Don't go. I'm his sister. Honest."

Mandy hesitated.

Austin nodded. "It's true. Underneath that bottled red hair is a blonde just like me."

Audra stood up and grimaced. "Forget the beer, little brother. I'll grab a cab. See you at the house later."

Then his five-years-older sister went completely off script. She stepped around him and took both of Mandy's hands in hers. "Here's the thing, ma'am. I know it's sometimes scary to meet men these days. Getting hit on in a bar can be dangerous."

"*She* was hitting on *me*," Austin muttered.

Both women ignored him.

Audra continued. "My brother is a good, decent man. He doesn't have any diseases, and he doesn't assault women. You don't have to be afraid of him."

"Audra!" His head threatened to explode from embarrassment.

Mandy barely glanced at him. "I see."

Audra nodded. "He doesn't live here. He's in town visiting me, and we came out tonight to…well…"

For once, his outrageous sister looked abashed.

Mandy gave him a puzzled look. "To what?"

Dear Lord. He gritted his teeth. If he didn't tell her, Audra would. "Today is the anniversary of my wife's death. She's been gone for six years. I finally took my wedding ring off, thanks to my sister's badgering. That's it. That's all."

Tears welled in Mandy's eyes. She blinked them back,

but one rolled down her cheek. "I had no idea. I am so sorry."

Audra patted her shoulder. "It was a long time ago. He's fine."

Austin got to his feet and grabbed his sister's arm none too gently despite her glowing character testimonial. "You're leaving. Now."

He glanced back at Mandy. "Don't move."

On the way to the door, Audra smirked at him. "I won't wait up for you. Have fun tonight."

"You are such a brat."

Outside on the sidewalk, he hugged her. "I won't discuss my love life with you. A man has boundaries."

Audra kissed his cheek. "Understood. I just want you to be happy, that's all."

"I am happy," he said.

"Liar."

"I'm happier than I was."

"Go back in there before she gets cold feet."

"I love you, sis."

"I love you, too."

He watched his only sibling get into a cab, and then he looked through the window into the bar where not one but two men had taken advantage of his absence to move in on Mandy.

No way. No way in hell. The little blonde was his. At least for tonight.

Brooke breathed a sigh of relief when her cowboy returned and dispersed the crowd that had gathered around her. Apparently if the hour was late enough and the man drunk enough, even the most vehement no didn't register.

When it was just the two of them again, the cowboy

gave her a slow, intimate smile that curled her toes. "May I buy you another drink?"

"No, thanks. I wasn't drinking. Not really. Alcohol clouds a person's judgment. I wanted to be clearheaded tonight."

"I see." He cocked his head and studied her. "Do you live here in Joplin?"

"Nope."

"So we're both just passing through?"

"It would seem that way."

A small grin teased the corners of his mouth. The man had a great mouth. Really great. She could imagine kissing that mouth all night long.

Finally, he shook his head, bemusement in his baffled gaze. "I know what *I'm* doing here, *Mandy*, but I'm still not clear about why you showed up at this bar tonight."

"Does it matter?" She hadn't expected a man to quiz her. The fact that her cowboy was slowing things down rattled her.

He nodded. "It does to me."

"Maybe I'm horny."

He snorted out a laugh and tried to turn it into a cough… unsuccessfully. Then he rubbed two fingers in the center of his forehead and sighed. "I'm not asking for your life story. But I'd like to know why me and why tonight. Is this a rebound thing? Are you trying to teach someone a lesson? Am I even warm?"

"Ninety-nine men out of a hundred would already have me in bed right now."

"Sorry to disappoint you."

The look in his eyes made her feel like a naughty schoolgirl. And not in a good way. She drained the last of her melted daiquiri and wrinkled her nose. "My life is boring. I'm having some family issues. For once I wanted to do something wild and exciting and totally out of character. Plus, you're really hot."

"So you *don't* frequent bars as a rule?"

"You know I don't," she grumbled, "or I wouldn't be so bad at it."

He flicked the end of her ponytail. "I never said you were bad at it."

Some deep note in his voice caught her stomach and sent it into a free fall of excitement and anticipation. "So are we good now?" she asked.

The cowboy stared at her. He stared at her for so long that her nipples pebbled and her thighs clenched. "What makes you believe that you and I will be wild and exciting? What if you chose wrong?"

She gaped. Words escaped her.

He closed her mouth with a finger below her chin. "It would seem prudent to take me out for a test drive ahead of time…don't you think?"

Before she could do more than inhale a sharp, startled breath, he slid one big hand beneath her ponytail, cupped the base of her neck and pulled her toward him just far enough for their mouths to meet comfortably.

Actually, *comfortable* was a misnomer for what happened next. Fireworks shot toward the ceiling in all directions. Angel choirs sang. A million dizzying pinwheels shot through her veins and rocketed into her pelvis.

The man was kissing her. Nothing more. So why was the earth shaking beneath her feet?

He tasted of whiskey and temptation. If she'd had any remaining reservations about her plan, they vanished in the heat of his lips on hers. It was possible she whimpered. She definitely leaned in and wordlessly begged for more.

Somewhere in the distance catcalls and whoops and hollers signaled an appreciative audience. But Brooke barely noticed. Her hands settled on the cowboy's shoulders. "Take off your hat," she begged.

"I only take off the hat in bed," he said, the words rough with lust and determination.

"Oh."

His smile was more of a grimace. "It's not too late for you to walk away. In fact, it's never too late. You started this little fantasy, but you can say no whenever you want."

She looked up at him, feeling the oddest combination of confidence and stomach-curling uncertainty. "I don't want to say no."

"Do you have a hotel room?"

"Not yet."

"Any preference?"

"Not somewhere fancy." Translation—nowhere that the staff might know her parents.

His terse nod seemed to indicate agreement. "Let's go, then." He tossed money on the bar for the tab and took her elbow as they walked out.

Outside, they paused on the sidewalk. It was August, and the air was pleasant at this hour. He pointed at a late-model pickup truck. "Would you like me to drive?"

Brooke shook her head. Who knew that the mechanics of a one-night stand were so tricky? "My things are in my car. I'll meet you there. How about the Sherwood Hotel? Two streets over?"

"I know it."

"I'm sorry," she said, feeling brutally young and stupid.

"For what?"

"I'm sorry you lost your wife."

He cursed beneath his breath, rolled his shoulders and stared up at the moon, his profile starkly masculine. "You told me we weren't going to use our real names," he said. "That was *your* rule. Well, mine is no rehashing the past.

This is sex, Mandy. Wild and exciting and temporary—if that's not what you want, walk away."

His entire body vibrated with tension. She honestly couldn't tell if he was angry or sexually frustrated or both.

In that moment, she realized that her reasons for coming to Joplin no longer existed. She wasn't here to flirt or to pick up a stranger or to have an anonymous tryst to prove to herself that she wasn't boring.

Right here, right now…with her limbs shaking and her mouth dry and her nerves shot…the only thing she wanted was to undress this cowboy and to have him return the favor. Because this man, this beautiful, hauntingly complicated man, tugged at her heartstrings. She wanted to know him in every way there was to know a lover.

She only had one night. It would have to be enough.

Daringly, she reached out and put a hand on his arm. She could feel his taut, warm muscles through the soft cotton fabric of his shirt. "I don't want to walk away, Cowboy. I'll meet you at the hotel. Don't make me wait."

Two

Austin Bradshaw couldn't be entirely sure he wasn't dreaming. This night was like nothing he had ever experienced. He glanced in his rearview mirror to make sure Mandy's little navy Honda was still behind him. He chuckled to himself, because he had a hunch the car was a rental. His mystery woman struck him as the kind of person who would attend to the details of a plan with great care.

The desk clerk at the midrange hotel was neither curious nor particularly friendly. He swiped Austin's credit card, handed over two keys and immediately returned his focus to whatever show he was watching on his laptop.

When Austin went back outside, he found Mandy leaning against the side of his pickup, an overnight case in her hand. She shifted from one foot to the other. "All set?"

He stared at her. "Are you sure you want to do this?"

"Quit asking me that," she huffed. "I'm here, aren't I?"

Releasing a slow, steady breath, he took the bag out of her death grip and set it on the ground. Then he cupped her head in his hands, tilted her face up to his and crushed his mouth over hers. He'd been in a state of arousal now for the better part of two hours. The faint scent of her perfume and the taste of her lips were imprinted on his brain.

He wanted her. Naked. Hungry. Begging. The more he thought about the night to come, the more he unraveled. At the rate they were going, there wasn't going to be much of the night left.

Reluctantly, he let her go. "Hurry," he said.

The hotel was three stories tall with indoor corridors and modern decor. At this point, Austin could have taken her up against the wall in the stairwell, but he resisted.

They rode the elevator to the top floor. Their room was at the end on the corner. His hand shook so badly it took him three tries to get the key in the door. He expected Mandy to give him grief about it, but she never said a word.

When they were finally inside, he closed the door carefully in deference to their fellow guests and leaned against it.

Mandy frowned. "Where's your bag?"

"I don't have one."

"Why not?"

"That's not really how a one-night stand works, honey."

She looked mortified. "Why didn't you tell me?"

"I thought you'd be more comfortable if you had your bag. Women like to have their little bits and pieces with them."

Mandy wrapped her arms around her waist and scanned the room like she was casing it for fire exits.

"What's wrong?" he asked, reminding himself that patience was a virtue.

Her bottom lip trembled. "I just realized something. If tonight is your first time to have sex in six years, I can't go through with this. That's too much pressure for me. Honestly."

He burst out laughing, and then laughed even harder at

the look of indignation on her face. "Not to worry," he said, wiping his cheeks and trying to get himself under control. His companion clearly didn't see the humor in the situation. "I've had sex. Occasionally. And besides, if what you said were true, we'd never have made it out of the parking lot back at the bar. So no pressure, okay? Just you and me and all that wild excitement you wanted."

Some of the tension drained from her body. "Oh. Well, that's good. I guess."

"Come here, honey." He held out his hand.

She came to him willingly. But her gaze didn't quite meet his, and her cheeks were flushed.

He unbuttoned the top button of her shirt. "Your skin is like cream. Beautiful and smooth." Brushing the tops of her breasts with his fingertips, he smiled inwardly when she sighed.

"You're still wearing your hat," she said.

"And we're still not in bed."

"Close enough." She reached up and took off his Stetson. After tossing it on the nearest chair, she massaged his head with both hands. "You shouldn't cover up your hair. Women would kill for this color."

He could tell she was more comfortable with him now. That was a very good thing, because he didn't want a timid partner in bed. "Feel free to take off anything else that catches your fancy."

"Very funny." She toyed with his belt buckle. "Why aren't you calling me Mandy?"

"Because you don't look like a Mandy. It's not your real name. So I'll stick with *honey*. Unless you want to fess up and tell me the truth. It's not like I'm going to stalk you."

"I know that." The snippy response was the tiniest bit sulky. And her bottom lip stuck out. It was so damned cute, he wanted to suck on it.

Gently, he pulled her shirt loose from the waistband of her jeans and slid his hands underneath. Her skin was warm and soft. So soft. He wanted to make this night good for her.

He unhooked her bra. It still bothered him that he didn't know why she was here…not really. But his brain was losing the battle with the driving urge to give her what she wanted. What *he* wanted.

When he slipped her shirt from her shoulders and took her bra right along with it, she didn't protest. The sight of her standing there, all white creamy skin and big gray eyes and rosy pink nipples, stole his breath and tightened his gut. "God, you're gorgeous," he said huskily, breathing it like a prayer.

He hadn't lied to her. There had been a handful of women in six years. But those had been *real* one-night stands. Women whose names and faces he barely remembered. Divorcées. Widows hurting like he was. The sex had slaked a momentary physical need, but afterward, his grief had been just as deep, just as raw.

In a way, it had been easier *not* to have sex, because that way he didn't have to be reminded of all he had lost.

He scooped her up in his arms and carried her to the bed. Something about tonight felt different. Maybe because his mystery woman was ridiculously charming and vulnerable and maybe even a little bit naive. She brought out his protective instincts and tapped into raw emotions inside him that he would have sworn were dead and buried.

With her he felt the need to be tender.

"Hang on, honey." Hitching her higher on his chest, he grabbed for the comforter with one hand and dragged it and the sheet halfway down the bed. Then he dropped the big-eyed blonde on the mattress and tried not to pounce on her. Instead, he came down beside her and propped his head on his hand.

Lazily, he traced a fingertip from her collarbone, down between her breasts, over her concave belly to her tiny cute navel. "Tell me what you're thinking, sweet lady. I swear I don't bite."

Her body was so rigid it was giving *him* a headache.

She gnawed her lower lip. "I forgot about protection."

"Not to worry. We're good for two rounds." He reached in his back pocket and extracted a duo of condom packets. "I had these in the truck."

"Oh. That's nice."

"Tell me your name," he coaxed. He bent over her and kissed his way from her navel up along her rib cage, pausing just at the slope of her breast and waiting until her breathing ratcheted up a notch and a shudder worked its way through her body.

"You're not playing fair…" She gazed up at him from underneath sultry lashes.

Did she have any idea what that look did to a man? He flicked his tongue across her nipple…barely a graze. "I play to win, honey. You wanted wild and exciting? That usually means breaking the rules."

He was breathing hard, barely holding it together. Playing this game was fun, more fun than he'd had in a hell of a long time. But he wasn't sure how much longer he could last. Already he wanted her so badly he was shaking.

"Brooke," she whispered. "My name is Brooke."

The trust on her face made him ashamed. She was doing something out of character. He knew it. And he was prepared to help her in her quest for a night of reckless passion. What kind of man did that make him?

He swallowed hard. "Brooke. I like it. With an *e* or no *e*?"

She smiled. "Does it matter?"

"It does to me." And it did. When this was over and they

went their separate ways, he wanted to remember her exactly like this. He wanted to know everything there was to know.

She caressed his chin, feeling the stubble. He'd shaved at six that morning. "With an *e*, Cowboy. Now it's your turn."

He didn't pretend to misunderstand. "Austin," he groaned. "My name is Austin." Moving his lips across her breast, he kissed his way up hills and down valleys and back again until Brooke panted and whimpered and begged. That was the sign he had been waiting for.

He rolled to his feet and ripped at his shirt, dragging it over his head in one frustrated motion. Then he toed off his boots and shucked out of his jeans and boxers. When he was buck-ass naked, he stood beside the bed and tried to catch his breath. It was embarrassing to be so winded when he hadn't even started yet.

Brooke came up on her knees and stared. "Are you normal?"

He blinked. "Excuse me?"

She waved a hand. "Your, um…you know. It seems kind of big."

A slither of unease sent ice water through his veins. "You wouldn't lie to me about that virgin thing. Would you?"

She straightened her shoulders, her eyes flashing. "I am *not* a liar."

"So you've definitely had sex."

"Of course."

"How many times?"

"That's none of your business." She unbuttoned her jeans and shimmied them down her thighs.

His mouth went dry. "I was gonna do that."

She gave him a look. "You were taking too long. I'm not sure I picked the right man. Are you positive you know what you're doing?"

He didn't know whether to laugh or howl with frustration. "God, you're a piece of work."

"You promised me wild and exciting. I'm still wearing panties."

He grabbed her around the waist and tumbled them both to the bed, rolling so they landed with Brooke on top. She was easily eight inches shorter than he was and forty pounds lighter. She pretended to struggle. He pretended to let her. When they were both breathless, he kissed her hard.

She melted into him, purring his name with soft, erotic yearning that made every cell in his body ache.

He rubbed her back. "I'm glad you walked into my life tonight, Brooke with no last name." Her ponytail had come loose. Pale, sunshiny hair tumbled around them, soft and silky. It smelled like lilacs and innocence and happy summer afternoons.

She nibbled his chin. "Me, too. I nearly chickened out, but then I saw you sitting there, and I felt something."

"Something?" He palmed her bottom. It was a perfect bottom. Plump and pert and exactly the right size for a man's hands.

"A zing, I guess. Animal attraction." She shifted her weight and nearly injured him. He was so hard his balls ached. The condom was in arm's reach. All he had to do was grab it. But he didn't want this to be over. He didn't want the night to end.

Without warning, Brooke rolled off him, settled onto her side, and took his sex in her hand. "I like the way you look, Cowboy." She stroked him slowly, her gaze focused on the task at hand.

The feel of her cool slender fingers on his taut flesh skated the line between pleasure and pain. He gritted his teeth and tried not to come. "I told you my name," he groaned.

She rested her cheek on his shoulder and continued her torture. "Yes, you did." She gripped him tightly. "Austin." She whispered it low and sweet.

Sweat broke out on his brow. This woman was killing him slowly…

Brooke was hot and dizzy and elated. For an idea that had begun so badly, this was turning out to be a night to remember. Austin was everything she could have asked for in a lover. Demanding and yet tender. Tough and masculine, but still considerate of her insecurities.

He grabbed her wrist and moved it away from his erection. "Enough," he croaked.

Before she could protest, he reached for the condom, rolled it on and dragged her panties down her legs. Then he was on top of her and in her and she forgot how to breathe.

He was heavy and wildly aroused. Thankfully, she was equally excited. Despite his impressive stats, her body accepted him easily. It had been a long time for her, but he didn't have to know that. She canted her hips, tried to relax and concentrated on the incredible sensation of fullness as her body became one with his.

Something about the moment dampened her eyes and tightened her throat. Maybe it was the thought of all he had lost. Maybe it was a breathless yearning to have a man like this for her own one day. Whatever it was, it made her weepy and left her feeling raw and vulnerable. As if it were impossible to hide from him.

He came quickly, with a muttered apology, his chest heaving. Brooke tried to squelch her disappointment. After a quick trip to the bathroom to dispose of the condom, he returned. In their hurry, they had left the lamp on. Now, he flipped the switch, plunging the room into darkness. Only an automatic night-light in the bathroom dispersed some of the gloom as their eyes adjusted.

Austin smoothed the hair from her face. "I'm sorry about that, honey. You had me pretty wound up, and it's been a little while for me."

"It's fine."

His grin was a flash of white. "It's *not* fine. But it will be. Spread your legs, darlin'. Let me show you the fireworks."

She moved her ankles apart obediently, but inside, she grimaced. This had never been her strong suit. It was too personal, too intimate. The only man who had ever gotten this far with her had been really bad at it.

Fortunately, Austin wasn't privy to her negative thoughts. He cradled her head in his arm and touched her with confidence, the confidence of a man who knew how to pleasure a woman and liked doing it. "Close your eyes," he crooned. "Relax, Brooke."

It was only when he said those two words that she realized her fingers were clenched in the sheets and her shoulders were rigid. "Sorry," she muttered. "You don't have to do this."

Austin frowned. "I need to touch you. Your body is beautiful and soft and so damn sexy. I want to hear you scream my name."

"Arrogant cowboy…"

He entered her with two fingers and used his thumb to stroke the spot where she ached the most. The keening cry that escaped her throat was embarrassing. But soon, embarrassment was the furthest thing from her mind.

Austin decimated her. He whispered naughty things and caressed her with sure steady touches until her own responses shocked her and her body became a stranger. Just as her spine arched off the bed, she did indeed scream his name. Moments later, he moved on top of her and entered her a second time.

The orgasm was incredible. On a scale of one to ten, it was some imaginary number that only scientists from outer space could decipher.

This time, Austin was just getting started as she tumbled down the far side of the hill. He laughed roughly and shoved her up the peak again, thrusting harder and faster and holding her tightly until they both found the pinnacle at almost the same moment and lost themselves in the fiery pleasure.

Brooke was boneless, elated and utterly spent. Never again would she settle for the kind of relationship that was boring and mundane. This wonderful cowboy had given her that.

They lay together in a tangle of arms and legs as their bodies cooled and their heartbeats slowed.

At last, Austin shifted so she wasn't bearing his full weight. "You okay?" he asked, sounding sleepy and sated and maybe a little bit smug.

She nuzzled her head against his warm, hard shoulder. "Oh, yeah. Better than okay." Tomorrow morning, she was going to get online and give this hotel five stars across the board.

He groaned and rolled away. "Don't move. I'm coming back."

She heard the water run in the bathroom. Then silence. Then a low curse.

"What's wrong?" she said, raising her voice in alarm.

He stumbled back into bed, his skin chilled. "The condom broke." His voice was flat. She couldn't read him at all.

"Oh."

"I'm sorry."

"It's okay. I'm on the pill. For other reasons. And besides, it's the wrong time of the month." She was due to start her period any day, actually.

"I'm healthy, Brooke. Nothing to worry about there."

"Then we're in the clear."

He yawned and pulled her into his arms, spooning her from behind. "Let me sleep for an hour, and we can go again."

"You're out of condoms."

He kissed the nape of her neck. "We'll improvise."

Brooke lay perfectly still and felt the exact moment when Austin crashed hard. His breathing deepened. The arm that encircled her became heavy.

She knew the time had come for her to go home, but she couldn't leave him. Not yet. This night had turned into something she hadn't anticipated, something she hadn't really wanted.

Here was a man who had known pain and loss. Even if they lived in the same town, he wouldn't want a woman like her. She couldn't even stand up to her parents. She had her own battles to fight. And she would have to do it without this sweet, gruff cowboy.

She inhaled his scent. Tried to memorize it. The way his body held hers seemed fated somehow. But that was a lie. He was a man she had picked up in a bar. A man with demons, like any other man.

Carefully, with her chest tight and her hands shaking, she extracted herself from his arms one heartbeat at a time. It wasn't easy. Fortunately, Austin slept like the dead. Once she was out of the bed, the rest went smoothly.

She visited the bathroom. She dressed quietly. She took her bag and her purse and slipped out into the hall.

On the other side of the door, she started to shake. Leaving her one-night stand cowboy was the hardest thing she had ever had to do.

The drive from Joplin to Royal in the middle of the night seemed surreal. Punching in the alarm code and sneaking into the house was almost anticlimactic. She was too tired to shower. Instead, she tumbled into bed and fell asleep instantly.

Three

Two months later

Austin parked his truck across the street from the Texas Cattleman's Club, got out and stretched. It had been three years...maybe four...since he had last been in Royal, Texas. Not much had changed. An F4 tornado a while back had destroyed a few homes and businesses and damaged others, but the town had rebuilt.

The club itself was a historic structure over a hundred years old. The rambling single-story building with its dark stone-and-wood exterior and tall slate roof was an icon in the area. Ordinarily, Austin wouldn't be the kind of guy to darken the doors, but he was meeting Gus Slade here at 10:00 a.m.

Austin had plenty of money in the bank...likely more than he would ever need. But he didn't have the blue-blooded ranching pedigree that men like Gus respected. Still, Gus had invited him here to do a job, and Austin had agreed.

Audra was right. He'd been drifting since Jenny died. It was time to get his business back on track. He'd rambled all over a five-county area in recent years doing odd jobs to pay the bills. The truth was, he was a damned good architect and had been wasting his skills.

Even this job with Gus was a throwaway. But it could open the doors to something more significant, so he had jumped at the chance.

He took his time crossing the street. No need to look too eager. Already, he had made concessions. Instead of his usual jeans and flannel shirt, he had worn neatly pressed khakis, a spotless white dress shirt with the sleeves rolled up and his best pair of boots. Cowboys came in all shapes and sizes in Texas. Austin was shooting for ambitious professional for today's meeting.

It was who he had been once upon a time. Until Jenny got sick…

Shoving away the unhappy memories, he ran a hand through his hair, flipped his phone to silent mode and strode through the imposing front doors. A smiling receptionist directed him to one of the private meeting rooms partway down the hall.

Augustus "Gus" Slade was already there, deep in conversation with two other men. When Austin appeared, Gus's two companions said their goodbyes and exited.

Gus held out his hand. "There you are, boy. Right on the money. Thanks for coming. It's been a long time."

"It's good to see you, sir. Thanks for offering me the job."

Gus was an imposing figure of a man. He was tall and solidly built with a full head of snow-white hair. Piercing eyes that were blue like the Texas sky reflected a keen intelligence.

By Austin's calculations, the man was probably sixty-eight or sixty-nine. He could have passed for a decade younger were it not for the leatherlike quality of his skin. He'd spent decades working in the sun long before warnings about skin cancer were the norm.

At a time in life when many men his age began to think about traveling or playing golf or simply taking things easy, Gus still worked his cattle ranch, the Lone Wolf, and wielded his influence in Royal. He had plenty of the latter to go around and had even served a few terms as TCC president. Though the burly rancher loved his family and was well respected by the community at large, most people knew he could be fierce when crossed or angered.

Austin had no plans to do either.

At Gus's urging, Austin settled into one of a pair of wing-backed chairs situated in front of a large fireplace. The weather in Royal was notably mercurial. Yesterday, it had been in the fifties and raining. Today, the temperature was pushing seventy, and the skies were sunny, so no fire.

Gus took the second chair with a grimace and rubbed his knee. "Got kicked by a damned bull. Should have known better."

Austin nodded and smiled. "I worked cattle during the summers when I was in college. It was a great job, but I went to bed sore many a night." He hesitated half a breath and plunged on. "So tell me about this job you want me to do."

When he had been in Royal before, Gus had wanted him to design and build an addition onto his home. Austin had still been paying for Jenny's medical bills, and he had needed the money. So he had worked his ass off for six months...or maybe it was seven.

He'd been proud of the job, and Gus had been pleased.

The older man twisted his mouth into a slight grimace. "I may have brought you here under false pretenses. It's not like last time. This will be a one-and-done project. But as I mentioned on the phone, I think being here at the club for a few weeks will give you the chance to meet some folks in Royal who are movers and shakers. These are the kind of men and women who have contacts. They know people and can make things happen to push work your way."

Austin wasn't sure how he felt about that. On the one hand, it made sense to rebuild his career. It had stalled out when he made the choice to stay home with Jenny during what turned out to be the last months of her life. It was a choice he had never regretted.

Even in the depths of his grief, when he had drifted from town to town and job to job, his skill set and work ethic had made it possible for him to command significant compensation for his quality work.

Did he really want to go back to a more structured way of life?

He honestly didn't know.

And because he didn't, he equivocated. "I appreciate that, sir. But how about you tell me the details of this particular project?"

"The club is hoping to do more with the outside space than we have in the past. Professional landscapers are in the process of developing a site plan for the area around the gardens and the pool. What I want from you is a permanent outdoor venue that will serve as the stage for the charity auction and can later be used for weddings, etc. The audience, or the guests, will be out front…under a circus tent if the weather demands it."

"So open air, but covered."

"You got it. Plus, we want the stage to have at least two or three rooms behind the scenes with bathrooms and changing areas…you get the idea."

"And what is this auction exactly?"

Gus chuckled. "It's a mouthful...the Great Royal Bachelor Auction." He sobered. "To benefit the Pancreatic Cancer Foundation. That's what my Sarah died of, you know. My granddaughter Alexis is on the foundation board. I'd like for you to meet her. Your wife has been gone a long time. It's not good for a man to be alone."

"I mean no disrespect, sir, but you don't seem to be taking your own advice. And beyond that, I have no interest at all in a relationship, though I'm sure your granddaughter is delightful."

Gus scowled at him. "Maybe you shouldn't be so quick to turn her down. A lot of men would jump at the chance to have my blessing."

Austin smiled. "If Alexis is anything like her grandfather, I'm guessing she doesn't appreciate you meddling in her affairs."

"That's true enough," Gus said. "She seems determined to fritter away her time with a man who is all wrong for her."

They had strayed off topic again, which made Austin realize that Gus was inordinately interested in matchmaking. He sighed. "I'll need a budget. And the exact specs of the area where I'm allowed to build."

"Money's no object," the older man said. "We want top-of-the-line all the way. And make sure to include some kind of outdoor heating units, concealed if possible. You know how it is in Texas. We might wear shorts on Christmas Day, and it can snow eight hours later."

"What's my timetable?" Austin asked.

"The auction is the last Saturday in November."

Austin tried to conceal his shock. "Cutting it a little close, aren't you?"

Gus nodded. "I know. It will be tight. But the club's custodial staff has been given instructions to help you in any way possible, and we've also allotted extra funds to hire part-time carpenters to rough in the framing and anything else you need. I have faith in you, boy."

"Thank you, sir. I won't let you down."

"Call me Gus. I insist."

After that, they made their way outside so Austin could see exactly what he had to work with. Despite his reservations about the quick turnaround, excitement bubbled up in his chest. This was always one of his favorite phases of a project—looking at a bare plot of ground and imagining the possibilities.

The gardens were soggy, but Austin could see that someone had already begun placing markers and lining off planting areas.

Gus pointed. "Over there is where the stage will be."

Austin nodded. "I can work with that."

In the distance, he could see the pool, now closed for the season. The new structure would tie in with the gardens and the rear of the original building to create a peaceful, idyllic setting for entertaining.

To their left, a small figure in stained overalls stood three feet off the ground on a stepladder painting a colorful mural on an outer wall of the club. Gus waved a hand. "Let's go say hello," he said.

It was only a matter of fifteen yards. Twenty at the most. They were close enough for Austin to recognize the pale, silky ponytail when it hit him.

The woman turned around as Gus hailed her. The paintbrush in her hand clattered to the ground. Her face turned white. She clutched the top of the ladder.

Austin sucked in a shocked breath. It was *her*. Brooke. His mystery lover.

Only a clueless fool would have missed the tension, and

Gus was no fool. He frowned. "Do you two know each other?"

Austin waited. Ladies first. Brooke stared at him, her eyes curiously blank. "Not at all," she said politely. "How do you do? I'm Brooke Goodman."

What the hell? Austin had no choice but to follow her lead. Or else call her a liar. He stuck out his hand. "Austin Bradshaw. Nice to meet you."

The air crackled with electricity. Brooke didn't take his hand. She held up both of hers, palms out, to show they were paint streaked. "You'll have to excuse me. I don't want to get you dirty." She shifted her attention to Gus. "If you two don't mind, I'm trying to get this section finished quickly. They tell me another band of showers is going to move in tonight, so the paint needs to dry."

And just like that, she turned her back and shut him out.

Four

Brooke felt so ill she was afraid she might pass out right there on the ladder. She stood perfectly still and pretended to paint the same four-inch square of wall until she heard a door open and shut. Out of the corner of her eye she saw the two men disappear inside the building.

What was Austin doing in Royal? Had he come to find her? Surely not. He'd been with Gus Slade. If she put two and two together, maybe Austin was the architect Gus had hired to build the fancy stage and outdoor annex. How did Gus even know Austin?

Who could she ask? Alexis? Then again, did she really want to draw attention to the fact that she was interested in Austin? She wasn't. Not at all.

Liar.

What made the situation even worse was the expression on Austin's face when he saw her. He'd been equal parts flabbergasted and horrified. Not the look a woman wanted to see from a man she'd spent the night with.

And see what he'd done to her, damn it…now he had *her* ending sentences with prepositions.

When the coast was clear, she wiped her brush and gathered her supplies. Ordinarily, she went inside the club to a utility sink and cleaned up before going home. Today, she couldn't take that chance.

For the rest of the afternoon and all night long, she fretted. She'd spent the last eight weeks trying to forget about her one-night-stand cowboy. Now he had appeared in Royal, completely out of the blue, and looking about ten times as gorgeous and sexy as she remembered. If he really was the new architect, she was going to be forced to see him repeatedly.

Her body thought that was a darned good idea. Heat sizzled through her veins. But her brain was smarter and more sensible. This was a bad development. Really bad.

The following morning, when the sun came up on another beautiful October day, she wanted to pull the covers over her head and not have to *think*. Still, the memories came rushing back. An intimate hotel room. A rugged cowboy. Two naked bodies. What was she going to do? With yummy Austin in town, there would be hell to pay if her secret came out.

More than ever, she needed to get her own place to live. With the money Alexis was paying her for the murals, there would soon be enough in her modest bank account for first and last month's rent on a decent apartment. In three and a half years, she would receive her inheritance from her grandmother and thus be able to start her after-school art program. Everybody took dance lessons and played sports—Brooke wanted to build a small studio where dreamy kids like she had been could dabble in clay and paint to their heart's content.

All she had to do in the meantime was find a permanent job, any job, that would give her financial independence from her parents. That task was tough in a town where the

Goodmans pulled strings right and left. Brooke had been unofficially blacklisted time and again.

Her parents' behind-the-scenes manipulations were humiliating and infuriating. And all because they wanted her to be the kind of high-powered entrepreneurs they were.

It was never going to happen. Brooke liked who she was. It wasn't that she lacked ambition. She simply saw a different path for herself.

Fortunately, her parents were both early risers and left for the office at the crack of dawn. Brooke was able to enjoy her toast and coffee in peace. Her stomach rebelled at the thought of food this morning, probably because she was so upset about the prospect of seeing Austin again.

What was she supposed to say to him?

Could she simply avoid him altogether?

She was small. Maybe she could hide.

When she couldn't put it off any longer, she drove into town. Her parents' Pine Valley mansion had been her childhood home. She'd left it only to go to college and grad school. Now it had become a prison. Her whole family was seriously broken in her estimation. Her brother Jared's poor fiancée had been forced to run away from her own wedding to escape.

Brooke was still trying to find a way out. It wasn't as easy as it sounded. But she was at least working on a plan.

When she arrived at the club, she parked one street over and gathered up the canvas totes that contained her supplies. At least she knew what Austin's truck looked like. So far, she didn't see it anywhere around. Maybe he was at his hotel doing whatever architects did on their laptops before they started a new job.

Hopefully she could get her murals done before he showed up again. Didn't a project like this require site prep? Surely an architect wasn't involved in that phase.

Her heart slugged in her chest. This was exactly why she had gone to another town for her secret fling. She hadn't wanted to face any ramifications of her indiscretion afterward.

Remembering that night was both mortifying and deeply arousing. What thoughts had gone through his head when he woke up and found her missing? She had second-guessed that decision a thousand times.

In the end, though, it had been the only choice. She and Austin had been strangers passing in the night. Joplin wasn't home for either of them. It had been the perfect anonymous scenario.

Except now it wasn't.

To access the gardens, it was first necessary to go through the club. She greeted the receptionist and made her way down the corridor hung with hunting trophies and artifacts. Both of her parents had been members here for years. The building was familiar.

What wasn't so familiar was the sensation of apprehension and excitement. She told herself she didn't want to see Austin Bradshaw again. But the lie wasn't very believable, even in her head.

It was almost anticlimactic to arrive in the gardens and find herself completely alone. The landscaping crew came and went at odd hours. This morning, no one was around to disturb Brooke's concentration. Up until now, she had enjoyed the time to focus on her creations, to dream and to let her imagination run wild. Today, the solitude felt disconcerting.

Doggedly, she uncapped her paints and planned the section she would work on next. It was a large-scale, multilevel task. Instead of two long gray stucco walls at right angles to one another, Alexis had charged Brooke with creating a whimsical extension of the gardens. When spring came and the flowers bloomed, there would be no delineation between the actual gardens and Brooke's fantasy world.

The work challenged her creativity and her vision. Not only did she have to paint on a very large canvas, but she had to think in bold, thematic strokes. It was the most ambitious project she had ever tackled, and she was honored that Alexis trusted her to handle the makeover.

When the stage was built, the new landscaping was complete and Brooke's paintings were finished, the outdoor area would be spectacular. It felt good to be part of something that would provide enjoyment to so many people.

She selected the appropriate brush and tucked it behind her ear. Soon she would need a taller ladder, but for now, she was going to finish the portion she had abandoned yesterday. It was a border of daisies and baby rabbits that repeated along one edge of her mural.

Grabbing the metal frame that held four small paint pots, she climbed up three steps and cocked her head. White first. Then the yellow centers.

"Are you avoiding me, Brooke?"

The voice startled her so badly she flung paint all over herself and a huge section of blank wall and the grass below. "Austin," she cried.

He took her by the waist, lifted her and set her on the ground. "So you *do* know who I am." He smirked. "Yesterday, I wasn't so sure."

She scowled at him, trying not to notice the way sunlight picked out strands of gold in his hair without his hat. "What was I supposed to do? I couldn't tell Gus how we met."

Austin's lips quirked in the kind of superior male smile that made her want to smack him. "Most people would have come up with a polite lie."

"I'm a terrible liar," she said.

"I'll have to remember that. It might come in handy."

The intimate light in his warm brown eyes and the way he looked at her as if he were remembering every nanosecond of their night together made heat curl in her sex. "Why are you here, Austin?"

"I have a job to do. Why are *you* here, Brooke Goodman?"

"I live in Royal. And I have a job to do as well. So that makes this terribly awkward."

"Not at all." He eyed her mural. "This is your work? It's fabulous. You're very talented."

His praise warmed her. Other than Alexis, few people knew what she was capable of doing—at least, few people in Royal. "Thank you," she said. "I still have a long way to go."

"Which means I'll get to watch as I build the stage."

Her heart stuttered. He didn't mean anything by that statement...did he? "Austin, I—"

He held up his hand. "You don't have to say a word. I can see it on your face. You're afraid I'll spill your secret. But I won't, Brooke, I swear. You had your reasons for what happened in Joplin, and so did I." He cleared his throat, then went on. "The truth is, as much as I like you, we need to leave the past in the past. I'm done with relationships, trust me. And in a town like this, you clearly can't do anything without the whole world knowing your business."

He was saying all the right things. Exactly what she needed to hear.

So why did she have a knot in her stomach?

"I should get started," she said.

"For the record, I was damned disappointed when I woke up and you were gone."

"You were?" She searched his face.

He nodded slowly. "Yes."

"It was an amazing night for me, but I didn't have much basis for comparison."

He chuckled. "Your instincts were spot-on. If I were in the market for a girlfriend and you were five years older, we might give it a go."

Her temper flared. "Do you have any idea how arrogant you sound? I'm getting very tired of everybody in my life thinking they know what's best for me."

"Define *everybody*."

Brooke looked over his shoulder and grimaced. "Here comes one now."

Margaret Goodman was dressed impeccably from head to toe. Though she was well into her fifties, she could easily pass for a much younger woman. Her blond hair, sprinkled with only the slightest gray, received the attention of an expensive stylist every three weeks, and she had both a personal trainer and a dietitian on her payroll.

Brooke's mother was ambitious, driven and ice-cold. She was also—at the moment—clearly furious. A tiny splotch of red on each cheekbone betrayed her agitation.

"What are you doing here, Mama?" Brooke stepped forward, away from the cowboy architect, hoping to defuse the situation and at the same time possibly avoid any interaction between her mother and Austin.

Her mother lifted her chin. "Are you trying to spite me on purpose? Do you have any idea how humiliating it is to know that my only daughter is grubbing around in the gardens of the Texas Cattleman's Club like a common laborer?"

Brooke straightened her backbone. "Alexis Slade hired me to do a job. That's what I'm doing."

"Don't be naive and ridiculous. This isn't a job." Her mother flung a hand toward the partially painted wall in a dramatic gesture. "A child could do this. You're avoiding your potential, Brooke. Your father and I won't have it. It was bad enough that you changed your major in college without telling us. We paid for you to get a serious education, not a worthless art degree. Goodmans are businesspeople, Brooke. We *make* money, we don't squander it. When will you realize that playing with paint isn't a valid life choice?"

Her mother was shouting now, her disdain and reproach both vicious and hurtful.

Brooke had heard it all before, but with Austin as a witness, it was even more upsetting. Her eyes stung. "This *is* a real job, Mama. I'm proud of the work I'm doing. And for the record, I'm planning on moving out of the house, so you and Daddy might as well get used to the idea."

"Don't you speak to me in that tone."

"You don't listen any other way. I'm twenty-six years old. The boys moved out when they were twenty-one."

"Don't bring your brothers into this. They were both far more mature than you at this age. Neither of them gave us any grief."

Brooke shook her head, incredulous. Her brothers were sycophants and weasels who coasted by on their family connections and their willingness to suck up to Mommy and Daddy. "I won't discuss this with you right now. You're embarrassing me."

For the first time, Margaret looked at Austin. "Who is this?" she demanded, her nose twitching as if sniffing out an impostor in her blue-blooded world.

Before Brooke could stop him, Austin stepped forward, hand outstretched. "I'm Austin Bradshaw, ma'am…the architect Gus Slade hired to build the stage addition for the bachelor auction. I'm pleased to meet you."

His sun-kissed good looks and blinding smile caught Margaret midtirade. Her mouth opened and shut. "Um…"

Brooke sensed trouble brewing. She took her mother's arm and tried to steer her toward the building. "You don't want to get paint on your clothes, Mama, and I really need to get back to work. We'll discuss this tonight."

Margaret bristled. "I'm not finished talking to you, young lady. Put this mess away and come home."

"I won't," Brooke said. She felt ill, but she couldn't let her dislike of confrontation or the fact that they had an audience allow her mother to steamroll her. "I've made a commitment, and I intend to honor it."

Margaret scowled. When Brooke's mother was on a rant, people scattered. She could be terrifying. "I demand that you come with me this instant."

Brooke swallowed hard as bile rose in her throat. She wasn't wearing a hat, so the sun beat down on her head. Little yellow spots danced in front of her eyes, and her knees wobbled.

This was a nightmare.

But then, to her complete and utter shock, Austin intervened. He literally inserted himself between Brooke and her mother, shielding Brooke with his body. "You're out of line, Mrs. Goodman. Your daughter is a grown woman. She's a gifted artist, and she's being paid to use that talent for the good of the community. I won't have you bullying her."

"Who the hell are you to talk to me that way?" Margaret shrieked. "I'll have you fired on the spot. Wait until Gus Slade hears about this. You'll never work in this town again."

The whole thing might have been funny if it wasn't so miserably tragic. Brooke's mother was used to getting her way with threats and intimidation. Her face was ugly beneath her makeup.

Austin simply ignored her bluster. "I'd like you to leave

now," he said politely. "Brooke and I both have work to do for the club, and you are delaying our progress."

Margaret raised her fist…she actually raised her fist.

Austin stared at her.

To Brooke's amazement, her mother backed down. She dropped her arm, turned on her heel and simply walked away.

"Oh my God, you've done it now." Brooke felt her legs crumpling.

Austin whirled and caught her around the waist, supporting her as she went down. She didn't faint, but she sat down hard on the grass and put her head on her knees. "She's going to make your life a living hell."

"Sounds like you know something about that." He crouched beside her and stroked her back, his presence a quiet, steady comfort after the ugly scene.

"I appreciate your standing up for me, but you shouldn't have done it. She doesn't make idle threats. She'll try to get you fired."

"I've dealt with bullies before. But I confess that I've never had to deal with it in my own home. I'm sorry, Brooke."

She wiped her eyes and sniffled, too upset to be embarrassed anymore. "I've applied for six different jobs here in Royal since I finished school, and in every instance I got some flimsy excuse about why I wasn't qualified. The first couple of times I wrote it off to the fact that I was straight out of college and grad school and had no experience, but then I got turned down for a waitressing gig at a place where one of my friends worked. I knew she had put in a good word for me." She released a quavering breath. "So I couldn't understand what I had done wrong…how I had interviewed so poorly that they didn't want me."

"Did you ever find out what happened?" he prodded gently.

"Yes. I couldn't let it go, so I screwed up my courage and went back to the restaurant and talked to the manager. He admitted that my mother had called him and threatened him."

"Son of a bitch."

Austin's vehement shock summed up Brooke's reaction in a nutshell. "Yep. Who does that to their own kid?"

"What exactly is it that she wants you to do?"

"Daddy would be happy if I went to law school and joined him in his firm. Mama is Maverick County royalty. Her family owns one of the richest ranches in Texas. I'm supposed to play the part of the wealthy socialite. Wear the right clothes. Hang out with the right people. Marry the right man."

He grimaced. "Sounds wretched."

"You have no idea. And my mother is relentless. I have an inheritance coming to me from my grandmother's estate when I turn thirty. All that's necessary for me to get my money sooner is to be married or to have my parents' permission. But my mother has convinced my father not to let that happen." She lifted her chin. "So I've decided I'll do whatever it takes to get out from under their roof. This job is the first step toward my liberation. Alexis isn't afraid of my mother. This is real employment with a real paycheck."

"But it won't last long, surely."

"No. The garden part will only take a few weeks. After that, Alexis wants me to do the walls in the childcare center. I'm saving every penny so I can rent an apartment."

He put the back of his hand to her cheek and gazed down at her in concern. "You don't look good, honey. Maybe you should go home."

Brooke struggled to her feet. "Absolutely not. I won't let Alexis down."

He sighed. "When do you quit for the day?"

"Around four."

"How about afterward we grab some food and take a picnic out in the country…find a quiet place where we can talk?"

"What if someone sees us and asks questions?"

His grin was remarkably carefree for a man who had recently tangled with the Goodman matriarch. "Let's live dangerously."

Five

Gus peered through the French doors and frowned when he spotted Brooke Goodman getting chummy with Austin Bradshaw. He'd have to nip that in the bud. Austin was on his radar as the perfect match for Alexis, even if neither of them knew it yet.

Impulsively, he strode out to the parking lot and climbed into his truck. There was one person who shared his goals, one woman who would understand his frustration. He drove out to Rose Clayton's Silver C Ranch feeling more than a little regret for all the years of bitterness and recrimination that lay between him and Rose. She had hurt him badly when he was a young man. Betrayed him. Broken his heart.

Still, five decades was a long time to carry a grudge.

The only reason they were speaking now was because they were both determined to keep their grandchildren from *hooking up*. Wasn't that what the kids called it these days?

Hell would freeze over before Gus Slade would let his beloved granddaughter Alexis marry a Clayton.

Rose answered the door almost immediately after his knock. She had aged well, her frame slim and regal. Chin-length brown hair showed only a touch of gray at the temples. Her gaze was wary. "Gus. Won't you come in?"

He followed her back to the kitchen. "I found a good prospect for Alexis," he said.

Rose waved him to a chair and poured him a cup of coffee. "Do tell."

"His name is Austin Bradshaw. Architect. Widower. Did some work for me a few years back...a handsome lad."

"And what does Alexis think?"

Rose's knowing smile irritated him. "She doesn't know my plans for the two of them yet, but she will. I need some time, that's all. As long as you keep Daniel occupied, we'll be fine."

"You can rest easy on that score. I'm sure there will be any number of eligible women bidding on him at the bachelor auction."

Gus drained his cup and leaned his chair back on two legs. "Did Daniel actually agree to the auction thing? It doesn't sound like his cup of tea."

Rose's face fell. "Well, I had to coax him. I did point out that he and Tessa Noble would make a lovely couple, if she bids on him."

"I agree. Makes perfect sense."

"Unfortunately, Daniel gets quite frustrated with me when I try to give him advice about his love life. He has come very close to telling me to stay out of his business. Imagine that. His own grandmother."

Gus snorted. "The world would run a lot more smoothly if young people did what their elders told them to."

Rose went white, her expression agitated. "You don't know what you're talking about, old man."

Her demeanor shocked him. "What did I say, Rose?" The change in her was dramatic. He felt guilty and didn't know why.

"I'd like you to leave now. Please."

Her startling about-face stunned him. He thought they had worked through some of their issues. After all, she had wronged *him*, not the other way around. Was she implying somehow that she had been manipulated by her father? Gus had worked for Jedediah Clayton. To a sixteen-year-old kid, the ranch owner had been both vengeful and terrifying. Yet that hadn't stopped Gus from falling in love with the boss's daughter.

Gus had finally made the decision to leave the Clayton ranch. He'd spent four years on the rodeo circuit, saving every dime. Then he'd returned to Royal, bought a small parcel of land and gone back to claim the woman he loved.

His world had come crashing down when he discovered his childhood sweetheart had married another man. Even worse was Rose's crushing rejection of the love they had once shared. The long-ago heartache was still vivid to him.

He had married her best friend.

But now he was confused.

"Go," she cried, tears gleaming in her eyes.

He caught her hands in his and held them tightly, even when she tried to yank away. "Did your father do something to you, Rosie?" His heart sank.

Her lower lip trembled. Suddenly, she looked every one of her sixty-seven years. "None of you cared," she whispered. "I was a prisoner, and you and Sarah never saw through my facade."

"I don't understand." His chest hurt. He couldn't breathe.

"He threatened me. My mother was desperately ill. He was going to let her die if I married you, refuse to pay for her treatments. So I had no choice. I had to pretend. I had to choose my mother's life over my happiness. I had to marry another man."

"My God."

Rose stared at him, her eyes filled with something close to hatred and loathing. Or maybe it was simply grief. "Go, Augustus. We'll continue our plan to keep Daniel and Alexis apart. But please don't come to my house again."

Somehow Brooke managed to work on her mural hour after hour without passing out or giving up, but it wasn't easy. The episode with her mother had upset her deeply. She felt wretched. Even now, her legs trembled and her stomach roiled. Her life was a damned soap opera. Why couldn't her family be normal and boring?

She paused in the middle of the day to eat the peanut butter sandwich she had packed for her lunch. The club had a perfectly wonderful restaurant, but dining there would have meant changing out of her paint-stained clothes, and Brooke simply didn't have it in her today. So she sat on the ground with her back to the wall and ate her sandwich in the shade.

She half hoped Austin would show up to keep her company. But clearly, he was very busy with the new project. She saw him at a distance a time or two. That was all.

On the one hand, it was good that he didn't hover. She would have hated that. She was a grown woman. Still, she'd be lying if she didn't say she was looking forward to their picnic.

By the time she finished a section at three thirty and cleaned her brushes, she was wiped out. Today's temperature had been ten degrees above normal for mid-October. It was no wonder she was dragging. And she had forgotten to wear sunscreen. So she would probably have a pink nose by the end of the day.

She stashed her supplies in her car, changed out of her work clothes into a cute top and jeans, and went in search of Austin. Her palms were damp and her heart beat faster than normal. The last time the two of them had spent any amount of time together, they'd been naked.

Despite that anomaly, they really were little more than strangers. Perhaps if she treated this picnic as a first date, she could pretend that she hadn't propositioned him in a bar and made wild, passionate love to the handsome cowboy.

That was probably impossible, given the fact that she trembled every time he got close to her.

She rounded a corner in the gardens and ran straight into the man who occupied her tumultuous thoughts.

He steadied her with two big hands on her shoulders. "Slow down, honey. I was just coming to find you."

She wiggled free, trying not to let him see how his touch burned right through her. "Here I am. Shall we swing by the corner market and pick up a few supplies for our picnic?"

Austin took her elbow and steered her back inside the club, down the corridor and out the front door. "I've already got it covered," he said. "I called the diner and had them make us a basket of fried chicken and everything to go with it."

Brooke raised an eyebrow. "I'm impressed." The Royal Diner was one of her favorite places for good old-fashioned comfort food. "I hope you asked for some of Amanda Battle's buttermilk pie."

Austin grinned. "I wasn't sure what kind of dessert you preferred, so I had them include four different slices."

"I like a man with a plan."

They were flirting. It was easy and fun. Something inside her relaxed for the first time all day.

Of course, it made sense to take Austin's truck. It was the nicer, bigger, newer vehicle. He stepped into the diner to pick up their order, and then they were on their way. It was a perfect fall afternoon. The sky was the color of a

Texas bluebonnet, and the clouds were soft white cotton balls drifting across the sky.

Brooke was content to let Austin choose their route until it occurred to her that he didn't live in Royal. "Do you even know where you're going?" she asked.

"More or less. I did a big job for Gus some years ago. It's been a little while, but this part of the county has stayed the same."

They drove for miles. The radio was on but the volume was turned down, so the music barely intruded. Brooke sighed deeply. She hadn't realized how tightly she was wound.

Austin shot her a sideways glance. "Has your mother always been like that?"

"Oh, yeah."

He reached across the small space separating them and put a hand on her arm. Briefly. Just a touch of warm, masculine fingers. But the simple gesture made her nerves hum with pleasure.

"Tell me why you came to Joplin that night," he asked softly.

"It was a stupid thing to do," she muttered.

"You don't hear me complaining."

The sexy teasing made her cheeks hot. "I was furious at my parents and furious at myself. Some people might have gotten stinking drunk, but that's not my style."

"So you decided to seduce a stranger."

"I didn't seduce you…did I?"

He parked the truck beneath a lone cottonwood tree and put the gear shift in Park. Half turning in his seat, he propped a big, muscular arm on the steering wheel and faced her. He chuckled, scratching his chin and shaking his head. "I don't know what else you would call it. I came in with my sister and left with you."

"Oh." When you put it like that, it made Brooke sound like the kind of woman who could command a man's interest with a crook of her finger. That was certainly never an image she'd had of herself. She kind of liked it. "Well," she said, "the thing is, I was upset and angry, and I let myself get carried away."

"Had something happened at home? Was that it? After what I witnessed today, I can only imagine."

"You're very perceptive. It's a long story. Are you sure you want to hear it?"

He leaned over without warning and kissed her. It was a friendly kiss. Gentle. Casual. Thrilling. His lips were warm and firm. "I've got all night."

She blinked at him. He sat back in his seat as if nothing out of the ordinary had happened. Her toes curled in her shoes. "Well, okay, then." It was difficult to gather her thoughts when what she really wanted to do was unbutton his shirt and see if that broad, strong chest was as wonderfully sculpted and kissable as she remembered.

"Brooke?"

Apparently she had lapsed into a sex-starved, befuddled stupor. "Sorry. I'll start with Grammy, my dad's mother. She died when I was seventeen, but she and I were soul mates. It was Grammy who first introduced me to art. In fact, when I was twelve, she took me with her to Paris, and we toured the Louvre. I remember walking through the galleries in a daze. It was the most extraordinary experience. The light the artists had captured on canvas…and all the colors. The sculptures. Something clicked for me. It was as if—for the first time in my life—I was where I was supposed to be."

"She must have been a very special lady."

"She was. I was crushed when she died, utterly heartbroken. But I made several decisions over the next few years.

First, that I wanted to become an artist. And secondly, that I wanted to take part of my inheritance and tour the great art museums of Europe in Grammy's honor."

"And was there more?"

She smiled, for the moment actually believing it might happen. "Yes. Yes, there was…there *is*. I want to open an art studio in Royal that caters to children and youth. Families pay for piano lessons and ballet lessons and soccer and football all the time. Yet there are tons of children like me who need a creative outlet, but their parents don't know what to do for them."

"I think that's a phenomenal idea."

"I did, too. I even went to the bank and filled out the paperwork for a small business loan to get things started. My inheritance would serve as collateral, but I was hoping my parents would see the sense in letting me have part of the money now as an investment in my future."

"I'm guessing they didn't share your vision."

She shook her head and swallowed against the sudden dryness in her throat. "I might have swayed my father… eventually. But my mother was outraged, and he does whatever she tells him to. That ugly scene went down the day I showed up in Joplin."

"Ah. So you were trying to punish them?"

"No. It wasn't that. I was just so very tired of them controlling my life. I'm sure you think I'm exaggerating or overreacting, but I'm not. Did you know that my brother was engaged to be married recently? His poor fiancée, Shelby, ran away from the church, and then my parents tried to blackmail her into coming back by freezing all her assets and hunting her down like an animal."

"Good Lord."

"I know! It's Machiavellian."

"Come on, darlin'," Austin said. "We need to take your mind off your troubles. Let's get some fresh air."

Brooke climbed out of the truck and stretched. Actually, she had to jump down. Being vertically challenged meant that half of the vehicles in Royal were too big for her to get in and out of comfortably.

The thing about an impromptu picnic was that a person couldn't be too picky. Instead of an antique quilt smelling of laundry detergent and sunshine, Austin grabbed a faded horse blanket from the back.

"I think this is fairly clean," he said.

They spread the wool blanket beneath the tree and anchored one corner with the wicker basket. The diner had recently begun offering these romantic carryout meals for a small deposit.

Austin handed her one container at a time. "Here you go. See what we've got." Brooke's stomach rumbled as the wonderful smells wafted up from the basket.

The meal was perfect, but no more so than the late-afternoon sunshine and the ruggedly handsome man at her side. She fantasized about what it would be like to kiss him again. Really kiss him.

Austin ate in silence. His profile was unequivocally masculine. Lounging on one elbow, he personified the Texas cowboy, right down to the Stetson.

"Will you tell me about your wife?" Brooke asked.

Austin winced inwardly. He'd been expecting this question. Under the circumstances, it was a reasonable request, and nothing about Brooke's tentative query reflected anything but concern.

The diner was famous for its fresh-squeezed lemonade. It was served in retro-looking thermoses that kept the liquid ice-cold. Austin drained the last of his and set it aside.

Wiping his hands on his jeans, he sat up and rested his forearms on his knees. "Jenny was the best. You would have liked her. She had a big heart, but she had a temper to match. When we were younger, we fought like cats and dogs." He laughed softly, staring into the past. "But the making up was always fun."

"Where did you meet?"

"College. Pretty ordinary love story. I always knew I was going to be an architect. Jenny was in education. She taught high school Spanish until she got sick."

"When was that?"

"We'd been married almost five years and were living in Dallas. She had a cold one winter that never seemed to go away. We didn't think anything about it. But it got worse, and by the time I made her go to the doctor, the news was bad. Stage-four lung cancer. She'd never smoked a day in her life. None of her family had. It was a rare cancer. Just one of those things."

"I'm so sorry, Austin."

He shook his head, even now feeling the tentacles of dread and fear left over from that time. "We went through two years of hell. The only saving grace was that we hadn't started a family. Jenny was so glad about that. She didn't want to leave a child behind without a mother."

"But what about you?" Brooke said, her gray eyes filled with an ache that was all for him. "Wouldn't a baby have been a comfort to you?"

He stared at her. No one had ever asked him that. Not Jenny. Not Audra. No one. Sometimes—way back then—the thought had crossed his mind. The idea of holding a baby girl who looked like Jenny—teaching her to fish when she was a little kid—had rooted deep inside him, but then the chemo started and fertility was a moot point.

"It wouldn't have worked out," he said gruffly. "What did I know about babies?"

"I suppose…"

"In the end, Jenny was ready to go, and I was ready to let her go. There are some things no one should have to endure. She fought until there was no reason to fight anymore." He swallowed convulsively. "When it was over, I didn't feel much of anything for a few days. Nothing seemed real. Not the funeral. Nothing. I didn't even have our house to go back to."

"What happened to your home?" she asked quietly.

"When Jenny's disease had progressed to the point that I couldn't work and care for her, we sold everything and moved to Joplin. Audra and I cobbled together a schedule for looking after Jenny and filled in the gaps with temp nurses and hospice toward the end."

"You and your sister are close."

"She saved my life," he said simply. "I don't know what I would have done without her. I had no rudder, no reason to get out of bed in the mornings. Audra forced me into the world even when I didn't want to go. Eventually, I started picking up work here and there. I didn't mind traveling."

"But what about your career in Dallas?"

"It had been too long. I didn't want to go back there. But Joplin was where Jenny died, so I didn't want to live there, either."

"Then you've bounced around?"

He nodded slowly. "For six years. Pathetic, isn't it?"

Brooke scooted closer and laid her head on his shoulder. "No. I can't imagine loving someone that much and losing them."

He wrapped an arm around her waist and inhaled the scent of her hair. Today it smelled like strawberries. Arousal curled in his gut, but it simmered on low, overlaid with a feeling of peace. It had taken him a long time, but he had survived the depths of despair. He would never allow himself to be that vulnerable again.

"Brooke?" he said quietly.

"Yes?"

"I know you're feeling sorry for me right now, and I don't want to take advantage of your good nature."

She pulled back and looked up at him. Her hair tumbled around her shoulders, pale gold and soft as silk. A wary gray gaze searched his face. "I don't understand."

"I want you." He laid it out bluntly. There didn't need to be any misunderstandings between them. If she was interested in a sexual liaison with him, he was definitely on board, but he wouldn't be accused of wrapping things up in romantic words that might be misconstrued.

Brooke frowned. "I heard you say very clearly that you weren't interested in a relationship."

He rubbed his thumb across her lower lip, tugging on it ever so slightly. "Men and women have sex all the time without relationships. I like you. We have chemistry in bed. If you're interested, I'm available."

Six

Brooke stepped outside her body for a moment. At least that's how it seemed in that split second. The scene was worthy of the finest cinema. A remote setting. Romantic accoutrements. Handsome cowboy. Erotic proposition.

This was the part where the heroine was supposed to melt into the hero's arms, and if it were a family-friendly film, the screen would fade to black. The trouble with that scenario was that Brooke didn't see herself as heroine material in this picture.

You had the leading man who was most likely still in love with his dead wife. A second woman who was far too young for him—case in point, she was having trouble extracting herself from under her parents' oppressive influence. And a red-hot, clandestine one-night stand that had catapulted an unlikely couple way too far in one direction and not nearly far enough in another.

Brooke knew the size and shape of the mole on Austin's right butt cheek, but she had no idea if he put mayo on his roast beef sandwiches.

That was a problem.

She tasted his thumb with the tip of her tongue, her heart racing. How bad could it be if she had naughty daytime sex with this man? He needed her, and that was a powerful aphrodisiac.

Putting a hand on his denim-clad thigh, she leaned in and kissed him. "I could get on board with that idea."

A shudder ripped its way through Austin's body. She felt it. And she heard his ragged breathing. "Are you sure? What changed your mind?"

She reached up and knocked his Stetson off his head. "I'm sure. I can't resist you, Cowboy. I don't even want to try."

They were parked beside a wet weather stream. The land was flat for miles in either direction. No one was going to sneak up on them.

Austin eased her onto her back. "I need to tell you something."

Alarm skittered through her veins. "What is it?

He leaned over her, his big frame blocking out the sun. "I haven't slept with any other women since you. I was serious when I said I'm not looking for a relationship. But I didn't want you to think you were one in a long line."

"Thank you for telling me that."

She couldn't decide if his little speech made her feel better or worse, but soon, she forgot to worry about it. Austin dispatched her clothes with impressive speed and prowess. The air was cool on her belly and thighs. When she complained, he only laughed.

He sheathed himself, came down between her legs and thrust slowly. Oh, man. She was in deep trouble.

Austin Bradshaw was the real deal. He kissed her and stroked her and moved inside her as if she were his last chance at happiness and maybe the world was even coming to an end. That was heady stuff for a woman whose only real boyfriend had lasted barely six months...during senior year in college.

She wrapped her legs around his back. Her fingers flexed on his warm shoulders. He had shed his shirt and his pants, but he was still wearing socks. For some odd reason, that struck her as wildly sexy.

Sex had never seemed all that special to her. Oh, sure, she thought about it sometimes. When she was lonely or bored or reading a hot book. But her life was full and busy, and the only experience she'd had up until two months ago had convinced her that the movie version of sex was not realistic.

As it turned out, that was true.

Sex with Austin Bradshaw was way *better* than the movies.

He nibbled the side of her neck right below her ear. "Am I squashing you, honey? This isn't exactly a soft mattress at the Ritz."

She tried to catch her breath, but the words still came out on a moan. "No. I'm good. I think there may be a small rock under my right hip bone, but my leg went numb a few minutes ago, so no worries."

"You should have said something." He rolled to his back, taking Brooke with him.

"Oh, gosh." Now she was on top. Exposed. Bare-assed naked. In the daytime. Well, the sun was *trying* to go down, but there was still plenty of light if anyone was looking.

This was far different from dimly lit motel sex in the middle of the night. Austin noticed, too. He suckled each of her breasts in turn, murmuring his pleasure and sending liquid heat from there to every other bit of her. "I love your body, Brooke. Do you know how beautiful you are?"

How was a woman supposed to answer that? Brooke wasn't a slug. She worked out and she was healthy. But beautiful? She had always wanted to be taller and more confident and to have a less pointy chin. "I'm glad you think so," she said diplomatically.

He bit a sensitive nipple, making her yelp. "If we're going to have sex with each other on a regular basis, you have to promise me you'll love your body." He ran his hands over her bottom, pulling her a little closer against him, filling her incrementally more.

"Yes, sir," she said, kissing his nose and his eyebrows and his beautiful, gold-tipped eyelashes.

He thrust upward. "We'll be exclusive," he groaned. "No one else while we're together. Understood?"

Was he insane? What woman was going to fool around when she had Austin Bradshaw in her bed? Nevertheless, Brooke nodded. A plan began forming in her head, but it was hard to focus on anything sensible when her body was like hot wax.

He gripped her hips tightly and moved her against him. Need flared, hot and urgent and breathless. She was burning up from the inside out, even though parts of her were definitely cold.

It was dusk now. The stars were coming out one by one. Or maybe she was the starry-eyed dreamer. How had she gotten so lucky? Like a rare comet, men of Austin's caliber came around once in a long time. She wouldn't be greedy. She wouldn't ask for more than he had to give.

He kissed her roughly, his lips warm, his breath feathering the hair at her temple where it fell across his face. "I don't want to send you home tonight, Brooke. But I'm staying in one of Gus's bunkhouses. We're gonna have to figure something out."

She nodded again, the speech centers in her brain misfiring. "Working on it," she stuttered. His fingers slid deep into her hair, tipping her head so he could nip her earlobe. He sucked on the tiny gold stud. "You make me want things, honey."

"Like what?" She was breathless, yearning.

"If I tell you, you might run away."

"I won't, I swear."

She ran her hands over his arms. Despite the plummeting temperatures, his skin was hot. His muscles were impressive for a man who called himself an architect. Clearly he did more than wield a pencil all day.

He was barely moving now, his body rigid. His chest heaved. "Damn it."

"What's wrong?" She probably should be alarmed, but she was concentrating too hard on the finish line to care.

"I only have one condom," he growled.

The pique in his voice struck her as funny. "We'll improvise later," she said, laughing softly. "Make me come, Cowboy. Send me over the edge."

Austin Bradshaw was clearly a man who liked a challenge. With a groan, he rolled her beneath him again and pistoned his hips, driving into her over and over until they both went up in a flare of heat. Brooke unraveled first, clutching Austin because he was the only steady point in a spiraling universe.

She was barely aware of his muffled shout and the way he shuddered against her as he came.

It took a long time for reality to intrude. Gradually, her breathing settled into something approaching normal. Her heartbeat dropped below a hundred.

Austin grunted and shifted to one side, dragging her against him. "Damn, girl, you're freezing."

"I don't care," she mumbled, burrowing into his rib cage. The man smelled amazing.

He yawned and lifted his arm to stare at his watch. "It's late."

"Yeah." Apparently, neither of them cared, because they didn't move for the longest time.

Eons later, he stirred. "Is there any food left?"

The man must be starving after burning all those calories. "Probably." Her heart began to race. She had reached a pivotal moment in her life, and she didn't want to screw it up. "Austin?"

"Hmm?"

"I want to ask you a question, but you have to promise me you'll think about it, and you won't freak out."

He chuckled. "I'm feeling pretty mellow at the moment. Ask me anything, honey."

"Will you marry me?"

Austin rolled to his feet and reached for his clothes, panic slugging in his chest. "We need to get in the truck. I think you have hypothermia."

"I'm serious," Brooke said, her voice steady and determined.

"Get dressed before you freeze to death." That was the thing about October. It could be really warm on a nice afternoon, but when the sun went down and the skies were clear, it got cold fast.

They found all their clothing. Between them, they repacked the picnic basket. "We can snack in the truck," Brooke said.

He folded up the blanket and tossed it in the back. They climbed into the cab. The picnic hamper was between them. Austin found a lone chicken leg and munched on it. He wasn't about to say a word at the moment. Not after that bomb she had just tossed at him.

Brooke finished off a bag of potato chips and stared out through the windshield into the inky darkness. "I was serious," she said at last.

"Why?" He could barely force the word from his throat. He'd done the marriage thing, and it had nearly destroyed him.

She reached up and turned on the small reading light that cast a dim glow over the intimate space. With the doors closed and the body heat from two adults, they were plenty warm now.

Brooke looked tired. She had smudges of exhaustion beneath her eyes and her cheekbones were hollow, as if she had lost some weight. "I'm not in love with you, Austin, and I don't plan to be. You can rest easy on that score. But I could use your help. You told me yourself that you've been bouncing from town to town since your wife died. Royal is as good a place as any to put down temporary roots."

"And why would I do that?"

"To help me get my inheritance. You met my mother today. You saw what she's like. You actually made her back down, Austin. You were the alpha dog, and she respected that. Marry me. Not for long. Six months. Maybe twelve. By then I'll have my inheritance and I can have my art studio up and running."

"What's in it for me?" It was a rude, terrible question, but he was trying to shock her into seeing how outrageous her plan was.

She smiled at him, a surprisingly sweet, guileless smile given the topic of conversation. "Regular sex. Home-cooked meals. Companionship if you want it. But most of all, the knowledge that you're doing the right thing. You're making a difference in my life."

Well, hell. When she put it like that… He cleared his throat, alarmed by how appealing it was to contemplate having Brooke Goodman in his bed every night. "Your parents will go ballistic," he pointed out. "I'm nobody on their radar. To be honest, I'll be seen as a fortune hunter by the whole town. That's not a role I'm keen to play."

She nodded slowly. "I understand that. But my parents have no say in the matter when it comes to marriage. I'm well past the age of consent, and my grandmother's will is very clear. The money is mine if I'm married. As for the other…if it would make you feel better, we could sign a prenup, and I could spread the word that you insisted on having one because you're such a Boy Scout."

"You seem to have thought of everything."

"Not really. The idea only began percolating this morning when I saw how you handled my mother."

"I can't *make* her hand over your inheritance."

"Exactly. That's why I began thinking about a temporary marriage." She reached out and stroked his arm. "You're a good man, Austin Bradshaw. Life has knocked you down once. I won't give you any grief, I swear. We'll make our agreement, and when the time is up, you'll walk away free and clear, no regrets. You have my word."

He looked down at her slender fingers pressed against the fabric of his shirt. Her touch burned, as if it were on his bare skin. Already, he could see the flaw in this plan. Brooke Goodman tempted him more than any woman had since Jenny died. He didn't want to *need* anybody else. He didn't want to crave that human connection. Being alone had been comfortable and safe.

"I'll think about it," he said gruffly. "But don't get your hopes up."

Seven

Austin avoided Brooke for an entire week. He was ashamed to admit it, even to himself, but it was true.

He saw her, of course. Across the courtyard garden. They were both working at the same outdoor location. But he kept his distance. Because he didn't know how the hell he was going to respond to her proposal.

With each hour and day that passed, he wanted more and more to say yes to her wild and crazy idea. That was insane enough to stop him in his tracks.

Fortunately, Gus's job kept Austin legitimately busy. Getting the stage ready in time for the upcoming auction required long hours and plenty of focus. Thanks to having an inside track, the plans were approved by the zoning board immediately. Austin had ordered the materials on the spot, and they had already begun arriving pallet by pallet. Soon, the first saws would start humming.

Gus had hired a foreman, but Austin was the boss. He liked the hands-on aspect of the project, and he was a bit of a control freak. It was his design, his baby. In the end, any problems would fall to him. He intended to make sure everything was perfect.

It amused him to realize that a number of the club members had taken to dropping by during the week to gauge the progress on the new stage addition. At first he thought it was to check up on him. Later, he realized that most of them, the men in particular, were simply interested.

One of the younger guys, Ryan Bateman, turned out to be very friendly. He even wrangled Austin into joining a pickup basketball game one evening. After that, when Austin was still avoiding Brooke later in the week, Ryan issued a lunch invitation.

"Let's eat in the club dining room," the other man said. "My treat. I think I know someone who could throw some work your way. You'll like him a lot."

"I don't know that I'm planning on staying in Royal," Austin said, wondering if Brooke had put Ryan up to this. Ryan was a club member, of course. Austin was not.

"At least come for the free food," Ryan chuckled. "What could it hurt?"

Austin glanced down ruefully at his dusty work clothes. "I'm not exactly dressed for the club dining room."

Ryan shook his head. "No worries. The old-school days with the rigid dress code are long gone—well, at least during lunchtime."

The other man looked pretty scruffy as well, to be honest. He had a day's growth of beard, and his green eyes twinkled beneath shaggy brown hair. His broad shoulders stretched the seams of a plain navy Henley shirt.

"A decent meal sounds good," Austin said, giving in gracefully. "Let me wash up, and I'll meet you inside."

At the end of the building where he was working, there was an outdoor faucet. He shoved his shirtsleeves to his elbows and threw water on his face and arms. Using a spare T-shirt to dry off, he tucked his white button-up shirt into his ancient khakis and scraped his hands through his hair.

Rich people didn't spook him. They had their problems, same as anybody else.

Up until now, he'd been swinging by the convenience mart at the end of town each morning and picking up a pre-packaged sandwich for his lunch so he didn't waste time on a midday meal. But he had to admit, he was looking forward to something more substantial.

Ryan was leaning against a wall in the hallway waiting on him. The two men made their way into the dining room where a uniformed maître d' seated them at a table over-looking the gardens. Except for a variety of chrysanthe-mums and a few evergreens, the area was dull and brown. Presumably the landscapers would bring in some tempo-rary plants and foliage for the auction, ones that could be whisked away for the winter.

Just as they got settled, another club member joined them. If Ryan and Austin were on the scruffy side, this guy was a young George Clooney who had just stepped off his yacht. He was easily six foot three. Black hair. Blue eyes. A ripple of feminine interest circled the din-ing room.

Ryan grinned broadly. "Austin, meet Matt Galloway. Matt, Austin Bradshaw. Austin is new in town. He's the architect Gus hired to do the stage addition out in the gar-dens."

Matt shook Austin's hand. "It's a pleasure. I like what you've done so far out there."

"Thank you," Austin said. "Are you a cattle rancher like Ryan here?"

Ryan snorted. "Not hardly. Galloway is an oil tycoon. And did I mention that he's newly engaged?"

Despite his sophisticated appearance, Matt's sheepish smile reflected genuine happiness. "I am, indeed."

Austin smiled. "Congratulations."

Ryan summoned the waiter. "A bottle of champagne, please. We need to toast the groom-to-be."

While they placed their lunch orders and waited for the drinks to be poured, Ryan pushed his agenda. "Austin, Matt's going to be needing a house. Tell him, Matt."

Matt nodded. "My fiancée and I do want to build. We have ideas, but neither of us has the skill set to get our vision on paper, so to speak. I was hoping you might be the person to help us."

Austin frowned slightly. "The stage addition is hardly a true showcase of my work. You do realize that, right?"

"Of course." Matt grinned. "But Ryan here is a pretty damn good judge of character, and if he likes you, that's good enough for me. Rachel and I want someone we feel comfortable with, someone who can guide us without taking over."

"I don't even know if I'm planning on sticking around," Austin admitted, feeling the sand eroding beneath his feet.

Ryan jumped in. "Where's home?"

"Dallas originally. And I've spent time in Joplin."

Matt paused as the waiter delivered their appetizers. "Are you footloose and fancy-free like Bateman here?"

Austin hesitated. He never knew quite how to answer this question. "I was married," he said simply. "But my wife died some years back. Cancer. I've moved around since then."

Ryan sobered. "Sorry, man. I didn't know."

Matt stared at him. "I'm sorry, too. But I have to tell you, Royal is a great place to live. Maybe it's time to put down a few roots."

"It's possible." Austin flashed back suddenly to a vision of Brooke's naked body and her unexpected proposal.

"Take your time," Matt said. "I'm not in a huge rush. When the auction is done, maybe you could have dinner with Rachel and me and we could kick around a few ideas. No pressure."

Austin nodded slowly. "That's doable. Thank you for the offer, and I'll be in touch."

The conversation moved away from personal topics after that. Austin realized that he had missed the camaraderie with other guys since he had given up his formal career. He had bounced from job to job, keeping to himself and walling off his emotions. Perhaps it was time to let the past go…

Still, it was a hell of a jump from moving on to being stupid enough to put his heart on the line again. Losing Jenny had ripped him in two and nearly made him give up on life. For several years, he had done little more than go through the motions.

He was not the same man he had been before Jenny died.

With an effort, he dragged his attention back to the present. Ryan and Matt seemed to enjoy poking at each other. While they dived into a heated argument about the upcoming World Series, Austin gazed through the large plate-glass window nearby, looking for Brooke. She had finished one entire section of her mural this week. Unicorns and fairies danced with odd little creatures that must be trolls or something like that.

He loved seeing Brooke's art. It gave him an insight into her fascinating brain. Suddenly, there was movement at the far end of the wall on the other side of the garden.

There she was. Her small aluminum stepladder caught the sun for a moment and cast a blinding reflection. He squinted. What the hell? She was working all the way up under the eaves. Surely the club had an extension ladder. Brooke wasn't tall enough to reach that section…was she?

He couldn't really tell from the angle where he was sitting. Austin stood up abruptly, an odd premonition of danger making him jumpy. All three men had finished their meals. Ryan had already signed his name and put the lunches on his account. "I should get back out there," he said. "Thanks for lunch, guys. I'm sure I'll see you around." He shot out of the dining room so fast he was probably being rude, but he couldn't get over the sight of Brooke stretching up on her tiptoes six feet off the ground.

He strode down the hall and through the terrace doors. At first he didn't see her at all. But then he spotted her. After doing his damnedest to ignore her for an entire week, suddenly he felt compelled to hunt her down.

"What do you think you're doing?" he called out, irritation in every syllable.

She looked over her shoulder at him, one eyebrow raised. "Painting a mural." With one dismissive wrinkle of her cute little nose, she returned to her task.

"Don't you think you need a taller ladder?"

"Don't you think you need to mind your own business?"

He counted to ten. "I'm looking out for your well-being."

"That's odd. I could have sworn you've been avoiding me. Why the sudden change?"

The tops of his ears got hot. "I've been busy."

"Uh-huh."

Pale denim overalls cupped her ass in an extremely distracting fashion. Her silky, straight blond hair was caught up in its usual ponytail, but today a streak of blue paint decorated the tips, as if she had brushed up against something.

"I like what you've done so far."

"Super."

"Are you mad at me?"

"I'm not *happy*."

He grinned, feeling better than he had all week. "I've missed you," he said softly.

Brooke turned around on the ladder. It wasn't an easy

task. She rested her brush on the open container of paint and stared at him. "I thought you were done with me."

Beneath the flat statement lay a world of hurt. His heart turned over in his chest. "Don't be ridiculous."

She lifted one shoulder and let it fall. "I let you do wicked things to my naked body. And that's the last I saw or heard from you. How would you read that situation?"

"I was thinking about stuff," he protested.

"You mean the marriage proposal?"

He looked around to see if anyone was listening. "Keep your voice down, for God's sake. Of course that's what I mean. You can't throw something like that at a man and expect an answer right off the bat."

"Ah." She looked at him as if he were a slightly dim student. "It doesn't matter anyway," she said. "I've changed my mind. You're off the hook."

"What the hell." He bristled. "I thought I was your best shot?"

She shrugged. "I read the situation wrong. I'm working on a backup plan."

"I didn't even give you an answer."

"My offer had an expiration date," she said, giving him a sweet smile that was patently false. "No need to worry. Your bachelorhood is safe from me."

"You really are pissed, aren't you?"

"I'm nothing, Mr. Bradshaw. You and I are nothing. Now go away and let me work."

With her on the ladder and him on the ground, the conversation was literally not on equal footing. He ground his teeth in frustration. One quick glance at his watch told him now was not the time to push the confrontation to a satisfactory conclusion. "We're not done with this topic," he said firmly. He had people waiting on him. Otherwise, he would have yanked her off that ladder and indulged in a good old-fashioned shouting match. The woman was driving him crazy.

She turned and looked down her nose at him. "It's *my* topic, Austin. You're merely an incidental."

When Austin strode away, his face like a thundercloud, Brooke tasted shame, but only for a moment. She was not a vindictive person. If anything, she leaned too far in the direction of being a people pleaser. But in this case, self-preservation was paramount.

Already her eyes stung with tears and her stomach felt queasy. She was letting herself get in too deep with Austin Bradshaw. Too intimate. Too fast. Too everything.

It was a good thing he hadn't accepted her stupid, impulsive proposal. His heart was ironclad, safely in the care of his dead wife. But Brooke was vulnerable. She liked Austin. A lot. Given enough time, she might fall in love with him. And therein lay the recipe for disaster.

Suddenly, she needed to put some space between them. Even knowing that he was at the far side of the club grounds wasn't enough. She felt wounded and raw. After capping her paint tin and wiping her brush, she climbed down the ladder and headed inside.

Her next project would be painting murals on the inner and outer walls of the club's day-care center. She kept a notepad and pencil in her back pocket. Maybe now was a good time to take a few measurements and begin sketching out ideas for the traditional nursery rhyme motifs she planned to use.

She had already received permission and a visitor's badge to enter the day care itself. Since two classrooms were outside playing, it turned out to be a perfect time for her to eye the walls and brainstorm a bit.

The creative process calmed her. Gradually, she began

to feel better. Everything was fine. It was a good thing that he hadn't accepted her proposal. She wouldn't see Austin socially again. It was better that way.

He was clearly on board with the idea of having recreational sex, but Brooke had never been that kind of woman.

Tons of people were. It wasn't that she was a prude. Despite what she'd agreed to the other day in the heat of the moment, though, she simply didn't have the personality to throw herself into a relationship that was strictly physical. She didn't know how to separate emotional responses from physical ones.

Perhaps she was too needy. A lifetime in a family that thought she wasn't good enough had given her some issues. Maybe instead of having hot, no-strings sex, she should find a good shrink.

Was it so wrong to want to be loved without reservation?

When Austin talked about his late wife, she could hear that deep, abiding love in his voice. Even though the end had been horrible, Austin had experienced the kind of relationship Brooke wanted.

Unfortunately, he wasn't keen to get involved again. Which meant that Brooke would be foolish to let herself fall for him. The best thing for her to do was concentrate on her current job and also to keep the bigger picture in focus. Somehow, some way, she was going to make her dreams come true.

She finished up her notes. Realizing she couldn't put off her outside project any longer, she headed for the door, only to run into James Harris, the current president of the TCC. "Hi, James," she said. The two of them were friends and moved in the same social circles, but she hadn't seen him in some time.

"Hey, Brooke." The tall, African American man gave her

a smile that was strained at best. Clinging to his leg was a cute toddler about a year and a half, give or take.

"I was so sorry to hear about your brother and his wife." They had been killed in a terrible car accident and had left James custody of their infant son. "That must have been a dreadful time for you."

James exhaled. Lines of exhaustion marked his handsome face. "You could say that. Little Teddy here is a bit of a terror. And to be honest, I don't think I would have agreed to be president of the club if I had known what was coming. I'm barely keeping my head above water. Nannies are coming and going at the speed of light."

Brooke crouched and smiled at the boy. His golden-brown eyes were solemn. She didn't try to touch him but instead spoke in a soft, steady voice, aiming her remarks toward the child's uncle. "You'd be a terror, too, if your world had been turned upside down...don't you think?"

James nodded slowly. "That's true. I know you're right. The poor kid is stuck with me, though, and I know squat about how to care for him. I don't suppose you'd be interested in a job?"

The hopeful light in his eyes, mixed with desperation, made Brooke grin. She stood and squeezed his arm lightly. "Thanks, but no, thanks. I probably know less than you do about kids. Things will get better. They always do."

"I hope so. At least he likes coming here to the day-care center. I kept him at home this morning so he could have a good nap, but I think getting out of the house is good for him. He's incredibly smart."

"See," Brooke said, grinning. "You're already talking like a proud parent."

"But he *is* smart," James insisted.

"I believe you." She brushed Teddy's soft cheek with a

fingertip. "Have fun in there, little one. Maybe you'll see me with my paintbrush soon."

James scooped up his nephew and held him close. "I just want to do right by him. What if I screw this up?"

For a moment, she glimpsed his fear. "You won't," she said firmly. "This isn't what you expected from life, James, but we all make adjustments along the way. Deep down, you know that. I have confidence in you. So did your brother, or he never would have left Teddy in your keeping."

James nodded tersely, as if embarrassed that he had let down his guard even for a moment. "Thanks, Brooke."

She gave him a quick hug. "I've got to get back to my murals. Don't give up. It's always darkest before the dawn and all that."

His grin flashed. "Maybe I'll get you to paint that on one of my stables."

"Don't laugh," she said. "I might just do it."

Eight

Austin stood in the shadows, unobserved, and watched as Brooke said her goodbyes to the man and the boy and headed back outside. He couldn't quite identify the feelings in his chest. None of them were ones he wanted to claim. Was Brooke seriously already moving on in her quest to find a convenient husband?

The wealthy horse breeder was a far more logical match for Brooke than Austin, even on a temporary basis. Gus had introduced Austin to James several days ago and had filled Austin's ear about the current TCC president. James Harris was charismatic, intelligent and a darling of Royal's social scene. To be honest, the guy needed a woman in his life. He had inherited a kid.

Brooke needed a husband. It all made a dreadful kind of sense.

Watching the two of them as they chatted casually told Austin that Brooke was comfortable with the other man. Was she thinking about proposing to James now that Austin had turned her down?

To be fair, Austin hadn't said no. He hadn't said anything at all. He'd been too damned shocked.

He was torn…completely torn. The smart thing to do would be to stay as far away from Brooke as possible until the job was done and he could hit the road again. He was used to being a wanderer now. It was the man he had become.

Even so, something inside him couldn't let Brooke go. Her innocence drew him like a gentle flame. Innocence was more than virginity. Brooke had an outlook on life that Austin had lost. Despite her parents' inability to see her worth, Brooke had not become bitter.

He went back to work, but his brain was a million miles away. Somehow, he had to mend the rift he had caused. Before he did that, he had to decide how to respond to Brooke's shocking request.

He possessed the power to make her life better. She had told him so. Having met her mother, Austin believed that statement to be true.

The only real question was—could he serve as Brooke's pretend husband and still barricade his heart?

Daniel Clayton pulled up at his grandmother's house and cut the engine, leaning back in his seat with a sigh. He loved Rose Clayton and owed his grandmother everything good in his life, but things were getting way too complicated.

After swallowing a couple of headache tablets with a swig of bottled water, he wiped his mouth and got out. The Silver C Ranch was home…always would be. Still, no one had ever told him how the older generation could muck things up.

Knowing he couldn't ignore the summons any longer, he strode up to the porch and rang the bell.

His grandmother answered immediately, looking as if she had just spent several hours at a spa. "Hello, sweetheart. Come on in. I made a pie, and I have coffee brewing."

Though she was sixty-seven, she didn't look her age. Her soft voice did little to disguise her iron will. He had both adored her and feared her since he was a child.

They made their way to the warm, inviting kitchen and sat down. While Rose poured the coffee and served the warm apple pastry, Daniel studied his grandmother, wondering why he couldn't just say no to her and be done with it.

He didn't have long to wait. Rose sat down beside him, pinned him with a pointed stare and ignored her dessert. "You haven't had much to say about the upcoming bachelor auction."

"No, ma'am. To be entirely honest, I was hoping I could convince you to get someone to take my place. I really don't want to do it. At all."

"I've told all of my friends that you've agreed to participate."

She said it slyly, using guilt as a sharp weapon. Daring him to protest.

He set down his fork, no longer hungry. "It's not my thing, Grandmother. I know I said yes, but I've changed my mind."

"The money will benefit the Pancreatic Cancer Foundation, a very worthy cause."

"Then I'll write a check."

"Our family has to be front and center. The Slades are integral parts of this event, and we will be as well."

"So it's a competition."

"Nonsense. I am a long-standing member of the Texas Cattleman's Club and a well-known citizen of Royal. Of *course* I volunteered my dear bachelor grandson for the auction. It was the least I could do. Surely you want to support me in this. And don't forget, I was hoping sweet Tessa Noble might bid on you. That would be a lovely outcome."

Daniel's headache increased despite the medication. He rubbed the center of his forehead. "Please don't try to play Cupid, Grandmother. That never ends well for anyone. Besides, I'm pretty sure Tessa is interested in her best friend, Ryan."

"Ryan Bateman?" Her eyebrows rose.

"Yes. But don't go spreading that around."

"Of course not." His grandmother seemed disappointed.

"I really don't want to do this bachelor thing," he said, trying desperately for one last chance to escape the inevitable.

Her eyes flashed. "Is it because *you're* interested in someone, Daniel?"

His stomach clenched. No matter how he answered, he was in trouble. And besides, what did it matter now? His love life was toast.

With a big show of glancing at his watch, he stood up and drained his coffee cup. He had barely touched the dessert. "If I can't change your mind, then yes…of course you can count on me."

His grandmother beamed. "You're a wonderful grandson. This will be fun. You'll see."

Brooke painted one last daisy petal and stood back to examine her work. She was proud of what she had accomplished…very proud. So why did the memory of her mother's harsh criticism still sting?

As she was gathering her things in preparation for heading home, she saw a familiar figure striding toward her across the open space that would soon be planted with lush garden foliage. Her heart beat faster. Austin.

Unfortunately, he didn't look too happy. He stopped six feet away and jammed his hands in his pockets. "We need to talk," he declared.

Her heart plunged to her feet. "No," she said. "We really don't. It's okay, Austin. I shouldn't have asked you. It wasn't fair. I'd like to pretend it never happened."

He gave her a lopsided grin. "All of it?"

Her knees went weak. How could he do that to her so easily? Three sexy words and suddenly she was back in his arms, breathless and dizzy and insane with wanting him.

She swallowed. "Be serious."

He inched closer. "You don't look good, Brooke."

"Gee, thanks."

"I'm serious. You're pale and a little green around the gills. Do you feel okay?"

She definitely did *not* feel okay. She was queasy and light-headed. She had been for several days now. But that was nothing, right? "I'm fine," she insisted.

Now he eliminated the last of the buffer between them and took her in his arms. "I'm sorry, Brooke."

His gentle apology broke down her defenses. Her throat tightened with tears. "Someone might be watching from the windows," she choked out.

"I don't really give a damn. Relax, sweetheart. You're so tense it's giving *me* a headache."

She started to shake. A terrible notion had occurred to her this afternoon—a dreadful prospect she had been refusing to acknowledge for the past two weeks. Though it was the last thing she wanted to do, she made herself pull away from his comforting embrace. "I need to go home now. Goodbye, Austin."

He scowled. "You're in no shape to drive. I'll take you."

Hysteria threatened. She had to get away from him. Her stomach heaved and sweat beaded her forehead. "I'll take it easy…roll the windows down. It's not far." Tiny yellow spots began to dance in front of her eyes. "Excuse me," she said, feeling her knees wobble and her hands turn to ice.

With a moan of mortification and misery, she darted into the narrow space where an air-conditioning unit loomed and proceeded to vomit until there was nothing left but dry heaves.

When her knees buckled, strong arms came around her from behind and eased her to the ground. "I've got you, Brooke. It's going to be okay."

They sat there on the dead grass for what seemed like an eternity. Only the ugly industrial metal protected them from prying eyes. Brooke leaned against Austin's shoulder and stared at an ant who was oblivious to their presence.

He stroked her hair, for once completely silent.

At last, a huge sigh lifted his chest, and he exhaled. "Brooke?"

"Y-yes?"

"Are you pregnant?"

The shaking got worse. "I don't know. Maybe."

Austin cursed beneath his breath and then felt like scum when Brooke went whiter still. He wanted to scoop her up in his arms and carry her to a safe, comfortable place where they could talk, but they were trapped. The three exits at the rear of the property were delivery bays that would be locked by now. The only way out was to march through the French doors, into the club and out the front entrance.

He stroked Brooke's arms, concerned by how cool her skin felt to the touch. "Do you feel like you're going to be sick again?"

She shook her head. "No. I don't think so."

"Can you walk if I keep my arm around you? I can't have you fainting on me."

"I won't faint."

"All we have to do is make it out to my truck. We can we leave your paints here, can't we?"

"I suppose."

He stood and pulled her with him, waiting to see if she really was steady. Brushing her hair back from her face, he bent to look into her eyes. "One step at a time, honey. Look at me and tell me you're okay."

Brooke sniffed. "I'm swell," she muttered. "But don't be nice to me or I'm going to cry all over your beautiful blue shirt."

"Duly noted."

"Get me out of here. Please." Her skin was translucent. Her bottom lip trembled ever so slightly.

Austin wrapped an arm around her waist and said a quick prayer that no one would stop them. He sensed that Brooke was close to the breaking point.

Fortunately, the clock was on their side. They were too early to run into the dinner crowd, and most of the daytime regulars were gone already. Austin whisked his companion inside, down the hall and into the reception area. Other than a few quick greetings and a wave, no one stopped them.

In moments, they were outside on the street. Austin steered her toward his vehicle. When she didn't balk, his anxiety grew. "I think we need some expert advice, Brooke. Do you have a doctor here in Royal?"

Her eyes rounded. "Are you kidding me? I can't walk into some clinic and tell them I might be pregnant. My parents would know before I got back home."

"You're not a child. And besides, there are privacy laws."

"That's cute. Clearly you don't know my mother."

"Then I have a suggestion to make."

Brooke climbed into the passenger seat and covered her face with her hands. "Oh…" The strangled moan made him wince.

"What if we drive over to Joplin? My sister is a nurse. We can talk this over with her."

Brooke wiped her face with the back of her hand, her big-eyed gaze chagrined. "What's to talk about? Either I am, or I'm not."

He kept his voice gentle. "You can't even say the *P* word out loud. Do you want *me* asking the questions, or would you feel more comfortable with another woman?"

"You think I'm an idiot, don't you?"

"No," he said carefully. "But from what you've told me, you haven't been sexually active recently, and I think this thing took you by surprise. I know the condom broke, but you told me you were on birth control."

Her face turned red. "The morning I left the hotel I was so flustered I forgot to take my pill. I didn't realize it until a few days later when I got to the end of the pack and had one left over."

He frowned. "And your period?"

"It started eventually… Well, there was…" She bowed her head. "This is so embarrassing."

"You're saying you had some bleeding."

She nodded, her expression mortified. "Yes."

He drummed his fingers on the steering wheel. "Stay here for a minute. Try to relax. Let me call my sister. I won't mention your name, but I'll ask a few questions."

Without waiting for Brooke to answer, he hopped out of the truck and dialed Audra's number. The conversation that followed was not one a man liked having with his sister, but it was necessary. The longer Audra talked, the more his stomach sank. At last, he got back in the truck.

Brooke was curled in a ball, her head resting on her knees.

He touched her shoulder. "Look at me, honey."

She sat up, her expression wary, and exhaled. "Well, what did she say?"

He shrugged. "According to Audra, you can get pregnant on any day of the month, even if you only miss one pill. It's far less likely, of course, but it happens."

"And the bleeding?"

"It could be spotting from hormonal fluctuations during implantation and not a real period. The only way to know for sure is to take a test."

A single tear rolled down her cheek.

Austin felt helplessness and anger engulf him in equal measures. *This* was exactly why he didn't let himself get involved with sweet young things who didn't know the score. Brooke was vulnerable. She'd been under her parents' intimidating influence for far too long.

To her credit, she'd been doing everything she could to strike out on her own. But the gap between her and Austin was still too great. He was worlds ahead of her in life experience. He knew what it was like to love and to suffer and to lose everything. He wouldn't allow that to happen to him again. Ever.

No matter how much Brooke tugged at his heartstrings, he had no place for her in his life. In his bed, maybe. But only for a season.

So what now?

"I'm sorry," she said, the words dull. "I take full responsibility. This has nothing to do with you."

"Don't be stupid." His temper flared out of nowhere. "Of course it does. I could have said no at the bar. I should have. But I wanted you." He touched her cheek, stroking it lightly. His heart turned over in his chest when she tilted her head and nuzzled her face in his palm like a kitten seeking warmth. He pulled her across the bench seat and into his arms. "Don't be scared, Brooke. We'll figure this out." He paused, afraid to ask the next question but knowing he wouldn't be able to move forward without the answer. "Did you propose to me because you thought you might be pregnant?"

She stiffened in his embrace and jerked backward. Her indignation was too genuine to be feigned. "Of course not. I need my inheritance. That's all."

"Okay. Don't get your feathers ruffled."

She bit her lip. "Oh, hell, Austin. I don't know. Maybe I did. I've been feeling weird for the past week. But I've ignored all the signs. It seemed too impossible to be true. I didn't want it to be true."

They sat there in silence for what seemed like forever. Outside, the sky turned gold then navy then completely dark. Brooke's stomach rumbled audibly.

"Here's what we're going to do," Austin said, trying to sound more confident than he felt. "There's a truck stop halfway between Royal and Joplin. We can get a meal there. It will be reasonably private, and if we're lucky, the convenience mart will have a pregnancy test. How does that sound?"

"Like a bad after-school movie."

He chuckled. The fact that she could find a snippet of humor in their situation gave him hope. "That's my girl. Where's your purse?"

"In my car. One street over and around the corner."

Once they had retrieved what she needed, they set out. Austin tuned the radio to an easy listening station, pulled onto the highway and drove just over the speed limit. His stomach was jittery with nerves.

Brooke was quiet—too quiet. Guilt swamped him, though he had done nothing wrong, not really. Other than not resisting temptation, perhaps.

The truck stop was hopping on this particular night. That was a good thing. Brooke and Austin were able to blend into the crowd. The hostess seated them at a booth with faux leather seats and handed them plastic-coated menus that were only slightly sticky.

Brooke studied hers dubiously.

He cocked his head. "What's wrong?"

"I'm starving, but I'm afraid to eat."

"Start with a few small bites. We've got all night. Or will your parents be expecting you home?"

"No. I told them I was spending the evening with a friend. They don't really care what I do on a small scale. It's the big picture they want to control."

After the waitress took their order, Austin reached across the table and gripped Brooke's hand. "I won't leave you to face this alone," he said carefully. "I need you to know that."

Her eyes shone with tears again. "Thank you."

"Do you want me to go buy the test now and get it over with, or would you rather wait until after dinner?"

She seemed stricken by his question. "Let's eat first. Then maybe we could book a room? Even if we only use it for a couple of hours?" She winced. "OMG. That sounds sleazy, doesn't it?"

The look on her face made him laugh. "I think it's a fine idea. In the meantime, let's talk about your inheritance and what you hope to do with it. I really want to know."

Brooke sat up straighter, and some of the strain left her face. "Well, I told you about starting the art school."

He nodded. "Yes. Do you have a business plan?"

"Actually, I do," she said proudly. "I even have my eye on a small piece of property near the center of town. It's zoned for commercial and residential both, but the woman who owns the land is partial to small-business owners. She and I have talked in confidence, and she really wants me to have it. The only missing piece is capital."

"Which marrying me will provide."

"Exactly."

"Even without a possible pregnancy, I'm surprised you're not more worried about your parents' reactions to me being your fiancé," he said quietly. "I'm not exactly upper-crust. Audra and I have done well for ourselves, but our mom cleaned houses for a living, and our dad was a plumber."

"They're both gone? But you're so young."

"Mom and Dad were never able to have kids. They adopted Audra and me when they were forty-nine. We lost them both within six months of each other last year. Pneumonia."

"I'm so sorry." Her empathy was almost palpable. "That must have been devastating, especially for you. Did it bring back bad memories of losing your wife?"

Nine

As soon as the words left her mouth, Brooke wanted to snatch them back. The flash of bleak remembrance she saw in Austin's eyes crushed her. It was as if the grief was fresh and new. Did he carry it always like a millstone around his neck, or did it come and go only when insensitive friends, like her, for instance, brought it up out of the blue?

Fortunately, the waitress arrived with their meals, and the moment passed.

Brooke, though she was leery of getting sick again, couldn't resist the sight and smell of the comfort food. She was starving and, thankfully, was able to eat without consequences. Austin cleared his plate as well.

The truck stop was as close to a good ole Texas honky-tonk as a place could get. The atmosphere was rowdy and warm and filled with laughter and the scents of cold beer and warm sweat.

It was not the kind of spot Brooke frequented, but to-night, it was perfect. As long as she didn't move from this booth, she was insulated from the consequences of her actions.

Unfortunately, though, the clock continued to move. The check was paid. The evening waned. Though Austin had said little during the meal, his gaze had stayed on her constantly. In his eyes she saw concern and more. Certainly a flash of sexual awareness. They were both thinking about the escapade that had brought them to this moment.

She bit her lip. "Have you heard of Schrödinger's cat?"

Austin sighed. "Here we go."

"What?" she said, indignant.

"Everyone who's ever watched a certain TV sitcom has heard of Schrödinger's cat. You're saying that as long as we sit in this booth and never leave, you're both pregnant and *not* pregnant. Have I got that?"

"Works for me," she said, stirring the melting ice in her Coke moodily.

"You're not a coward, Brooke Goodman. Knowledge is power. One step at a time. I can quote you clichés till the cows come home. Let's go buy that test and see what we're facing."

"It might be negative," she said, desperately clinging to one last shred of hope.

"It might be…"

His impassive expression told her nothing.

The minimart, unlike the truck stop, was *not* crowded. Brooke, her face hot with embarrassment, snatched two boxes—different brands—off the shelf, plunked down her credit card and hastily signed the receipt. Fortunately for her, the employee manning the counter was more interested in his video game than he was in her purchases.

Soon after, Austin secured two keys to room twenty-four, the last unit on the far right end. They parked in front of their home away from home. He unlocked the door and waited for Brooke to enter.

Could have been better. Could have been worse.

The decor was late '80s, but everything appeared to be clean.

She stood, irresolute, in the middle of the floor.

Austin locked the door, took her in his arms and kissed her forehead. "Get it over with. I'll be right here."

The list of humiliating things she had experienced today was growing. Now she had to add peeing on a stick with a tall, handsome cowboy just on the other side of the door. Fortunately, directions for pregnancy tests were straightforward. She read them, did what had to be done and waited.

After the first result, she ripped open the second box. Pee and repeat.

There was no mistaking the perfect match.

She didn't feel like throwing up. She didn't feel anything at all.

Austin knocked on the door. "You okay in there, honey?"

"Yes," she croaked. "Give me just a minute." She dried them, hoping to erase the evidence. Still the same. Taking a deep breath, she opened the bathroom door and leaned against the frame, feeling breathless and dizzy and incredulous. "Well," she said, "I'm pregnant."

Austin went white under his tan. Which was really pretty funny, because it wasn't exactly a huge surprise. Apparently, like her, he had been hoping against hope that her barfing had been a fluke.

He swallowed visibly. "I see."

"Say something," she begged. Why couldn't this be like the commercials where the woman showed the man the stick and they both danced around the room?

"What do you want me to say?" His gaze was stoic, his stance guarded.

"I keep feeling the need to apologize," she whispered. The tears started then in earnest. They rolled down her cheeks and onto her shirt. Austin didn't want a wife, not even a temporary one. And he surely didn't want a child. This man had been badly hurt. All he wanted was his freedom.

Though she didn't make a sound, her distress galvanized him. He closed the space between them and scooped her up in his arms, carrying her to the bed. He sat down and held her on his lap. "Things happen, Brooke. This situation isn't your fault. It isn't mine."

Time passed. Maybe five minutes, maybe an entire day. So many thoughts and feelings rushed through her body. Having Austin hold her like this was both comforting and at the same time wildly arousing. Her body tensed in heated reaction. In his arms, she felt as if she could handle any obstacle in her path. But at the same time, he made her want things that were dangerous to her peace of mind.

Beneath her, his sex hardened. The fact that Austin Bradshaw was now unmistakably *excited* made her want to strip him and take him without a single thought for the future.

Instead, she scooted off his lap and stood, scrubbing her face with her hands, trying not to compound her mistakes. One thing she knew for sure. "I know I have…options, but I want this baby. Maybe *want* is the wrong word. I'm responsible for this baby. I'm the one who walked into a bar to do something foolish. Now I'm pregnant. So I'll deal with the consequences."

"A baby will change everything about your life," Austin said. His dark gaze was watchful. "It will be a hell of a long time before you can take that months-long trip to Europe to visit art galleries and study the grand masters."

The enormity of the truth in his words squeezed her stomach. "Yes. But that was a selfish bucket list item and one that can wait indefinitely."

"I'll provide for the child financially. You don't have to worry about money."

She winced. "I appreciate the sentiment, but with my inheritance, that won't be necessary. I'm assuming this pregnancy will tip the balance in my favor. My parents are not fond of babies. They won't want me in the house, so I think they'll have no choice but to turn over what is legally mine."

"Having met your mother, I think you're being naive. If I had to guess, I'd say they'll use your child as a bargaining chip to control you. Your situation hasn't gotten better, Brooke. It's gotten worse."

She gaped at him, studying the grim certainty on his face and processing the truth of his words. "I hadn't thought of it that way."

He stood as well, jamming his hands in his pockets and pacing. "We'll get through this…"

"We?" she asked faintly, feeling as if she were an actor in a very bad play.

He shot her a hard glance, his face carved in planes and angles that suggested strong emotion tightly under wraps. "*We.*" His forceful tone brooked no argument. "We're a family now, Brooke…whether we want to be or not. Our only choice is how to handle the way forward. You asked me to marry you. Now I'm saying yes."

"This isn't your problem," she insisted. "It's *my* baby."

He stopped in front of her, their breath mingling, he was so close. At last, the rigid posture of his big frame relaxed, and a small smile tilted those masculine lips that knew how to turn a woman inside out. "Sorry, honey. It doesn't work that way. There were two of us in that bed."

"But you don't want to be here," she cried. "You're only planning to stay in Royal for a couple of months at the most."

He slid his hands into her hair and cupped her neck, tilting her head, finding her lips with his. "So I'll change my plans," he said, kissing her lazily. "Some women sail through pregnancy. But a lot of them don't. You need someone to care for you and support you. Right now, that someone is going to be me."

Kissing Austin was never what she expected. He could take her from gentle bliss to shuddering need in a heartbeat. Tonight, he gave her something in between. He held her and made her believe, even if for only a moment, that everything was going to turn out okay.

She rested her cheek against his chest, feeling and hearing the steady *ka-thud* of his heartbeat. "I can't ask you to do that." Even if the prospect of having Austin in her corner made her soul sing.

"You don't really have a choice." When he chuckled, the sound reverberated beneath her ear. He was so big and hard and warm. Nothing in her life had ever felt so good, so perfect.

But the perfection was a mirage. Her heart screamed at her to proceed with caution. Austin was being kind. Honorable. He was the sort of man who did the right thing regardless of the cost.

That didn't mean he wouldn't inadvertently break her heart.

She pulled away, needing physical distance to be strong. "I'll talk to my parents tomorrow. If they agree to give me the inheritance, the baby and I can have a home of our own. You don't even have to be involved."

Austin shook his head, his smile self-mocking. "I'm involved up to my neck, Brooke. And I'm not going anywhere for the moment."

For the moment... Those three words were ominous but truthful. She'd do well to plaster them on her heart, so she didn't get any foolish ideas. Suddenly, her knees felt weak. She staggered two steps toward the bed and sat down hard.

His gaze sharpened. "What's wrong?"

"Nothing. Not really. Just a little light-headed. It will pass."

He crossed his arms over his chest. "Do you want to stay here until morning? I can buy what we need at the convenience mart."

From his expression, she hadn't a clue what *he* wanted to do. Probably run far and fast in the opposite direction.

The prospect of spending the night with Austin, even in this unappealing motel room, was almost impossible to resist. It was easy to imagine making love to him all night long and waking up naked in his arms. Her breath caught.

Austin's gaze narrowed. "Are you sure you're okay? You're all flushed."

"I'm fine."

If she were going to be a mother, she had to start making mature decisions. "We can't stay here," she said slowly. "I need to be at the club tomorrow to work on the murals. And before that, I'll have to face my parents at breakfast and tell them the news."

"Don't you want to give yourself time to get used to the idea first? You've had a shock, Brooke."

"I can't have this hanging over my head. I believe in ripping off the Band-Aid."

"Fair enough." He nodded slowly. "And you won't be alone. I plan on being there beside you when you break the news."

"Oh my gosh, no," she squeaked, already imagining the fireworks. "That's a terrible idea. I'm not going to tell them about you."

"Don't be ridiculous. We've already established that I

can handle your mother. Besides, the truth will get out sooner or later. This isn't going to be our guilty secret."

Though she was skeptical, she nodded. "If you insist. But don't say I didn't warn you."

Austin took Brooke home. Dropping her off at her parents' house was more difficult than he had expected. Already he felt possessive. Even if he kept himself emotionally divested, Brooke was the mother of his child. That meant something.

The following morning, he dragged himself out of bed, wondering if she had slept any more than he had. A shower did little to offset the effects of insomnia. He shaved and dressed carefully, not wanting to give the Goodmans any overt opportunity to look down their noses at him. Not for his sake, but for Brooke's.

Austin had already seen firsthand how her mother treated her. It didn't take a genius to deduce that a man like Austin would not be on their list of suitable husbands for their daughter.

Brooke had insisted that she be the one to do all the talking, because she knew how to handle her mother and father. Austin had reluctantly agreed.

When he showed up at the imposing Goodman residence, the house looked even more opulent than it had the night before. As an architect, Austin knew plenty about price points and quality building materials. The Goodmans had spared no expense in building their Pine Valley mansion. He wondered if Brooke had lived here her entire life.

He rang the bell. A uniformed maid answered the summons and escorted him through the house. A full hot breakfast was in the process of being laid out on a mahogany sideboard. Sunlight flooded the room through Frenchpaned windows. The dining table was set with china, crystal and antique silver that sparkled and gleamed.

Brooke greeted him with a smile, though he could see the strain beneath the surface. The elder Goodmans were cool but polite in their welcomes. Once everyone was seated, the grilling commenced.

Simon Goodman eyed Austin with more than a hint of suspicion. "My wife tells me you're doing a temporary job for Gus Slade."

No mistaking the emphasis on *temporary*.

"Yes, sir. Or for the Cattleman's Club, to be more exact. I'm overseeing the outdoor addition to the facilities."

"And you have the suitable credentials?"

Austin swallowed his ire. "An advanced degree in architecture and a number of years' experience at a firm in Dallas."

"But you're no longer with that firm?"

"Daddy!"

Brooke's indignant interruption had no discernable effect on the interrogation. For some inexplicable reason, Margaret Goodman was oddly silent. Austin sighed inwardly. "When my wife became very ill, I worked until she needed constant care, and then I quit my job. Since she passed away six years ago, I've chosen to be a bit of a nomad."

"I can't believe this." Brooke stood up so abruptly, her chair wobbled. She glared at her father. "You're embarrassing me. And you're being horribly rude. Austin is my friend. He doesn't deserve the Spanish Inquisition."

Brooke's mother waved a hand. "Sit down and eat, Brooke. You aren't fooling anyone. Your father is well within his rights to ask as many questions as he sees fit. That's why you've brought Austin here, isn't it? To convince us that you've fallen madly in love with a handyman?

And that we're supposed to throw you a lavish wedding and hand over your inheritance?"

The silence that fell was deafening. Scrambled eggs congealed on four plates. Though every bit of the breakfast was spectacularly prepared and worthy of a five-star restaurant, Austin suspected that most of the food would end up in the trash. *He* had certainly lost his appetite. And poor Brooke looked much as she had yesterday when she had gotten sick behind the club.

Every instinct he possessed told him to take charge of the situation, but he had promised to let Brooke do the talking, so he held his tongue. It wasn't easy.

She sat down slowly. Her face was the color of the skim milk Mrs. Goodman was adding to her coffee from a tiny silver pitcher. Brooke cleared her throat. "I was going to broach the subject more gently than Daddy did, but yes, Austin and I are going to get married. We haven't talked about a ceremony yet. I don't even know if I want a big wedding. I'm telling you because you're my parents, not because I expect you to pay for anything."

Poor Brooke looked frazzled. Austin swallowed a bite of biscuit that threatened to stick in his throat. "I am perfectly capable of paying for our wedding. All Brooke needs from you is your blessing and your support. She loves her family and wants to include you."

Austin infused his words with steel. Though it might have gone over Brooke's head given her current physical discomfort, it was clear from Margaret and Simon's expressions that they heard his ultimatum. They could treat Brooke well, or they could lose her…their choice.

Unfortunately, Brooke's mother refused to go down without a fight. "Please understand, Mr. Bradshaw. It's a parent's obligation to protect his or her child from fortune hunters."

The blatant insult was almost humorous. How could sweet, openhearted Brooke have come from such a dreadful woman?

Fortunately, Austin had always relished a good battle. "In that vein, I'm sure you'll understand it's *my* job to make Brooke happy. And by God, that's what I intend to do."

Simon's face turned an ugly shade of puce. "You don't know who you're dealing with, Bradshaw."

"I know that you've blackballed your daughter. That you've made her a prisoner in her own home. That you've deliberately sabotaged her search for meaningful employment. That you've refused to acknowledge she's an adult and one who deserves respect and autonomy."

Margaret slammed her fist on the table. "Get out," she hissed, her gaze shooting fire at him as if she could incinerate him on the spot.

Austin looked across the table at Brooke. He smiled at her, trying to telegraph his unending support and compassion. "Do you want me to go, honey?"

Brooke stood up, seeming to wobble the tiniest bit. She dabbed her lips with a snowy damask napkin and rounded the table to put a hand on his shoulder. "Yes. But not yet. I'll leave with you in a moment."

He heard her take a quavering breath. Now he knew what was coming. Her tension was palpable. Quickly, he got to his feet and put an arm around her waist. Not speaking, just offering his silent support.

Brooke stared at her mother, then her father. She cleared her throat. Her eyes glistened with tears. Austin wanted to curse. This should be a joyful moment. He hated that it was playing out like a melodrama with Brooke's parents as the wicked villains.

"Here's the thing," she said quietly. "Austin and I are getting married. Very soon. After that, I will petition the court for my inheritance. You know it's mine. For you to interfere would be criminal, mean-spirited and petty."

Her fathered puffed out his chest. He glared. "You'll squander every penny in six months. Don't think you can come crawling back for more."

Austin's arm tightened around Brooke. He could literally *feel* the blow of her father's cruel words. "I won't come back home, Daddy," she said. "At least not to stay. I'm a grown woman."

Margaret shoved back from the table and approached Brooke, using her physical presence as a threat, just as she had in the club gardens. Her smile was cold and merciless. "You're a child. This man doesn't love you. He's using you. All I've ever wanted is what's best for you, baby. Let's put this awful business behind us. Start over. Turn back the clock."

Brooke's spine straightened a millimeter. She slid her hand into Austin's and gripped it so hard her fingernails dug into his skin. "I can't turn back the clock, Mama. I'm pregnant."

Ten

Margaret's infuriated shriek reverberated in the confines of the room. For one terrible moment, Austin thought she was going to strike her own daughter. He thrust Brooke behind him and confronted her mother. "Tread carefully, Mrs. Goodman. There are some bridges you don't want to burn. I think it's best if we continue this conversation at another time."

Without giving anyone a chance to protest, he grabbed Brooke's hand and hurried her out of the room and away from the house. After he hustled her down the front walk to where his truck was parked, he cursed beneath his breath when she leaned against the hood of the vehicle and covered her face with her hands. A pregnant woman needed sustenance. Between morning sickness and emotional trauma, Brooke had barely swallowed a bite as far as he could tell.

He tucked her into the passenger seat and ran around to the other side. Once the engine started, he sighed. Taking her hand in his once again, he lifted it and kissed her fingers. "I am so very sorry, sweetheart."

Brooke shrugged, her gaze trained somewhere beyond the windshield. "It's nothing new. Not really."

"I have a proposition for you," he said, wanting desperately to erase her sorrow.

"Isn't that what got us into this mess?" she said wryly.

Something inside him eased. If she could joke about it, even now, all was not lost. "You can't stay there anymore, Brooke. It's not healthy for you or the baby. Gus has been hosting me in the bunkhouse out at the ranch, but frankly, that's getting old. I've taken a look at some new rental condos on the east side of town. They're really nice. What if we go right now and sign a twelve-month lease?"

Her eyes rounded. "*Live together?*"

"You already proposed to me. This seems like a logical step."

Her face turned pink. "I'm sorry I've complicated your life."

"Stop it," he said. "And relax. Stress isn't good for a woman who's expecting. If nothing else, my job is to pamper you and make sure you have a healthy pregnancy. We enjoy each other's company. What do you say?"

Half an hour later, Brooke took slow, shallow breaths and tried to convince herself she wasn't going to barf. After escaping the uncomfortable breakfast with her parents, she and Austin had used the drive-through at a fast food restaurant and picked up sausage biscuits and coffee.

They sat in the parking lot and ate the yummy food, barely speaking. Even so, the silence was comfortable. Austin didn't *crowd* her. Most men in this situation would be demanding an answer.

He finished his meal and crumpled up the paper wrapper. "How's your stomach?"

She held out her hand and dipped it left and right. "So-so."

"I can't read your mind, honey. What are you thinking?"

"Honestly?" She grimaced. "As soon as you and I look at condos together, the gossip will be all over town."

"Doesn't change anything, does it?"

"I can't afford to rent a condo. I don't have any money, Austin," she said bluntly. "And even if we were to get married today, the process to claim my inheritance would take longer than you think to work its way through the court system."

"Forget about that," he said, his voice quiet but firm. "I've lived very frugally for six years. I've got money in the bank. Plenty for you and me and the baby."

She felt her face heat. "I've tried so hard to be independent. This feels like a step backward."

"Not at all. This is *us* making a home for our baby. If you don't leave that house, your parents will only find more ways to make your life miserable and to try and control you."

"I want to be clear about our expectations," Brooke said slowly. "Are you suggesting cohabitation or marriage or both?"

His expression shuttered suddenly, every nuance of his real feelings erased. That sculpted masculine jaw turned to granite. "This would be a practical marriage partnership between two consenting adults. I was considering your proposal even before we found out you were pregnant. Now, it makes sense all the way around. Once the baby comes and you're back on your feet physically, emotionally and financially, we'll reassess the situation."

"You mean divorce."

He winced visibly. "That's what you suggested earlier, yes. But even if we separate, I'll always be part of your life on some level. Because of the child."

So clinical. So sensible. Why did his blunt, rational speech take all the color and sunshine out of the day?

"What will you do when the project at the club is finished?"

"Matt Galloway has talked to me about building a house for him. That would take the better part of a year. After that, I don't know. I suppose I may want to stay in Royal because of the baby. I can't imagine not seeing my son or daughter on a regular basis."

And what about me? She wanted him to tell her how hard it would be to walk away from *her*.

Swallowing all her nausea and her misgivings and the pained understanding that Austin was offering so much less than forever, Brooke summoned a smile. "Okay, Cowboy. Let's go look at these condos. Window-shopping doesn't cost a thing."

An hour later, she ran her hand along the windowsill of a cheery, sun-filled room overlooking a koi pond and a weeping willow. The backyard was small but adequate. And it was fenced in. Perfect for a toddler to stagger across the grass chasing a ball or laughing as soap bubbles popped.

This particular condo, the fourth one they had looked at, had three bedrooms—plenty of space for a loner, a new baby and a woman whose life was in chaos. The complex was brand-new, the paint smell still lingering in the air. The rentals were designed primarily for oil company executives who came to Royal for several months at a time and wanted all the comforts of home.

The agent had stepped outside to give them privacy.

Austin put a hand on her arm. "You like it, don't you? I can see it on your face."

She shot him a wry glance over her shoulder. "What's not to like? But these places have to be far too expensive."

The units were over three thousand square feet each. They weren't the type of starter homes young newlyweds sought out. Each condo Brooke and Austin had toured was outfitted with high-end everything, from the luxurious marble bathrooms and the fancy kitchens to the spacious family rooms wired for every possible entertainment convenience.

"I told you. Money is not a problem."

Panic fluttered in her chest. "I'll pay you back. Half of everything. As soon as I have my inheritance."

He frowned. "That's not necessary.

"Those are my terms."

Even to her own ears she sounded petulant and ungrateful. But she was scrambling for steady ground, needing something to hold on to, some way to pretend she was in control.

"So we'll get married?" He stood there staring at her with his hands in his pockets and a cocky attitude that said *take me or leave me.*

"You don't have to do this, Austin."

"You promised me home-cooked meals and hot sex."

He was teasing. She knew that. But suddenly, she couldn't make light of their situation. Tears clogged her throat. Creating a home with a baby on the way should be something a man and a woman did that was almost sacred. Brooke and Austin were making a mockery of marriage and family. "I need to visit the restroom," she muttered. "Will you see how long we can wait to give them an answer?"

She locked herself in the nearest bathroom, sat on the closed commode lid and cried. Not long. Three minutes, max. But it was enough to make her eyes puffy. Afterward, she splashed water on her face and tried to repair the damage with her compact.

In the mirror over the sink, she looked haggard and scared. Poor Austin hadn't signed on for all this drama.

She used a tissue to wipe away a smudge of mascara and dried her hands on her pants.

Then—because she quite literally had no other choice—she unlocked the door and went in search of her cowboy.

Austin and the rental agent, an attractive woman in her early forties, were chatting comfortably when Brooke emerged onto the front porch. The other woman gave her a searching look. "Everything okay? I have bottled water in my car."

Brooke nodded. "I'm fine."

Austin curled an arm around Brooke's waist, drawing her close. She leaned into his warmth and strength unashamedly. He smelled good, though his nearness made her knees wobble. She couldn't seem to stop wanting him despite everything that had happened.

The agent eyed them both with a practiced smile. "I was telling Mr. Bradshaw that there are three other couples on the books to see this unit today, two this afternoon and one tonight. As you probably know, decent rental property is hard to come by in Royal. This new development is very popular, and this particular condo was only finished two days ago. This one is outfitted as a model, though you certainly don't have to take the furniture if it's not your taste. If you're interested, though, I wouldn't wait too long."

Austin tightened his arm around Brooke. "Give us a few minutes, would you?"

The woman walked down the steps and out to her car.

"Well," he said. "What do you think?"

Brooke wriggled free, needing a clear head. She couldn't get *that* standing so close to the man who made her breathe faster. He rattled her. "You know it's perfect. Of course, it's perfect. But that's not really the point. Aren't we rushing into this?"

He lifted an eyebrow. "You're already pregnant. The clock is ticking. You're the one who asked for marriage. I'm happy for the both of us to move in here either way. I'm already imagining all the ways we can use that big Jacuzzi tub."

So could she. The intensity of her need for him made her shiver.

She licked her lips. "I don't think pregnant women are supposed to use hot tubs."

"Then we'll improvise in the shower."

The heat in his gaze threatened to melt her on the spot.

"How can you be so cavalier about the situation?" she cried. There was absolutely nothing she could do about the panic in her voice. The fact that Austin was cool and unruffled told her his emotional involvement was nil. It was Brooke who was unraveling bit by bit.

Austin shook his head slowly. "Take it easy. I didn't mean to pressure you. But it made me so damn mad to see your parents play the bully. Sit, honey. Breathe."

He summoned the agent with a crook of his finger. Brooke sank onto the porch swing, half numb, half scared.

Austin gave the woman a blinding smile. "I'll take it," he said.

The agent faltered. "You?" She glanced at Brooke. "But I thought…"

"The contract will be in my name only," Austin said cheerfully. "Just mine. I asked Ms. Goodman to come along and give me advice. She likes all those flopping and flipping shows, don't you, sweetheart?"

Brooke nodded. Austin was giving her a way out. Was she being a coward? Maybe so. But his gesture touched her deeply, because it told her he understood her fears.

While Austin wrote a check for first and last month's rent and signed a dozen pages of an official-looking contract, Brooke moved the swing lazily, pushing her foot against the crisply painted boards of the porch. Halloween was only a few days away. This house would need a smiling jack-o'-lantern.

Was she going to live here? For real? Or was this some kind of bizarre fantasy?

She tried to imagine it. Coming home each night to Austin Bradshaw. Sharing his bed.

Every scenario that played in her head was more delicious and tempting than the last. Under this roof, she and Austin would be *alone*. She could indulge her lust for his magnificent body over and over and over again. Intimate candlelit dinners for two. Watching movies on the couch and pausing the action on the screen when they couldn't resist touching each other. Lazy Saturday morning sex when neither of them had responsibilities. It would be one long, sizzling affair.

She blinked and came back to reality with a mental thud.

In one blinding instant, she saw the impossibility of her situation. She *did* need Austin. Marrying him would free up her inheritance and thus finance her dreams of owning an art studio in Royal…of training and inspiring the next generation of artists and dreamers.

Marrying him would make her child legitimate in the eyes of the law, an outdated concept no doubt, but one that was nevertheless appealing. Marrying Austin would give her the freedom to finally be her own person.

But at what cost? Living with him would end up breaking her heart.

She watched him as he talked and laughed with the rental agent. He was making a concerted effort to charm the woman, to keep her from spending too much time wondering why Brooke was not signing on the dotted line, as well. Hoping, perhaps, to deflect the inevitable gossip.

Everything about this man was dangerous. From the very first moment Brooke saw him in that crowded bar in Joplin, something about him had spoken to her deepest needs. She was already half in love with him. The only remedy was to stay far, far away.

Instead, she was about to do the exact opposite.

With a sigh, she pulled out her phone and tried to distract herself with emails while she waited for Austin to finish up. At last, the formalities were done. The agent locked up the property and drove away.

Austin sat down beside Brooke and stretched his long arms along the back of the swing. Yawning hugely, he dropped his head back and sighed. "She's going to meet me here at 8:00 a.m. on Monday to pick up the keys. I'll pack my stuff at Gus's this weekend, so I can move in after work that afternoon."

"And me?"

He curled one hand around her shoulder and caressed her bare arm below the sleeve of her top. His fingers were warm against her chilled skin, eliciting delicious shivers. She'd left her jacket in the car, so she snuggled closer, welcoming his body heat.

"Well," he said slowly. "I suppose that's up to you. I hate the thought of you going back to that house."

"It's my home, Austin. They're not going to poison my soup or lock me in my room."

"Don't be too sure. I wouldn't put anything past your mother." He shuddered theatrically. "She scares me."

His nonsense lightened the mood. "Do you really think we can make this work?"

"I do. We're reasonable adults with busy schedules, so we won't be together 24/7. We both have plenty of work ahead of us at the club, not to mention the fact that we have to get ready for a baby. And when it comes to that, by the way, I can be involved as much or as little as you want me to…"

"Okay." She was feeling weepy again. Lost and unsure of herself. Not an auspicious start to a *convenient* relationship. She swallowed. "Are you still willing to marry me?"

His gaze remained fixed out on the street where two delivery trucks were wrangling about parking privileges. "Yes." The word was low but firm.

"Not a church wedding," she said. "Something small. And very simple."

"The courthouse?"

"Yes." Sadness curled in her stomach. If she were marrying the love of her life, even a courthouse wedding would be romantic. However, under these circumstances, it seemed sad and a bit tawdry.

"I have one requirement."

She stiffened. "Oh?"

He shifted finally, half turning so he could see her face. "I want you to buy a special dress. It's doesn't have to be a traditional gown. But something to mark the day as an occasion. Will you do that for me?"

He leaned forward and brushed her cheek with his thumb. Suddenly, her heart thudded so loudly in her chest she was sure he could hear the ragged thumps. "Yes," she croaked. "I'll go tomorrow."

"Brooke?" He leaned in as he said her name, his lips brushing hers once…twice. "I care about you. I'll never do anything to hurt you, I swear. And I will protect you and this baby with my life."

It was as solemn and sacred a vow as any she had ever heard. Even without the word *love*, it would have to be enough. Austin had already made that other vow on another day with another woman. Brooke would have to be satisfied with these very special promises he had given to her as the father of her baby.

She kissed him softly. "Yes," she said. "I will marry you, and I will live with you. For this one year. And I will do everything in my power to make sure that you don't regret your decision. Thank you, Austin." Curling her arms around his neck, she let herself go, gave herself permission to lower her defenses and simply enjoy the moment.

He wrapped her in his arms tenderly, as if she were breakable…as if all the passion between them had to be kept in check, muted, held at bay to keep from crushing her. Paradoxically, his gentleness made the moment all the more arousing. Their heartbeats, their longing clashed, and like an almost palpable force, the wanting grew and multiplied.

Emboldened, she slid a hand beneath his shirt and caressed the hard, warm planes of his back.

They were outside. In public. Only the confines of the porch gave them any privacy at all.

Austin groaned.

"What?" she whispered, pressing into him, needing him so badly she shook with it.

"I should have written her a check for three more days and taken the keys right now."

Brooke pulled back and stared at him. "That was an *option*?"

His sheepish smile softened the moment, though not the intensity of her desire for him. On the other side of the door lay at least two brand-new, fully serviceable beds. "I wasn't thinking too clearly. It's not every day a man buys a house for his wife and child."

"Rents," she corrected, reminding herself of the tenuous nature of their agreement.

"Whatever." He glanced at his watch and muttered a curse. His disgruntled expression was almost amusing.

"I take it we're through here?"

He stood and stretched. "I have to meet someone at the club. It's important. Or I wouldn't leave you."

The odd choice of words gave her pause. "I have to go, too. I want to finish up the last outdoor mural so I can start on the daycare walls next week. The weather is supposed to turn dreary."

Austin tugged her to her feet. He rested his forehead on hers. "Will you be here with me Monday night?"

Her heart beat faster. Moving out of her parents' house would be no picnic. "Yes," she said clearly. "You can count on it."

Eleven

They wasted no time in heading for the Texas Cattleman's Club. Austin found a prime parking spot, gave Brooke a quick kiss and ran off for his appointment. She stopped by her own car—still parked where it had been overnight—grabbed a couple of items she needed out of the trunk and went inside to change into her work clothes, engulfed in a haze of giddy anticipation and cautious optimism.

The sun was shining, and the temps were balmy. It was a perfect day to paint, though she missed Austin already. In the distance, she could see the stage addition taking shape. It was going to be a push, but Austin swore he would have everything ready in time for the auction. Already, the landscapers were putting down sod and laying out string and markers for the plants, both temporary and permanent, that would turn the gardens into a fall foliage paradise.

The whole thing was exciting. Not that Brooke would attend the auction itself. At least she didn't think so. She certainly wasn't going to bid on a bachelor. She would, however, make an extremely modest donation to the charity, despite her financial woes. This event was important to

Alexis, and Brooke wanted to support her friend in every way she could.

Because she was so close to finishing the entire outdoor project, she opted for peanut butter crackers at lunch. To appease her conscience, she resolved to have a healthy dinner when she got home.

The day flew by. She was in the zone. Anytime her heart was in the midst of a painting, it was as if the brush moved on its own. At four o'clock, she was limp with exhaustion but filled with elation. Two huge outdoor walls now burst with life and color.

As she cleaned up her supplies and packed everything away, she kept an eye out for Austin, but he was nowhere to be found. She told herself not to be silly. Going home to face her parents was something she could do on her own. She didn't need a man to help with that.

In the end, the expected confrontation never materialized. She had completely forgotten that her mother had a huge real estate conference in Las Vegas. Her father had gone along to play golf. Brooke glanced at the calendar in the pantry. They had flown out at 3:00 p.m. Wouldn't be back until Monday night.

She stood in the empty kitchen with an odd feeling in the pit of her stomach. Instead of facing an unpleasant weekend of arguments and emotional upheaval, all she had to do was pack her things and say goodbye to her childhood home. This time when she walked out, it would be for good.

There were sweet memories in the huge house. Not everything had been a struggle. But unfortunately, the lovelier moments of her childhood had been somewhat obliterated by events in recent years.

The cook had left two different casseroles in the fridge. Brooke picked the one with carrots and other veggies. She needed to eat well. Unfortunately, the smell of the food heating in the microwave made her stomach heave. She rushed outside and leaned against the house, breathing in the night air. No one had ever told her that morning sickness could last all day.

On a whim, she sent a text to Alexis…

Are you busy? Want to come over? I haven't seen you in ages…

Alexis's response was almost immediate.

Sounds great. Are your parents home?

Brooke grinned. Alexis was no more a fan of Simon and Margaret Goodman than Austin was. She typed a single-word reply and threw in a few happy-face emojis for good measure…

NO! ☺ ☺ ☺

Alexis replied quickly.

See you soon.

While Brooke cleaned up the kitchen and waited for her friend, she debated how much of the truth to share. She could trust Alexis with her secrets. She had no doubts about that. But she didn't want to feel disloyal to Austin. The confusion was a dilemma she hadn't expected.

Alexis arrived barely half an hour later. After the two women hugged, Brooke led the way into the comfy den. "You want something to drink?" she asked. "A glass of wine, maybe?"

The other woman plopped down on the sofa with a sigh. "What are you having?"

Brooke felt her cheeks get hot. "Just water. Trying to be healthier. You know."

"Yeah. Probably a good idea. This whole bachelor auction may turn me into a raving alcoholic before it's over anyway."

Brooke curled up in an adjoining chair. "How are things going?"

Alexis shrugged. "I suppose you could say we're on schedule. Still, I'm putting out new fires every day. I can't imagine why there are people who *want* to do event planning for a living."

Brooke laughed, but she sympathized with her friend's frustration. Gus Slade, Alexis's grandfather, had insisted his granddaughter be in charge of the bachelor auction. No one ever said no to Gus, least of all his beleaguered family members.

Alexis was similar in height and build to Brooke, though Alexis was a bit taller, and her eyes were blue, not gray. The two women had been friends since childhood. Alexis was the same age as Brooke, but unlike Brooke, Alexis had been sent away to school at a young age and had developed a sophistication and confidence Brooke wondered if she herself would ever match.

Brooke studied the lines of exhaustion on her friend's face. "Sounds like you need a break. Have you seen Daniel lately?"

"No," Alexis said sharply. "Daniel and I are history. End of story."

"Sorry for bringing him up," Brooke muttered.

"No, I'm sorry," Alexis said quickly. Her guilty smile was apologetic. "But let's talk about you."

"Okay." Brooke paused, struggling for words. There

really was no way to dance around the subject. "I'm pregnant."

Alexis's jaw dropped. She sat up straight and stared. "You're joking."

"No." Brooke shook her head.

"But who?" Her friend was understandably bewildered.

"Austin Bradshaw. The architect your grandfather hired to design and oversee the new club addition."

"I've run into him. Briefly." Alexis frowned. "He only arrived two weeks ago. Maybe not even that long."

"We met in Joplin just before Labor Day. It was never supposed to be anything more than a…" The words stuck in her throat.

"A one-night stand?" Alexis winced.

"Yes. The pregnancy was an accident."

"Are you okay, Brookie?"

The childhood nickname suddenly made Brooke want to bawl, but at the same time, it was comforting in an odd way. This woman had known her forever. They had been through a lot.

"I've been sick. It's not fun, I'll tell you that. But I've decided I want the baby. I really do. Before we found out about the pregnancy, I was trying to talk Austin into a temporary marriage, so I could get my inheritance." Alexis knew all about the money from Brooke's grandmother and how her parents were refusing to let her open an art school.

"Do you think you can trust this man? He's practically a stranger. I don't like the idea of him having a shot at all those millions."

Brooke frowned. Alexis's concern made perfect sense, but she felt the need to defend her husband-to-be. "Austin is a decent, wonderful person. I have no worries on that score at all. In fact, he was the one who insisted on a prenup. He doesn't want people thinking he's a fortune hunter."

"Maybe he's just saying that to win your trust."

"He's not like that. He's a widower who loved his wife."

Alexis snorted. "And widowers can't be villains?"

"He's not a villain. He's a great guy."

"But he knocked you up, so there's that."

"It was an accident," Brooke said. "Neither of us did anything wrong. It just happened."

"Are you in love with him?" Alexis asked.

"No. We hardly know each other."

"Then why are you blushing?"

"I *could* love him, I think," Brooke said. "But he's still hung up on his dead wife." She released a heavy sigh. "They were college sweethearts. I can't compete with that. Besides, Austin has told me flat out that he's not interested in a relationship."

"Was that before or after you found out about the baby?"

Brooke gaped, trying to remember. "It doesn't matter. We've been very careful to talk about everything as *short-term*. I'll admit that the baby complicates things."

"I've got a bad feeling about this, Brooke. I understand why you need to get married. But this can't be a paper commitment only…not with the baby. You and Austin are going to be inextricably involved, indefinitely. Life will be messy. Particularly if you fall in love with him."

Having all her doubts spoken aloud was sobering. "I hear what you're saying… I do. But I have to make the best of a difficult situation. Austin has offered to support me until the inheritance comes through the courts. He's renting a house for the three of us."

Alexis arched a brow. "He's being awfully accommodating for a guy who buried his heart with his dead wife."

"Don't be like that."

"Like what?" Alexis's cynical smile was disturbing.

"I want the fairy-tale romance," Brooke cried. "Don't

you think I do? When you and Daniel tried to run away as teenagers and then everything went south, I ached for you. And then all these years later you reconnected. Of *course* I want a love like that. But not everyone gets that chance. I have to make do with what I have."

Alexis stood and prowled, her expression tight. "You can forget about Daniel and me. Nothing has changed even though we're back in the same town. Ours was no grand love affair, believe me. All the reasons we couldn't make it work as teenagers are still there." She thumped her fist on the mantel. "I told you I don't want to talk about Daniel." She wiped her face, though Brooke hadn't realized until then that Alexis had been crying. "When is the wedding?" she asked.

Brooke pulled her knees to her chest. "I don't know," she said glumly. "We'll go the courthouse, I suppose. In Joplin, maybe. Not here."

"Do you want me to be there with you?"

Brooke nodded, her throat tight. "I'd like that."

"Okay, then." Alexis sighed, visibly shaking off her mood. "What can I do to help tonight?"

"Well," Brooke said, "I have two large suitcases and four boxes upstairs ready to be packed. I wouldn't mind a hand with that."

"Only two suitcases?"

"None of my clothes are going to fit…remember? I'll get the other stuff later. When my parents have had a chance to get used to the idea of me being gone."

"And being pregnant. And being married."

"You're not making me feel better."

"Sorry." On the way up to Brooke's room, Alexis ran her hand along the banister. "I wonder how many nights I spent in this house over the years."

"Who knows? But it was certainly a lot. I think my parents liked having you here, because you were a Slade and thus a good influence on me."

"Not after I tried to run off with the help and got banished for my indiscretions." The bitterness in her voice was impossible to miss.

Brooke paused on the top step and turned, looking down at Alexis. "I'm really sorry. This stupid town puts far too much emphasis on social standing. My mother actually called Austin a *handyman*. As if that was the worst insult she could come up with at the moment."

They walked down the hall and into Brooke's childhood bedroom. The toys and school trophies had long since been packed away. The room had been professionally redecorated and painted. But Disney posters still hung inside her walk-in closet. At one time, Brooke had considered becoming a graphic artist. She loved color and design.

Alexis flopped down on the bed and stretched her arms over her head. "I feel like I should throw you a party. After all this time, you're finally escaping your parents' clutches."

"I love my mom and dad."

"I know you do, darlin', and that's why I love *you*. Despite the way they've treated you, you won't turn your back on them. Not everyone is as forgiving as you are."

Brooke gave her friend a pointed look. "Don't make me out to be a saint. I'm not inviting them to the wedding. In fact, I'm not even telling them when it is. My mother would probably call in a mock bomb threat to the courthouse."

"Or she'd have your father fake a heart attack."

They dissolved into laughter, and the conversation moved onto lighter topics. In an hour, the packing was done.

Alexis studied the partially denuded bedroom. "Do you want to come to my place tonight? I hate to think of you staying here all by yourself."

"I appreciate the offer. But honestly, I need some time to think. To make sure I'm doing the right thing."

"It sounds like you've already made up your mind."

There was no criticism in Alexis's statement…only quiet concern.

Brooke shrugged. "I guess I have. I like Austin. He's willing to help me get my inheritance. He's interested in supporting his child, and he wants to play a role in the baby's future."

"What about you, Brooke? What do you want?"

"I'm not entirely sure. But I'll figure it out soon. I'm running out of time."

Austin drove to Joplin on Saturday. He didn't have to. There sure as hell was plenty going on at the club that needed his attention. But he had learned—when Jenny was ill—there was more to life than work.

His sister was thrilled to see him. A pot of his favorite chili bubbled on the stove, and she had gone the extra mile to make chocolate chip cookies. He shrugged out of his light jacket and hung it on the hook by the back door. "Hey, sis. Smells great in here."

Audra hugged him. "It's a sad day when I have to bribe you to get a visit."

Not for the world would he ever tell her this house held too many painful memories. Jenny had died in the bedroom just down the hall. Six years had passed. The raw grief had healed. Still, the house was not comfortable to him. Perhaps it never would be.

They had lunch together, talking, laughing, catching up. Audra was almost six years older than he was. In many ways she had been a second mother to him. She had been married briefly when he was in high school. But apparently the guy was a jackass, because the relationship ended after eighteen months. Audra never spoke of it, and she never dated seriously since.

Come to think of it, she and Austin had a lot in common. Too much pain in their pasts. Too little inclination to try again.

He knew that sooner or later she would grill him because of the phone call he had made to her the day he discovered Brooke was pregnant. She waited until he was on his second cup of coffee and his third cookie.

"So," she said, leaning her chair back on two legs and looking at him over the rim of her pink earthenware mug with the huge daisy painted on the side. "You want to tell me what's going on?"

He sighed inwardly. "Brooke's pregnant."

"The cute blonde from the bar?"

"Yep."

"Did she set you up?" Audra's suspicious frown had *mother hen* written all over it.

"Stand down, sis. This was entirely an accident. I won't go into details, but the kid is mine."

"What now?"

He told her about Brooke's inheritance and her dream of opening an art school and her crazy-ass parents. "I've rented a condo as of Monday. And I've offered to marry Brooke so she can get her money. Temporarily only."

Audra scowled. "You are so full of crap."

"Hey…" He held up his hands. "Why the attitude? I'm the good guy in this scenario."

"Are you planning on sleeping with her?"

"The condo has three bedrooms."

"That's not an answer and you know it. Tread carefully, Austin."

His neck got hot. "I don't follow."

She leaned forward and rested her elbows on the table.

"I love you, little brother. But you're not the same man you were before Jenny got sick. When you were younger, you were the life of the party, always joking and laughing. After she died, you changed. I miss that old Austin. Honestly, though, I doubt if he's ever coming back."

His stomach curled. Nothing she had said was news to him. "What's your point?"

"Don't hurt this girl."

"I don't plan to hurt anyone."

"But that's the problem, kiddo. You think everything can stay light and easy. But you're not able to see this from a young woman's perspective, especially the one I remember from the bar. She still had stars in her eyes, Austin. I'll bet when she looks at you, her heart races and she starts imagining a future where the two of you grow old together."

"That's where you're wrong," he said defensively. "I've been very clear about that. I told her I don't want another relationship."

Audra's visible skepticism underscored his own doubts. But what could he do? The course was set. He and Brooke were getting married.

Twelve

While Austin was busy with his own agenda Saturday morning, Brooke sat in her car in front of Natalie Valentine's bridal shop and tried to think of a cover story that wouldn't sound too unbelievable. Her phone said it was 9:57. The store opened at ten.

After Alexis left last night, Brooke had spent an hour wandering from room to room of her family home, wondering if she was jumping from the proverbial frying pan into the fire. How could she marry a man she barely knew?

On the other hand, how could she not?

She had eventually slept from midnight until seven and then spent an hour in the bathroom that morning retching miserably. This pregnancy thing was taking a toll on her body already. Her weight was down five pounds.

When she saw the hanging placard in the glass doorway flip from *Closed* to *Open*, she climbed out of the car and marched inside.

Natalie greeted her with a smile. "Hi, Brooke. You're out early. Can I help you find a dress for the auction? I assume that's why you're here. I've sold ten gowns in the last week already. If my business is any indicator, the charity bachelor gig is going to be a huge success."

"I'll just browse for a bit if that's okay," Brooke said, avoiding the question.

"Of course. Make yourself at home. There's coffee in the next room if you get thirsty."

When Natalie moved to greet another customer, Brooke breathed a sigh of relief. She wasn't prepared to explain why she needed a dress. The traditional wedding gowns in the back half of the salon beckoned with their satin and lace and bridal splendor, but she wouldn't let her wistful imagination go there. Reality was her currency. She had plans to make and a future to plot out.

She tried on six dresses before she found one that didn't make her feel self-conscious. The winning number was an ivory silk affair, strapless, nipped in at the waist, ending just below the knee. It was sophisticated, elegant and bridal enough for an informal courthouse wedding.

With the dress draped over her arm, she bumped open the fitting room door with her hip and nearly ran into Tessa Noble. The curvy African American woman with the sweet smile greeted Brooke warmly. "Hey, Brooke. I haven't seen you in forever. Are you shopping for a charity auction dress...like me?"

Brooke hugged the other woman. "*You're* going? Tripp, too?" Tessa's brother was as popular as his sister, though Tripp was an extrovert, and Tessa definitely preferred staying out of the limelight.

Tessa chuckled. "Would you believe that Ryan Bateman has talked Tripp into being one of the bachelors?"

"Oh, wow. Your brother is a hunk. The bidding will go wild."

Tessa rolled her eyes. "Yeah. That's what I think. He'll eat it up. But it's all for a good cause."

"So what kind of dress do you want? I bet you would look amazing in hot pink. Or scarlet maybe. Even emerald green."

Tessa chewed her bottom lip. "Oh, I don't know, Brooke. I was thinking something a little less flashy."

"I can understand that. But every woman deserves to look her best. Do you mind if I hang around and see what you try on?" She sensed that Tessa might need a gentle push in the right direction.

"Of course not. Is that what you're going to wear?"

Brooke felt her face get hot. "Maybe. I have a couple of other occasions coming up during the holidays, so I wanted to be prepared. Here," she said, pulling two outfits off the rack when she saw what size Tessa was eyeing. "Humor me." The red or the fuchsia—either choice would be sensational.

Tessa seemed dubious. "I'd prefer something with a little less wattage. This one might work." She held out an unexceptional gown that was perfectly plain.

Brooke wrinkled her nose. "Basic black is acceptable for a formal occasion, of course, but you have a majestic figure, Tessa. Play to your strengths. Don't hide in the shadows."

"I'm not hiding," Tessa insisted. "I love my body. Or at least as much as any woman does." She grinned. "But that doesn't mean I want everyone gawking at it."

"Isn't there something in between? Then again, my life isn't exactly going according to plan lately, so who am I to hand out advice?" Brooke admitted the truth ruefully.

Natalie had apparently been watching the good-natured standoff. She joined them and gave Tessa a reassuring smile. "You're not the first woman to be nervous about stepping out of your comfort zone. Here's an idea. Take all three possibilities home overnight, plus another one or two if you like. Try them on in the comfort of your own bedroom with your own shoes and jewelry. Keep the tags attached, of course. I think—under those circumstances— you'll end up with exactly the right outfit for the occasion."

While Tessa took her time selecting from a wide array of choices, Brooke said her goodbyes and followed Natalie back to the cash register to pay for her purchases. Natalie took Brooke's credit card, then slid the dress into a clear garment bag. "This one is lovely. You can dress it up or down so many ways. And if it's a cooler evening, some kind of golden, gauzy shawl would be pretty."

Brooke nodded. "Yes." She was almost tongue-tied. It had never been her intention to hide her pregnancy forever. But now it seemed difficult to dump the news on people without divulging far more than she wanted to about her personal life.

By the time she made it back to her car and spread the dress bag out in the trunk, she was starving. She still had two stops to make, but they would have to wait. Instead, she drove the short distance to the diner and grabbed chicken noodle soup and a chicken pita sandwich to go.

It wasn't the easiest meal to eat in the car, but she didn't want to run into anyone she knew. How was she going to explain Austin to the world? How was she going to explain her pregnancy? The deeper she got into the chaotic whirl of events she herself had set in motion with one crazy night in Joplin, the more out of control she felt.

Babies were amazing and wonderful. She truly believed that. But this little one was turning Brooke's world upside down and backward in a big way.

She parked beside the courthouse and ate her lunch slowly, huddling in her navy wool sweater and wishing she had dressed more warmly for the day. The weather, as predicted, had taken a nasty turn. The skies were dull and gray. The temperature had dropped at least fifteen degrees. A steady, driving rain stripped any remaining leaves from the trees. Fall, her favorite season, would soon turn to winter.

Royal's winters were mild, for the most part. Still, it was a good thing she had finished the outdoor murals. She couldn't risk getting sick. Not with so much at stake.

What was Austin doing right now? Was he at the club? Working on the new addition? It pained her that she had no idea.

When she couldn't put it off any longer, she got out and locked the car. The wind made her umbrella virtually useless. The lawyer her parents used occupied an office in the annex across the street from the courthouse. Brooke had an appointment.

The dour older gentleman took her back to his overly formal suite right on time. He didn't seem happy to see her, particularly after a tense fifteen-minute conversation. "So you see," Brooke said, "I'll need the prenup right away. And I'll need your assurance that what we've discussed doesn't leave this room. I know my mother tries to twist people to her way of thinking, but you are obligated to keep my confidence. Right? I've told her I'm getting married. I just haven't said when."

The lawyer blustered a bit, pretending to be insulted, but Brooke knew there was a better than even chance he would dial her mother's cell number as soon as Brooke walked out of the room.

The man scowled. "Your parents are looking out for your best interests, Miss Goodman."

"It's *Ms.*," she said. "I'm twenty-six years old. Plenty old enough to know my own mind. I'll bring you the marriage license as soon as I have it. And then?"

He shrugged. "I'll file the paperwork. Barring any kind of hiccups, the transfer of your grandmother's assets should be fairly straightforward."

"What kind of hiccups?" Brooke asked, mildly alarmed.

"Merely a figure of speech."

She left the office soon after. This time the queasiness in her stomach had nothing to do with her pregnancy. Surely her parents wouldn't try to contest her grandmother's will. It was ironclad. Wasn't it?

Unfortunately, the meeting with the lawyer directly preceded her first visit with the ob-gyn who would be caring for Brooke during her pregnancy and birth. The woman frowned when she saw Brooke's blood pressure. "Have you had issues with your BP in the past, Ms. Goodman?"

Brooke flushed. "No, ma'am. I had kind of an upsetting afternoon. That's all. I'll be fine."

The appointment lasted almost an hour. Brooke was poked and prodded and examined from head to toe. Except for the blood pressure thing, she was in perfect health. The doctor gave her a stern lecture about stress and demonstrated a few relaxation techniques. At the very last, Brooke received the piece of information she had been waiting for.

The doctor smiled. "Since you seem to know the exact date you conceived, it makes things easier. I've marked your due date as May 14. Congratulations, Ms. Goodman. I'll see you in another month."

Brooke took her paperwork, handed over the copay and walked out of the office on unsteady legs. Deep down, perhaps she had been hoping that the whole pregnancy thing was a mistake. Except for the nausea and occasional light-headedness, she still didn't *feel* pregnant.

But now, there was no doubt.

She stopped at the pharmacy to pick up her new vitamins—tablets the size of horse pills—and then she drove by the piece of property she hoped to buy soon. The empty lot sat forlorn. Brooke leaned her arms on the steering wheel and stared through the rain-spattered windshield.

Her art center would be the kind of place where she could bring her infant to work. Being her own boss would be the best of both worlds. She could be a parent and still create her dream of a thriving studio for children and young teens to pursue their artistic endeavors.

She wished she had brought Austin here. He needed to see what he was helping her accomplish. And besides, she missed him. Her body yearned for his in a way that was physical and real and impossible to ignore. Already, her life seemed empty when he wasn't around.

That thought should have alarmed her, but she was too tired to wrestle with the ramifications of falling for the handsome cowboy. She would try to protect her heart. It was all she could do.

When she returned home, it was as if her wistful thoughts had conjured a man out of thin air. Austin was sitting on the front porch when she walked up the path. Her parents had given the house staff the weekend off, not out of any sense of altruism but because they didn't want to pay hourly employees when they were out of town.

Hence, there had been no one to answer the door.

Austin unfolded his lean, lanky body and stretched. "I was beginning to think you weren't coming back."

"I live here," she pointed out calmly, trying not to let him see that her palms were sweaty and her heart was beating far too fast.

He grinned. "Not for long." He dropped a kiss on her forehead. "I have a surprise for you. Will you come with me? No questions asked?"

She hadn't been looking forward to an evening all alone. "Yes. Do I need to change?"

"Nope." He steered her back down the walk in the direction she had come moments before. Her wedding dress was still in the trunk of her car, so she used her keys to beep the lock. It would be fine for the moment. Before she could climb into the cab of the truck, Austin put his hands at her waist, lifted her and set her gently on the seat.

She wanted to make a joke about how strong he was and that he was her prince charming, but she stopped herself. This wasn't an ordinary flirtation. They weren't an ordinary couple.

Once they began driving, it didn't take long for her to realize that Austin was taking her to their new condo. When he parked at the curb, she shot him a teasing glance. "Breaking and entering? Not really my style."

Austin reached in his pocket and dangled a set of keys in front of her face. "I sweet-talked the rental agent into the giving me the keys early. She made me swear we wouldn't move in until Monday. Insurance regulations, you know. But tonight, it's all ours."

On the top step sat a jaunty pumpkin. His jack-o'-lantern face had been carved into a perpetual glare.

Brooke laughed softly. "You did this?"

Austin nodded. "Yes."

"I love it." Warmth seeped into her soul. That and the reassurance that she wasn't being entirely foolish. All her doubts settled for the moment, lost in the excitement of being with Austin. "Did you mention dinner? I seem to be perpetually hungry these days."

"Follow me." He unlocked the front door with a flourish. In the living room, he had somehow managed to procure a romantic meal, complete with candles and strawberries and a crystal vase filled with daisies. "You've had a lot of stress lately, darlin'. I thought we both deserved a break."

She looked up at him through damp eyes. "A lovely idea. Thank you, Austin."

He cocked his head, a slight frown appearing between his eyebrows. "Something's wrong."

Brooke sat down on the floor and leaned back against the sofa, stretching out her legs. "Not really. Just a lot of *adulting* today."

"Like what?" he asked, joining her.

"Well, the lawyer's office, for one."

His gaze sharpened. "The prenup?"

"Yes."

"Good."

"And I got a dress for our wedding."

"Excellent."

"And I also had my first visit with my ob-gyn."

His lips twitched. "I'm impressed."

"No, you're not," she said slowly. "You're making fun of me."

"I'm not, I swear. You're a list maker, aren't you?"

"To the bone. Is that a bad thing?"

He leaned over and kissed the side of her neck, sending shivers down her spine. "I like a woman who can focus."

She moaned when he pulled her close and found her mouth with his. His lips were warm and firm and masculine. Arching her neck, she leaned into him and, for a few exciting moments, let herself indulge in the magic that was Austin.

But when the kiss threatened to burn out of control, she pulled back, still hesitant, still unsure of the big picture, no matter how much she craved his touch.

She cleared her throat. "Will I seem needy if I say I missed you today?"

"I missed you, too, Brooke." His smile was lopsided, almost rueful. "In fact, I should have taken you with me, I think."

"Taken me where?"

He hesitated briefly before responding. "I went to see my sister, Audra."

"The tall redhead?"

"The one and only."

"Was it a friendly, low-key visit, or an I'm-about-to-get-married announcement?" she asked.

He scraped his hands through his hair. "The second one. Audra thinks I'm making a big mistake."

"Oh." Brooke's stomach curled into a tight knot of hurt and embarrassment. "She's probably right."

"Audra didn't have all the facts. I filled her in. And of course, the baby was the tipping point."

"Oh, goody. She's probably out right now getting my sister-in-law-of-the-year T-shirt."

"You're getting cranky," he said. "Eat a taco."

Austin must have had help with this picnic, because the food was still warm. Even so, her stomach revolted. She took one bite and set the plate aside. "Alexis thinks we're making a big mistake, too."

"Alexis Slade? Gus's granddaughter?"

"I told you she's my friend. She gave me the mural job, remember?"

He nodded. "I do. What's her beef with me?"

"It's not you," Brooke said. She rested her chin on her knees. "She thinks I'll let my gratitude for what you're doing cause me to confuse sexual attraction with love."

He went still, his entire body frozen for a full three seconds. At last he sighed, almost silently. "But you told her we've been very clear about our expectations…right?"

"I told her."

"Then what's the problem?"

The problem was that Austin Bradshaw was a gorgeous, sexy, intensely masculine man who also happened to be a decent, hardworking, kind human being. A platonic relationship might have worked if Brooke had thought of him as a brother. But from the first moment she'd set eyes on him in that bar in Joplin, she had wanted him. Badly.

Wanting was a short step to needing. And needing segued into loving with no trouble at all.

She managed a smile. "We don't have a problem. I think everything is going exactly according to plan."

Thirteen

In hindsight, Austin had to admit that preparing a romantic indoor picnic for a woman might be sending mixed signals. All he had wanted to do was reassure Brooke about moving in with him. To let her know that leaving her parents' house was the right thing to do.

But now she seemed skittish around him, especially after that kiss.

Making Brooke smile and laugh was rapidly becoming an obsession. The way her gray eyes lit up when she was happy. The excitement in her voice when she told him about her plans. Even her shy anticipation about having a baby she had never meant to conceive at all.

Perhaps he was the one in danger.

He filled his plate in hopes that Brooke would follow suit. She had been so very sick these last few days, she was losing weight already. Her petite frame didn't have pounds to spare. Right now, her cheekbones were far too pronounced—her collarbone, too.

She carried an air of exhaustion, though he had a hunch her fatigue was as much emotional as it was physical. Hearing and seeing what her parents had put her through in recent months made him angry on her behalf.

Out of the corner of his eye, he saw her take a bite of the savory shredded-pork taco. Soon, she finished the entire thing, including most of the brown rice alongside it.

"Another one?" he asked.

Brooke eyed the platter longingly. "I don't know. I don't want to push it. The food is amazing, though. Where did you get it?"

"One of my carpenters is from Mexico. He and his family just opened a new restaurant on the south side of town. I told him what I was doing tonight, and he helped me get everything together."

"Give that man a raise." She put a hand on her stomach and grimaced. "I'll wait fifteen minutes, and if everything stays down, I'm going to have a second." She wiped a dollop of sour cream from the edge of her mouth, eyeing him with an expression he couldn't decipher. "I've been thinking," she said slowly.

"About what?" He dunked a chip in cheese sauce and ate it.

"Marriage. My art studio. Us."

His gut tightened. "I thought we settled all that."

"Well, when the two most important people in our lives wave red flags, it *should* make us think twice."

"Our business is our business, Brooke. Neither of them understand where we stand on this."

"At least hear me out. You don't want to be married again. And you don't want to have a child. I can't do anything about that second part, but I did think of a way we could skip walking down the aisle."

He stood up and folded his arms across his chest. "Oh?"

"The terms of Grammy's will state that I get the money when I marry or on my thirtieth birthday. I'll hit that mark three years and two months from now. Instead of marrying me, you *could* simply cosign the loan for my art studio with me. Then my parents wouldn't try to contest the will or stop the wedding. You wouldn't be legally tied to a woman who isn't Jenny. And I wouldn't have to feel guilty for ruining your life."

Austin stared at her, feeling shifting sand beneath his feet. Everything she said made sense. Yet he hated every word. "Come here, woman." He reached down, grabbed her hand and drew her to her feet. He put his hands on her face, cupping her cheeks in his palms. "No one," he said firmly, "makes me do something I don't want to do. I'm not marrying you because I *have* to. I don't feel trapped. You're not taking advantage of my good nature."

Her eyes widened. "I'm not?"

He dragged her against him, letting her feel the full extent of his arousal. His erection throbbed between them, pressing into her soft belly, telegraphing his intent. "This marriage is convenient for me, too," he drawled. "I want you in my bed every night. I want you in a million different ways. I want to take you over and over again and make you cry out my name until neither of us can remember to breathe. You're a fire in my blood."

He paused, his chest heaving. The words had poured out of him like hot lava, churning to the surface without warning.

Brooke stared at him, eyes wide, lips parted. He put a hand on her flat belly. "This baby is *ours*," he said softly. "Yours and mine. I never had that with Jenny. So that makes you pretty damned rare and unique. I don't have it in me to love again. I won't lie about that. But I'll be good to you, Brooke. Can't that be enough?"

Her lower lip wobbled. "I suppose." Dampness sheened her eyes. He could fall into those deep gray pools and never come up for air. For six long years he had wandered in a wasteland of despair and pain. Every part of his soul was awakening now. The rebirth hurt in a different kind of way, which was why he had put safeguards in place.

This thing with Brooke was special, but he wouldn't let it drag him under.

He scooped her into his arms and walked toward the master bedroom. The house had been staged for showing. Only a bedspread covered the mattress. Austin didn't care. It had been too long since he'd been intimate with Brooke and felt her soft body strain against his.

Brooke was silent. For once, he couldn't tell what she was thinking. He laid her down and lowered himself beside her, settling onto his right hip and propping his head on his hand. "I didn't ask," he said slowly, suddenly unsure of the situation. "I want to make love to you. Is that okay?"

She chewed her lip. "Have sex, you mean?"

"Don't do that."

"Do what?"

"Pick at words. You know what I mean."

She laughed softly, though he was convinced he saw doubts in her eyes. "I do know what you mean," she said. "And yes. I want to have sex."

He winced inwardly at her insistence on the more clinical phrase. Was she trying to make a point, or was the *L* word as much a problem for her as it was for him?

Shaking off the worrisome thoughts, he unbuttoned her designer jeans and placed a hand flat on her belly. "This is the first time we've done this knowing that you're…" The word stuck in his throat. With some consternation, it occurred to him that he had *never* made love to a woman who was growing another human.

Brooke grinned. "Pregnant? Is that the word you're looking for? All the parts still work the same. The doctor said

I have no restrictions in that area. And the good news is…
I can't get pregnant *again*."

"Very funny."

He leaned over and kissed her taut stomach. "You have
a cute navel, Ms. Goodman. I can't wait to see it grow."

"I'll have to finish the day-care murals soon before I get
too fat to climb up a ladder."

"Not fat," he muttered, reaching underneath her to un-
fasten her bra. "Rounded. Voluptuous. Gorgeous."

Brooke giggled until he took one nipple in his mouth
and suckled it. Her tiny cry of pleasure sank claws of hunger into his gut. She tasted like temptation and sin, a heady
cocktail.

"Tell me you want this."

"I already did."

"Beg me…"

The gruff demand showed Brooke a side of her cowboy
she had never experienced before tonight. He wasn't above
torturing her. The rough slide of his tongue across her sensitive flesh was exquisite.

She cradled his head in her hands, sliding her fingers
into his silky hair and pulling him closer. "Please," she
whispered. "Please, please, please make love to me, Austin."

"I thought you'd never ask."

He undressed her slowly. The house was warm. Even
so, the erotic pace covered her body in gooseflesh. Austin's hooded gaze and flushed cheekbones signaled a man
on the edge.

In the silence, his ragged breathing was unsteady.
Brooke, on the other hand, wasn't sure she was breathing at all.

She hadn't expected this time with Austin to be any

different. But the baby was changing things already. This tiny life growing inside her had seemed like an ephemeral idea…a hard-to-believe notion.

Here…now, though, the child was almost tangible. She and Austin had created something magical. Was it her imagination, or was the tenderness in his gaze more pronounced tonight? Despite the unmistakable hunger in his touch, he had reined in his need. He was handling her like spun glass.

Unbuttoning his shirt was the next logical step. It was easier now to touch him, easier than it had been the first time, or even the second. She was beginning to know what he liked, what brushes of her fingertips made him groan.

He had undressed her down to her bikini underwear. She straddled him and leaned forward to stroke the planes of his chest. His skin was hot. The place where his heart thudded beneath her fingertips beckoned. She kissed him there, lingering to absorb his strength, his wildly beating life force.

"I won't regret this," she whispered. "I won't regret *you*." She hoped it was a vow she could keep.

Austin lifted her aside and rolled to his feet…just long enough to strip off his remaining clothes. He was magnificent in his nudity. Not even the scar on his left thigh from a childhood injury could detract from his power and virile beauty.

He came back to her, scooted her up in the bed and settled between her thighs. "I can't wait," he growled. He took her in one forceful thrust, stealing her breath. The connection was electric, the moment cataclysmic.

For a panicked instant, Brooke saw the folly of her plan. Doggedly, she shoved the painful vision aside. She had Austin in this moment. Nothing could ruin that.

The condo faded away. Not even the smell of fresh paint nor the faint sounds of laughter and traffic on the street outside could impinge on her consciousness. Nothing existed but the feel of Austin's big, warm body loving hers.

Emotion rose in her chest, hectic and sweet. She wanted to call out his name, to tell him how much he gave her, how much she wanted still.

But she bit her tongue. She kept silent. She would not offer what he did not want or need.

Perhaps pregnancy made her body more receptive, more attuned to the give and take between them. She felt as if she had climbed inside his skin...as though the air in his lungs was hers and the beat of her heart was his.

They moved together slowly, all urgency gone. It was as if they had been lovers for a hundred years. Because despite the differences that kept them apart, she knew him. *Intimately.* And in that moment, she fell all the way into the deep. She loved Austin Bradshaw.

The knowledge was neither sweet nor comforting. It was a raw, jagged blade that ripped at her serenity, severing her hope for the future.

Her arms tightened around his neck. "Don't stop," she groaned. "Please don't stop." She concentrated on the physical bliss, shoving aside all else that would have to be dealt with later.

This was Austin, her Austin. And she loved him.

Her climax was explosive and deeply satisfying. Austin groaned and found his release. Seconds later, he reached for a corner of the bedspread and pulled it over their naked bodies. Rolling onto his back, he tucked her against his right side. In moments, she heard the gentle sound of his breathing as he slid into sleep.

Presumably he had been up early for the drive to Joplin. Chances were, he had gone by the club to check on his big project before arranging this surprise. The man worked hard.

His left hand rested flat on his chest. She lifted it and played with his fingers, twining hers with his. Then she saw something that somehow she had never noticed before— perhaps because it was the kind of thing a person could only see if they were staring closely.

On the third finger of Austin's left hand, there was a white indentation where his wedding ring had resided. The sight shocked her. She rubbed the shallow groove. Austin never moved. His hand was lax in hers, trusting.

Pain like she had never known strangled her. She swallowed a moan. The night she had met him was the first time he had been without that ring. She had coaxed him into bed that night. Or maybe he had coaxed her. The lines were fuzzy. If they were to marry this week, would he be expecting a wedding band from Brooke?

She couldn't do it. She couldn't replace a man's devotion to the love of his life with an empty symbol of a convenient union.

Stricken and confused, she climbed out of bed and dressed. Ironically, despite her emotional upheaval, her stomach now cooperated and announced its displeasure by growling loudly.

The sparsely outfitted kitchen did have a microwave. She fixed a plate of leftover food, nuked it and sat at the table.

Austin found her minutes later. He had dressed, but his shirt was still unbuttoned, giving her glimpses of his hard chest. He yawned and dropped a kiss on top of her head. "Sorry. I've had a few late nights recently. This project is one snag after the other."

She murmured something noncommittal.

He grabbed seconds for himself as well and joined her. "You okay, honey?"

"Yes." It was a humongous lie, but under the circumstances, perhaps the Almighty would forgive her.

Austin wiped his mouth. "I don't see any point in post-poning our wedding. Does Wednesday work for you? I thought I'd tell my crew I have personal business that day. I happen to know that Audra is free. Do you think Alexis can join us?"

Brooke's throat was so tight it was difficult to speak. "I'll ask her. But I'm sure her schedule is flexible."

He frowned, staring off into space. "I know there will be gossip. Can't be helped. People will wonder why we're not taking a honeymoon. We'll simply say that the club-addition project is under a tight deadline so we're waiting until after Thanksgiving."

"That makes sense."

"What about your parents? I don't want you to have re-grets, Brooke."

Too late for that. Hysteria bubbled in her throat. "The old me would have invited them. Even knowing what I know, I would have invited them because it's the proper thing to do. But they don't want to come, and even worse, they would almost definitely give us grief."

"Your brothers?"

She shook her head. "They won't have any interest in this, believe me. Alexis is all I need."

"Okay, then." He reached across the table and took her hand. "What kind of flowers do you like? I want you to have a bouquet." His gaze was open, warm…nothing at all to suggest that this wedding ceremony—modest though it was to be—might bring back memories of another, happier day.

"That's not necessary."

He squeezed her fingers, his smile teasing and intimate. "You'll be my bride, Brooke. Despite the circumstances, that's a fact. If you don't tell me, I'll get something atro-ciously gaudy, like purple carnations."

She laughed in spite of herself. "Oh, heck, no. Make

it white roses." She paused. "And maybe white heather." Once upon a time she had researched flower meanings for an art project in college. White heather symbolized protection and a promise that wishes do come true. If any of that nonsense were real, she needed all the good karma and mojo she could summon.

"I'll do my best," he said.

They gathered up the remains of the dinner. Darkness had fallen.

"We should go," Brooke muttered. "I have a few more things to pack." She didn't really want to leave, but the longer she stayed, the more she felt the pull of that bed and this man and those impossible dreams.

"How 'bout I come with you now and load up the boxes you already have finished?"

"You wouldn't rather do that tomorrow?"

"No. I plan to spend most of the day at the club. Since I'm missing work Wednesday, I want to get a jump on this week's schedule. Things are moving fast now."

They *were* moving fast…too fast. "That makes sense," she said.

"And what about you?"

"Me? Um…"

He grinned. "Sorry. Didn't know it was a hard question."

"Alexis and I usually go to early mass and then have brunch. But she's not available this Sunday. I thought I'd finish the last of my packing and then maybe call my parents. I won't be there when they get home Monday night. Might as well break the news to them now."

"That won't be pleasant." He sobered, his jaw tightening.

"No. But it has to be done."

He pulled her into his arms and held her close. "They should be proud of you, Brooke. I'm sorry your mom and dad haven't been there to support you. I wish things were different."

The painful irony of his statement mocked her. *I wish things were different.* So did she. A million times over. No matter how much she told herself she was making the best of a difficult situation, she couldn't escape the gut-clenching certainty that she was making the biggest mistake of her life.

Fourteen

Sunday felt like the equivalent of a condemned man's last meal. Tomorrow Brooke would move into a new home with Austin. Wednesday she would legally become his wife.

These last peaceful hours in her childhood house constituted one final chance to make a run for it…to change the course of her destiny. Had it not been for a broken condom and a forgotten birth-control pill, perhaps she would have done just that. Maybe she would have found other businesspeople in Royal besides Alexis who were willing to stand up to Margaret Goodman and give Brooke a job. Maybe Brooke could have then found a roommate and a simple, inexpensive apartment.

Maybe she could have been free.

Her dream of an art studio would have been majorly postponed, but that was the case with a lot of people's dreams. And then some just never came true.

Now she faced the prospect of being trapped in a loveless marriage with the one man she wanted more than life itself. Her body craved his lovemaking. She yearned for his smiles, his teasing touch. But she was very much afraid that she had no future with Austin. How could she compete with the memory of his dead wife?

She slept fitfully and woke up sick. The routine was becoming familiar to her now—lukewarm tea and plain crackers after she emptied her stomach. The doctor had told her the nausea might subside in another few weeks as she entered her second trimester. Then again, it might not.

Eventually, her energy returned, at least enough to finish cleaning out the last of her bedroom closets and bathroom drawers. Though the housekeeper would return tomorrow, Brooke did all the vacuuming anyway. By two o'clock, her presence in the Goodman mansion was virtually erased. All that remained were her toiletries and one small overnight case.

Because Austin had loaded her boxes and large suitcases into his truck last night, tomorrow morning would be almost anticlimactic. All she would have to do on her way to work would be to walk out and shut the door.

She was putting the vacuum away in the utility closet off the kitchen when she heard a commotion in the garage. Her heart jumped. The alarm beeped, signaling that someone had shut it off.

Moments later Brooke's parents walked into the kitchen.

She gaped at them, glanced at the calendar and frowned. "I thought you weren't coming back until tomorrow." Her stomach clenched. That last awful meal with her parents and Austin had been a dreadful experience. She didn't want a repeat. The one saving grace was that her mother's temper usually burned hot and quick, and then she moved on to her next victim.

Either that or her parents were biding their time, preparing for their next military offensive. Brooke would be on her guard, just in case.

Margaret Goodman waved a hand and dumped her purse

and tote on the island, her expression harried. "Your father wasn't feeling well. We managed to book an earlier flight. I'm going to call Henrietta immediately and have her come fix dinner."

Brooke winced inwardly. Her mother was essentially helpless in the domestic arena. "I don't mind cooking for you, Mama. Something simple, anyway. Baked chicken? A nice salad?"

Her father's face brightened, but her mother was already shaking her head. "I pay for the privilege of having my staff on call. It's not like I'm dragging her out of bed at midnight. Henrietta won't mind at all."

Maybe she would and maybe she wouldn't. It was a moot point. When Margaret Goodman delivered an edict, everyone jumped.

Despite what Brooke had told Austin about making a phone call to her parents today, she changed her mind. She had been preparing herself mentally to come over at dinnertime tomorrow before going to the condo. She had concluded that the conversation was one she needed to have face-to-face. Now fate, or her father's indigestion, had offered a much quicker and easier solution.

But it also meant delaying the inevitable for several hours, a nerve-inducing span of time in which she rehearsed her speech a dozen times. She had to wait for her mother to take a shower and change out of her *nasty* travel clothes. The Goodmans always flew first-class, so it was hard to imagine how much nastiness there could be on Margaret's powder-blue Chanel pantsuit. Still…

And her father had to catch up on sporting events he had missed while he was gone. He holed up in his man cave immediately.

Brooke was left to hide out in her room with her laptop researching baby furniture online. It was a delightful pastime. Even so, it wasn't enough of a distraction to calm her nerves.

Too bad she couldn't be over at the new condo handing out candy to trick-or-treaters. That would be fun. The Goodman home was in a gated community where the houses were spread far apart. No little ghosts and goblins would be ringing the doorbell here tonight.

The minutes on the clock crept by. Henrietta arrived. Brooke saw the cook's car out her window. Soon afterward, appetizing smells began wafting upstairs. Dinner was almost invariably served at six thirty. Margaret's doctor had told her that eating too late would make her gain weight.

At last, the three Goodmans sat down together in the formal dining room, and the first course was served. Brooke would have far preferred eating at the cozy kitchen table in the breakfast nook. Her mother, however, believed in keeping up appearances. Brooke's father didn't have a dog in the fight, but he had given up caring about such things years ago.

Because Brooke was uncomfortable talking about very personal subjects in front of staff, she waited until dessert was served. Fresh apple tarts with cream. The timing meant Henrietta would be in the kitchen for at least the next half hour cleaning up the dishes.

Brooke took a deep breath. "Mom, Dad… I wanted to let you know that I'm moving out tomorrow."

Her father never lifted his head. He continued to eat his dessert as if afraid someone was going to snatch it away from him. Since it was definitely not on his approved diet, perhaps that was a valid fear.

Margaret, however, swallowed a bite, took a sip of wine and sat back in her chair. "Where on earth would you go, Brooke? You haven't a dollar to your name."

"And whose fault is that, Mama? You've deliberately sabotaged every attempt I've made to be independent."

Her mother didn't deny the charge. "Perhaps I'm afraid of the empty-nest syndrome."

Brooke rolled her eyes. "Oh, please."

Her mother lifted a shoulder. "I'm told that's a *thing*."

"Not for you. You're too busy conquering the world. And that's not bad," Brooke said quickly. "You've always set a good example for me as a woman who can do anything she sets her mind to…"

"I sense your compliment is wrapped around a piece of rotting fish."

Margaret Goodman had always been a drama queen, a larger-than-life figure. She ruled her world by the sheer force of her personality—along with fear and intimidation.

"The compliment is sincere, Mother. But I'm telling you it's time for me to find my own way in the world."

"With this *handyman*?"

"Austin is a highly trained architect. He's brilliant, in fact."

"He hasn't held down a job in over six years. Your father and I had him investigated."

Brooke swallowed her anger with difficulty. "He nursed his dying wife. He told you that."

Her father looked up. "People say a lot of things, Brooke. Don't be naive. We won't apologize for being concerned."

Margaret nodded. "Besides, the wife has been gone a long time."

"My God, Mama. Have some compassion. He loved her. I think he still does."

For once, a tinge of genuine concern flickered in her mother's expression. "Then why, in God's name, Brooke, are you so hell-bent on throwing in your lot with this cowboy? He'll break your heart. Tell her, Simon."

Brooke's father grimaced. "Your mother may sometimes be prone to overstating the facts, but in this instance, I happen to agree with her. The man got you pregnant, Brooke, fully aware that you're an heiress. It looks bad, baby. And I know you. You've got romance in your soul. You want the happily-ever-after. But this architect isn't it. Give it time, Brooke. Someone else will come along."

The fact that they weren't yelling was actually worse. To have her parents speak to her as an adult was such an anomaly she felt as if the universe had tilted. "I appreciate everything you both have done for me. And even now, I appreciate the fact that you want me to be happy. I do. But I have to stand on my own feet. I'm going to be a mother."

"You could put the baby up for adoption," Margaret said. "Privately. In Dallas. This will change your whole life, Brooke."

"Yes, Mama. You're right. I didn't want to get pregnant. I didn't plan to have a baby so soon. Still, that's where I am. Despite the circumstances, I do want this child. He or she will be the next in a new line of Goodmans. Doesn't that excite you even a little bit?"

Both of her parents stared at her. Her father's expression was conflicted. With Brooke gone, there would be no one around to deflect Margaret's crazy train.

Brooke's mother's seemed to age suddenly. "I've never seen you like this, Brooke. So calm. So grown-up."

"Well, Mom, it had to happen sometime. I don't want to fight with either of you. I love you. But I have new priorities now. If you can respect those, I think we'll all be happier."

Her father grimaced. "It's not too late to break things off with the Bradshaw man. If this art studio business is so important to you, I can fund that, whether or not your mother agrees."

"Simon!" Margaret's outrage turned her face crimson.

He gave his wife a truculent stare. "Well, I can." He shrugged sheepishly, coming around to hug Brooke before releasing her and pouring himself another scotch. "I've let your mother take the reins, but I won't stand by and see you heartbroken by a bad relationship. You're my baby girl."

Brooke was completely caught off guard. "Thank you, Daddy. That means the world to me. I'll keep your offer in mind."

Margaret Goodman stared at her daughter. "I hope you won't do anything to tarnish our standing in the community."

Brooke flinched. The chilly words were their own condemnation. "I understand your concern, Mother. I'll do my best."

Monday morning, Brooke didn't see either of her parents when she came downstairs. While she had been in her bathroom miserably ill, Margaret and Simon Goodman had left for work.

The much-dreaded confrontation was over. Brooke had faced her two-headed nemesis and won. Or so it seemed.

Shouldn't there be some kind of trophy for what happened last night? When an adult child navigated the chilly waters of independence, surely there needed to be some permanent marker. The feeling of anticlimax as she said goodbye to her childhood home and climbed into her car was disheartening.

She had been counting on an exciting day at the club to boost her spirits. Fortunately, that was an understatement. While she was outdoors taking one last critical look at her garden murals, a crew showed up from a regional magazine to do a story about the bachelor auction and all the renovations.

The reporter interviewed Brooke. The photographer took dozens of shots. Alexis was escorting the duo.

While the two professionals conferred, Brooke pulled Alexis aside. "Any chance you're free to be my maid of honor on Wednesday morning?"

She'd been hoping Alexis would squeal with excitement. Unfortunately, nothing had changed. Her friend wrinkled her nose. "You realize I can't say no to you, Brookie. But I have strong reservations."

"Duly noted."

"What time?"

"I don't know. We'll probably leave for Joplin first thing. Austin and I will talk tonight."

"So you're really moving in with him?"

"I am."

Alexis gnawed her lower lip. "I wish I could talk you out of this. But I'm hardly in a position to hand out romantic advice. Just promise me you'll be careful."

"What does that even mean? The man is only trying to do right by me and his child. He's not some wacko ax murderer."

"I'm not worried about your physical safety. I'm afraid he'll break your heart."

I'm afraid he'll break your heart.

Alexis's words reverberated in Brooke's head for the remainder of the day. Perhaps because they echoed Brooke's worst fears.

Could she keep her emotional distance? Was that even possible?

Austin met her on the front steps of the club just after five. They had texted back and forth during the afternoon, and his mood was upbeat.

When she stepped outside, he gave her a big grin. "I

skipped lunch. What if I take you to dinner at La Maison? To celebrate?"

What exactly were they celebrating? She was afraid to ask.

Instead, she looked down at her black pants and cream sweater. "I'm not really dressed for that place." La Maison was one of Royal's premier dining establishments.

Austin waved a dismissive hand. "It's Monday night. Nobody will care."

Again, they left her car behind. The restaurant was in the opposite direction from the condo, so they could pick up the vehicle later.

Once they were seated at a table for two beside the window, Brooke felt herself relax. "This was a great idea," she said. "I didn't realize how stressful it was going to be to talk to my parents. They didn't go ballistic, but it wasn't easy."

Austin poured her a glass of sparkling water from the crystal carafe the waiter had left on their table. "You should be proud of yourself."

"I am," she said, sipping her water slowly and gazing absently at their fellow diners. It was true. Despite her current circumstances, she felt in control of her life. It was a heady feeling.

They stuck to innocuous topics during dinner. Austin had changed out of his work gear into a sport coat and dark slacks. His white shirt and blue tie showed off his tan.

The man was too handsome for his own good.

Despite her best efforts, Brooke couldn't keep herself from repeatedly sneaking a peek at that tiny, telltale white line on the third finger of Austin's left hand. She noticed it every time he reached for the bread basket or picked up the saltshaker.

"I should tell you something," she said, the words threatening to stick in her throat.

Austin stilled, perhaps alerted by the note of gravity in her voice. "Oh?"

"My father stood up to my mother. It was remarkable, really. He said he would fund my art studio despite her wishes."

"What are you telling me, Brooke?"

Now she felt like a bug on the end of a pin. Austin's piercing gaze dissected her and found her wanting. "Just that my dreams are within reach with or without a marriage license."

That was a lie. A whopper, really. Her dreams were no longer limited to an empty, weed-choked lot in downtown Royal. Now they included a cowboy architect with a big smile and a closed-off heart.

The man in question picked up a silver iced teaspoon and rolled it between his long fingers. The repetitive motion mesmerized her.

"I thought we had a deal, Brooke. You've bought a dress. I've ordered flowers. The appointment with the judge is on the books."

She reached across the table and took the spoon out of his hand. Then she linked his fingers with hers, feeling his warm, comforting grasp ground her…give her courage. "I know what we said. But I want you to know there's an escape clause. You can bail right now. Free and clear."

Part of her wanted him to take the bait. So that she would no longer be clinging to this terrible, fruitless yearning to lay claim to this man's heart and soul.

Austin squeezed her fingers. His smile was both sweet and mockingly erotic. "I know what I want, Brooke. You're the only one dithering."

And there it was. The challenge.

She took a deep breath. "Okay, then. If you're sure. I asked Alexis about Wednesday morning. She's free."

"Good."

He reached into his pocket and extracted a slim white envelope. "This is for you, Brooke."

She took it from him gingerly. "What is it?"

"Open it, honey. You'll see."

Inside was a gift certificate to a baby store in Dallas. The certificate had a lot of zeroes at the end. "Austin," she said softly. "This is too much."

"Get everything you need for the nursery. Everything. You can wait until we know if it's a boy or a girl, or you can go with a unisex theme and start shopping now. I want you to have plenty of time to get the baby's room ready. If you'd like to paint, I can handle that on the weekends."

"I don't know what to say."

He rubbed the back of her hand with his thumb, sending tingles down her spine. "Tell me you're happy, Brooke."

That was a heck of an order. Why did he have to ask for so much?

"I'm happy," she whispered, her throat tight. "Of course I'm happy."

It was clear from his face that her words were not entirely convincing.

Even so, he smiled. "Ready to get settled into our new digs?"

"Oh, yes. I forgot we'll have to make up beds."

"Nope. I had a service come in today. They've outfitted the entire house with the basics, so we'll be all set until we have time to pick out our own things. And they've stocked the fridge and cabinets with staples and perishable items."

"Looks like you've thought of everything."

"I tried," he said. "We'll see how well I did."

Fifteen

Austin kept waiting for the other shoe to drop. Brooke seemed matter-of-fact about their new living arrangements, but he couldn't be sure what she was thinking. The woman had learned to hide her emotions and feelings from him. He didn't like the change. Not one bit.

On a more positive note, she was less frazzled now. Clearly she had come to terms with her pregnancy. He could almost see the mental switch that had flipped inside her. Deciding to embrace motherhood wholeheartedly was a huge step.

At the condo, she flitted from room to room, examining every nook and cranny, though she had seen it all twice before. He gave her space. She was nervous. Understandably so.

For his part, Austin was glad not to be living in the bunkhouse at the Lone Wolf anymore. He had appreciated Gus's hospitality, but it was time to put down more permanent roots, at least for the short term. The irony of that equivocation didn't escape him.

As the hour grew later, Brooke got quieter. It occurred to

him that she was on edge about the sleeping arrangements. That was easy enough to fix. He didn't want her coming to him out of any sense of obligation.

When they passed in the hall for the fifth or sixth time, he put out a hand and caught her by the wrist. Her bones felt small and fragile in his grasp. "Relax, honey. You have your own room."

She chewed her lower lip, making no pretense of misunderstanding. "I know. But I thought we agreed this would be a real marriage."

Her anxiety caught him off guard. And though he would be loath to admit such a thing, it hurt. "I'm not buying a wife," he said, the words sharper than he had intended.

She flinched. "I didn't mean it like that."

"Look," he said. He stopped, scraped his fingers through his hair and pressed the heel of his hand to his forehead. He sighed. "I need to go to Dallas tomorrow. Just for the day. Why don't you come with me?"

"No," she said quickly. "There's lots to do here." She grimaced. "Do you have to go?"

He shrugged. "Jenny's father died this past weekend. They've asked me to say a word at the funeral. I don't want to. Not really. But I couldn't think of a polite way to say no."

"I'm so sorry." Brooke's expression was stricken. "We should postpone the wedding. You'll be expected to stay longer than one day, surely."

"Brooke…"

She stood there staring at him. "What?"

"This isn't because of Jenny. It's not, I swear. I'm not doing this for her. But her mom…well, she…"

"She loves you," Brooke said, her voice flat.

"Yes. I know it's been a long time. It shouldn't matter."

"People are entitled to their feelings, Austin. I understand that. You should be honored."

"I wanted this to be a special week for you and me."

She wrapped her arms around her waist. "I'm not a child. Things happen. Please don't worry about me. Do what you have to do."

Austin went to bed alone that night. He lay in the darkness on an unfamiliar mattress with his hands linked behind his head and tried not to think about Brooke sleeping just a few feet down the hall.

His sex hardened as he imagined her soft body tucked up against his. The scent of her hair was familiar to him now. The curve of her bottom. The way her breasts warmed in his palms.

In less than forty-eight hours, she would be his wife. At one time, that notion would have scared him. Now he was confident he could handle it. Brooke knew the score. She understood what he could give and what he couldn't.

Despite his very real aversion to opening himself up to an intimate relationship, this was going to be a good thing.

He was looking forward to fatherhood. Brooke was going to be an amazing mom, even though she was understandably scared. Hell, so was he. What did he know about raising a kid? But it was something he wanted, something he had always wanted.

Jenny's death had been the death of that dream, too.

In the silence of the darkened room, he could hear himself breathing. Soon, Brooke would be here beside him. He couldn't deny the rush of pleasure and anticipation in his gut at that thought.

Brooke was awakening feelings in him that he'd been sure he would never experience again. Affection. Warmth. The need to protect.

To say that he was conflicted was like saying Texas was

a big state. He was looking forward to his new future. But at the same time, he was skittish.

He didn't want to hurt Brooke. But his heart wasn't up for grabs. Period.

Though it pissed him off, Brooke managed to avoid him the following morning. He was forced to head for the airport without seeing her at all. Leaving town with things rocky between them made him uneasy.

They were supposed to be getting married tomorrow, so why was that prospect seeming less and less likely?

The funeral was difficult and sad. Seeing Jenny's mother even more so. He had dreaded coming, because he thought it would cause him to relive every minute of Jenny's funeral. In the end, that didn't happen. Not really.

His grief was different now. It would always be a part of his past, but it was no longer a searing pain that controlled his days.

The realization brought first dumb shock, then quiet gratitude.

At last the funeral and the accompanying social niceties were over. Traffic on the way back to the airport made him miss his flight. He cooled his heels for an hour and a half and finally caught a later flight. After a hot, crowded hop to Royal, he landed and retrieved his truck for the drive to his new home.

The condo was dark when he arrived. It was after eleven. It made sense that Brooke would be asleep.

Disappointment flooded his stomach as he unlocked the front door and let himself in quietly. He stood in the foyer and listened. Not a sound broke the silence.

With a sigh, he carried his bag to his bedroom and tossed it on the chair beside the bed. After a long, hot shower, he felt marginally more human.

His lonely bed held no attraction at all. Wearing nothing but a pair of clean boxers, he tiptoed down the hall and stopped at Brooke's door. It was not closed completely. He eased it open and stood in the doorway until his eyes grew accustomed to the semidark. Her body was a small lump under the covers. A dim night-light cast illumination from the bathroom.

This entire day he had been driven by a need to return home. Here. To this house. A place where he had slept only one night so far and that could not—by any conceivable standard—possibly be considered home already.

What had drawn him back from Dallas was more than drywall and shingles and wooden studs. The invisible homing beacon was wrapped up in a petite woman with a big heart and an endless capacity for hope.

Guilt flooded him without warning, leaving sickness in its wake. He was about to marry her tomorrow for no other reason than because she drove the cold away. And he needed that. He needed her.

But it wasn't love. It couldn't be. Never again.

He couldn't even pretend to himself that he was her savior. Brooke's father had offered to finance her studio dream. Brooke didn't need Austin at all anymore. The best he could offer was giving the baby his name.

He must have inadvertently made a sound. The lump beneath the covers moved. Brooke sat up in bed, scrubbing her face like a child. "Austin? Sorry. I was waiting up for you. I must have dozed off."

Her hair was loose around her shoulders. The scent of her shampoo reached him where he stood. She was wearing an ivory camisole that clung to her small breasts.

"I didn't mean to wake you."

"It's okay. How was the funeral?"

He shrugged, one hand clenched on the door frame

to keep himself in check. "It was fine. Saw a lot of old friends."

"And your mother-in-law?"

"She'll be okay, I think. Her sister is going to move in with her. She's a widow, too."

The silence built for a few seconds.

Then Brooke held out a hand. "You must be exhausted. And cold. Come get in bed with me."

He stumbled toward the promise of salvation, knowing full well that he was a selfish bastard who would take and take and give nothing in return.

Brooke lifted the covers and squeaked when he climbed in. "Your feet are like ice," she said.

"Sorry." He spooned her from behind, dragging her close and wrapping his arms around her so tightly she protested. His world was spinning. Brooke was his anchor. He rested his cheek on the smooth plane of her back. "Go to sleep, honey. It's after midnight."

"But you're..."

He had an erection. Pike hard. Impossible to hide.

"Doesn't matter," he said.

For hours he drifted in and out of sleep. It was as if he was afraid to let down his guard. He'd been half convinced she would bolt when he was out of town. Until he had his ring on her finger, he couldn't be sure this peace would last.

Exhaustion finally claimed him. When he next awoke in the faint gray light of dawn, Brooke had scooted on top of him and joined their bodies. She kissed him lazily, nipping his bottom lip and sucking it until he groaned aloud.

He was too aroused for gentleness. He gripped her ass and pulled her into him. Feeling her from this angle was sensory overload. He shoved up her camisole and toyed with her raspberry nipples.

Brooke's head fell back. She cried out. He felt the ripple of inner muscles caressing his hard length as she found her release.

Groaning and cursing, he rolled them in a tumble of covers. Lifting her leg onto his shoulder, he went deeper still, thrusting all the way to the mouth of her womb, claiming her, marking her, saying with his body what the words would never offer. She was his.

They slept again.

The next time they surfaced, pale sunshine spilled into the room.

Brooke stirred drowsily, yawning and stretching like a little cat. She burrowed her face into his side. "Don't wanna get up," she mumbled.

He tightened an arm around her and kissed the top of her head, feeling a bone-deep contentment inexplicably overlaid with dread. "It's your wedding day, sweetheart."

She opened one eyelid. "Don't you mean *our* wedding day?"

His face heated. "Yes. Of course." Pressure built in his chest. He wanted to *do* something, *say* something.

But he couldn't.

Instead, he nuzzled her cheek with his and climbed out from under the covers. It was an asinine thing to do. Any man with an ounce of testosterone would have stayed right there and claimed what was his.

But a chasm had opened at his feet. Terrifying. Endlessly deep.

He'd been down that canyon once before.

"How long before you'll be ready to leave?" he asked, feigning cheerfulness.

Brooke rolled to her back, her expression hard to read, though she seemed more resigned than delighted about her upcoming nuptials. "Half an hour, I guess."

"Sounds good."

He shaved and dressed with little recollection of his jerky, automatic movements. Putting on his newest suit with a crisp white shirt and a royal blue tie made him marginally calmer.

He'd worn a tux when he married Jenny. This was not the same at all.

The florist delivered Brooke's bouquet right on time. Austin signed for it and tipped the guy.

In the meantime, he texted back and forth with Audra. She was meeting them in Joplin. At her insistence, she had procured a small cake for afterward at her house.

Austin was completely unprepared when Brooke walked out of the bedroom. The sight of her as a bride, even a less than formal one, slammed into his chest like a gunshot. And was equally painful.

Her blond hair was caught up on top of her head in one of those fancy knots women manage, with little wisps artfully framing her flushed cheeks. Subtle makeup emphasized smoky gray eyes. Soft lips covered in pale raspberry gloss made him want to snatch her up before any other man caught a glimpse of her delicate beauty.

The dress she had chosen was perfection. Her shoulders were bare. Ivory silk flattered her delicate curves. The skirt was narrow with a hint of swish. Her legs, those legs that could twine around his back and take him to heaven, looked a million miles long. Ivory pumps to match her dress had three-inch stiletto heels that gave her more height than usual.

He tried to swallow the boulder in his throat. "You look breathtaking."

Her smile was more cautious than radiant. "At least the dress still fits. I suppose that's the upside of being sick every morning."

"Is it awful? Even now?"

She lifted one pale, perfect shoulder. "I think we may be getting past the worst of it. We'll see."

"Good."

He hated the stilted conversation, hated the distance she had set between them.

He knew why the awkward wall was there. Brooke was protecting herself. Austin had insisted on a sterile, emotionless union, so his bride was doing her best not to *care*.

His own jacked-up psyche had created this mess.

Brooke reached for her clutch purse. "We should go. Alexis will be waiting."

Alexis had offered to meet them in Joplin, but Brooke had insisted her friend travel with them. Austin wasn't an idiot. His bride didn't want an intimate car ride with him.

Outside on the front porch, they both huddled into their coats. If the weather was any harbinger of marital luck, they were doomed. November had come in with steel-gray skies and chilling rain.

Austin struggled to lock the front door. The new key wanted to stick. "Damn it," he said, after it got stuck a third time and he had to take it out and try again.

Brooke hopped from one foot to the other. "I'm going to wait in the truck. I'm freezing."

"Wait," he said. "You'll ruin your dress. Let me hold the umbrella."

At the last moment, the dead bolt finally clunked as it was supposed to. He dropped the keys in his jacket pocket and reached for the large black umbrella. But Brooke had already taken it and stepped off the porch.

In slow motion, her shoe hit the top step—the newly painted top step that was slick as glass in the pouring rain. Her flimsy heels wobbled, giving no purchase as all. As he watched in horror, unable to reach her, she fell down seven stairs, striking her shoulder and her head and finally crumpling onto the sidewalk.

His entire body was paralyzed. A roaring in his head made it almost impossible to think. To breathe.

He was at her side in seconds, calling 9-1-1. Feeling like a fool because he couldn't remember his new address.

"Brooke. Brooke, sweetheart."

Her eyes were closed. A large, ugly bruise already bloomed on her right cheekbone. Blood seeped from a gash just above it. He wanted to scoop her up and hold her, but he was terrified to risk further injuries.

He knew the first-aid drill. Brooke might have damaged her spine during the fall. To lift her limp body could do irreparable harm.

Shrugging out of his coat, he draped it over her, covering as much of her small, broken body as he could. He left her only long enough to retrieve the damned umbrella. Then he opened it and crouched beside her, keeping the rain at bay as best he could.

With one hand, he stroked her face, held her wrist, felt her pulse. "Hang on, Brooke. Help is on the way. You're going to be fine." Though it seemed her heart beat strongly, what did he know?

Royal's emergency services were top-notch. Austin knew they must have arrived in mere minutes. But the delay seemed like an eternity.

When at last they pulled up with a cacophony of sirens and a barrage of flashing lights, he should have felt relief. Instead, he was numb. The fear had overtaken him…had frozen every cell in his body.

Forced to step back, he watched, agonized, as they eased Brooke onto a board and strapped her down. Started an IV. Wrapped her in a blanket.

"She's pregnant," he blurted out suddenly. "She's pregnant."

One of the female EMTs gave him a sympathetic smile. "We'll take good care of her, sir. You can meet us at the hospital. Okay?"

He nodded. Hospital. Right. Not a courthouse. Not today.

He should call Audra. And Alexis.

The idea of making meaningful conversation was beyond him.

Instead, he took Brooke's phone from her purse and found Alexis's info. Adding Audra's number to the text, he sent word to both of them.

Brooke fell. We're at the hospital. I don't know about the baby.

His own cell phone rang immediately. He didn't answer. He couldn't speak. He was so cold and so scared and so damned helpless.

He couldn't lose someone again. He couldn't.

In retrospect, he shouldn't have driven himself to the hospital. There was no time to waste, though, so he did it anyway.

The emergency room waiting area was crowded. After struggling to find a parking space, he was then forced to cool his heels for several minutes before it was finally his turn at the counter.

"They brought my fiancée in by ambulance," he said. "Brooke Goodman?"

The woman consulted her computer. "The triage nurses are with her now. As soon as they get her in a cubicle, I can send you back."

"Can you tell me anything?"

The middle-aged woman, harried, impersonal, glanced

at him a second time, and whatever she saw on his face must have cut through her professional reserve, because her expression softened. "I'm sorry. I can't give out any information like that. But it won't be long. Please take a seat, and I'll call you."

Sixteen

Brooke stirred, tried to breathe and groaned as a sharp pain lanced through her chest. A feminine voice broke through the fog. "Easy, Brookie. Not so fast. I'll hold a straw to your mouth. Open your lips."

It was simpler to cooperate than to protest. A trickle of cool liquid soothed her parched throat.

Why was she here? What happened to her?

Moments later, she sank back into sleep.

Her dreams were not pleasant. In them, she struggled. She cried out. And always, the pain.

Gradually, the fog receded. But the pain did not. Breathing was agony. "Alexis?" Her voice sounded thin and reedy.

"I'm here, baby. What do you need?"

"More water, please."

Swallowing didn't hurt. As long as she stayed perfectly still.

Unfortunately, that wasn't going to be an option for much longer. An overly cheerful nurse came in and unhooked an IV. "Gotta get this young lady up and moving around before pneumonia sets in. I'll be back shortly."

Brooke put an arm over her face. "Damn, that hurts."

Alexis pulled a chair closer to the bed. "You have two cracked ribs. And a broken wrist. The wrist required surgery. But everything is going to heal nicely. Those ribs will give you hell, though. Nothing they can do about that."

Gradually, snippets began to return. Her wedding day. The rainy morning. A slow-motion tumble off the porch. She remembered hearing Austin's panicked shout. Her own scream. And then multiple jolts of pain before she blacked out.

"The baby?" she croaked, suddenly terrified. "What about the baby?"

Alexis stroked her hand. "The doctor says the baby is fine. There was a bit of bleeding initially. They were concerned you might lose the pregnancy, but that has settled down. Your poor body took the brunt of the damage. They can't give you the best pain meds, though, because of the pregnancy. That's why you're hurting."

"Ah…"

Brooke turned her head slowly and scanned the room. As far as she could tell, she was in one of the very luxurious private suites at Royal Memorial Hospital.

Alexis hovered. "Can I get you anything?"

"What day is it?"

"Thursday afternoon. They'll bring you dinner shortly. You didn't get to eat yesterday because of the surgery. Then today when you woke up, the morning sickness kicked in. They're concerned about your weight."

"Where's Austin?" She couldn't hold back the words any longer.

Alexis blanched. "Well, um…"

The door opened and a familiar redhead walked into the room. She smiled gently at Brooke. "We've met. I'm Audra."

"Austin's sister."

"Yes."

"Where is he?"

The other two women looked at each other and back at Brooke. Alexis swallowed. "We're not exactly sure, honey. He took off."

Brook tried to sit up in the bed, alarmed. "What do you mean?" Pain forced her back down.

Audra took over the narrative. "Austin was here with you when Alexis and I arrived. He stayed through the surgery, until the doctor assured all of us you were safe and out of the woods. And then he…"

"Then he left." Alexis had a militant look in her eyes. "No one knows where he is. I'm sorry, Brooke."

Before Brooke could process that extraordinary information, the officious nurse was back. With the help of Audra and Alexis, the uniformed professional hustled Brooke out of bed and into a robe before making her stand and take a stroll down the corridor and back.

At first the pain was enough to make Brooke's forehead bead with sweat. Gradually, it subsided to a dull ache. Her legs moved slowly, as if she had been bedridden for a week and not a mere thirty-six hours.

Finally, the ordeal was over and she was allowed to return to her bed.

She fell asleep almost instantly.

When she awoke, Brooke instinctively looked for Austin, but her heart cried out in disbelief. He was nowhere in sight. Only Audra was in the room.

Austin's sister was as gentle as Alexis and even more comfortable with the routine. Brooke remembered that she had been—or still was—a nurse. "Thank you for helping me," Brooke said. She didn't know the protocol for dealing with Austin's sister.

All she could think about was Austin admitting that Audra had said marrying Brooke was a bad idea.

Great. Just great.

The dinner trays were delivered. As darkness fell outside the window, Brooke made herself eat.

Audra didn't say much.

When Brooke had finished half a baked chicken breast and some mashed potatoes, Audra sighed. "My brother isn't answering his cell phone. But while you were sleeping, this was delivered by hand to the front desk."

It was a plain white envelope with the word *Brooke* scribbled on the front. Though Brooke had never actually seen Austin's handwriting, the bold masculine scrawl was somehow familiar.

Her hands shook as she opened it.

Dear Brooke,
I've moved my things out of the condo for the moment. I want you to be comfortable there. And I'm trying to clear my head. If you need anything at all, Audra has access to my accounts. I'll be in touch soon.
AB

Brooke handed the single sheet of paper to Austin's sister. "I don't really know what this means." Horrible feelings assaulted her. Hurt. Abandonment. A deep sense of betrayal.

Audra glanced at the terse note and winced. "Nor do I. But he was a mess yesterday. Don't give up on him, Brooke. Please. I love my brother, and I want him to be happy."

Brooke's throat hurt. Some aspects about this interlude were going to take far longer to heal than a broken wrist.

"The songwriters and poets tell us we each have one great love in our lives."

"That's bull crap. Austin loved Jenny. Of course he did. But I've seen a change in him since he met you. I have to believe that means something."

"Wishing doesn't make it so." The facts were damning.

Both Austin and Brooke had struggled with mixed emotions about marrying for the baby's sake. Austin had been willing to help Brooke secure her inheritance, but once her father relented, that excuse was no longer valid.

In the end, the wedding hadn't happened. Now, it likely never would. Even though she knew it was probably for the best, the crushing weight in her chest made it hard to breathe.

The following morning Brooke convinced Alexis to take her home—to the condo, though Brooke's friend was not at all happy about it. "Come to my house, damn it," Alexis said. "We have a million servants. You'll recover in the lap of luxury. I don't want you spending time alone."

Actually, time alone sounded heavenly. Brooke needed to be on her own to lick her wounds and regroup. "I'll be fine," she insisted. "The doctor said I don't have any special restrictions. They gave me plastic to wrap around the cast when I shower, and the ribs themselves will be self-limiting. I have to move slowly or pay the price."

"You are *so* stubborn."

Brooke grinned. "Pot. Kettle." She slipped her arms into the loose cardigan Alexis had brought to the hospital. That, along with a solid T-shirt and knit stretchy pants were destined to be Brooke's wardrobe for the near future.

At the moment, she and Alexis were waiting on the nurse to bring the discharge forms.

Audra had driven back to Joplin late last night.

Austin had been spotted on the job site at the club this morning, but that was the only information Brooke had been able to pry out of her closemouthed friend.

Brooke picked at a loose thread on her sweater. "Where's my wedding dress? Is it ruined?"

Alexis grimaced. "I won't lie. It was a mess. Blood. Mud. A rip or two. But my dry cleaner is a miracle worker. I took it to him yesterday and promised him a pair of tickets to the charity gala if he could work his magic."

"You didn't have to do that."

"For you, Brookie, anything." Alexis paced the confines of the small room. "You won't be able to work at the club for a few weeks, but not to worry. I'll pay you anyway. You know…sick leave."

"Don't be absurd. I'm on contract. Sick leave wasn't part of our agreement."

Alexis bristled, her eyes flashing. At times like this, Brooke could see the resemblance to her grandfather. "It's *my* budget and *my* event. I can do as I please."

Brooke blinked back tears. She was dispirited and exhausted and barely hanging on to hope for the future. In spite of everything, she missed Austin's steady, comforting presence, his support. And she missed *him*. He was like a drug her body craved without ceasing.

To have Alexis in her corner meant everything. "Thank you. At least it was my left hand. I can still work on pencil sketches for the day-care murals. So I won't fall completely behind."

"Well, there you go."

Soon, the paperwork was complete, and they were on their way.

The most logical route from the hospital to the condo would have taken them directly past the Cattleman's Club. Instead, Alexis drove three blocks out of the way.

Brooke pretended not to notice.

When they reached the street where Austin had leased a home for himself and his child and his temporary wife, Brooke struggled with a great wave of sadness. She had tried so hard to do the right things in her life.

Yet lately, everything she touched seemed to turn to ashes.

The attached garage at the back of the house made it possible for Brooke to enter the condo by negotiating only two steps. If she and Austin had gone out this way on Wednesday, the accident never would have happened. She would be his wife by now.

A shiver snaked its way down her spine, though the day was warm. In true Royal fashion, the cold snap had moved on. Now November was showing her balmy side. Who knew how long it would last? And who knew if Brooke would ever again share Austin's bed?

Alexis helped her inside and went back to unload Brooke's few personal possessions from the car. In the meantime, Brooke stood in the doorway of Austin's bedroom and surveyed the emptiness. He hadn't been kidding. Every trace of his presence had been erased from the condo.

Was he avoiding *her*? Or a ghost who wouldn't let go?

Alexis made a pass through the kitchen, muttering to herself. "You have the basics," she said. "But I'll send over meals, at least for a few days. The doctor says you're to do nothing but rest and get light exercise."

"Yes, ma'am." Brooke smiled. "I would hug you, but I don't think I can."

Alexis smirked. "I'll take a rain check. Seriously, Brookie. Promise me you'll text any time, night or day. I won't sleep a wink worrying about you."

"I swear. I'll be a model patient."

"Okay. I've got to get to the club. I'll send over lunch, and I'll check on you midafternoon."

The day dragged by. Brooke had never been much of a TV fan. She wasn't in the mood for a movie, either.

Instead, she listened to music, talked to the baby, worked on her sketches and pondered her immediate life choices. The past three months had changed her. She was done letting other people control her fate. She and her child were a unit. A family. It was up to Brooke to create a home and a future for her son or daughter.

Saturday ambled along as slowly as the day before. Some tiny part of her hoped to see Austin, but it was a futile wish. He had missed a day of work for his father-in-law's funeral and another day of work for the almost wedding and the hospital kerfuffle. He would need today to catch up, especially in light of the glorious weather.

By the time Sunday rolled around, Brooke was feeling much better physically. The jagged fissure in her heart was another matter. Every time she walked past Austin's door, the empty room mocked her.

For all her brave notions of independence, she hadn't quite figured out her next step when it came to housing. Should she stay? Should she go? Would Austin ever want to come back to the condo?

With every hour that passed, more questions arose.

Around three in the afternoon, the sunshine was so bright and so beautiful, she couldn't resist any longer. Grabbing a blanket from the closet, she made her way to the small, private backyard, spread her cover on the ground and stretched out on her back.

Getting down was harder than she'd anticipated. Her damaged ribs protested vociferously. But once she was settled, she closed her eyes and sighed. She had slathered her face and arms with sunscreen, so she had no qualms about soaking up the warm rays.

With her hands tucked behind her head and her legs crossed at the ankles, she concentrated on relaxing her entire body, muscle by muscle. Peace came slowly but surely.

No one had ever died from a broken heart.

Loving Austin was a gift. A bright, wonderful gift. As much as it hurt to contemplate letting him go, knowing him had brought her immeasurable joy.

Still, knowing that didn't stop the flood of aching regret and the stab of agony over everything she had lost.

When she awoke, the angle of the sun told her she had slept for a long time. It was no wonder. Her body was still playing catch-up.

Instead of rolling to her feet—a move that would most certainly involve a sharp jolt of pain—she stayed very still and amused herself by cataloging the myriad sounds in her new neighborhood.

Despite the calendar, someone nearby was mowing their lawn. Dogs, more than one, barked. Staking a claim. Marking territory.

Childish laughter was harder to catch in the distance, but it was there.

As she wrinkled her brow and concentrated on the odd plinking sound nearby, a shadow fell across her body.

She shielded her eyes. "Alexis?" No one else had a key. No one but Austin.

He crouched beside her. "No. It's me."

If she tried to sit up, it would hurt. He would try to help, and he would touch her, and she would fall apart.

So she didn't move. "What are you doing here?"

"I live here," he said.

"Do you? I wasn't sure."

"You're angry," he said.

"No. Not angry. Confused maybe. And sad." She shielded her eyes. The sun was low on the horizon. "What time is it?"

"Almost five."

"No wonder I'm hungry."

She tried to speak matter-of-factly, but her heart was racing. No matter his reasons for coming, this conversation was going to be tough.

Austin sat down on his butt, propped up one knee and slung an arm over it. "Aren't you cold?"

"I wasn't earlier. I guess it's cooling off now."

"Can I help you up?"

She shook her head. "I can do it myself. Please don't touch me."

He flinched. Perhaps the words had come out too harshly. That wasn't her problem. She was in self-preservation mode.

Taking a deep breath, she rolled to her side, scrambled to her knees and cursed as pain grabbed her middle and squeezed. Then at last, she was on her feet. "We should go inside," she said. "It's going to get dark."

Without waiting to see if he would follow her, she clung to the stair rail and hobbled up the steps one at a time, as if she were an old lady.

Inside the house, she made her way to the den. One of the recliners had become her nest of choice. It was relatively easy to get in and out of, and once she was settled, it didn't put pressure on her ribs.

She stood behind the chair, using it as a shield. "Is this going to take long?"

"Stop doing that," he said, the words laced with irritation.

"Doing what?"

"Acting weird."

Her eyebrows shot to her hairline. "*I'm* acting weird? Give me a break, Austin. I'm not the one who disappeared into thin air."

She tried to study him dispassionately, as a stranger would. His face was haggard, as if he had aged ten years in a handful of days. He looked thinner. Paler. There was an air of suffering about him.

He was wearing an ancient leather aviator's jacket and jeans. The soft, long-sleeved Henley shirt underneath was a caramel color that complemented his dark brown eyes.

Everything about him was intensely masculine. The casual clothes, slightly unkempt blond hair and ruggedly handsome stance made him the poster boy for *lone wolf.* Brooke got the message loud and clear.

She was trembling inside, but she dared not let it show. Not for anything in the world would she let him think his desertion had crippled her. She could stand on her own.

She *would* stand on her own. She had no other choice.

Seventeen

Austin wasn't sure what he had been expecting, but it wasn't this. Brooke looked at him as if they were strangers. She didn't appear to be angry. If anything, all of her usual animation had been erased.

He was accustomed to her laughter and her quick wit and her zest for life. This woman was a shadow.

"How are you feeling?" he asked gruffly. It had infuriated him to find out that Brooke was alone…that neither Alexis nor Audra was by her side.

"I'm fine," Brooke said. "Sore, of course, but that will pass. This little cast isn't too much of a bother since it's on my left wrist. I won't have to wear it very long."

"And the baby?"

"One hundred percent perfect."

"Good."

His chest ached. His throat hurt. His head throbbed.

Brooke was so beautiful, he wanted to grab her up and hold her until the terrible ice inside him melted. But the fear was greater than the wanting.

She bit her bottom lip, a sure sign she was nervous or upset or both. "Where do we go from here, Austin?"

He hadn't expected the blunt question.

"Stay as long as you like," he muttered.

"So you're going to support the baby and me out of the goodness of your heart?"

The snippy sarcasm raked his raw mood. "I'm trying to be the good guy in this situation."

"News flash. You failed."

He reared back, affronted. "What do you want from me, damn it?"

"An explanation would be nice. I never tried to trap you into anything, Austin. I'm not sure why you felt the need to hide out."

"It's complicated."

"Try me." Brooke glared at him, her gray gaze stormy. Her cheekbones were too pronounced. Her turquoise knit top and cream sweater swallowed her small, delicate frame. Even though she wore thin black leggings, there was no visible sign of a baby bump yet.

"Do we have any coffee?" he asked.

Brooke frowned. "That's all you're going to say?"

He put a hand to the top of his head, where a jackhammer burrowed into his skull. "Let me have some caffeine," he pleaded. "And I'll make us a couple of sandwiches. After that, I'll answer all your questions."

It was a magnanimous offer and one he might later regret. But he needed sustenance.

He followed Brooke to the kitchen, careful to keep his distance. Despite her injured ribs, she moved gracefully, putting coffee on to brew, getting out cups and saucers, directing him to what he needed for cobbling together thick roast beef sandwiches with slices of freshly cut Swiss cheese.

At last, they sat down at the table together.

He fell on the sandwich with a groan of appreciation.

Brooke ate hers with more finesse, though she eyed him with a frown. "When was the last time you had a real meal?"

"I don't know," he said. "Breakfast with you Wednesday morning, maybe? I've had a few packs of peanut butter crackers along the way. It's been busy at the club. Haven't felt much like eating."

Without another word she stood and fixed him a second sandwich.

Three cups of coffee later, he felt marginally more human.

When the plates were empty, there was nothing left but the silence.

He stood and paced again.

Brooke remained seated. He had already noticed that standing and sitting aggravated her ribs. It was a wonder she hadn't punctured a lung when she fell.

Dizziness assailed him, and he sat down hard. The image of Brooke tumbling down those damn stairs was one he couldn't shake. It haunted his dreams.

Her expression softened, as if she could see his inner turmoil. "Talk to me, Austin."

He dropped his head in his hands and groaned. "I lied to you from the beginning," he said.

She blinked at him. "I don't understand."

"You made the assumption that I was still in love with Jenny. That fiction suited my purposes, so I let you believe it. Even though I knew the lie caused you pain. So there. Now you know what kind of man I am."

Brooke's bottom lip trembled. "The day I met you was the first time you had taken off your wedding ring."

"That much was true. But I continued wearing the ring as long as I did because it kept women like you from getting ideas."

"Oh."

"I loved Jenny. Of course I did. But that wasn't why I wore my wedding ring for six long years. I wasn't still wallowing in my grief or clinging to her memory, not by that point. All I wanted was to be left alone. The ring was a useful deterrent."

He laid out the facts baldly, painting himself in the worst possible light. Brooke needed to know the whole truth.

"But you had taken it off that night when I met you."

He nodded. "Audra wouldn't let up. She said I was turning into a soulless jackass, and she insisted I return to the land of the living."

"I see."

"I *knew* you thought I was still in love with Jenny, Brooke. And I let you believe it. Aren't you going to ask me why?"

Her eyes were huge, her face pale. "Why, Austin?"

He scraped his hands through his hair. "Because you scared me more than anything that had happened to me in forever. You gave me a glimpse of light and warmth and happiness, and I wanted it. God, Brooke, I wanted it."

"But…"

"I was terrified," he said simply. "I don't know if I can make you understand. I don't know if anyone can understand unless they go through it. Watching a loved one die like Jenny died is worse than being sick yourself. She waded through hell. The truth is, I would literally have cut off one of my limbs, Brooke, to have spared her even a day of the agony. But I couldn't. She had to walk that road alone, and the best I could do was walk beside her."

"Walking beside someone is a lot. It's *everything*."

"It didn't seem that way. I've never felt so helpless in my life. So when I met you with your sunshiny spirit and your sweet smile and your utter joy for life, I wanted to let you into my heart and into my soul, but I was too damned scared."

"Scared of what?" she asked softly.

"Scared to care. I never want to feel that pain again."

Her heart sank. "But then I got pregnant and you had to come up with plan B."

"Exactly. Even then, I hedged my bets. I told myself I could sleep with you and provide for the baby, but that was my line in the sand."

"Then why marry me?"

He jumped to his feet, pacing again. Restless. Over-whelmed with a million conflicting emotions. "I don't know."

Brooke stood up slowly, wincing. "I think you do know, Austin." Her smile was wistful. As if her endless fount of hope had dried up.

"I wanted our child to be legitimate," he said.

"No one cares about that kind of thing anymore."

"They do in Royal."

"Maybe. But that's not why you agreed to my proposal, is it?"

"It was one reason." The other reason was harder to admit. Almost impossible, in fact.

He shoved his hands in his pockets to keep from reach-ing for her. "Are you sure the baby is okay?"

"Yes. Quit changing the subject." Brooke leaned back against the fridge, gingerly shifting her weight from one foot to the other. "Tell me how it felt when you saw me fall."

He gaped at her. *No!* Reliving that moment made him light-headed. "I was worried," he said. "It all happened so fast. I was afraid you were seriously injured. That you might never wake up. That you could have a miscarriage."

Big gray eyes stared at him, eyes that seemed to see deep

inside to every screwed-up corner of his psyche. "Did you blame yourself, Austin?"

He started to shake. Ah. There it was. The truth. Again, he saw her tumbling down those damn stairs. He should have been close, holding her arm. "You didn't wait for me," he croaked.

"Exactly. And Jenny was a grown woman who could have made an appointment and gone to the doctor for her cough long before she actually did." She released a shuddering breath. "I'm sorry I scared you. Truly, I am. But you're not in control of the world, Austin. You never were."

"You were unconscious," he said, reliving that horrific moment four days ago when he had lost his shit completely. "It was raining and you were wearing that beautiful silky wedding dress, and all I could do was crouch over you and pray you didn't lose the baby."

"Losing the baby would have solved your problem."

Fury rose in him, choked him, sickened him. "By God, don't you say that. Don't you *dare* say that!"

She wrapped her arms around her slender waist, fearless and unflinchingly brave in the face of his wrath.

"Why not, Austin? It's true."

The chasm was there at his feet again. No matter how much he backpedaled, he couldn't escape it. Brooke kept pushing him and pushing him. As though she thought he was brave enough to jump across. He wasn't brave. He was blind with fear.

She held out her hand, her smile tremulous. "Tell me why you were so upset when I fell. Tell me why you weren't at the hospital when I woke up. Tell me why you rented this beautiful condo for us and then moved out so I'm forced to sleep here all alone at night. Tell me, Austin. Why?"

He couldn't say it. If he did, fate would smack him down again…would bring him to his knees and punish him for daring to believe he might find happiness one more time in his life.

But he owed Brooke something for what he had put her through. She at least deserved the truth. Even if Austin had not turned out to be the man she thought he was.

Before he could speak, Brooke came to him and laid her head on his shoulder. She slid her arms around his waist. "You've given me so much, Austin. I wanted to break free of my parents' influence and stand on my own two feet. You helped me get there. I'll always be grateful to you for supporting me."

"*You* did that," he said. "You're brave and determined and so strong." He held her tightly, but with infinite gentleness. Her warmth broke through the last of his painful walls. "I love you, Brooke Goodman," he whispered. "Body and soul. Jenny was my first love, the love of my youth. You're my forever love, the mother of my child, the woman who will, please God, grow old with me."

"I love you, too, stupid cowboy. Don't ever leave me again."

Her voice broke on the last word, and she cried. The tears were cathartic for both of them. They clung to each other—forever, it seemed.

At last, Brooke pulled back and looked up at him, her eyelashes damp and spiky, her eyes red rimmed. "I'm not jealous of Jenny. I'm really not. I'm glad she had you when it mattered most."

Austin shook his head slowly, rescuing one last teardrop with his fingertip. "You are an extraordinary woman. But hear this, my sweet. I'm going to spend the next fifty years making up for the fact that your family hasn't appreciated you. I'm going to shower you with love and affection, and it's entirely possible that I may spoil you rotten."

A tiny grin tipped the corners of Brooke's mouth. "Is that a threat or a promise?"

He sighed deeply, feeling contentment roll through him like a golden river. "Either works. How do you feel about an after-Christmas wedding? With all the trimmings. I'm not a fan of the way we were headed the first time."

Brooke pouted. "I don't want to wait that long to be your wife."

"I'm open to debate, but we're staring down the gun at this auction thing. I have promises to keep. More importantly, I've decided you and I are going to take a grand honeymoon. Like in the old days, when couples went to Europe for a month. I want to take you to all those art galleries before the baby comes. How does that sound?"

She beamed up at him. "I think it sounds amazing. But I'd still be willing to do a quickie courthouse ceremony."

"Nope. We're going the whole nine yards. An engagement ring, for starters. And a bridal gown that will be the envy of every woman in Royal. Empire waisted, of course," he said with a grin.

"I love it." Brooke tried to dance around the kitchen and had to stop and grab the counter when her ribs protested.

"Plus," he said, "I'd like for my bride to be able to take a deep breath without being in pain."

"Details, details." Brooke waved a dismissive hand, but she was pale beneath her excitement-flushed cheeks.

"Then it's settled." He took her in his arms and kissed her slowly, long and deep. Lust filtered through his body, overlaid with gratitude and tenderness. Brooke's lips clung to his, her ragged breaths matching his own.

He wanted her so badly, he trembled.

But her injury made his hunger for her problematic. He released her and brushed a strand of hair from her forehead. "I can't sweep you off your feet right now, can I?"

"Not unless you want me to pass out."

"Duly noted. How do you feel about really, really careful sex?"

"I thought you'd never ask."

Brooke climbed up onto the mattress and watched Austin undress. She would suffer a dozen broken ribs if this were the payoff. Hearing Austin say he loved her made up for endless days of heartache.

He ditched the last of his clothing and joined her. Brooke had done her own restrained striptease moments earlier, because Austin was afraid of hurting her.

Now here they were. Both of them bruised and broken in different ways.

She ran a hand down his warm, hair-dusted thigh. "Did I ever tell you that my grandmother was a twin?"

Austin raised one eyebrow as he coaxed her nipples into tightly furled buds with his thumbs. "You might have forgotten to mention that."

"How do you feel about multiple babies?"

He nibbled the side of her neck. His big body was a furnace. "I like making them. A lot. And though I prefer them to arrive one at a time, I'll keep an open mind."

He scooted lower in the bed and kissed her still-flat tummy. "You're going to be the most beautiful pregnant woman in Royal."

"You might be a tad prejudiced."

"Maybe." He kissed the inside of her thigh.

Her breath hitched. "When you finish Matt Galloway's house, will you design one for us? I thought we could start looking for land in the meantime. And don't get all prissy about my inheritance. We can split the price fifty-fifty if it makes you feel better."

His grin was brilliant. Carefree. It made her heart swell

with happiness and pride. "I could live with that." He eased her onto her side and scooted in behind her, joining their bodies with one gentle push. "Is this hurting you?"

She gasped as he shifted and his firm length hit a sensitive spot in her sex. "Yes, Cowboy. But only in the best possible way."

He kissed the nape of her neck, his breath warm. "I adore you, Brooke."

Pleasure rolled through her body in a shimmering wave. "You're mine, Austin. Now and forever. Don't you forget it."

Then, with a gentle, thorough loving, he took them home...

* * * * *

COMING SOON!

We really hope you enjoyed reading this book. If you're looking for more romance, be sure to head to the shops when new books are available on

Thursday 15th November

LET'S TALK
Romance

For exclusive extracts, competitions
and special offers, find us online:

- ▣ facebook.com/millsandboon
- 🐦 @MillsandBoon
- 📷 @MillsandBoonUK

Get in touch on 01413 063232

For all the latest titles coming soon, visit
millsandboon.co.uk/nextmonth